Mary, Mary, Shut the Door

Mary, Mary, Shut the Door

and Other Stories

Benjamin M. Schutz

Author of THE MONGOL REPLY

Five Star • Waterville, Maine

First Edition, Second Printing.

Published in 2005 in conjunction with
Tekno Books and Ed Gorman.

Set in 11 pt. Plantin.

Printed in the United States on permanent paper.

Library of Congress Cataloging-in-Publication Data

Schutz, Benjamin M.
    Mary, Mary, shut the door, and other stories / by Benjamin M. Schutz.—1st ed.
       p. cm.
    ISBN 1-59414-371-4 (hc : alk. paper)
    1. Detective and mystery stories, American.   I. Title.
PS3569.C5556A6 2005
  813'.54—dc22   2005019743

Dedication

For JoAnne,
my best friend and
the love of my life

Table of Contents

Introduction

I did not start out writing short stories. I had already written three Leo Haggerty novels, when I was invited to submit a short story to the centenary celebration volume: *Raymond Chandler's Philip Marlowe*. I did not learn my craft from doing short stories and then tackle the transformation to the novel, a format without limits. Rather, I had already developed a style (I think you will see a consistency across these stories, written over the span of seventeen years) and had to learn to adapt this style to the rigors of the short story.

As I reread these stories, some for the first time in fifteen years, I saw commonalities in how I structure short stories and as a consequence what the major tasks are that I deal with in writing them.

Generally, they are time-bound tales; the clock is ticking; something terrible must be averted. I use time to compress my stories, to give them shape and limit. As such they function as mini-thrillers. Pace is very important. You have to lay out the challenge, introduce the protagonist and get moving. Without that, the heart will not race. Many stories begin with the hero *already* engaged in the central action of the story.

Time also provides the pressure for Hemingway's dictum "Courage is grace under pressure." What is that "grace"? For me, and my characters, it's the ability to keep a clear head and fashion effective actions when there are very high stakes, and "failure is not an option." It's also the ability to keep a clear moral compass, when the gales of seduction and danger threaten to throw you off course. That's a tall order for twenty pages. So economy of language is important; you don't have any words to waste. Misdirection of the reader to preserve suspense is often the result of ambiguity in the text. Ambiguity is achieved by precision in expression. What is revealed and what is omitted, and how that is done. These were elements I had to learn and relearn as I wrote short stories; pace, economy, precision.

I spend a substantial amount of time researching my short stories. For a thriller to work, there has to be an ever-present sense of inevitability to the increasing peril. Nothing deflates the blood pressure cuff on a thriller faster than a stupid protagonist. My research helps me understand how an experienced, knowledgeable person would respond to the predicaments I construct. I then use that "insider" knowledge to be creative in how they resolve it. I want the reader to feel that they would have done all the same things as the hero, would still be facing the impending danger with only two pages to go, and be surprised at the very end.

I think that style is especially important in genre fiction. The major dangers of genre fiction are cliché and boredom. A genre's conventions are a contract. Like all contracts, they tell you what is the *minimum* you can expect from the tale— not the maximum. The minimum is a Sisyphean reading experience—you push the same tale with the same characters up that damn hill. Style, a unique way of telling the story, provides freshness and vitality to not-so-novel plots or characters. For me, I try to use dialogue and metaphors to make the story fresh; to put memorable lines in my characters' mouths; provide resonant images for the readers' minds, and pithy insights into the human condition. When successful, these tools create a depth to the story without adding length or slowing the pace.

My debt to Raymond Chandler is obvious in what I have just written. In fact, when I wrote my first short story, I reflected on what attracted me to Chandler's writing. I wrote:

Chandler brought a poet's intensity to the mystery. His images made the "same old scenes" fresh and vibrant and lodged them firmly in my memory. He wrote dialogue in the language we wished we spoke and he made it sound natural anyway. Sometimes I would read pages out loud just to savor the sound of those words.

I'd settle for being remembered that way.

I've grouped this collection around different protagonists: Private Eyes; Forensic Psychologists; Police Officers; and last, the anomaly in my writings, a story without a hero of any sort; the last tango of two serial killers.

The private eye stories start with two about the Ellis brothers, Matt and Sean. They are based on my sons, who worked as private eyes/process servers for a couple of summers in college. I remember what they said about the job. They liked it because it had consequences; it had impact; and you had to think on the run. Not like mis-flipping a burger. The first, "Whatever it Takes," was a finalist for the Ellery Queen Mystery Magazine Reader's Award. The second story, "Til Death Do Us Part," was written for this collection. Next are my three Leo Haggerty short stories. The second one, "Mary, Mary, Shut the Door," is my best-known short story. It won both the Edgar and Shamus awards for short story (1992). Only Lawrence Block's "By the Dawn's Early Light" (1984) has also pulled off that double. Trying to emulate Lawrence Block is always a pathway to excellence. The third Leo Haggerty story, "Lost and Found," gave me a chance to tie up loose ends from "Mary, Mary, Shut the Door," and the last Haggerty novel, *Mexico is Forever*. It was reprinted in *A Century of Noir*, chosen by Max Collins and Mickey Spillane. The last story, "The Black Eyed Blonde," has been changed slightly from the original. The detective is no longer Philip Marlowe, but now his lesser known, but equally effective, fellow L.A. gumshoe, Max Barlow. Other characters' names taken from Marlowe short stories have also been changed. In all other respects it is the original story, from the collection *Raymond Chandler's Philip Marlowe*.

That collection was the subject of an interesting research paper. "The Not So Simple Art of Imitation: Pastiche, Literary Style, and Raymond Chandler" by Sigelman and Jacoby in *Computers and the Humanities*, volume thirty, pages eleven through twenty-eight, 1996. It's a fascinating computer analysis of style and concludes, unsurprisingly, that none of us who wrote stories for that volume would be mistaken for Chandler. Of the twenty-three stories in the collection, mine was rated fifth closest to Chandler's style. I was pleased to learn that I had achieved a modicum of success in carrying my appreciation of Chandler into my own work.

The next section is my forensic psychologist stories. The first two feature Dr. Ransom Triplett (Who is in a peer supervision group with Dr. Morgan Reece of *The Mongol Reply*). "Expert Opinion" was cited as a distinguished story in *Best American Mystery Stories of 2000*, and the other, "Not Enough Monkeys," was chosen by long time *Ellery Queen Mystery Magazine* editor, Janet Hutchings, for her anthology, *Crème de la Crime*. This section ends with my one foray into science fiction. I retold the story of Frankenstein's monster as a forensic pre-sentencing report. I've always seen the story as that of the unloved child, cursed by the gift of life, who destroys himself and those who reject him. We have thousands of such children in our jails and hospitals.

The next section has two stories infused with my brother's experiences as a Washington D.C. police officer. "Open and Shut" was chosen by Jon Breen for his anthology *Mystery: The Best of 2001*.

The last section has one short story in it. "Meeting of the Minds" or what happens when two cats mistake each other for mice.

I'd like to thank my agent and friend Lynn "Swifty" Myers, Jr., for all his help bringing this project to fruition. The leap from legal pad to computer disk was long indeed. My wife, JoAnne Lindenberger, was as always, an enthusiastic researcher and my best editor. What crosses other people's desks has had the benefit of her tempering of my excesses.

Time to let the stories speak for themselves. I hope you find them gripping, surprising, and that they linger longer than the reading.

Benjamin M. Schutz
Woodbridge, Virginia
February 2005

PRIVATE EYES

MATT AND SEAN ELLIS

LEO HAGGERTY

MAX BARLOW

Whatever It Takes

"Wake up, Sean, Mickey called. We've got work."

His brother, Matthew, prodded him with a toe.

"You need a shower too. You've still got paint in your hair."

Sean Ellis grunted but didn't move. He entered each day with the ease of a twelve-pound breech birth.

"You better get a move on. I'm not waiting. I'll take all the work myself."

"Like hell you will." He rolled over, swung his legs over the side and followed his brother out of the bedroom. He went into the shower and watched his brother go into the kitchen.

Matthew Ellis opened the refrigerator, took out two bagels and a block of cream cheese. Dropping a bagel into the toaster, he reached up and got down two coffee mugs and poured a cup for himself and one for his brother. He carried his cup, milked and sugared, into the living room.

His mother lay asleep on the sofa. Matthew walked around the living room chairs and turned off the television. More and more often he found her asleep in her clothes in the living room, as if she had only enough energy to get inside the front door.

Chris Ellis was a petite woman, barely over a hundred pounds. Her son thought she was slipping from lean to frail but hoped that he was wrong. Her blanket had slipped down to her waist and her book was open on her chest.

He sipped his coffee and looked at himself in the mirror over the sofa. Stocky and muscular, he was dressed in khaki shorts and a dark blue T-shirt from his stint at the medical ex-

17

aminer's office. Across his chest ran the unofficial motto of that office:

Homicide?
Suicide?
I decide.

He looked down at his mother's tiny fists, clenched in her sleep like a baby's. Her thumbs were tucked inside her fingers. He wondered if she had been fighting in her sleep and hoped that she had won. He wanted to cover them but knew that if he adjusted her blanket, she'd startle and waken.

The phone in the kitchen rang and he rushed to answer it.

"Hello," he said.

"Matthew, boy. Is that you?"

"Yeah. Who is this?"

"It's your dad. Don't you recognize my voice?"

He did, but denied it so that his father would have to identify himself. Every little bit of distance helped. "What do you want?"

"I'd like to see you and your brother. Talk about things. See where we stand."

"Not a chance. You made your choices, now live with them. We sure as hell had to."

"Look, Matt, I know you're angry . . ."

"Angry? I'm homicidal, you bastard."

"Put your brother on."

"Sorry, I can't hear you. You seem to be breaking up."

He hung up the phone and began to massage his temples with his fingertips.

"What's up, Matt?" His brother asked as he walked into the kitchen.

"What else? That was Dad with his Monday morning

overture. Let's talk boys, let's start over, let's forget every-thing that happened. I'm a changed man. I've found Jesus." He squeezed his eyes shut and began to use his palms. "I get such a headache talking to him. You gotta take the next one, man."

"Whatever." He fixed his coffee, handed Matt the bagel from the toaster and put one in for himself.

He was as long, lean and fair as his brother was short, wide and dark. Like his brother, he'd dressed in shorts and a T-shirt. August around D.C. made anything else unbearable without air conditioning.

"Sean, let me ask you a question."

"Okay."

"Have you noticed how gray mom is getting? She's only forty. Do you think stress can do that to you?"

"I don't know man. I'm the art major, remember. I didn't take psychology."

They ate in silence, washed their cups and plates, stacked them to dry, and turned out the lights before they left the apartment. Matt stood by the door, his hand on the light switch looking at his mother's shape on the sofa.

"You know Sean, when I was little, I thought the worst times of my life were those nights mom came home with a date. I was wrong. I'd give anything for her to come home with somebody now. She doesn't even use the bed for herself any more."

"Let it be, Matt. We've got work to do."

Their ten-year-old Subaru had all the pickup of a pair of drunken oxen. Like their previous car, they had bought it at an auction for less than a hundred bucks, planned to drive it 'til it stopped and then get another one. Maintenance had no place in their plans. It was just delaying the inevitable. Like a respirator or a feeding tube. Besides, it cost money.

Mickey Sloan's office was tidy and well organized. He had a sofa along one wall for his field agents to sit on and read the papers they were going out to serve. He sat facing them inside a U-shaped desk. His desk phone had five lines. A missed call was a job lost and so he carried a cell phone and a pager with him at all times. A copy machine sat on top of a wall of file cabinets. On the opposite wall next to the window was a large map of the metropolitan region. Through the blinds, Mickey could see the courthouse across the street; a giant paper factory, without any smokestacks. His computer screen had a screen-saver design of a bearded caveman with a piece of paper in his hands, trotting forever across a barren landscape.

Matt and Sean came in, took their packets off of Mickey's desk, and sat down to read their day's work.

First up was a notice of judgment against Mohammed Ben Zekri out in Herndon, then a witness subpoena for Vu Tran Nguyen in Falls Church. Vu had seen an automobile accident. Lorelei Petty was going to get a notice of deposition in the divorce case of Truman and Molly Wing. She was going to be asked about her affair in excruciating detail. Truman's attorney had a very limited imagination and the mechanics of lesbian love had to be repeated over and over before he got it. A restraining order was today's bit of sunshine for Gustavo Martin, courtesy of his girlfriend Mirabella Montoya of the bloodied nose and chipped-tooth Montoyas. Last but not least was a subpoena *duces tecum* for the records of Lowell Gorman, DDS, pioneer in the use of anesthetic-shrouded fellatio as a dental procedure.

"How much for these, Mickey?"

"Ben Zekri, Nguyen, and Petty are twenty-five each; Gorman is thirty, and Martin is fifty."

"Anything special we should know?"

"Watch out for Martin. Serve him together. This isn't the

first girl he's slapped around. He's out on bond and looking at some time inside for this one. He won't be in a good mood when you find him."

Mickey cleared his throat. "Uh, I've got a piece of bad news for you guys. You know that case you've been working on for Barton and Hammon?"

"Yeah," they said, drawing the syllable out slowly. They had been working for days to find a way to serve Byron Putnam, who oscillated between his gated condominium in McLean and a security office building on K Street. He was now worth $4.00 an hour and sinking fast.

"They want it back. They know you've had trouble getting to Putnam. There's another agency that says they can get into his building."

"Who?" Matt asked.

"Amanda Marshall."

"Right. She thinks one of her hos in hot pants and a halter is gonna do the job."

"Yep."

The boys shook their heads. "She's probably right," Sean said. "The gimp at the gate will go brain dead, drool down her cleavage and the chemical reaction will make her invisible. I remember reading about that."

"Hey, I'm sorry. I know you guys put a lot of time on that one, but they're the clients. They can take the paper back."

"Fine, fine. It's out in the car. We'll drop it by their office later today. Any more good news?" Sean muttered.

"No. That's it."

"How about letting us into the 'Icebox'. We've been here almost three months already. You know we can do the job. How about it?" Matt asked.

Mickey mulled it over. They were leaving soon to go back

to school. He wanted to hold it out as a carrot to get them to come back over the Christmas break. On the other hand, they were reliable and hard working. Maybe a taste of bigger things now would whet their appetite. Christmas gifts could run into beaucoup dollars.

"Alright. Here's the rules. The 'Icebox' has papers we haven't been able to serve. They may not even be valid anymore. You'll have to check with the lawyer and the client to see if they still want them served. If they do and you're successful, you keep all the money. So check with the attorney on that too, some are worth more than others. But it's strictly a sideline—something you do after you hit the current jobs. I like keeping that box small. That means we tag all the fresh ones. Understood?"

"Understood."

Sean took the box down and sat it on his lap. Matt leaned over as they thumbed through the papers. They were filed alphabetically.

"We'll come back when we're done today and research these, see which ones we want to pursue," Sean said.

"Good hunting. You better hit the streets. One last word about the 'Icebox', even though I don't think you need it. One reason I don't let everybody in there is because of the risk of sewer service."

"What?"

"Sewer Service. I once had a guy claim he'd served a paper when he'd flushed it down the toilet. He figured we couldn't find the guy so he wasn't gonna show. Easy money. Well we couldn't find him because he was dead. That came up at the hearing. Not a shining moment. I got a reprimand and he got sixty days. My reputation rides along with you two every day, but hey, I don't need to say that, that's why I'm letting you into the 'Icebox'."

★ ★ ★ ★ ★

Mickey's office was in one of the faux colonial buildings that ring the courthouse and public safety building. They took I-66 west from there to the parkway, then across the county over the Dulles Access road into Herndon. Matt drove and his brother navigated.

"Right here, Matt, into this development. Take the first left and go straight to the end."

"Where do we stand, Sean?"

"You're up thirty-five. I figured to take two of the twenty-fives and the doctor. You take the other two and we're even."

"Alright. This one's yours."

They drove past a row of McMansions, five hundred thousand dollar pseudo-Georgians so close together you'd have to mow on alternate days, and looked for house numbers painted on the curb. Sean began to count by twos and started to shake his head. The houses came to a halt just short of the address for Mohammed Ben Zekri. They pulled up to the curb and looked at the hole in the ground, awaiting a foundation. Mr. Ben Zekri was gone along with ten thousand cubic feet of dirt.

Matt got out of the car and walked over to the last house and headed up the stairs to the front door. Sean pulled out the cell phone, looked at the signature page on the notice, and called the attorney.

"Klompus, Bogans, and Hess. How may I help you?"

"Jack Klompus please."

"Who may I say is calling?"

"Sean Ellis of AAA Process Service."

"This is Linda, Mr. Klompus's secretary. How may I help you?"

"I'm here at the address your office provided for Mohammed Ben Zekri and what it is is a hole in the ground."

Matt stood next to him and mouthed, "Empty for six months."

"In fact it's been a hole in the ground for six months. We'd appreciate it if Mr. Klompus could check his file and see if he has a more current address for Mr. Ben Zekri."

"I'm sorry, Mr. Klompus is on vacation. I'll leave a message for him. His assistant will call you back."

"Thank you."

Sean put the phone back in his pocket. "You know for three hundred dollars an hour, they could check their addresses every six months. That wouldn't be too much to ask, would it?"

They got back in the car and plotted a course to the next address, a red brick apartment box in Falls Church, on the edge of "Little Saigon." There was no grass on the lawn, only dirt, rocks, and glass. The one tree was long dead. A number of windows had broken panes. The chain-link fence lacked only a razor wire frosting to complete the detention-center look of the place. The boys walked through the graffitied door and looked at the mailboxes. There wasn't a name on a single one.

"You take the top floor and work down. I'll go up," Matt said.

They met on the second floor at the only door that was opened to them. Inside was an elderly Vietnamese woman, her streaked gray hair pulled into a tight bun. She had a young child on her hip and two others behind her. All three children were in diapers with fingers in their mouths.

"Uh, ma'am, we're looking for Mr. Vu Tran Nguyen. Can you tell us what apartment is his?" Sean asked.

Her face was utterly impassive, an appropriate reaction when assailed by gibberish.

Sean proceeded, "Do you speak English?"

Nothing.

"I thought so. So if I tell you I'm going to rip this child out of your arms and eat him, your eyes won't widen and you won't slam the door in my face, will you? Of course not, and so you haven't. Have a nice day. Welcome to America."

They turned away and trotted down the stairs. "Didn't I tell you to take Vietnamese as your foreign language elective, Matt? No, you had to take French. Have you noticed any place called 'Little Paris' around here?"

"Let me think. No, I don't think so."

"Me neither. Who's next?"

"Lorelei Petty over in McLean. Good bet she speaks English."

"Lucky you, Matt."

They drove slowly through Falls Church towards Tyson's Corner and McLean. Tyson's Corner was the largest commercial center in America not located in the heart of a city. Falls Church sat between Washington D.C. and Tyson's, and its one main thoroughfare was always distended with traffic, a perpetual aneurysm.

Forty-five minutes later they pulled up in front of Lorelei Petty's townhouse on the Tyson's-McLean frontier, where the proper zip code could mean a twenty thousand dollar difference from the other side of the street.

Matt read the paper. "This is a notice of deposition, so the shit's been hitting the fan for quite awhile. We don't have the advantage of surprise here."

"So, call her. See if she's here. Do we have a description?"

"Yeah, five feet six inches, hundred forty-five pounds, light brown hair, wears glasses."

Matt dialed directory assistance, got the number for an L. Petty, and then dialed that.

"Hello?"

"Lorelei Petty?"

"Yes."

"Hi, my name is Matt Ellis, I'm a process server. I have a subpoena for you in the Wings matter. I'm on my way over. I'll be there in about twenty minutes, is that okay with you?"

"Uh, sure, whatever."

Matt set the phone down. "What do you think, Sean?"

"A guy, he'd be outta there three minutes tops. A woman, I'd say six."

They looked down at their watches. The adjacent townhouse had a contractor's sign hung from the front porch railing. It proclaimed: "Another fine project from the master craftsmen at DNT Contractors. Call Burle Hitchens at (703) 555-9400."

Five minutes later, Matt rolled up the paper, stuck it in his back pocket and got out of the car. He was going up the stairs when the front door opened. A woman stepped out, and turned back to lock the dead bolt. Matt closed ground.

"Lorelei, is that you?" He asked, eagerly but uncertain.

"Yes," she said and turned to face her caller.

Matt whipped out the papers and handed them to her.

"You've been served, ma'am."

She backed away, waving her hands at the paper like it was an angry insect.

"No, I haven't. I haven't taken these."

"That's TV, ma'am. You answered to the name, you match the description, you live at the right address. You've been served."

Matt dropped them at her feet. "I'd advise you to read them and call a lawyer. Have a nice day."

"I hope your dick falls off, you miserable little bastard."

"Duly noted ma'am, and my affidavit of service will include your kind words."

Matt jumped into the car and it pulled away. "What next?" he asked.

"Our Latino lady-killer, over in Arlington."

"Where are we serving him?"

"Work. He's a janitor at a motel in Arlington."

Their cell phone rang.

"Hello?" Sean said.

"Sean, is that you? It's Chuck Pruitt. You and your brother want to do some surveillance?"

"Hold on Chuck, I'll ask him."

He covered the mouthpiece. "Matt, it's Chuck Pruitt, he wants us to do surveillance, what do you say?"

"I say no. He hasn't paid us for our last two jobs. Working for him is working for free. It's been over two months he's owed us."

"You sure? It's work."

"Work? It's charity. Slow pay is no pay. You can do it. I'll pass."

"Uh, Chuck, we'll pass. You still owe us about two hundred and fifty bucks for work we did in May."

"Hey, guys, it's not me. I bill the clients. I've gotta chase them to pay me so I can pay you. Every check I get that you're owed a piece of, I pass it straight on."

"Chuck, I'm not saying you're stiffing us. But none of this is gonna pay my tuition bill. Summer's almost over. I need money now. The school could give a damn. It's due when it's due. Sorry."

"I hate being the asshole of the food chain. The pâté's at the other end, down here it's all bullshit," Sean snapped.

"Well, we've got two more chances for today. Let's make 'em count."

Gustavo Martin was a janitor at the Arlington Inn, which operated on the same principles as its neighbor, the Pentagon: Don't Ask, Don't Tell.

"You take the front desk, Matt. I'll find a maid, see if she knows where he is."

"Wait for me if you find him. He might think twice about going off."

"Sure." They exited the car, Matt going to the office, Sean heading upstairs where he had seen a maid's cart in the hallway. He went up the stairs three at a time, grabbed the rusting metal railing and swung up and around on to the second floor. The ice machine had its bin door open and a sign taped to the front that said, 'Broken'. He walked down to the maid's cart and looked into the room it was parked outside of.

"Excuse me, can I talk to you?" he said into the darkened room.

"*¿Si, quien es?*" A woman replied. She was bent over, making the bed.

"*Donde esta Gustavo Martin?*"

"*No entiendes ni jota.*"

"I know he works here. Just tell me where he is?"

"He's around. I don't know."

"Okay. What does he look like?"

"He's short, curly black hair, mustache . . ."

As she spoke, her words coalesced in the space at the end of the hall. The man looked at Sean, saw him take a step towards him, turned, and started down the stairs. Sean leaned over the railing and saw his brother step out of the motel office.

"That's him, Matt."

Glancing over his shoulder at his second pursuer, the man ran across the parking lot towards the high grass along the railroad tracks. There were no trains in sight. He would have to run all the way to El Salvador. Matt took off after him. The guy was wind-milling his arms through the high grass, bobbing back and forth above his churning bowlegs. Matt had no speed to speak of, but he and his brother ran five miles a night through their neighborhood. The longer Gustavo ran, the better Matt's chances of catching him. He heard the slap of footsteps behind him, each one louder than the last. He came out on the dusty path alongside the tracks.

"Hold on, Matt. I'm coming." Sean ate up ground, each stride longer and faster than those of either of the others.

Committed to a sprint, Matt accelerated. Even if he didn't catch Martin, he'd make him run flat-out to escape him, and then watch his brother run him down, even if it took ten miles.

Matt figured Martin for a chain-smoking couch potato who'd smack Mirabella if she didn't get him a Dos Equis with each trip to the kitchen. Four hundred yards in his boots with their two inch heels and he was doubled over, holding his side and gasping for breath.

Matt and Sean slowed down and approached him.

"Gustavo Martin?"

"No. *Yo soy Carlos Gonzalez.*"

"Bullshit. We've got something for you, Mr. Martin." Matt reached for the papers in his pants pocket.

"No, no." Gonzalez spun towards them, his hand digging into his pocket.

"Oh shit," they both thought. It had to happen. Someday they'd serve someone with a gun. Sean leaped with both arms outstretched to pin the man's hands in his pants. His brother stepped up behind him, planted his feet, and threw a right hand that hit Gonzalez flush on the chin. Helped by the weight of the other boy on his chest, he slammed backwards into the earth and lay still.

Sean grabbed the man's hand and pulled it out. He was clutching a wallet. While Sean squatted and flipped through it, Matt patted the man down. He had a six-inch switchblade in his right back pocket.

Sean handed him the wallet. "Woops."

All the cards read "Carlos Gonzalez." He too was short, mustachioed with curly black hair. They tucked the wallet back into his pants and pulled him away from the tracks.

Gonzalez came around in a couple of minutes. Sean said, "We're sorry Mr. Gonzalez. We were looking for Gustavo Martin."

"Yo soy Carlos Gonzalez."

"We believe you. Why'd you run?"

No reply.

"Le cremos. ¿Porque corrio?"

He pointed at Matt's shirt. *"Policia."*

"No. No policia."

"¿Sos de la Migra?"

"No. *No Immigration.*"

Gonzalez stood up, rubbing his jaw.

"Sorry about that. I thought you were going for a gun. Uh, *perdone me, pense que usted buscaba una pistola.*"

"No, si tuviera una pistola les hubiera pegado un balazo." Gonzalez imitated shooting them both.

"I'm sure you would have," Sean replied. "No guns. No INS. Why don't we call it a draw and all go away happy."

They walked away and left him there rubbing his jaw.

"Why are we doing this, Matt? Run it by me one more time."

"Because the chicks love it. We're dangerous men. We're hard and shifty. Men to be reckoned with."

"Thanks. It's all coming back now. I must have lost it when I was shitting myself back there, and by the way, don't wear that shirt again. We're not the Hardy boys. I don't want to die in a hail of irony, gunned down by some ESL dropout."

"No problem. It's history."

"And we still have to find Gustavo Martin."

"Not today. We'll get his home address and try him there."

"This doctor, did you arrange to serve him?"

"Called his office, set up an appointment for four o'clock. Should be a piece of cake."

"With a ground glass crust. Let's do it."

Dr. Gorman's office was in Tyson's Corner, a three-story box of solo practitioners: doctors, dentists, accountants, architects, insurance salesman, and an individual who advertised himself as a Failure Analyst.

"That's the best job title I've ever seen. You make a living analyzing other people's screw-ups. How do you train for that? What was his major?" Matt mused.

"We can ask on the way out. You go on ahead. I've got to take a leak," Sean said and ducked into the men's room.

When Sean entered Dr. Gorman's office, there were four other people in the waiting room. It was a battleship gray, with tubular metal chairs arranged around the edges of a purple carpet flecked with white. A central coffee table had a green flowerless plant and a pile of worn magazines.

"Dr. Gorman, please. I've got some papers for him," Sean said.

"I'm sorry, Dr. Gorman isn't here," the secretary said, closing her appointment book. She sat behind a sliding-glass panel in the wall, next to an unmarked door.

"What about all these people?"

"We have another doctor covering for him today."

"Really? I called to set up this appointment. I was told he'd be here."

"I'm sorry, who are you with?"

"Short Fuse Process Service. How about I leave this with you Ms. . . . ?"

"Not a chance. I'm not authorized to accept service and I'm not taking it. You get out of here or I'll call the police." The last part she whispered fiercely.

"Okay. I'll go, but you tell Dr. Gorman I'm going to his house next. I know he's got a teenage daughter. She should be home soon from school. I'll serve her. She'll love reading this stuff."

"Get out of here you despicable piece of . . ."

"Don't say it. You'll piss me off. Right now this is just a job. Don't make it personal."

He pulled the door closed behind him. As soon as it settled, the secretary pushed a button on her phone and whispered into the mouthpiece as she pulled the glass panel closed. A bald man with a precisely shaped beard and half-glasses near the end of his nose came up from the back office. They spoke briefly. He grimaced and shook his head at each thing she said. A patient, his hand to his jaw, approached the window and rapped on the glass. The secretary slid it back.

"Excuse me, Dr. Gorman, how long a wait do you think it's gonna be. My tooth is killing me," he mumbled.

"I don't know, I'm running a little behind today," he snapped irritably.

The patient smiled at this, reached through the opening with the hand he'd held to his face, and dropped a folded piece of paper on to the desk.

"Dr. Gorman, you've been served." The secretary opened her mouth. He pointed at her. "Don't say a word. If you hadn't lied to us, we wouldn't have lied to you. Have a nice day."

Matt left the doctor's office and headed to the elevator. He pushed the down button and the doors opened. Sean was leaning against the far wall. They both raised their arms and slapped palms. Sean started to sing, "Nowhere to run to, baby, nowhere to hide."

"Short Fuse Process Service. That was good. You make that up on the spot?"

"Yeah, she was pissing me off. If she'd gotten the doctor or agreed to accept it, I'd just have asked you for the paper. Once she started that shit, I just ad-libbed it and hoped you'd find a place to step in. If not, I figured we'd stake out his house."

"Does he have a daughter?"

"Hell if I know. I was on a roll."

"That got my attention. I wasn't so sure I wanted to serve the daughter. This is ugly stuff. She didn't do anything."

"Hey, whatever it takes, Matt. Nobody cares about stiffing us."

"What is that, our motto? Short Fuse Process Service: Whatever it takes."

"Sure, why not."

Matt shook his head. "Yeah, why not. We're young. We're hard core."

"Let's go back to the office, file the paperwork and look at the 'Icebox'. Have you figured out how much we've made? Tuition's due at the end of August, we've only got a week left," Sean said.

"Yeah, I've checked. We're short. We'll need to take everything we can get. Night jobs, the weekend. If we don't make it, we can see if they'll put us on the monthly plan, that'll give us some more time to come up with the balance."

"You know for white male oppressors, we're not having a lot of fun running this country."

"Our turn will come. Until then, we go home, grab a bite to eat, and go to the gym. The state bench press meet is Thanksgiving. If we're going to have any chance, we can't let our training slack."

"What if we get a call at the gym?"

"We go. And we bitch the whole way. That's why we're Short Fuse, remember?"

They sat in Mickey's office and filled out affidavits of service and billing sheets for the day. Each one rummaged through the "Icebox" as the other recorded his work. Mickey double-checked the forms and countersigned them.

"Find anything?" He asked nonchalantly.

"Yeah. One," Sean said.

"Who is it? Let me see."

Sean handed him the papers.

"I remember this guy. A deadbeat dad. You guys'll love tagging him. Good hunting. Remember, call the attorney first, make sure it's still valid and what they'll pay. Get it in writing and see if they'll pick up your expenses. Remember when you had to eat that all day parking bill? See you tomorrow."

Sean took the papers back, nodded to Mickey, and the brothers left his office. In the car, Sean pointed to the case citation.

"See that. Chelsea Lyn Dougan v. Burle Hitchens."

"Yeah, so what?"

"I saw that name today. On a sign. It was the house next to Lorelei Petty. The contractor's sign. He was remodeling the house. It said, 'Burle Hitchens'; it even had a phone number."

"That's crazy. If this guy was doing business openly in this county, Mickey would have found him. DBA's, corporation lists. That's the first thing he does."

"Maybe he wasn't working back then. Time passed, he got more confident, used his name, no one came after him."

"Or it isn't the right guy. Same name, wrong guy. We already tagged the wrong man once today. That's plenty."

"Two Burle Hitchens? Maybe. We'll check it out to-morrow at the courthouse."

"What do you think we can get for this?"

"The original fee was two hundred. All for us. It may be worth more now."

"That would be sweet."

They pulled into their apartment complex, hurried by the pool they rarely had time to visit and bounded up the stairs of their building. The apartment was empty when they entered. Their mother had left a note on the refrigerator.

"I'm working the late shift. It's a favor for Marge. I owe her one. Don't worry about me. It'll be fine. Love, Mom."

"Look at this, Matt," Sean said, handing his brother the note.

"Don't worry, my ass. When will she get off?"

"Eleven."

"We're going over."

"Matt, they have escorts now."

"I don't care."

"Hey, okay. I'm not arguing with you."

Their mother's parking-lot rape four years earlier at the hospital was never far from either of their minds. Nor the fact that her attacker was never caught.

"Let's change and go to the gym. We can come back and eat later," Matt said.

"What's the rush?"

"Might be some chicks we can impress. I mean we almost got shot, right?" He joked.

They impressed no one that evening. Matt put up 315 at a body weight of 162. His brother, with his longer arms, did 245 at the same weight. The only women in the gym were a couple of Spandex encased Barbies being fondled between reps by their Kens and a bodybuilder who outweighed them by fifty pounds. At eleven they were in the hospital parking lot where they could watch their mother leave the emergency-room staff exit and walk all the way to her car. She'd never have let them come to pick her up, saying they couldn't run over to protect her all the time; she had to be able to go to work; that's why they have the escort service. And they'd never rely on anyone else. So she wrote them notes and ad-monitions that they silently ignored. If she ever saw them in the shadows, she never said.

Matt was profoundly agitated at these times, a small part of himself wanting someone to try and accost her, to give him the reason to release four years of fury. He imagined that there'd be nothing but melted steel around a crater where he and the attacker had both vaporized.

They recognized her escort as Lucius Weems and watched her go to her car. Matt waited for her to back out and head for the exit as Sean swung by in the Subaru. He jumped in and they left by another exit and were home, watching *Wild Things*, nodding in solemn agreement that Denise Richards was the hottest woman they'd ever seen when they heard her key in the door.

The next morning, they were on the phone at nine to the law office of Joe Anthony, who told them that the Motion for Judgment was still valid. They had served papers for other cases Anthony had handled.

"Do you know where this guy is?" he asked.

Matt said, "No. We're just cleaning house for Mickey. Toss out the ones that aren't servable, get updates on what-ever we haven't served yet. We're still looking; we want to be the ones to get this guy."

"Well you better get on it. The statute of limitations is running out on this one."

"When does that happen?"

"End of the month. If you don't find him, he walks away scot-free on this."

"What does that mean?"

"He hasn't paid child support in ten years. With interest, he owes his ex-wife over a hundred thousand dollars. This is an out-of-state case. The judgment was in Louisiana. They've got a statute of limitations of ten years. Even with the Uniform Interstate Family Support Act, Virginia can't enforce an out-of-state judgment after ten years. So he gets to give his wife, his kids, the state of Louisiana the finger. That's what it means. The paper you have is a Motion for Judgment. It has its own clock, a year. Once we filed that, it stopped the clock on the statute of limitations, but if we don't serve him in a year, then the wife's suit is dismissed and his clock starts up again. Our year is up in a week. I could non-suit the case and re-file it in six months, but his ten years is up in two weeks, so there'd be no point. It's now or never."

"What if he gets served and runs again?"

"That's the biggest problem. You find him, we have to keep an eye on him until we get into court. He has twenty-one days to file a reply. In that time he can liquidate his assets and flee. We go into court, we win the legal battle. But it means nothing. She doesn't get a cent. What I'd love to do is have you serve him, then go get an ABJ on him. I could file that on any motions day."

"What's an ABJ?" Matt asked.

"Attachment before Judgment. If I could go in and show he was a flight risk, I could get the court to attach all his assets immediately, so even if he goes, all his money stays here. It might not cover all he owes, but it's a start."

"What do you need for that?"

"Evidence that he would not honor the notice of suit. See,

this guy hasn't been served yet, you haven't been able to find him, so I can't argue that. That's why we'd need to keep him under surveillance. So we'd know where he went if he ran, and he will. If you boys did the surveillance, what would it cost?"

"Uh, we're twenty-five dollars an hour each, plus expenses. If we did it in shifts, that'd be six hundred dollars a day for three weeks, uh, twelve thousand, six hundred dollars." Matt was woozy just saying the number. He wrote it on a pad for Sean to see.

"My client can't afford that."

"Well, we could only do it for a week. We've got to go back to school."

Sean shook his head and grabbed the paper. He wrote, "I'll go back late. My friends'll cover for me. This is too good to pass up."

"That's still four grand. She can't afford that. If she could, we wouldn't be chasing him."

"We have a deal with Mickey. On these old papers, if we can serve them we get to keep all the money. How much was he getting for this one?"

"Because of the amount of money at stake, he was getting two hundred for the paper. That would have been a hundred for you. I'll tell you what, since we're almost out of time. If you find this guy, it's worth five hundred dollars, all to you."

"How about our expenses?"

"Like what?"

"I don't know. Money to informants, stuff like that."

"Up to a hundred dollars, with an invoice."

"Okay, we've got a deal. We'll send you a letter to confirm this."

"Good luck guys, you're running out of time."

"Is there any information you can give us on this guy? A description, work history."

"Yeah, he's a big guy, about 6 feet, over two hundred pounds. White, brown hair, brown eyes. Anything other than that would be ten years old. He was a custom builder back in Louisiana. There was a significant discrepancy between his declared income and what his clients said they paid him, as I recall from the filings. That was a big issue in establishing the child support. He was getting paid in cash a lot. I'll check the file, see if we have anything else that would be useful. If I come up with anything, how do I get in touch with you?"

Matt gave him the cell-phone number. "It's on all the time."

He hung up the phone and pumped his fists. "Yes. Five hundred and a hundred for expenses."

"Let's go to the courthouse and see what they have on this guy. It's like you said, he had to be in hiding until recently or Mickey'd have found him," Sean said.

They grabbed their jackets and line danced out of the apartment, singing, "Nowhere to run to baby, nowhere to hide."

Matt said, "If that's our theme song, we ought to find out whose song it is."

Their mother rolled over in bed, her arms clasped across her chest, her fists under her chin and said, "Martha and the Vandellas. Good luck, boys," as she heard the door quietly close.

Two hours later they sat in the cafeteria of the Fairfax County Circuit Court building reviewing their notes. They had a home address and phone, office address and phone, and state corporation filings for the last two years for Burle Hitchens and DNT Contracting.

"This makes no sense. He hasn't been hiding. We should have found him first time out of the box a year ago."

"Who cares, Matt. Whoever Mickey gave this to didn't. They screwed up and it's our good fortune. Let's call him, make sure he's at the job site or at his office, and go pay him a visit. Easiest five hundred bucks we've ever earned."

In the car they dialed DNT's office number from the sign.

"DNT Contracting."

"Is this Burle Hitchens?"

"Who's calling?"

"My name is Sean Ellis. I saw your sign on a house in my neighborhood. I'm thinking about adding a deck on to the back of my house, maybe making it a covered porch. I was wondering if I could talk to you about the job."

"Sure. Why don't you come by the office? I'll show you some pictures of other projects we've done."

"Great. What's the address?"

Hitchens gave it to them and they hung up. His office was in his house, on Route 123, down near Lorton, Washington, D.C.'s prison. They pulled into the dirt driveway and parked next to a white pickup truck. The house had a wide, raised front porch that ran across the front, supported by columns at the corners. It was a white wooden salt-box with dormers on the second floor. The windows were open, and gauzy white curtains billowed with the breeze. The backyard had a chain link fence with a 'Beware of Dog' sign. The truck had a bumper sticker that read, "White men can't jump. We don't have to. We hire black men to do that."

"I'm gonna love tagging this guy," Matt said.

"You want to do it?" Sean asked.

"I don't care. We're splitting the money, right?"

"Of course."

"You can do it. It should only take a minute."

"Okay, you write notes for the affidavit."

Sean climbed out of the car, walked across the packed dirt yard, up the steps to the porch and knocked on the door. The door was opened by a large man and Sean stepped inside.

Matt flipped over his pad and began to note the address, time of day, and who went to serve the papers, when he began to realize that Sean was gone longer than a simple "Tag, you're served." Hitchens knew they were coming. He'd be ready to meet Sean. Maybe he was on a phone call and Sean had to wait outside the office. Matt reached down and felt around for the foot long steel bar by the edge of the front seat. He looked around to see if there were other vehicles out back. There were none. If Hitchens made a run for it he'd have to come out the front to get to his truck. Matt thought he'd just slide out and liberate some air from one of the truck's rear tires.

Just as he opened the car door, he saw Sean walk out of the front door. He bounded down the stairs and strode briskly to the car like he was all done and ready to go, but he wasn't smiling. He should have been smiling.

Sean slid into the car.

"What's the matter? Wrong guy?"

"Oh no, he's the right guy. That's the problem. I know why he wasn't served before."

"Yeah?"

"He just offered me a thousand dollars to forget that I found him. He said, 'Oh, you guys again.' Somebody in the office found him and he bought them off."

"Yeah, so what, you papered him, right?"

"Not exactly. I told him I'd come out here with someone else who knew where he was. So he offered you a thousand, too. I told him I had to come out and get you to agree. He says he can get the money, in cash, of course, this afternoon.

Anyway, I started thinking."

"You can stop thinking. We aren't doing this."

"Hear me out. This guy says taking the money isn't a crime. We're not sheriffs, we're not officers of the court. We can't be bribed. If we don't file an affidavit that says we couldn't find him, then we haven't committed fraud. We just walk away. That's all he's asking. Walk away with two thousand dollars. Somebody else has already done it."

"Sean, we can't do this. Mickey gave us this chance. We'd be stabbing him in the back. Hell, we have to tell him that somebody else sold him out. We're doing this for the summer, we're passing through. This is his life. We can't ruin his reputation."

"Yeah, but two grand sure would make our lives easier."

"No doubt. What do you think a hundred grand would do? We'll make more money some day. So this year we'll eat a lot of ramen, we'll mooch off all our friends, we'll go inactive at the fraternity. It'll pass. If we do this, that woman and her kids will never get that money."

"I know, I know. There's got to be a way to take the money and then paper him. I have no problem lying to a weasel like him."

"I don't know man. That's real iffy. We've just got his word that it's not a crime. If you take it, maybe it's some kind of conspiracy to commit fraud even if we don't do it. It's his word against ours. We'd spend all the money in legal fees just trying to hold onto it or stay out of jail. Let it rest. Go back inside, tag him and go. Agreed?"

"Agreed. Anyway, if I did it what kind of motto would we have? Whatever it takes or best offer."

Sean walked back to the house and knocked on the front door. Hitchens yelled, "Come on in. Have a seat. I'm on the phone. Just be a couple of minutes."

Sean sat with the papers rolled up batting them against his open palm. Five hundred bucks wasn't bad. Two grand was a whole lot better. But Matt was right. He'd known it before he opened his mouth but sometimes, just talking things out, they'd come up with better plans than either one of them had on his own. They'd served a lot of papers that way. The perfect solution was keeping the money and serving the guy, but that wasn't an option. He wondered how much they still needed for tuition. Their campus job in the cafeteria covered meals, and loans took care of room. That left tuition and books; oh well.

"All right, kid, come on in."

Sean walked into Hitchens's office. He was a big man, now well over two hundred pounds, Sean guessed, with long mutton-chop sideburns and a droopy left eye.

"What'll it be? If I was you I'd take the money. If you serve me, I'll just get a friend to say I was at their job site when you claimed to serve me. Some place nice and isolated, no witnesses, just me and a friend. Your service'll be dismissed, my ten years'll run out. That bitch isn't getting one penny of my money. No way. Paying you off is just the cost of doing business. I accept that. It's easier, cleaner that way. No publicity, no court appearances, no hassles. Do the right thing, kid. Easiest two grand you'll ever make. It's a win-win situation. What do you say?"

Sean was adrift in this new sea of words. If the service was dismissed as bad, would they lose the five hundred? Could this turn out to be a complete loss, no service, no money? This guy had beaten the system for ten years. He sure sounded like he knew what he was talking about. Sean had to make a decision. The wrong one would carry a lifetime of consequences. Wasn't this why they got the big bucks?

"Okay, this is what I'm going to do . . ." Sean spoke slowly, laying down a path of words like breadcrumbs; maybe someone would find him before he committed an irreversible act.

"What we're going to do is take the money. That's what we agreed to, Sean, right?"

He looked back at the doorway. Matt strode in and reached out his hand to shake Burle Hitchens's. "You're absolutely right, Mr. Hitchens. This is a win-win situation."

"What the hell?" Sean said, relieved, confused and angry all at the same time. He stared incredulously at his brother like the RCA dog, his head cocked to the side.

"Sean, what's our motto? Whatever it takes, right? Well this is what it takes. Trust me."

A mechanical chirp interrupted them. Matt pulled a phone out of his pocket and pushed a button to answer the call.

"No, not now. I can't talk. Look, I'll call you back in, say, fifteen minutes, okay? Fine. Goodbye." He disconnected the line.

"Sorry, another case. Look, Sean, serving papers can't be all that we're about. There's more to life. That's the way I see it. We can do better here. Mr. Hitchens has offered us a way to do that. I think we ought to take him up on it. You understand what I'm saying?" He pointed the phone at him for emphasis.

"Yeah, I guess." Sean had the faint feeling that he was having two conversations, in two languages, ones that he knew just well enough to misunderstand with confidence. He decided not to speak but just listen carefully.

Matt turned toward Hitchens. "I'm his brother. He told you that we found you together. Let me make sure I understand the deal. You'll give us a thousand dollars each. Cash money, that's right?"

Hitchens nodded, "Yeah."

"In exchange we just take this Notice of Judgment and re-file it as unserved, that's it, even though it is for you?"

"That's right."

"No false affidavits, and you don't want us to destroy the paper, just re-file it."

"Yeah, that's the beauty of it for you guys. No crime's been committed. You walk away with the money, no risk of having it confiscated, no risk of jail, painless."

"Okay. You have the money here?"

"No. I can get it easy enough. Meet you back here in, say, an hour, how's that?"

"Tell you what, Mr. Hitchens. As a good faith gesture, how about you give us whatever cash you've got in the office. That way we know you're serious about this, and when we take it, you know we're serious about our part. We're in this together."

"Good point. Let me see what I've got." He reached into the bottom left drawer of the desk and pulled out a metal box. He spun the combination lock, opened the lid, and took out a wad of bills.

He began to thumb the edges back, counting out loud, stopping at four hundred and eighty three. "That good enough for you boys?"

"That's fine," Matt said. He stuffed the phone back in his pocket, took the money and counted out half for his brother. "We'll see you in an hour."

"Nice doing business with you boys."

"Pleasure's all ours, Mr. Hitchens."

Matt led the way out the front door towards the car. Sean hurried to catch up.

"What the hell was that all about, Matt? We're in the shit now. We took the money."

"Keep walking Sean and don't say anything else. We'll talk in the car."

Matt opened the car door and walked around to let himself in. In the car, he pulled the phone out of his pocket, and spoke into the mouthpiece. "Did you get all that?"

"Every word. A warrant's been issued and a car should be there in ten minutes. You need to come straight down to the station and fill out a statement. He'll be booked and jailed."

"Great. We'll stay here until the car arrives, then we'll be straight over."

Matt pushed the off button.

"What did we just do?"

"We did 'better', is what we did. Remember what Joe Anthony told us about serving him and still not getting a penny. I was sitting in the car and I said to myself why am I letting a criminal tell me what is and what is not a crime. I called the police. His offering us money to not do our duty is a crime. It's corruption of an agent. Even if we aren't officers of the court, even if we don't commit a fraud. The officer said he could get a warrant and a car out here right away if a crime was committed in his presence. So I said, what if you hear it. He said that's enough."

"I told him to call me on both lines. First one, then the other. When I answered the first call in the office, all I did was switch to the other line to disconnect him. That line was open and they heard everything. That's why I was waving the phone around. It was a microphone. Hitchens couldn't know that we have a two-line phone—when I said goodbye and pushed a button he assumed I'd turned the phone off. I just moved my hand up to cover the lights."

Matt dialed Joe Anthony's office as the police cruiser pulled up next to them.

"Mr. Anthony. This is Matt Ellis of Short Fuse Process

Service. I have good news for you and your client. Not only did we find Mr. Hitchens, but we served him, and he's also being arrested, as we speak, for corruption of an agent. He offered us a thousand dollars each not to serve him. He'll be going straight to jail and I'd think that should be enough with our affidavits for you to get that ABJ you wanted."

"Christmas in August. Great work, guys. Come by as soon as you can. I'd like you to give my client the news directly. You just changed her life and her kids'."

The police were walking Hitchens out to the cruiser. Sean got out of the car and approached as they were getting ready to tuck him inside.

"Burle Hitchens. This is a Notice of Judgment against you served in the county of Fairfax on behalf of Chelsey Lyn Dougan." As Hitchens's hands were cuffed behind him, Sean tucked the papers in his front shirt pocket, arranging them as neatly as a foulard. The officer opened the door and guided Hitchens into the back seat.

"You were right Mr. Hitchens. This was a win-win situation. Only there were three sides to it, not two."

ACKNOWLEDGEMENTS: The author would like to thank the following people for the gracious donation of their expertise. Any errors are the responsibility of the author. Attorneys Joe Condo and Chanda Kinsey, Arlington County Magistrate Larry Black, Nancy Crawford, Regional Special Counsel for the Virginia Division of Child Support Enforcement, Mark Simons of Advance Process Service, Guillermo Solorzano, and my assistant, Jennifer Egen.

Til Death Do Us Part

"Boss, we're on our way to the airport."

"Do you guys have a credit card for your tickets?"

"No." Sean Ellis made it sound like 'moo'. "Would this be a good time to bring up giving us a company card?"

"Sure, we can beat that dead horse if you like. The answer is still no. It's not that I don't trust you, but I'd have to give them to everybody or explain why not. I tried it once and un-reimbursable expenses went up 14%. I'm not doing that again. Besides, you boys are short-timers. After you graduate, I'll just be left with the headaches.

"When you get to the airport and find out his flight number, call me and I'll purchase your tickets electronically, you can pick them up at the gate."

"You know, I don't think you should treat all your employees the same. Where's the payoff for doing a good job?"

"Tell you what, Sean, you promise not to ask me that again and I'll promise to lose sleep over it."

The Ellis brothers followed Damien Sylvester's car out the access road to Dulles International Airport. Inside Eero Saarinen's masterpiece, under the curved concrete canopy, barely tethered to the ground, Sylvester bought a ticket to Boston. Sean Ellis relayed this information to his employer, Sandra Jones, owner of Metro Detectives.

"You can't work in Massachusetts unless you're under the supervision of a licensed local agency. I'm going to call someone I know up there: James Gruber. He has an agency in Boston. We've covered for his people down here. I'll see if I can get him to meet you with a car at the airport. He'll have an affidavit you each have to fill out and sign. Remember, this is still our case. You call me first, then Jim. Got that?"

"Yes, ma'am," Sean said.

Sean's brother Matt had been watching Sylvester, whose toe-tapping angst threatened to break out in a full Ginger Baker solo at any minute.

Surveillance work had helped accelerate their growing up. You can't 'live in the now' on stakeout. It's all about 'what if?' and being three steps ahead of your target, anticipating the options, always planning ahead. This is the reason they had carry-ons in the trunk of their car and everything they needed to study for finals.

"When is your first exam?" Matt asked.

"Wednesday. But it's advanced drawing. I just have to turn in my portfolio. I've got plenty of work done already. How about you?"

"Biochem is on Thursday. I need to ace this one. It's important for my transcript."

Matt had decided he wanted to go to medical school. Since he also believed that 99 was zero, he had developed a studying jones that drove his brother bonkers. Sean could have benefited from a small transfusion of his drive. He approached deadlines as if they required a magic act. Voila! At the very last minute I shall pull an A out of my hat. The injustice of his successes drove his brother bonkers.

Once seated, five rows behind their target, Matt pulled out the file that Sandra had given them and began to read it. Damien Sylvester was a junior at Georgetown University. He majored in dissolution with a minor in squandering. He had bounced on and off of academic probation, without ever rising above a 2.0 GPA. He'd changed majors so often that he was faced with needing a fifth year to collect enough credits in anything to graduate. Sylvesters had been distinguishing themselves at Georgetown for generations, but he was putting an end to all that. His father, the late Senator Mark Sylvester, had died when Damien was eight years old. His mother, the appallingly wealthy Catarina Sylvester, nee Littbarski, had recently concluded that Damien was not going to pull himself out of his decade long slough of despond without a kick in the rear, and had administered that by announcing that she had changed her trust, and that for the rest of his days Damien's inheritance was to be administered by a consortium of Boston bankers hand picked for their penurious ways.

Damien exploded on the phone, with a tirade on the unfairness of her actions that was equal parts apoplectic rage and mendacious apology. After that, nothing. This nothing had gone on for three weeks and was starting to trouble Mrs. Sylvester. She had contacted Sandra Jones and asked her to keep an eye on her only child. She sent down an old picture of Damien, a hefty retainer check, his address and phone number. She didn't know anything about his friends or the places that he liked to hang out. She didn't want him doing anything rash and self-destructive while he tried to get his head around this monumental insult to his narcissism.

Matt gave the file to his brother to read. When he had finished, Sean turned in his seat and said, "So we just have to make sure he doesn't open a vein or besmirch the family honor?"

"I guess so. This could be a real short trip. His mother lives in Boston. He could be going home to make up with her."

"Oh, God, please don't let that happen. We're looking at easy money here. Twenty-five dollars an hour each; portal to portal billing. For tantrum control. How hard can that be?"

They landed at Logan on time. While Sean watched Damien at the Hertz desk, Matt met with Jim Gruber's field agent, got the keys to their rental car and scanned the affidavit he had to sign. Sure that he was felony free and had not dabbled in moral turpitude, he checked the appropriate spaces. When Sean walked out of the terminal, he handed the form to him, and he scribbled his signature. All the while he kept his eyes on Sylvester as he walked across the lot to get his car.

"Oh yeah, Jim said to give you this. Sandy vouched for you." It was a New England Investigative Services credit card.

Ninety minutes later they were on Route 6, following Damien down the spine of Cape Cod. Surrounded by trees, if you didn't notice the sand you'd have no idea that you were driving out the flexed arm of Massachusetts. That arm, bent at the elbow, ended in the upraised, balled fist of Provincetown, forty miles out into the cold Atlantic from all-seeing Boston.

The trees gave way to giant dunes on both sides of the road. In the distance a tower thin as an ice pick pierced the sandscape.

"The map says there's an ocean around here somewhere, but all I see is sand. We could be in Saudi Arabia, Matt."

The dunes flattened out and the horizon became a deep blue with dancing flashes of sunlight on the surface. Damien Sylvester entered Provincetown. He turned down Cornwell, then right on Bradford and right towards the ocean. Mid-block he pulled into a driveway. Matt stopped the car opposite the inn.

"What do you want to do?"

"Let's give him fifteen minutes. See if he gets a room here. Then we'll register. This whole thing will be a lot easier if we're all sleeping in the same place."

Sylvester left the office, took his bag out of the car and

jogged up to his room on the third floor.

"Excellent. Let's keep him above us. See what the room numbers are below his and ask for one of those by the stairs," Matt said.

Sean walked off to check the room numbers and they went in to register. They got room seventeen and were informed they could stay until next Thursday when the first of the Memorial Day weekend guests would arrive. From then until Labor Day the inn was sold out.

"I'll bring the bags up," Matt said. "Why don't you stay here and follow the trust fund. You do have your cell phone with you if he leaves?"

"Right here, Captain Anal," Sean said, tapping his pocket and then saluting.

Fifteen minutes later, Damien left the compound and headed for Commercial Street and the center of town. Matt and Sean watched him from the car, got out and followed him.

"Here's your room key. It also opens the gate to the grounds. They lock up at eight p.m.," Matt said.

"Anything else I should know?"

"Read this. I don't know if they give this out to everyone or just Virginians that have lost their way and don't know that they aren't the moral majority around here."

It was a brochure from the chief of police, welcoming tourists to Provincetown and alerting them, among other things, that people here enjoy freedom that might not have similar acceptance back home and that one issue for which they have absolutely zero tolerance is hate crimes. They are passionate about this topic.

"Did you know that in Virginia, being gay is unfitness per se to raise a child? Sandy was doing a custody case and told me that was the law," Sean said.

"And America is a vast country encompassing many contradictions, all blended together in our non-stick melting pot." Matt intoned with mock evangelical fervor.

The brothers followed Damien down the hill towards the beach. On Commercial he turned left and meandered into town, slaloming back and forth with the sidewalks that mysteriously appeared and disappeared from each side of the road without ever being on both sides at once.

"Do you think they do this on purpose? Like the way they steer shoppers so that you have to go through the entire store even if you only want one item."

"Does asymmetry affront you?" Sean asked.

"No. I just like irregularities to be rational. Is that so much to ask?"

Sean laughed at his brother. Matt was an inveterate pattern maker, while he was drawn to the eccentric, the unique, and the outliers. At their best they were complements, not opponents.

Up ahead, Damien sat down in a sidewalk café, ordered a beer and watched the parade of mankind pass by. Matt and Sean sat behind him and ordered two ginger ales.

There were tight-lipped New Englanders with fair skin reddened by the sun and salt cured by the sea spray. They wore hats and deck shoes. Sunglasses on straps hung from their necks. Foreign tourists, mostly young and judging by their accents, mostly Scandinavian, pirouetted in the street to take everything in. There were many same sex couples holding hands. Moms pushing their children in strollers. And then there was 'Leatherman,' he of the bovine britches and vest, collar and cuffs. The sides of his head were tattooed with flames and on top an open mouth with pointed teeth. He had his own 'Boy George' on a leash out for his afternoon walk. Outré meets quaint in Provincetown.

Sean smiled. "Strange stuff happens at the edges of America. Do you ever wonder why that is?"

"If it isn't on the MCAT, I don't want to know. Our boy is on the move." Matt pushed away from the table. Sean waved the waitress over and paid the bill.

Traffic was light and the crowds were thin. Maybe half of the shops were still closed. There were lots of construction vehicles out, their crews making last minute repairs before high season began.

"He has no idea he's being followed. He hasn't looked back once."

"We need a break. There's no crowd cover out here."

Sylvester wasn't into art and passed the galleries without even slowing down. Sean was in agony.

"Listen if he stops anywhere for awhile, how about you tail him alone and I'll hit some of these galleries. I saw really good stuff back there."

"Sure. But if you do that, look for a gift for mom. Maybe a necklace or something. She likes beads and shells."

"Good thought."

Sylvester passed the tattoo and piercing shops, the gay pride store and the windowless leather bar. He did stop to admire a little teddy in white lace, feathers and leather trim on a mannequin in the Erotique Boutique. Playtime Provincetown gave way to the city that works: town hall, police station, public library, post office.

Sylvester walked out to the town pier. Tour buses filled the parking lot. He stopped at the whale watch kiosk and then continued on to the end. He stood, hands in pockets, his jacket collar turned up and stared out to sea past the beckoning finger of Long Point and its lighthouse.

Sixty-five feet away the Ellis brothers rotated so that Sean could see Damien over Matt's shoulder.

"What do you think he's doing? He's been standing there too long for me. There isn't that much to see," Matt said.

"Maybe he's waiting for his ship to come in. I don't know."

"What if he's deciding to take a long walk off this short pier?"

"Then he's all yours big brother. You're a much better swimmer than I am."

"Shit. If that nimrod decides to pitch himself into the sea because mommy's teats have dried up, I will tie him to a piling and count his bubbles."

"Easy bro. Why don't we sidle up a little closer so we can blow our cover and tackle him before he enters the life aquatic?"

Just as they started to move forward, Sylvester spun away and began to walk back towards them. They turned towards a seafood carryout and pretended to pore over the menu.

"Why are we saying no to chicken lobster?" Sean asked as he pointed to a hand painted sign above the menu.

"Well I'm generally against interspecies breeding. I think that a chicken lobster would be both ugly and tasteless."

Sean saw Damien walk past in the carryout glass.

Sylvester went into a restaurant called The Lobster Pot. Matt sent Sean around to see if there was a back door to the place. He came back shaking his head.

"You want to get something to eat? We may not get a chance later on."

"Yeah, but not inside. I don't want him seeing us too often."

Across the street there was a sandwich shop. Matt got a lobster roll and Sean a bifana, a Portuguese pork loin sandwich. They sat in the shop and watched the door across the street. When Sylvester appeared, they followed him back to the inn.

Around eight, he came out of his room in a robe, went down to the Jacuzzi, dropped it on a lounge and joined two blondes in the water.

"He's not likely to go anywhere dressed like that. Let's just watch him from here," Sean said.

Matt nodded. He was on the phone. "Hi, Mom." He gave her the inn's name and their room number. It was she who had insisted that they get cell phones once they started to do surveillance work. The illusion that they were never out of touch let her get to sleep before they walked in to their apartment.

"We've got to be back before Thursday for exams. Anything you'd like us to get you from here? I'd recommend the lobster. It's as cheap as peanut butter up here, but I don't think it'll travel that well. Love you, bye."

"Did you call Sandy?"

"Yeah. She said to sit on him as long as we can. She'll send Tom and Bruce up before we have to leave. I also filed a report with Jim Gruber. What are you going to do?"

"There's not enough light to draw. I'll watch Damien if you want to study."

"Cool. Thanks. Tomorrow, if we're in town, why don't you go to some galleries? I picked up a couple of street maps at the front desk. Take one in case you have to find us in a hurry."

Sean sat back from the window, so he wasn't visible from the outside and watched Damien and the blondes cohere. At ten they separated and went to their rooms. He went out and sat by the Jacuzzi until Damien's light went out.

At five, Sean went for a run through town. On the way back, he scribbled the names and addresses of the galleries he wanted to visit. Matt left for his run at six-thirty. At eight they were having coffee and muffins by the pool when Damien walked into the dining room to get his breakfast.

Sylvester went back to his room and stayed put until noon. At a quarter past twelve he popped out of his room, took the stairs three at a time and dashed across the courtyard to his car. The Ellis brothers didn't even look up until he was in the driveway concentrating on traffic.

He turned right and two minutes later they did. Sylvester crossed Route 6, drove past the town dump and entered the national seashore. He parked near the visitor's center, walked quickly to it, entered and went upstairs. Sean followed while Matt sat in the car writing down the license tags of the other cars in the lot.

Sean wandered around the first floor displays alert to any sounds from above. After a few minutes he casually made his way to the observation deck. What's with this guy and precipices? He thought.

As he climbed out of the stairwell he saw Damien in an animated conversation with an older man. Sean turned away and went to the other side of the deck and busied himself learning about the eternal war between rapacious man and the vengeful dunes. Denuded of their trees to provide building materials and firewood, they became nomads bent on erasing all signs of our existence. The moving sands threatened to cover up the roads and encroached on the town until vegetation was planted to hold them in their place. Reparations for past crimes against nature.

The older man towered over Damien. Thin with deeply etched cheeks, his stubble of beard was white. He listened to whatever Damien had to say and responded both verbally and by tapping out his message with an insistent forefinger to the chest. The man pushed by Damien who said, "I couldn't get the money. I tried." He followed him downstairs and out to the beach. The older man trudged across the sand to his car.

Sean watched from inside the visitor center. The old man tapped his watch and pointed at Damien who nodded understanding.

Damien drove back to the inn with the Ellises in his wake. He spent the rest of the afternoon in his room. Matt studied by the pool and Sean wandered in and out of half a dozen galleries. When Damien left for town, Matt called to have his brother meet him. Damien met the old man on the sidewalk outside an upscale craft store on Commercial Street. They walked leisurely into town. The old guy stopped for an ice cream cone near city hall. He was handed a flyer by a volunteer helping with the flood of marriage license applications that had been taken out that weekend. He scanned the flyer, turned it over and looked to chuck it in the trash. He stopped, went back to the front and read it carefully. He slapped Damien in the chest, broke out in a big grin and walked across the street to city hall. Matt and Sean followed and watched as Damien Sylvester and his friend filled out an application for a license to wed. The brothers followed the lovebirds back out to the street.

"I know my 'gaydar' is jammed, but this makes no sense at all," Matt said.

"I know. I thought he was pretty interested in those two blondes at the pool."

"Which proves nothing. In case you hadn't noticed, not only is symmetry in short supply in this town but also nobody seems too keen on respecting the sanctity of categories either. Girls want to be guys. Guys want to be girls. Opposites attract and repel."

"Okay, so Damien Sylvester is bisexual. But why get married? Most of the couples in that line were a lot older. They probably wanted to do this for a long time. Better yet, why this guy? Provincetown is not Richmond and everyone is real comfortable expressing affection in public. These two haven't touched each other except for that one finger typing bit out on the dunes. They aren't even staying in the same hotel. Where's the romance?"

"It looked like the old guy's idea. Maybe it's some way to get the money Damien owes him."

"How? Blackmail mom? Give me money or I go public with your son's dirty little secret. A wedding license would add some heft to that claim."

"About the only thing we've ruled out here is true love."

"Did you see the sign in there for volunteers to help with the paperwork? Why don't you see if you can get a look at the application, ID the guy? I'll keep tabs on them out here," Sean said.

"Okay. If you get the chance, give Sandy a call. See if she has any ideas." Matt turned away and went back into city hall.

Sean nodded and set off behind his quarry. An hour later he was back at the inn, sitting by the pool when his phone rang. It was Matt's number.

"I'm on my way back. I got enlisted to help with the filing and let's just say I was successful. I'll tell you more when I get there."

When Matt made it back to the inn, he found Sean holding court with the two blondes. Their names were Merete and Helle, they were from Copenhagen and they were a couple. Sean's drawing had attracted their attention and they were vigorously debating whether post-modernism had been doomed from the start, a victim of its own faulty premises or had been assassinated by the academy in a backlash of corrupt classicism, or some such thing.

When the wind had died down and the girls had gone, Matt said, "You know, that art thing is as good as sitting a baby on your lap. Girls love that stuff. You gotta teach me some."

"Okay, I'll give you a cover story for your stick figures. Repeat after me: You're an outsider artist; you're into neo-primitivism; you're trying to recapture a child's view of the world before it was corrupted by society. Got it?"

"Yeah. What does that mean?"

"You can't draw worth a shit but you don't know it."

"And that'll work?"

"Just don't talk to any art majors. Don't worry, your time will come. I'll be a starving artist in some sketchy part of Brooklyn and you'll be a plastic surgeon in Malibu with a supermodel on each arm."

"I'll settle for just getting into medical school."

"You will. You've never failed at anything you set out to do."

"Then why do I think that failure is just way overdue in finding me?"

" 'Cause you're you, big brother."

"Where's our metrosexual?"

"Up in his room contemplating eternity with Ichabod Crane."

"What did you learn at city hall?"

Matt tapped his shirt pocket. "I Xeroxed the application. They're getting married at eight a.m. on Monday. You have to wait seventy-two hours after the application is filed. Buyer's remorse I guess."

Sean laughed. "We should get that info to Sandy."

"The application included name, address, DOB and social security number. For that marriage to be legal, all that info has to be correct."

"Christ, Sandy will know if he's boxers or briefs in ten minutes."

"Did you learn anything from those girls?"

"Not really. He hit on them at first. Over and above his anatomical handicaps, they found his boundless self-regard off-putting. There's no 'u' in 'the joy of me'."

"Did he tell them why he was here?"

"A fairytale about being in law school at Harvard, just down here for the weekend, catch a little sun, surf and sand, recharge the batteries before finals."

"Lifestyles of the rich and shameless. I'll call Sandy. Can you watch for Sylvester?" Matt asked.

Sean nodded and went back to his drawing of Merete and Helle's smiling faces, foreheads touching, happy through and through.

Matt returned with his biochem book. "Oh, by the way, I found this really cool bracelet in town. River stone, onyx and silver. The lady said that Uma Thurman's sister designed it."

"Did you touch it? That's as close as you'll ever get to 'The Divine Miss U'."

"I think mom would love it."

"How much was it?"

"Six hundred."

"Ouch. I know that this has been a great gig, but all the money we're making here is spoken for."

"I know. It would be nice to get her something special. A complete surprise. A reminder that good things can also happen to good people."

Matt's phone rang. "Hello. Oh hi Sandy. What do we know?"

"Nothing yet on Mr. Docherty. I've called Jim Gruber. He has lots of contacts in the Boston PD. We'll see if he has any criminal record. Maybe Damien owes him money for drugs, or its gambling losses. More importantly, I spoke with our client. She's not aware of any such problems with her son.

She says he likes to drink, to party; he's generally irresponsible but nothing criminal. However, she doesn't strike me as the most attentive of mothers. She is adamant that she does not want that wedding to take place and she doesn't care how we stop it. She'll be down to talk to Damien late on Monday. She has some business in Chicago and can't get away until then."

"Okay, she doesn't care how we do it. How about you?"

"I care. I don't want you breaking any laws. Be creative."

"How about a bonus if we pull it off?"

"Like what?"

"A thousand dollars."

"Total. Done. You stop the wedding and you don't wind up in jail and it's yours."

Matt hung up. "Hot damn. You hear that? A thousand dollar bonus if we stop the wedding."

"Got any ideas?"

"We don't know what the reasons are for them getting married, so we don't know what arguments would sway Damien away from that. We're only going to get one chance at this. If we don't succeed, Docherty will keep us away from him. He was the one who seemed to initiate the idea," Matt said.

Peter John Docherty stood in the doorway to the courtyard. His hands were stuffed into his trench coat pockets and his collar was turned up against the early evening breeze. He was slightly hunched over so it was difficult to gauge his true height. Six-three at least. Close-cropped gray hair stood out like magnetized metal filings on his head. His face was an unreadable hieroglyph of creases and slits.

Damien came down the stairs and the two men went off to town.

After a thirty count, Sean slapped his brother on the leg.

"Let's go save the day for Mother Sylvester." They tagged along trying to figure out how to separate the two men but came up empty.

In the middle of the street a conundrum in army boots, tutu, make-up and five o'clock shadow yowled and hiccupped, "I'll never call you again, you bitch," to the back of another equally transgressive soul, striding away, head up despite the terrible news.

The rejecter lurched drunkenly backwards and caromed off the Ellis brothers. Turning around, he crooned "Hello, boys. Here for the festival are you? I could make both of you very happy. What do you say we go to my place?" He tried to wriggle himself between the brothers and snake his arms through theirs. They both jumped back swatting at their arms as if they were covered in spider-webs. An immediate reaction of horror and revulsion.

"Get away from me, you . . ." Matt snarled.

"Unfortunately confused, extremely intoxicated, grief stricken inhabitant of this fair town," Sean said, pulling his brother away.

"What the . . ."

"Stay cool, man. We can't afford to lose Damien. They're going into that bar up ahead."

Docherty's height helped keep them in sight. They ducked into a doorway and followed a brick path to a recessed entrance. The brothers gave the cover charge to a bald guy sitting on a stool. Pinned to the wall behind him were the house rules. No murder, no mayhem. The usual.

The bar was to the left, tables to the right and a dance floor in between. Live music began at nine. The crowd was mixed, gays and straights. Docherty and Sylvester took a table at the edge of the dance floor and were engaged in a hushed conversation. Matt and Sean sat at the bar, nursed a couple of light beers and watched them in the mirror.

They'd stopped talking and Damien was scanning the crowd. He seemed interested in a quartet of girls seated across the dance floor. Spectacled twins in matching outfits. Sean wondered why they dressed like that. Why reinforce their sameness? The other two would never be mistaken for each other. The older woman had an angular, sharp-featured face that was all smiled out. Her hair was a crinkly cascade and her back was covered in a baroque tattoo with a weeping eye in the center. Her companion was a waif, with darting, anxious eyes who picked nervously at the label on her beer. Damien moved to get up. Docherty clamped his wrist to the table and he sat back down. Damien smiled at the girls and raised his beer in salute.

"I have an idea," Sean said, "but if we do this, the loser decides when it becomes a cool story to tell. No exceptions. Agreed?"

Matt nodded and leaned over while his brother whispered in his ear. They made fists and shook them three times. Matt's stayed a fist, Sean's became a sideways V. Sean shook his head. Matt pulled out his cell phone. Sean took a deep breath and pushed away from the bar.

He came up behind Damien Sylvester, put a hand across the back of his chair, smiled at Docherty, turned to Damien, and staring deeply into his eyes, said, "You're just the prettiest little thing in this whole room. I don't know what you're doing with Lurch here, but I'd love to . . ."

Sylvester spun around and took a swipe at Sean's head with his beer bottle. It grazed his head but did not stagger him. Docherty pushed away from the table as if he might join in then settled back down with a look of resigned indifference.

Sylvester stood, called Sean "a fucking faggot" and

launched a roundhouse that took forever to catch Sean high on the side of his head. Sean staggered back, fell on his butt and rolled over holding his head. Matt spoke loudly into his phone. The bar's bouncers separated the two of them and looked at Sean's head. Matt flipped his phone closed and watched his brother.

Three minutes later two policeman entered the bar. They took statements from Sylvester, Sean and other patrons. They asked Sean if he wanted to press charges, which he most assuredly did. Sylvester was read his rights and marched off to jail. Since it was Friday night, he couldn't be bailed out until Monday, when the court opened. Because of the huge number of civil ceremonies being performed each day, he'd have to wait until additional magistrates arrived to handle the overflow of work. Sean declined medical attention and returned to the bar.

"I don't know what was harder, coming on to him or waiting for that roundhouse to arrive."

"I'm proud of you little brother. You earned that bonus. Your plan and you executed it."

"I just thought about how immediate and unthinking our reaction was to that guy in the street. If we were right about Damien, that he wasn't gay and he's as impulsive as his mother described, it was worth a try. Remember it's my call when this gets to be a cool story. I don't care if you're trying to impress Uma Thurman."

"Look, Docherty's leaving."

"Let him, our work is done."

"Is it? We still don't know why they were going to get married. He's the only one who does. We can't get to talk to Damien. I'd like to know if we were on the right track."

"Do you think he'll tell us?"

"Maybe, maybe not. What's the harm in asking? He says

no and we're no worse off than when we started. He tells us and it might be useful to Mrs. Sylvester in fixing things with her son. And it might impress Sandy."

"That's always a good idea. I'd like to get more work like this."

They followed Docherty back through town to a chain motel near Route 6. He went into the motel's restaurant, slid into a booth and ordered a drink. The Ellis's approached him.

"Mind if we join you?"

"Who the fuck are you two clowns?"

"I'll take that as a yes," Matt said and slid into the booth.

"We're detectives, Mr. Docherty. And we have a mystery only you can solve."

"And what would that be?"

"Why were you and Damien Sylvester going to get married?"

The waitress returned with Docherty's drink and asked what they wanted. "Coffee. Two," Sean replied.

"I don't know what you're talking about."

"We got a copy of the application."

"You did? What else do you know?"

"We know that Damien owed you money. We don't know why."

"So you say."

"No. I heard you talking out at the visitor's center. We have photos of you two talking." He ad-libbed.

"You do?"

Matt's phone went off. He pulled it out. It was Sandy Jones. "I've got information on Peter Docherty. It's not good news."

Docherty sipped his drink. "You have any tapes of us talking?"

"No," Sean said. "So what was it? Did he owe you money for drugs or gambling?"

Docherty smiled and reached into his pocket.

"My theory was it was a plot to blackmail his mother into not changing her trust."

"Docherty's a contractor for the Boston mob. He's been linked to three killings but never indicted."

Matt nodded, never taking his eyes off of Docherty.

"That's great, Sandy. You have all the information we sent you on Docherty, right? The application, all our reports, the photos? Good. No, we'll be in the office, bright and early Monday to sign all those reports. We just have a couple of loose ends to tie up with Mr. Docherty. In fact, he's here with us right now. Anything you'd like to ask him?"

Docherty removed his hand from his jacket. "Put that away," he whispered.

"Tell you what, Sandy. Call me back here in five minutes. If I don't pick up, call the cops in Provincetown." He gave her the motel's name and address.

"Very smart. You know, one thing about our lines of work, you have to be able to improvise." Docherty finished his drink. "Lots of things happen when you get married. Like you inherit your spouse's estate, when they die, god forbid. Kind of a nice way to insure payment for services rendered. You also get the protection of spousal privilege. You can't be compelled to disclose a conversation you've had with your loved one. You can't even waive that protection. You're covered even if you're both engaged in a criminal conspiracy. They take the sanctity of marriage very seriously around here. It even survives after divorce. Like a lifetime vow of silence. Lesson's over. You're bright boys, you connect the dots."

The waitress arrived with the coffees. Docherty paid for his drink and stood up to leave.

"A final word. You got lucky here. You don't have any evidence of a crime. Nothing was said to Mr. Sylvester, because we weren't married yet. But you really fucked up my retirement plans. Cost me a lot of money. Too many people know about you and me for me to do anything about that now. But, if I ever see either of you again, I'll kill you, no questions asked. Have a nice trip home."

When they were sure he was gone, they slowly turned to face each other. It was Matt who broke the silence. "I don't know about you, Sean, but I think we just earned every penny."

ACKNOWLEDGEMENTS: I'd like to thank defense attorney extraordinaire Peter Greenspun and the queen of private investigators, Joan Beach, for their help with this story. Any errors are entirely my responsibility.

What Goes Around

In the darkness things always go away from you. Memory holds you down while regret and sorrow kick hell out of you.
James Sallis, The Long-Legged Fly

Trickle down was so much bullshit. If you let the rich get richer then some of that money just had to trickle down through their tightly clenched fists. The only thing that "trickled down" as the economy came to a halt was misery. A monsoon of misery. Lost jobs, lost homes, lost dreams, lost hopes. All of which was good for business. My business, private investigation.

I was going through our weekly collections, counting up the slow pays, deciding which ones we were going to put on hold, who we were going to introduce to our lawyers.

"Call for you, Leo, line one," my secretary, Kelly, announced over the intercom.

I picked up the phone. "This is Leo Haggerty, what can I do for you?"

"Mr. Haggerty, my name is Gina Logan, we met once before . . ."

"Where was that?"

"The Virginia Investigators License Course last year. You taught the section on professional ethics and liability."

"That's right."

"Well, I was the one who talked to you after the class."

"The adoptee, right?"

"Yes, that's right. I'm surprised you remembered me."

"You asked some very good questions. Did you ever find your mother?"

"Uh, yes I did."

69

I thought about asking her how it had gone, but didn't. A triumph she would have already declared; a fiasco was none of my business.

"Well, how can I help?"

"I'd like to buy a little of your time, if I could. I need a consultation. I think I've made a big mistake that might cost me my license."

"Okay. How much of a rush is there? I'm just about ready to leave the office. Can it wait until tomorrow?"

"I don't think so. Is there any way we can meet this evening?"

"Tell you what. I'm going over to Artie's for dinner. Can you meet me there in say thirty minutes?"

"Sure, whatever you say."

"Okay. The manager's name is John, tell him you're meeting me. If you get there first, ask for the last booth on the upper level and ask him to keep the one next to it empty."

"Sure thing. Listen, thank you very much. I'll look for you there."

Artie's was my favorite restaurant. Its fine food and bustling crowds were welcome antidotes to my life alone. A year's worth of meals there had earned me some consideration.

I finished my work with the billing logs, reviewed tomorrow's schedule with Kelly, and left to meet Gina Logan.

On the way over, I tried to remember what she had looked like. Nothing came to me. I'd check her ID anyway. I parked at Artie's, entered, and waved to John. The end booth was empty. I pointed to it and he nodded that it was fine.

I slid in and John came over. We shook hands and I asked him if he could keep the next booth empty.

"Sure. You working?"

"Yeah. I'll try to keep it brief."

"No problem. Just let us know when we can open it up."

"Thanks, John."

I ordered the calamari and waited for Gina Logan. Fifteen minutes later I looked up from my plate to see a woman standing there.

"Mr. Haggerty, I'm Gina Logan." She put out her hand. I stood partway up, shook it, and motioned for her to join me.

She set her bag aside, took off her raincoat and said, "Thanks for seeing me on such short notice. I really appreciate it."

"No problem. Why don't you tell me what your situation is? Don't give me any particulars, keep it real general," I said and forked some squid into my mouth.

"Okay. I'm a free-lance investigator. I've been trying to supplement that with direct referrals, maybe start my own shop some day. Anyway, about ten days ago I got one, my first one, in fact. So I met with the client. He tells me he thinks his wife is having an affair. He wants me to follow her to see if it's true. He's going out of town for the weekend, a business trip. It's the perfect opportunity for her if it's true. So I got the details on the wife, a retainer for two days of my time, and I tailed her."

"When did you start?"

"The next day. He was going from my office to the airport. This was Thursday evening. I started with her around eleven-thirty."

"In case she was having a nooner."

"Right."

"So what happened?"

"Well, she wasn't going out on her lunch break, but . . ."

A waiter appeared to fill her water glass and ask if she wanted a menu.

"No, thank you. A cup of coffee would be nice though."

"Anything else for you, Mr. Haggerty?"

Yeah, a refresher course on manners. "No, I'm fine for now." I set my fork down.

When the waiter left, I looked up from my plate. "Sorry, that was rude of me. I guess I've been eating alone too long."

"No need to apologize, I'm fine. I never eat this early anyway."

"Well, if you change your mind . . ."

"Thanks, but coffee will be fine."

"So, you were saying . . ."

"Where was I . . . oh, right, she didn't leave her office for lunch but at five she came out of the front of the building, stood on the sidewalk for a couple of minutes, and was met by a man."

"Not her husband."

"Not even close. They walked down the street to a restaurant with a bar, went in, had a few drinks, stayed for dinner, then went back to his car. He drove her to her car and followed her home. Where he spent the night, departing around ten-thirty the next morning."

"You've got opportunity and inclination. Job well done. You confirmed that the guy wasn't her cousin or brother, right?"

"Yes. I did stay awake through your lecture, you know." She smiled.

"Apparently. I hope it wasn't too difficult to do."

"Not at all. Your stories were a great relief. At least, to me they were. To know what kind of mistakes you'd made over the course of your career, and what you'd learned from them. That was why I called you. I figured that if anyone would understand how I'd gotten myself into this jam, you would. I even have a quote from your lecture on my desk. I start off each day looking at it."

"What did I say? I'll be honest, I didn't prepare that talk. I was winging it."

"You said, 'It's not the mistakes you make, but what you make of them that's important. Nothing will make you a better detective, faster, than a good mistake, if you let it.' "

I thought about all the qualifiers I'd trim that brave talk with now, but kept them to myself.

"So far, you've done everything right. Where's the mistake?"

"You asked if I checked the guy out, right? I did. I ran his plates through DMV and got his name, address, and so on. Monday I called him, posing as a cosmetics salesperson, and found out that he had no female family in the area who could use our free samples. Anyway, Monday evening my client calls me and I have to give him the bad news. I've done this before, so I go into my newscaster imitation, and give him the facts, no nonsense, straight out, boom-boom. I tell him I have pictures if he needs them. I was down in my bunker waiting for the explosion. You know how it is when they first find out. It's either hiccups and tears and it can't be true or they go ballistic and every other word is kill or fucking fill-in-the-blank. This guy was only interested in who the man was. He was convinced it was someone he knew, either at work or a friend. He just wanted to know who it was and whether he'd been betrayed twice."

"And you said that knowing who it was really wasn't going to help anything, that he needed to decide what he wanted to do about this and if he'd have his lawyer contact you, you'd discuss the evidence you had."

"Right, but he said he couldn't decide what he wanted to do until he knew what he was dealing with and then he started asking me questions, you know the gory-detail ones that nobody needs to know. Did they do this, did they do that. I couldn't stand it, he was tearing himself apart . . ."

"So, you told him the name of the guy."

She pursed her mouth and nodded. "Yeah, I told him who the guy was. He was real grateful, it wasn't anyone he knew. He said he'd discuss it with his lawyer and get back to me."

"And?"

"And I didn't hear back from the guy or his lawyer."

"How long has it been?"

"A week. That's too long. If you've got a lawyer and you tell him what's happened and what you've got, the lawyer is going to tell you to go with it. If you act on it immediately, you've got all the leverage."

"Maybe the guy hasn't called his attorney yet. Maybe he's mulling it over, maybe he and the wife are getting into therapy instead. Maybe he wasn't such a great husband in the first place."

"I wish. No, I got antsy and I started thinking about things. The more I thought about them the less I liked what I was thinking."

"Which was?"

"That the wife and her boyfriend didn't seem at all self-conscious about their displays of affection. They met right in front of her office and kissed very openly on the sidewalk. Suppose a co-worker came out? Anyway the kicker was when I called the DMV back. I ran her plates and asked for any other cars registered at that address. None. No car. No hubby."

"Did you have his plates?"

"No. He said he was leaving his car at the airport. She'd only have the other one to use."

"Maybe his car is a company car."

"No. I went by the house yesterday, caught the mailman. He says she lives alone. He never delivers mail to anyone but her at that address."

"So your client lied to you and you're afraid that . . ."

"He's a stalker and he's going to use the information I gave him to hurt someone, probably the boyfriend."

"What can I do for you?"

"First, can I tell the boyfriend what's happened and that he might be in danger? Is that a breach of client confidentiality? Secondly, am I at any risk if this guy hurts someone?"

"First things first. Let me see your investigator's license and your driver's license."

"Why?"

"Because all the time I've been listening I haven't been able to picture you at the lecture. Oh, I remember talking to someone but I can't physically place you, so before I open my mouth and get into this mess, I want to be sure you are you."

"Oh." She took being forgotten pretty well, and pulled her licenses out of her wallet and handed them to me.

Gina Logan was licensed by the State of Virginia as a private investigator. The start date was right for the course she claimed to have taken. I looked at the back of her driver's license and memorized her address, date of birth, and social security number. The picture was a good likeness: large deepset eyes ringed in shadows; pale skin contrasting with her plum red lips. Any more color on them would look like a hemorrhage. Her license said brown and brown, five-five and one hundred and ten pounds. My eyes agreed, but there were pewter streaks in her hair.

"Okay. First question. You don't owe your client squat. He hired you under false pretenses and that voids the contract, explicit or implicit, that governs your services. You won't be violating a client's confidence by talking to the target because your client's behavior has waived that protection.

"Second question. Are you at risk if someone gets hurt?

Yes. The vicarious liability laws would extend to you if information you gave led to an injury."

"So, I shouldn't have told him the guy's name."

"Yup."

"I guess I should contact the guy and warn him right away."

"Maybe."

"Why not?"

"Because this may be only half of the problem."

She frowned for a moment. Then she said, "I don't understand. What's the rest of the problem?"

"I've been doing this work for almost twenty years and this has happened to me two, maybe three times. Your first case and you get set up this well. I don't think so. How did this guy find you?"

"He said he looked me up in the yellow pages."

"Nobody referred him to you?"

"No."

"Think about that for a second. What does your listing say?"

"My name and number."

"Address?"

"No. I work out of—"

"Your home and you're a single woman, no ring on your left hand, and don't want clients to have that information. Just the way I recommended in the lecture.

"Without a referral, people go through the phone book and find an agency by location. Then they compare rates over the phone and go to the nearest and cheapest. If they feel comfortable after the first interview, you've got a client. Did you talk money over the phone with him?"

"No, I was so excited to have a client, I forgot. I made sure that we talked about it first thing when we met."

"And he had no problem with your fees, right?"

"That's right."

"What's your client's name?"

"Todd Berman."

"I'll tell you what else your client didn't do. He didn't go through the yellow pages alphabetically. Franklin Investigations would be before you and we didn't get a call like this in the last week. If we had, we'd have taken the case and it wouldn't have gotten to you. So it wasn't a referral, it wasn't your ad, and it wasn't alphabetical. Only one other way this guy found you."

"And that is?"

"Somebody sent him to you. Somebody who doesn't like you. Not one bit. If I was you, I'd like to know who that is. Then figure out what I want to do about it."

"Yeah, I'd like to know that. Do you have any ideas?"

"First, let's keep you away from the target. Your client knows what you look like. If he sees you near the guy, he'll know his story was blown. That's okay as far as him not hurting anyone, but once he backs off it'll be twice as hard to find out who set you up. Why don't I contact the guy? I can warn him without your client wising up. That way we may still be able to flush out whoever has it in for you."

"Okay. What can I do?"

"Right now, nothing. I'm going to call some other people in town tomorrow. See if any of them had contact with this Berman guy before you. Try to trace his steps looking for a P.I. If that turns anything up, you can do the legwork on it."

"Okay. How much do you charge?"

"I'm a hundred dollars an hour. This thing we just did here is on the house. I don't charge people to find out if I can help them. If we're agreed I can help you, my meter starts."

Gina Logan gave me her hand. As we shook hands, she

said, "Start your meter, Mr. Haggerty."

"Do you have the case file with you?"

"Yes, it's in my bag."

"Why don't you leave it with me. I'll get on this right after I finish eating. You can come by the office tomorrow, we'll do a fee-for-services agreement, and that'll make it official."

"Great. Thanks very much, Mr. Haggerty. I feel a lot better now that we've talked."

We shook hands again and smiled. This rush of optimism would recede after a while and her doubts, like roaches, would return, scurrying about in the dark recesses of her mind when she was alone, waiting for news. Optimism is just a by-product of activity, just another metabolite.

Gina Logan slipped into her coat, placed the case file on the table, fumbled around for some money for the coffee until I waved her off saying I'd pay for it, smiled again and left.

John came over. "Are you staying for dinner tonight?"

"Yeah, let me have the mixed grill and another cup of coffee. And I'm done working. Thanks, again."

"No problem."

I opened the case file on Todd Berman. Gina had his name, address, and phone number. Berman paid his retainer in cash. The information was probably all phony, but that was okay. The woman would know who he was and where to find him.

I flipped over the contact sheet and services agreement, to the information on her subjects. The woman's name was Tara McKinney. She worked as a secretary at a small trade association. Her work address and phone number were listed, so was a description of her car and tags. Gina's notes said Tara McKinney was five-seven, one hundred and twenty pounds. She had blonde hair worn straight, long, green eyes and pierced ears—all of her earrings dangled or were big hoops. She wore nonprescription sunglasses when out.

The next page was her surveillance notes and a Ziploc bag of photographs. I took them out and fanned them in my hand. There was a good one of Tara and her boyfriend. I stood that up against my water glass and filed the rest.

After she'd made her case, Gina listed the DMV information on the boyfriend: Stanley Calloway, address and phone and Social Security number.

The rest of her notes confirmed her story. After I finished eating, I tucked the file into my briefcase and left Artie's. I called Mr. Calloway from my car.

"Hello."

"Yes, is this Mr. Calloway?"

"Yes, this is Stan Calloway."

"My name is Leo Haggerty. I'm a private investigator and I have reason to believe that you are being watched by someone who may intend to do you and your girlfriend, Tara McKinney, some harm. I'd like to meet with you so we can discuss this further."

"Just who is it that's supposed to be watching me?"

"I'm not sure of his name. He calls himself Todd Berman. I have reason to believe that he's an ex-boyfriend of Ms. McKinney's."

"Jesus Christ, not him again. I thought we were finished with all this."

"What do you mean, 'finished with all this'?"

"Tara had him arrested the last time he harassed her. He got a suspended sentence and a fine. He was supposed to be in some kind of counseling. If he ever harassed her again he was going to jail."

"Maybe he's decided that the way to keep her for himself is to keep everyone else away from her. If no one else will go out with her because of his harassment, maybe he thinks he'll win her back. Did that judgment cover you?"

"No. How did you find out about this? Are you watching me, too?"

"No, Mr. Calloway. This information came to me through another investigation." Technically true. "And I felt it was important to alert you right away. I have some ideas on how to respond to this Mr. Berman."

"Don't bother calling him that. His name is Joel Silverman."

When Calloway didn't address my invitation, I repeated it.

"Can we talk about Mr. Silverman?"

"Why? I'm going to do what we did the last time, call the police and have him arrested, or get a lawyer to charge him with harassment."

"It's not that simple. He hasn't done anything to you yet. The police won't pick him up. Your lawyer might be more successful. He might get a restraining order issued, but you see what he's doing even with jail time hanging over him. He hasn't quit. He's just changed his approach. Besides, I believe that someone pointed Silverman at you for their own ends. They don't care what trouble he causes you if it helps them."

"Who is that?"

"I don't know yet. That's the other investigation I mentioned." Technical truth # 2. "I'm hoping to nail both Mr. Silverman and the person who is using him. I need your help to do that."

"How do I know that you aren't working with Silverman, that this whole story isn't a scheme to get me alone somewhere and kill me? That's what he threatened Tara with. That he'd kill her and anyone who went out with her."

"You don't know, Mr. Calloway. I'm willing to meet with

you anywhere, anytime, under any conditions you choose. I only ask one thing in terms of helping me understand and predict what Mr. Silverman might do. I'd like to meet with you and Tara McKinney. If not together this first time, that's fine. Do whatever you want to convince yourself that I'm who I say I am. But I think her input would be very helpful."

"Let me think about this. How can I get in touch with you?"

I gave him my office number and beeper, and got a dial tone in return.

Home was just where I'd left it. I tossed my mail, cleared the machine on the business line, and turned on the TV. I did laps around the dial until I found a movie.

I settled into my chair and watched a young couple attempt to flee a mob of the undead lurching forward with decayed features, carrying torches to find their prey. The young couple was not successful. Trapped in their car, they were pulled out through the shattered windows and devoured by the cannibals, who gorged themselves even as their own entrails followed behind.

Oh, for the good old days, when we were the mob, and Frankenstein the monster, the only one of his kind.

I fell asleep to an unhappy ending and the threat of a sequel.

Paula Zahn woke me up. I wish. Her broadcast image was bringing me up to date on the latest inhuman folly. The Duke of Cornhole had just been arrested for molesting his three daughters. Good-bye incestral home. I cut the sound off, started the coffee and went to shower and dress. With coffee and reheated pizza in hand, I just liked to watch her talk. She was so expressive, so obviously intelligent, so beautiful. The fact that she looked so much like my ex-something had nothing to do with it.

In the office, I flipped open to detectives in the yellow pages and began calling. Todd Berman had done just that. His first story wasn't nearly as slick as the one he gave Gina Logan. In fact, he was turned down cold by the first three agencies he talked to. They all told the same story. The guy had no right to information about an ex-girlfriend, so they passed on it. Nobody tried to wise him up, so they just said they were booked up. And nobody admitted to referring him to anyone else.

The next agency on the list was Excalibur Investigations, run by Rick Stone.

Rick was an encyclopedia of bad habits, moral turpitude, and unpunished felonies. A routine sideswiping by Rick on a female client would include a padded expense sheet, an offer to forgive the balance in the horizontal plane, a hold back on the photos for later blackmail, and leaking confidences like a shotgunned intestine. A woman under surveillance got the same treatment only in a different order.

His greatest talent was a nose for shame. That was probably what kept him in business. If he could smell it on a woman he went right after her. Win or lose, she'd never tell. While Rick had read way too many paperbacks, apparently so had his clients. He was macho cliché all the way up to his snow-white pompadour. To me he looked like a Q-Tip. Enough people bought the pebbled glass door, the bourbon in the desk, the shoulder holster in plain sight, and the "trouble is my business" motto to keep the lights on and the phone ringing.

Franklin Investigations followed Excalibur in the directory. Rick had fine-tuned "Todd Berman" and pointed him at Gina Logan. Why?

I picked up the phone to get an answer when Kelly announced over the intercom that a Ms. Logan was here to see me and there was a call from a Mr. Calloway. I asked Kelly to show Ms. Logan in and tell Calloway I'd return his call shortly.

Kelly pushed open the door and Gina Logan walked in. I motioned for her to sit, and pulled her case file out of my briefcase.

"Here is your file. I've talked to Mr. Calloway. That was him on the phone just now. We might be able to do something there, but first, do you know Rick Stone?"

"God, that slug. Yeah, I did some freelance work for him. I quit when he cornered me in his records room to discuss my taking advantage of some career opportunities. Apparently he thought I'd lost one up my skirt and he was gonna find it for me."

"That it?"

"No. I filed a grievance against Stone with the state licensing board. They found against him and suspended his license for three months."

"Well, guess what, Todd Berman was your thank-you note from Rick. Berman went through detectives alphabetically until he got to Rick. Rick didn't send him on to me, we're next on the list. He sent him on to you. And he gave Berman a much better cover story than the one he started out with."

"What can I do about that?"

"Unless we can get Berman to roll over on Rick, not much. You can bet there's nothing on paper. One meeting, no witnesses. Berman is frustrated. He tells Rick about his problems with the other detectives. Rick sees a way to sandbag you. So he tells Berman how to sell himself to you, gives you a good recommendation, then declines the case on account of he's booked up. The initial consultation, hey that's on the house, sorry, I couldn't help you more. Rick's cracking open the Post every day, hoping there's a disaster with your name on it. That I think we can avoid. Personally I'd like to play pin-the-tail-on-the-Ricky with this one. You interested?"

I watched her mull it over. What was Rick thinking when he put the moves on her? He must have had a head cold that day. I couldn't get a whiff of shame or even embarrassment off her. She seemed to have a good sense of who she was. But then I had no nose for women to start with.

"Yeah, I'm interested. What do you have in mind?"

"I'm going to call Calloway now. We'll need his help on this."

I got Calloway's number from Kelly and dialed it.

"Stan Calloway."

"Mr. Calloway, Leo Haggerty returning your call."

"Yes, thank you. I talked it over with Tara and we decided I should meet with you first. I'd prefer it to be someplace public."

"Fine. Where do you work?"

"In town, right near the zoo."

"Okay, how about the zoo, say forty-five minutes?"

"That's fine. Where should we meet?"

"How about the polar bears. The bench closest to the railing."

"What do you look like?"

"I'll be wearing a leather jacket, sunglasses, and a brown suede cap. I've got a beard and I'll be talking to the bears."

"I'll see you there, Mr. Haggerty."

I hung up the phone and Gina asked, "You want me there?"

"Yeah. I'd have preferred to meet someplace private where 'Berman' wouldn't see us together, but as a sign of good faith, I said I'd go anyplace Calloway was comfortable, so the zoo it is. Why don't you take a position where you can keep us in view and scan the area to see if 'Berman' is following him already? If he's there, come down, lean over the railing, and drop your purse on the ground. I'll bend over to help you and you let me know what he's wearing and where he is."

"Okay."

I got my jacket and cap and motioned for Gina to lead the way. When she asked, "What about a fee agreement? I thought you . . ."

"Yeah, well that was before this turned into an opportunity to put Stone out of business. I'd pay for a shot at that. We're both doing the profession a favor."

I took a seat above the bear pit. One of the older males immediately stood up and began sniffing the air. Once he realized I was where he couldn't get at me, he lost interest and lay back down on the rocks in the spread-eagle position, like a boned chicken, that they use to sneak up on seals.

I walked over to the railing and leaned on it. The male saw me and made eye contact. I met his eyes. I stood up with my arms down at my sides. He did the same thing. I kept my head up and stuck out my lower lip as a sign of submission. The next crazy step would be for me to vault the railing and play with the bear. Except that I'd be face-down, peeled and eaten like a banana in minutes.

"Uh . . . Mr. Haggerty?"

I snapped out of my reverie and turned to face a young man, late twenties or early thirties, wearing a long top coat, with his hands in his pockets. He had wavy reddish-brown hair, pale freckles, and a tight-lipped, serious look on his face.

"Mr. Calloway?"

"Yes."

"Why don't we sit and talk? My friends won't mind."

"I was going to apologize for meeting like this," he said, "but you seem to be very comfortable here."

"I am. I come here—oh two, three times a year—to see the bears. You like polar bears?"

"No, not really. Can't say I think too much about animals at all. The reason I was going to apologize was that Tara got back to me after we'd spoken and said that she'd talked to some attorneys about you and they'd all said the same things. That you were a straight shooter and honest. So I guess we didn't need to meet like this."

"No problem. As you can see, I'd as soon meet here as anywhere."

"You said you wanted my help in dealing with Joel Silverman and somebody else you felt was using him, is that right?"

"Yes. I believe Silverman was assisted in finding you by a private detective named Rick Stone. Stone showed Silverman how to dupe another detective into locating you by lying to that detective. He did this as revenge for her filing a grievance for sexual harassment against him. I'd like to put Stone out of business. This is just the latest stunt of his. He's bad news for all of us and for his clients and innocent people like you."

"Okay, obviously I'd like to get rid of Joel Silverman and you want to get rid of this Stone fella. How can I help?"

"Well, that depends on how you want to deal with Silverman. I have my own approach to stalkers, but it's not for everyone. How have you dealt with him?"

"I haven't had to deal with him, not directly. I helped Tara deal with him. You know—unlisted phone number, better security at her home and work, keeping neighbors notified, taking a lot of precautions when she's out, prosecuting as soon as he did anything threatening . . ."

"And anxious all the time. Right?"

"Yeah. But that's getting better. At least it was until this happened. Now, she's a wreck again. She's thinking about moving and starting over someplace else."

"How much does she mean to you? You willing to move with her?"

"I don't know. I mean we're not engaged or anything. It might turn out that way, but it's too soon to tell."

"So, you don't know how much of your life you're willing to get messed up for this girl," I went on, imagining Calloway's thoughts out loud. "If you get scared off, then it's proof to her that she's either Silverman's or no one's. And you already told her that wasn't true, that you wouldn't let him run you off, right?"

I turned to look at him. He wouldn't meet my eyes, but stared down at his lap. Bingo. Gotcha. Man or Mouse to the woman you love? What a trap.

"But this has scared you big time. If you don't stand up to this guy, you lose the girl. Maybe that's okay," I paused, "and you lose a little self-respect. That'll gnaw at you whether she's here or not. Is that okay?"

I had to be careful not to use Calloway for my own ends. I wanted Stone bad, but shaming Calloway into being a target wasn't right. My life didn't mean much to me these days so I could advocate recklessness. Maybe his did. Maybe he had things to lose. Cowardice is an easy call from the sidelines.

What'll it be, Mr. Calloway? We're waiting. You look like a kid who got run off a lot of playgrounds. Is this one too many or not enough yet?

I let Calloway take his time and walked over to the railing. A young male streamed up out of the pool onto the rocks, and then shook himself dry, his fur rippling and sliding like it was borrowed from a bigger bear.

"Ah, Mr. Haggerty, what do you have in mind?"

Was there an answer buried in that question?

"Stalking puts you on the defensive. Where is he? What does he want? When will he show up again? He has all the control, you have all the anxiety. I recommend to people that they take the control from the stalkers. Provoke a confrontation. But a well-planned one. Keep the risk to a minimum and maximize the chances that they'll be caught in the act and get some good jail time."

"What if it doesn't work?"

"What do you mean, doesn't work? He doesn't make a play, you try again. He does and doesn't get convicted?"

"Yeah and now he's angrier than before. Then what?"

Then you have him killed, that's what. "I don't know. You try again. You stalk him. Set him up in other ways. Keep him under scrutiny all the time."

"There goes your life. You're still chained to their obsession. How do you get free from that?"

"The same way every slave has ever gotten free. You turn on your masters and free yourselves. No master ever gave up slavery out of the goodness of his heart."

"I don't know. I need to think. If we did try to set Silverman up, you'd arrange it so we wouldn't get hurt, is that it?"

"Almost. I'd arrange it so there'd be only a small chance of you getting hurt. No guarantees."

"I have to talk with Tara about this. I'll call you back when we make a decision."

"Take your time, Mr. Calloway, this is serious business. I want you to be sure."

"No, I don't think sure will be possible. Willing, maybe."

"That's all you need. I'll wait to hear from you."

We stood up and shook hands. Calloway looked over his

shoulder as he left and turned back up the path toward Connecticut Avenue.

I sat back on the bench and waited for Gina Logan to return. The snow began to fall before she sat down. Large, soft flakes that melted on your tongue.

Gina shivered. "I hate snow," she informed me.

"Well?" I asked.

"Couldn't see anybody following him. But I'm not the best in the world at surveillance. He could have been there. What did you two talk about?"

"About how to turn things around on Mr. Silverman. He's thinking it over. If he agrees, the next step is yours. You'll be setting your client up. You ready for that?"

"It's like you said, once he lied to me and used me, all bets were off. How will I set him up?"

"You'll call him back, ask if he's talked to his attorney yet. You were concerned because you hadn't heard. He'll give you some line of shit. Then you tell him that if he wants to establish a pattern of infidelity that you know where they'll be this Friday night."

"And where is that?"

"I don't know yet. If Calloway goes for it, I'll ask the woman if she and Silverman had any special spot, someplace meaningful to him, or an activity they did together, anything that'll yank his chain. You'll tell him that's where they'll be."

"And how do I know this? I'm off the case, remember?"

"Yeah, but you overheard them talking about it in the restaurant last week when you were sitting behind them at the bar."

"Isn't this getting a bit risky, provoking him like that?"

"Yeah, but it's the only way to make sure he comes out of his hole. I want to be calling the shots, not him. That's the best way to get him off the streets for a while. We'll give him a reason to want to violate his restraining order and the opportunity, then we'll drop a net over him."

"How do we do that?"

"That's where Rick Stone comes in." I looked down at the snow starting to cover the sidewalk. The zoo was emptying out rapidly.

"And?"

"Oh, uh don't worry about that. If we get that far, I'll tell you all about it." The bears were up shuffling from one side of the cage to the other, their heads bobbing to pick out scents of interest.

"You know, you're doing a lot more than just helping me fix a mistake. You're trying to help put Silverman away and Stone, too. Why?"

"Just tying up loose ends. Old business. Rick Stone's needed fixing for a long time. This may be my one chance to do it. I want to make the most of it." I drifted away on an ice floe of memory, until her voice harpooned me.

"Listen, I'm going to go, okay. It's getting worse by the minute here. You'll call if anything comes up?"

"Sure. I want to thank you."

"What for?" she said, standing up and stamping her feet.

"Your problem has given me an opportunity to set some things right. I've waited a long time for this chance. I'm grateful."

Gina shook her head. "I'm not sure I like the way this is going. Do I want to know what's with you and Rick Stone?"

"No. You don't. Go on home. It's snowing. I'll call you."

Gina brushed her graying hair and hunched into the wind, moved carefully across the slick sidewalk, testing each step before taking another.

Well, Rick, this might just be my lucky day. The sun was going down and the light was seeping out of the slate sky. The air got colder and the snow fell faster. Do you ever think about Helen Burroughs? I think about her a lot, Rick. Especially that last night. I'd watched her in the bar, plenty of nights, just like you did. That was the job. Just watch her. Keep a log of how much she drank, how long she sat there. God, she was sad. All dressed up, hoping she was still pretty, and afraid to find out. How many guys did she turn down? Three, four a night.

That last night she had what, sixteen beers. No, that wasn't pretty at all. No way I could let her drive like that. I didn't have to pick her up, just hold her up. So there I am, at her front door, one arm around her waist, trying to hold her up while one of her breasts pops out of her top and I'm missing the keyhole like the porch is a North Sea oil rig.

When did you get the bright idea to call Mr. Burroughs? When I told you I was going to make sure she got home alive or after I left?

There you were, video rolling, lights, action, camera. Shouting at Mr. Burroughs. He was a welcome addition, going on like a thesaurus with one entry: whore, see the following. And then I hear you over it all. "I told you he couldn't be trusted, Mr. Burroughs. He lied about how much she drank and this is why."

You couldn't stop there though. No, why settle for a banality like winning a case when you can reach the sublime like ruining a life? I don't know whose face was more awful, hers when she saw him there, or his watching her collapse in a heap, clutching at my pants leg with one hand, trying to tuck her breast back in its mooring and throwing up in long yellow threads.

He was eight years old, Rick. A little young for such a complicated lesson, don't you think? That clinched it though. Divorce and custody hammered through without a whimper, much less a fight, from Helen Burroughs. The boy was too angry and she too ashamed to make the few visits work. You got a nice bonus, I got the boot, and seven months later Helen Burroughs, blood alcohol level .19, got a physics lesson in the rapid deceleration of deformable bodies at the base of the Springfield off-ramp. She did not pass.

I don't know about you, Rick, but I think about Helen Burroughs a lot. And about how you used to say we were friends.

I stood up, shook the snow loose, and shuffled off.

At the subway, an old man talking to himself invited me to referee. I listened for a minute and declared it a draw. This pleased him so much he asked if I could help him get something warm inside him to keep the cold away. He had the fuel located and held for him. All he needed was the money to liberate it.

His face was so lined and creased and seamed that if he had to blow his nose you thought he'd just wad up his face, do it, and then pat his features back into place.

There was a time I'd have brushed the old man off like a tick, thinking to myself, get a job, get a life, get away from me. Now that I've come to expect less of myself, I've extended the courtesy to others. Not compassion, just an allergy to hypocrisy.

I gave the old man five bucks to ransom himself for a night. Perhaps tomorrow he could aim higher.

I stopped off at Skyline and swam enough laps to leave me defenseless against sleep, then drove home to see if I could find it.

My answering machine had one message on it. Calloway had talked to Tara McKinney. Tara was interested in my plan, would I give them a call tonight or tomorrow to discuss it in detail. Women can stiffen a man up in more ways than one. Tonight was too much, tomorrow would do. I scribbled down the number and went to bed.

I called Calloway around eight.

"So, you've decided to take me up on my offer."

"I don't see how we have any choice. You're right, he won't go away, he won't abide by the law. It's really crazy, you know. You start out trying to decide if you even want a relationship and the next thing you know, you're imprisoned by their lunacy for life."

"Can you give me Tara McKinney's phone number?"

"Don't need to. She's right here. Hold on."

"Hello, this is Tara."

"Ms. McKinney, my name is Leo Haggerty. I'm the man who spoke to Stanley Calloway about Silverman."

"Yes. We talked about it last night. I think you're right. He won't leave me alone and I'm tired of being afraid all the time. If your plan will get him out of my life, I'm all for it."

"I think it will. The new stalking laws in Virginia call for a minimum sentence of a year and a twenty-five-hundred-dollar fine since he's already got a judgment against him. Once that lapses the sentence is six months. Now is as good a time as any to go after him."

"What are you proposing that we do?"

"Very simply, provoke him into making contact with you. Then have him arrested. The important thing is to provoke him into an attempt to harm you or Mr. Calloway but not let him be successful."

"How do you plan to do that?"

"First off, we'd have a bodyguard with you to intervene. Second, we'd set up the place and control the location so the ways that Mr. Silverman can approach you are limited, the ways he can do harm are limited. Third, we'd probably have you wearing body armor as a precaution."

"Can't you use a stand-in for us?"

"No. The stalking would hold only if you're there. That just requires his acting in a way that leaves you fearing for your safety. I don't want him to try to harm you. I'd like to intervene before then."

"Okay. So how do we provoke him?"

"Did you and he have any place special you went, anything you did together that would be especially infuriating if you did it with someone else?"

"You know, I've avoided every place we ever went together because all it does is bring back painful memories."

"That was probably a wise decision."

"I guess the first place he ever took me out. He said it was his favorite restaurant because of how well they treated him there. 'Like a king,' he said. He went there to celebrate all his successes, he said."

"What was the name?"

"Simon's."

A pretender to Morton's crown as the king of steak houses. However, the meat wasn't as good and the service, unlike Morton's, was intrusive and humorless.

"That's a good place to go. The parking lot is large, open, and well lit. I doubt that he'd try anything inside the restaurant. Too hard to get away without being seen, especially if he's known to them. No. I'd guess he'd do something to you or your car in the lot. What has he done to you already?"

"You mean before we broke up or after?"

"Both."

"Well, when we first went out, there were calls and hang-ups at all hours of the night, driving by to see if I was home. At first he said it was because he couldn't believe that a girl like

me would go out with him or fall for him. I tried to reassure
him that I liked him, that I was sincere."

"But it didn't work." It never does.

"No, it didn't. Pretty soon I got tired of it. The jealousy
when we were out, looking at other men to see if they were
looking at me. Then it got plain crazy, not letting me go to the
bathroom without waiting outside. I said that was it. I quit,
thanks but no thanks. Joel wouldn't hear of it. I couldn't leave
him. He wouldn't let me. He loved me. The farther away I
tried to get, the more he distorted the relationship. That was
what really scared me. The less he meant to me, the more I
meant to him. His phone calls got more threatening. He sent
me hate letters. I changed my phone number. He went to my
work and harassed my co-workers about me. That was when I
went to the police. My trash was dumped all over my lawn. A
dead squirrel was put in my mailbox, so I got a post office
box. My car had all the tires punctured and acid poured all
over the body. I had to buy a new car. My heat pump was
ruined when he poured cement into the fan housing. He ran
the garden hose into my dryer vent and flooded the basement.
My telephone lines were cut twice, my outside lights had the
bulbs removed. I had security cameras installed. That's what
caught him when he came up and sprayed graffiti on my
house. I tried to sell the house but the agents said no one
would buy for fear that Joel wouldn't quit and no one wanted
to deal with him. I felt cursed, absolutely cursed. I was afraid
to leave my house. I was afraid of what I'd find when I got
home. He parked in the neighborhood and followed me to
work. He'd drive up alongside and get almost to where he'd
sideswipe me, then he'd pull in front of me and hit the brakes.
I had to stop driving to work for a while and get picked up by a
car pool. Then he started leaving messages and mail for me at
work. He ordered pizzas for everyone in my name. Magazine

subscriptions. Anything you can order without paying for it came to the office. He was relentless. Thank God my employer was on my side. He filed complaints with the police, too. I was a basket case. I couldn't sleep. I was taking antidepressants and anti-anxiety pills. My job performance fell off. I lost a raise I should have gotten; I almost lost my job.

"I got the police to keep an eye out for him in my neighborhood. Then I told all my neighbors about him and what he was doing. That helped cut down on the vandalism. People yelled at him when they saw him a couple of times.

"I wasn't able to do anything. I couldn't relax. I just went to work and then went home. I had girlfriends come by to visit or I'd go to their houses, but they were scared, too.

"There was a time when things quieted down for a while. I don't know why. I thought he'd gotten it out of his system. It was quiet for months. I started going out a little bit. I met Stan. We started going out together. Then wham he's back. Now I wonder if he was out of town on a job."

"What does he do?"

"You'll love this. What better place for a paranoid. He does security work. He's a private consultant designing secure communications systems for industry and government. He told me that he got jobs out of the country that take months to do."

"He's threatened you and done a lot of damage to your property. Did he ever hurt you physically?"

"No. Joel never hit me when we were together. He hasn't really had an opportunity since then."

"Does he own a gun, or did he ever talk about having used one?"

"No. I never saw one. And he never talked about guns with me."

The guy had no history of direct physical confrontation or

violence, at least not with this woman. Plenty of damage to her property, but he hadn't broken in yet.

"Other than the squirrel, anything else killed? A pet?"

"No. I don't have any pets."

The guy likes to destroy things, when no one's looking. A bomb under the car would be his style. Poison in the food? Better not let them eat in the restaurant. If he doesn't make his play in the parking lot, have them come out of the restaurant after fifteen minutes and go home. Try again another day.

"Here's what I propose." I ran through my plans for Silverman and Rick Stone, covering all of my goals, most of my doubts, and some of my motives.

Tara McKinney and Stan Calloway agreed to my plan and I asked them to meet me at my office at ten o'clock. I called Gina Logan and asked her to join us to complete our preparations.

Kelly showed Stanley and Tara in. I introduced them to Gina Logan. Gina apologized to them. They dismissed it saying they knew how easily Silverman could fool people. They sat around my desk. I motioned to the coffeepot on the sideboard but they declined. I had two phones on my desk. Speaker phones change the sound of your voice and would alert Rick and Silverman.

"First, I want you, Tara, to call Rick Stone. Let's get him committed to this case, then we'll call Joel Silverman. Do you remember the scenario we outlined last night?"

"Yes."

"Okay. I'll keep listening in on this other phone. If he asks you a question you can't answer or wants to change the plan, I'll write you a note with what to say to him. Ready?"

"Let's go." She picked up the phone and dialed. I already

had the receiver to my ear.

"Excalibur Investigations. Rick Stone speaking."

"Yes, Mr. Stone, my name is Sarah Maginnes and you were referred to me by a friend, actually a friend of a friend. She said you did a great job for her and that you were the man I needed . . ."

Gina stuck her finger down her throat.

"What's your friend's name?"

"Oh, her name is CeCe, that's short for Cecilia Rodriguez, but it was a friend of hers that gave me your name."

"And what can I do for you?"

"I, well, my husband and I are going out for our anniversary dinner tomorrow and I've been getting some obscene phone calls at my home and office. This guy says he's been watching me and following me. They've got me really frightened. My husband suggested some security so that when we went out I'd be able to relax. I don't want the evening to be ruined. I don't know . . . do you think we're overreacting, Mr. Stone?"

"No, no. You know what I always say, better to be safe than sorry. I'd take care of something like this personally, ma'am. Invisible protection, you'd never know I was there. Satisfaction guaranteed. You and your husband would have the time of your lives. Afterward we could talk about installing some security devices to catch this creep and prosecute him."

Tara looked at me. I mouthed "Good idea."

"That sounds like a good idea to me, Mr. Stone. You know I feel better just talking to you. You sound so confident."

"Ma'am, I don't believe in false modesty. Let me assure you, I'm the best there is, at what I do."

My head slumped onto my chest.

"Now where is this anniversary party and what time?"

"Simon's Restaurant at 7 p.m. this Friday."

"All right, when can you and your husband—or you your-self, if he's not available—come by my office to discuss my ideas for security for the evening?"

"I could come by this morning, if that's okay with you?"

"That would be perfect. Do you know where my office is?"

"Yes, CeCe gave me the address. I know the area. How about eleven-thirty today?"

"Fine, I'm looking forward to meeting you, Sarah."

"And I'm looking forward to meeting you, Mr. Stone."

"Rick. Call me Rick."

"Okay, Rick, see you then."

Tara put down the phone. "Do you have any mouthwash I could use? Just talking to him felt sleazy."

Gina laughed. "To know him is to loathe him."

"What do I do at the appointment?"

"Pay him his retainer. Keep it to a minimum for the night. Leave anything else for later. Go along with his plans. Tell him you want to use your car. That's what Silverman will be looking for. As much as it nauseates me to say it, Rick does know how to do personal protection. It's not his competence that's in question, it's his ethics. Whatever he wants you to do will be good procedure. If you're really uncomfortable call me afterward and tell me what he said. I'll tell you if it's sound or not."

I turned to Gina. "Ready?" She nodded. I put the phone to my ear. Stanley reached over and took Tara's hand.

"Hello," a flat voice said.

"Uh, Mr. Berman, this is Gina Logan calling."

"Why?"

"Uh, well, I didn't hear from your attorney, so I thought

I'd check back with you, see if you'd decided what you wanted to do."

"Well, I haven't decided yet . . ."

"I understand. I just thought your attorney would want to know that I can establish a pattern of infidelity, not just one incident."

"I don't understand. I didn't ask you to work on this case anymore."

"Well, I haven't. It's just that when I was following your wife last week, I overheard her talking about how much she is looking forward to going out this Friday to celebrate something with her, uh, friend."

"Where were they going, did she say?"

"Yes, uh, let me look it up. I think I have it here. Yes. Simon's. She said something else about it but that's the name."

"What else did she say?"

"Look, Mr. Berman, like you said, I'm off the case. I don't think that information would be useful to anyone. I just thought I'd call to let you know we can make an airtight case against your wife. If you and your lawyer want to."

"Right, you just thought you'd drum up a little business for yourself, Ms. Logan. You don't fool me with that solicitous crap. Let me make it clear to you, you are no longer in my employ. I do not want you sticking your nose into my business. If I want any other work done I'll call you. Got that?"

"Loud and clear, Mr. Berman. I'm sorry you feel this way, I was only trying to help."

"Good-bye." He hung up.

"And fuck you too, you asshole." Gina's jaw muscles rolled back and forth under her ears. "I'll take a double on the mouthwash. You know, I really hate working for assholes."

"Well, I think we're in business. Friday night you'll go out to Simon's with Rick Stone. I expect Mr. Silverman to show up and try something in the parking lot. If it all goes well, you'll have a witness to your harassment by Silverman and Stone will be forced to clean up his own mess." And a whole lot more, if I get my way.

Tara checked her watch. "I'd better be going. I'll call you after my meeting with Mr. Stone."

"Fine, I'll be here in the office until one."

Stan Calloway stood up. We shook hands and they left.

Gina was staring into space when I sat down. "What's bothering you?"

"I hate taking shit like that from anybody, even if it's the smart thing to do."

"That's why it's important to get paid and paid well for this work. With the assholes, it's the only satisfaction you get."

Friday night arrived as promised. Gina and I were sitting in my car opposite Simon's lot at six-thirty watching to see if Silverman would show up.

"What do you think he'll do?" she asked anxiously.

"I really don't know. He may want to keep her out of Simon's so it won't be ruined by her eating there, or he may consider it ruined already. This is her first assault on him. I expect he'll be pretty angry and he'll make a direct confrontation this time. He's been pretty careful so far in avoiding consequences for his behavior, so I expect he'll do something he hopes he can get away with. Up to now that's been his pattern. That's your best predictor of future behavior. Not a great predictor, but the best we've got. We're changing some important parameters here, and he could go off in an entirely new direction."

"Okay, but what do you think he'll do? Your best guess?"

"A direct confrontation outside the restaurant. That's what I'm counting on."

"Isn't that risky?"

"Yes, but it offers great rewards, too."

I spent the next fifteen minutes scanning the lot for running cars, occupied cars, cars parked facing the exit. If Silverman made his move he'd need to see them come in and ideally be able to make a quick getaway. I pushed away the thought of him hiring someone to do a professional job. The consequences of that response would be disastrous.

Parking lots leave plenty of room for people to approach unseen between the cars, and getting out of a car is a slow, awkward movement, providing that moment of vulnerability so necessary for a successful attempt at harm.

"He either does it in the lot or he runs them down on the street, going to the restaurant. That's a longer shot. I'm still going for the lot," I said, reassuring myself.

"Rick will lose any tails he picks up and sweep the car, so I don't think it'll happen on the road. No, it's the lot. Car stopped, open, poor visibility. If he's going to preserve the sanctity of Simon's he'll deny her admission. That's my bet." My tongue was tossing verbal Valium all over the car. It dissolved on contact but had no effect.

At five minutes to seven, I pointed to a car parked just down from Simon's. "Gina, walk over to the restaurant and see what that car's plates are, also if it looks like Silverman. I'm going to call the restaurant and make sure Silverman or Berman doesn't have a reservation and isn't inside already."

"Good idea." Gina got out and walked briskly across the lot. I made two calls while she was gone.

Gina got back in the car. "It's not him." In fact, the car was easing away from the curb. "What about the restaurant?"

"No reservation for Silverman or Berman. Nor do they have one for people he's been known to dine with."

Tara's car was pulling into the lot.

"Showtime." I picked up the binoculars and scanned the lot again. "Look, over there." I pointed to a shadow moving low between a row of cars. "Here he comes."

Gina reached over and grabbed my arm. We were watching a shark attack coalescing. Each element moving into position, meaningless until the final conjunction. The bait dangling, one leg in the car, one leg out. The shark, a dark shape cutting through the night, picking up speed.

"Shouldn't we do something, warn them?" Gina gasped.

"Too late for that now. Hold on. Here comes the collision." We braced ourselves as if Silverman was running right at us.

Silverman sprinted across the aisle toward Tara McKinney. His arm was low and extended. Tara was screaming, her hands to her face. Then she was gone. A black shape rolled across the trunk of the car and slammed into Silverman. He disappeared. Columns of smoke drifted up by the car accompanied by shrill screams.

"My God, what's that?" Gina asked.

My wildest dreams, I thought, but didn't answer.

Sirens grew in the distance and two Fairfax County police cruisers pulled into view. One closed off the lot's exit, the other ventured in toward the screaming. They blocked Tara's car and turned their searchlights toward the ground. One officer crouched behind the hood, gun extended; the other spoke into a microphone.

"You on the ground. Put your hands up and come on out of there. Anyone in the car, put your hands up and come out one at a time."

I motioned to Gina. "Let's get out and see what happened." She scooted out of the car, closed the door quietly, and dashed across the street to the corner of the lot. I caught up with her and motioned to the shadows at the foot of the wall. Gina followed me, scuttling sideways between bumpers and bricks to a vantage point directly behind the police cruiser.

Stan Calloway and then Tara McKinney emerged slowly from the car, their hands overhead. Stan started to speak but was cut off.

"Hands on the roof and spread 'em. Then you can talk."

The other officer came around the cruiser and approached them from the rear.

First one pair of hands, then another appeared, rising up from the ground. The second pair was still smoking.

"Jesus Christ," the cop said and stepped out of the cruiser. "Put 'em on the roof, easy does it, and spread 'em. Get away from each other."

Tara and Stan had backed away from the car. The other cop was talking to them.

Rick was patted down, then Silverman.

He held up his ruined hands as he was turned away from the car. He was moaning over and over, like a scratched record from hell.

"John, we can't cuff this guy. I think he's burned his hand with acid or somethin'. You better call for an ambulance."

The officer speaking to Tara got back into the cruiser.

"What happened here?" the other cop asked.

"Look, Officer, my name is Rick Stone, I've got ID in my coat. I was hired by—"

"Stone, Stone. Yeah, you were the guy called in the report."

Silverman turned slowly and looked at Rick. He stopped moaning. The dawn of recognition in their faces was beautiful indeed, like someone had opened an umbrella up their asses.

"You, you set me up. All along. You did this to me!" Silverman waved his hands at Rick. "I'll kill you, you bastard!"

The cop pointed his nightstick at Silverman and backed him away from Rick.

"I don't know what you're talking about," Rick said. "I've never seen you in my life, you psycho!"

"Liar! Liar! Liar!" Silverman shrieked.

Rick's natural aversion to taking responsibility for anything was an easy match for Silverman's paranoia, especially without two burned hands to distract him. The more Stone did his backstroke in front of the cops, the more it fueled Silverman's rage.

Two minutes later, an ambulance pulled into the lot. Two paramedics jumped out and approached Silverman. They gave him an injection and ran an I.V. into him.

The cop and Rick followed Silverman into the ambulance.

"Listen," the cop said. "We appreciate your calling us in on this. A lot of you guys, you get headlines in your eyes, forget that we have to clean up your messes."

"Hey, I don't know what you're talking about. I never called you guys." Stone's face was white with anger.

"Liar!" Silverman bellowed from the ambulance. One of the paramedics was kneeling on him, trying unsuccessfully to get him to lie down. "Like you never saw me in your life. I'll get you, you son of a bitch! Just as soon as I get out of here. You'll wish you'd never seen me. I'll fix you. You'll—"

A closed door interrupted Silverman's recitation of things to come. The siren wailed.

"Honest, I don't know what you're talking about," Rick reiterated.

"All I know, your name was on the call-in. We need you and your clients to come over to the station, make statements. Then you can be on your way."

"Okay, we'll be right over," Rick said, shaking his head even as he agreed.

The two cruisers pulled away and after a brief conference, Tara, Stan, and Stone got into their car and followed.

When their taillights blurred in the distance, I stepped out of the shadows. Gina Logan joined me.

"Well, what do you think?" she said.

"I think you should savor this moment. It doesn't get any better than this."

Gina shivered. "Is that the good news or the bad?"

I smiled. "They're one and the same."

ACKNOWLEDGEMENTS: I'd like to thank Mike Jackson for all his help on this one. He's the real McCoy and welcome in Leo's shop any day.

Mary, Mary, Shut the Door

Enzo Scolari motored into my office and motioned me to sit. What the hell, I sat. He pulled around to the side of my desk, laced his fingers in his lap, and sized me up.

"I want to hire you, Mr. Haggerty," he announced.

"To do what, Mr. Scolari?"

"I want you to stop my niece's wedding."

"I see. And why is that?"

"She is making a terrible mistake, and I will not sit by and let her do it."

"Exactly what kind of mistake is she making?"

"She knows nothing about him. They just met. She is infatuated, nothing more. She knows nothing about men. Nothing. The first one to pay any attention to her and she wants to get married."

"You said they just met. How long ago, exactly?" Just a little reality check.

"Two weeks. Can you believe it? Two weeks. And I just found out about it yesterday. She brought him to the house last night. There was a party and she introduced him to everyone and told us she was going to marry him. How can you marry someone you've known for two weeks? That's ridiculous. It's a guarantee of failure and it'll break her heart. I can't let that happen."

"Mr. Scolari, I'm not sure we can help you with this. Your niece may be doing something foolish, but she has a right to do it. I understand your concern for her well-being, but I don't think you need a detective, maybe a priest or a therapist. We don't do premarital background checks. Our investigations are primarily criminal."

"The crime just hasn't happened yet, Mr. Haggerty. My niece may be a foolish girl, but he isn't. He knows exactly what he's doing."

"And what is that?"

"He's taking advantage of her naïveté, her innocence, her fears, her loneliness, so he can get her money. That's a crime, Mr. Haggerty."

And a damn hard one to prove. "What are you afraid of, Mr. Scolari? That he'll kill her for her money? That's quite a leap from an impulsive decision to marry. Do you have any reason to think that this guy is a killer?"

He straightened up and gave that one some thought. Enzo Scolari was wide and thick with shoulders so square and a head so flat he could have been a candelabra. His snow-white eyebrows and mustache hung like awnings for his eyes and lips.

"No. Not for that. But I can tell he doesn't love Gina. Last night I watched him. Every time Gina left his side, his eyes went somewhere else. A man in love, his eyes follow his woman everywhere. No, he's following the maid or Gina's best friend. Gina comes back and he smiles like she's the sunrise. And she believes it.

"He spent more time touching the tapestries than he did holding her hand. He went through the house like a creditor, not a guest. No, he doesn't want Gina, he wants her money. You're right, murder is quite a step from that, but there are easier ways to steal. Gina is a shy, quiet woman who has never had to make any decisions for herself. I don't blame her for that. My sister, God rest her soul, was terrified that something awful would happen to Gina and she tried to protect her from everything. It didn't work. My sister was the one who died and it devastated the girl. Now Gina has to live in the world and she doesn't know how. If this guy can talk her into marrying him so quickly, he'll have no trouble talking her into letting him handle her money."

"How much money are we talking about here?"

"Ten million dollars, Mr. Haggerty." Scolari smiled, having made his point. People have murdered or married for lots less.

"How did she get all this money?"

"It's in a trust for her. A trust set up by my father. My sister and I each inherited half of Scolari Enterprises. When she died, her share went to Gina as her only child."

"This trust, who manages it?"

"I do, of course."

Of course. Motive number two just came up for air. "So, where's the problem? If you control the money, this guy can't do anything."

"I control the money as trustee for my sister. I began that when Gina was still a little girl. Now she is of age and can control the money herself if she wants to."

"So you stand to lose the use of ten million dollars. Have I got that right?"

Scolari didn't even bother to debate that one with me. I liked that. I'll take naked self-interest over the delusions of altruism any day.

"If they've just met, how do you know that this guy even knows that your niece has all this money?"

Scolari stared at me, then spat out his bitter reply. "Why else would he have pursued her? She is a mousy little woman, dull and plain. She's afraid of men. She spent her life in those fancy girls' schools where they taught her how to set the table. She huddled with her mother in that house, afraid of everything. Well, now she is alone and I think she's latched onto the first person who will rescue her from that."

"Does she know how you feel?"

He nodded. "Yes, she does. I made it very clear to her last night."

"How did she take it?"

"She told me to mind my own business." Scolari snorted. "She doesn't even know that that's what I'm doing. She said she loved him and she was going to marry him, no matter what."

"Doesn't sound so mousy to me. She ever stand up to you before?"

"No, never. On anything else, I'd applaud it. But getting married shouldn't be the first decision you ever make."

"Anyone else that might talk to her that she'd listen to?"

"No. She's an only child. Her father died when she was two in the same explosion that killed my father and took my legs. Her mother died in an automobile accident a little over a year ago. I am a widower myself and Gina was never close to my sons. They frightened her as a little girl. They were loud and rough. They teased her and made her cry." Scolari shrugged as if boys would be boys. "I did not like that and would stop it whenever I caught them, but she was such a timid child, their cruelty sprouted whenever she was around. There is no other family."

I picked up the pipe from my desk, stuck it in my mouth, and chewed on it. A glorified pacifier. Kept me from chewing up the inside of my mouth, though. Wouldn't be much of a stretch to take this one on. What the hell, work is work.

"Okay, Mr. Scolari, we'll take the case. I want you to understand that we can't and we won't stop her wedding. There are guys who will do that, and I know who they are, but I wouldn't give you their names. We'll do a background check on this guy and see if we can find something that'll change her mind or your mind. Maybe they really love each other. That happens, you know. This may be a crazy start, but I'm not sure that's a handicap. What's the best way to run a race when you don't know where the finish is?" I sure didn't have an answer and Scolari offered none.

"Mr. Haggerty, I am not averse to taking a risk, but not a blind one. If there's information out there that will help me calculate the odds, then I want it. That's what I want you to get for me. I appreciate your open mind, Mr. Haggerty. Perhaps you will change my mind, but I doubt it."

"Okay, Mr. Scolari. I need a description of this guy, his name and anything else you know about him. First thing Monday morning, I'll assign an investigator and we'll get on this."

"That won't do, Mr. Haggerty. You need to start on this immediately, this minute."

"Why is that?"

"Because they flew to St. Mary's this morning to get married."

"Aren't we a little late, then?"

"No. You can't apply for a marriage license on St. Mary's until you've been on the island for two days."

"How long to get the application approved?"

"I called the embassy. They say it takes three days to process the application. I'm looking into delaying that, if possible. Once it's issued they say most people get married that day or the next."

"So we've got what, five or six days? Mr. Scolari, we can't run a complete background check in that period of time. Hell, no one can. There just isn't enough time."

"What if you put everyone you've got on this, round the clock?"

"That gets you a maybe and just barely that. He'd have to have a pimple on his backside the size of Mount Rushmore for us to find it that fast. If this guy's the sneaky, cunning opportunist that you think he is, then he's hidden that, maybe not perfectly, but deep enough that six days won't turn it up. Besides, I can't put everyone on this, we've got lots of other cases that need attention."

"So hire more staff, give them the other cases, and put everyone else on this. Money is no object, Mr. Haggerty. I want you to use all your resources on this."

My jaw hurt from clamping on the dead pipe. Scolari was old enough to make a foolish mistake. I told him it was a long shot at best. What more could I tell him? When did I become clairvoyant, and know how things would turn out? Suppose we did find something, like three dead ex-wives? Right! Let's not kid ourselves—all the staff for six days—round the clock—that's serious money. What was it Rocky said? When you run a business, money's always necessary but it's never sufficient. Don't confuse the two and what you do at the office won't keep you up at night.

I sorted everything into piles and then decided. "All right, Mr. Scolari, we'll do it. I can't even tell you what it'll cost. We'll bill you at our hourly rates plus all the expenses. I think a reasonable retainer would be thirty thousand dollars."

He didn't even blink. It probably wasn't a week's interest on ten million dollars.

"There's no guarantee that we'll find anything, Mr. Scolari, not under these circumstances. You'll know that you did everything you could, but that's all you'll know for sure."

"That's all you ever know for sure, Mr. Haggerty."

I pulled out a pad to make some notes. "Do you know where they went on St. Mary's?"

"Yes. A resort called the Banana Bay Beach Hotel. I have taken the liberty of registering you there."

"Excuse me." I felt like something under his front wheel.

"The resort is quite remote and perched on the side of a

cliff. I have been assured that I would not be able to make my way around. I need you to be my legs, my eyes. If your agents learn anything back here, someone has to be able to get that information to my niece. Someone has to be there. I want that someone to be you, Mr. Haggerty. That's what I'm paying for. Your brains, your eyes, your legs, to be there because I can't."

I stared at Scolari's withered legs and the motorized wheelchair he got around in. More than that he had money, lots of money. And money's the ultimate prosthesis.

"Let's start at the top. What's his name?"

The island of St. Mary's is one of lush green mountains that drop straight into the sea. What little flat land there is, is on the West Coast, and that's where almost all the people live. The central highlands and peaks are still wild and pristine.

My plane banked around the southern tip of the island and headed toward one of those flat spots, the international airport. I flipped through the file accumulated in those few hours between Enzo Scolari's visit and my plane's departure. While Kelly, my secretary, made travel arrangements I called everyone into the conference room and handed out jobs. Clancy Hopper was to rearrange caseloads and hire temporary staff to keep the other cases moving. Del Winslow was to start investigating our man Derek Marshall. We had a name, real or otherwise, an address, and a phone number. Del would do the house-to-house with the drawing we made from Scolari's description. Larry Burdette would be smilin' and dialin'. Calling every computerized database we could access to get more information. Every time Marshall's name appeared he'd take the information and hand it to another investigator to verify every fact and then backtrack each one by phone or in person until we could recreate the life of Derek Marshall. Our best chance was with the St. Mary's Department of Licenses. To apply for a marriage license Marshall had to file a copy of his passport, birth certificate, decrees of divorce if previously married, death certificate if widowed, and proof of legal name change, if any. If the records were open to the public, we'd get faxed copies or I'd go to the offices myself and look at them personally. I took one last look at the picture of Gina Dalesandro and then the sketch of Derek Marshall, closed the file, and slipped it into my bag as the runway appeared outside my window.

I climbed out of the plane and into the heat. A dry wind moved the heat around me as I walked into the airport. I showed my passport and had nothing to declare. They were delighted to have me on their island. I stepped out of the airport and the cab master introduced me to my driver. I followed him to a battered Toyota, climbed into the front seat, and stowed my bag between my feet. He slammed the door and asked where to.

"Banana Bay Beach Hotel," I said as he turned the engine on and pulled out.

"No problem."

"How much?" We bounced over a sleeping policeman.

"Eighty ecee."

Thirty-five dollars American. "How far is it?"

"Miles or time?"

"Both."

"Fifteen miles. An hour and a half."

I should have gotten out then. If the road to hell is paved at all, then it doesn't pass through St. Mary's. The coast road was a lattice of potholes winding around the sides of the mountains. There were no lanes, no lights, no signs, and no guardrails. The sea was a thousand feet below and we were never more than a few inches from visiting it.

Up and down the hills, there were blue bags on the trees.

"What are those bags?" I asked.

"Bananas. The bags keep the insects away while they ripen."

I scanned the slopes and tried to imagine going out there to put those bags on. Whoever did it, they couldn't possibly be paying him enough. Ninety minutes of bobbing and weaving on those roads like a fighter on the ropes and I was exhausted from defying gravity. I half expected to hear a bell to end the trip as we pulled up to the resort.

I checked in, put my valuables in a safe-deposit box, took my key and information packet, and headed up the hill to my room. Dinner was served in about an hour. Enough time to get oriented, unpack, and shower.

My room overlooked the upstairs bar and dining area and below that the beach, the bay, and the surrounding cliffs. I had a thatched-roof veranda with a hammock and clusters of flamboyant and chenille red-hot cattails close enough to pluck. The bathroom was clean and functional. The bedroom large and sparely furnished. Clearly, this was a place where the attractions were outdoors and rooms were for sleeping in. The mosquito netting over the bed and the coils on the dresser were not good signs. It was the rainy season and Caribbean mosquitoes can get pretty cheeky. In Antigua one caught me in the bathroom and pulled back the shower curtain like he was Norman Bates.

I unpacked quickly and read my information packet. It had a map of the resort, a list of services, operating hours, and tips on how to avoid common problems in the Caribbean such as sunburn, being swept out to sea, and a variety of bites, stings, and inedible fruits. I familiarized myself with the layout and took out the pictures of Gina and Derek. Job one was to find them and then tag along unobtrusively until the home office gave me something to work with.

I showered, changed, and lay down on the bed to wait for dinner. The best time to make an appearance was midway through the meal. Catch the early birds leaving and the stragglers on their way in.

Around eight-thirty, I sprayed myself with insect repellent, slipped my keys into my pocket, and headed down to dinner. The schedule said that it would be a barbecue on the beach.

At the reception area I stopped and looked over the low wall to the beach below. Scolari was right, he wouldn't be able to get around here. The rooms jutted out from the bluff and were connected by a steep roadway. However, from this point on, the hillside was a precipice. A staircase wound its way down to the beach. One hundred and twenty-six steps, the maid said.

I started down, stopping periodically to check the railing. There were no lights on the trail. Late at night, a little drunk on champagne, a new bride could have a terrible accident. I peered over the side at the concrete roadway below. She wouldn't bounce and she wouldn't survive.

I finished the zigzagging descent and noted that the return trip would be worse.

Kerosene lamps led the way to the beach restaurant and bar. I sat on a stool, ordered a yellowbird, and turned to look at the dining area. Almost everyone was in couples, the rest were families. All white, mostly Americans, Canadians, British, and German. At least that's what the brochure said.

I sipped my drink and scanned the room. No sign of them. No problem, the night was young even if I wasn't. I had downed a second drink when they came in out of the darkness. Our drawing of Marshall was pretty good. He was slight, pale, with brown hair parted down the middle, round-rimmed tortoiseshell glasses, and a deep dimpled smile he aimed at the woman he gripped by the elbow. He steered her between the tables as if she had a tiller.

They took a table and I looked about to position myself. I wanted to be able to watch Marshall's face and be close enough to overhear them without looking like it. One row over and two up a table was coming free. I took my drink from the bar and ambled over. The busboy cleared the table and I took a long sip from my drink and set it down.

Gina Dalesandro wore a long flower-print dress. Strapless, she had tan lines where her bathing suit had been. She ran a finger over her ear and flipped back her hair. In profile she was thin-lipped, hook-nosed, and high-browed. Her hand held Marshall's, and then, eyes on his, she pulled one to her and kissed it. She moved from one knuckle to the next, and when she was done she took a finger and slowly slid it into her mouth.

"Gina, please, people will look," he whispered.

"Let them," she said, smiling around his finger.

Marshall pulled back and flicked his eyes around. My waitress had arrived and I was ordering when he passed over me. I had the fish chowder, the grilled dolphin with stuffed christophine, and another drink.

Gina picked up Marshall's hand and held it to her cheek and said something soothing because he smiled and blew her a kiss. They ordered and talked in hushed tones punctuated with laughter and smiles. I sat nearby, watching, waiting, her uncle's gargoyle in residence.

When dessert arrived, Gina excused herself and went toward the ladies' room. Marshall watched her go. I read nothing in his face or eyes. When she disappeared into the bathroom, his eyes wandered around the room, but settled on no one. He locked in on her when she reappeared and led her back to the table with his eyes. All in all it proved nothing.

We all enjoyed the banana cake and coffee and after a discreet pause I followed them back toward the rooms. We trudged silently up the stairs, past the bar and the reception desk, and back into darkness. I kept them in view as I went toward my room and saw that they were in room 7, two levels up and one over from me. When their door clicked closed, I turned around and went back to the activities board outside the bar. I scanned the list of trips for tomorrow to see if they had signed up for any of them. They were down for the morning trip to the local volcano. I signed aboard and went to arrange a wake-up call for the morning.

After a quick shower, I lit the mosquito coils, dialed the lights way down, and crawled under the netting. I pulled the phone and my book inside, propped up the pillows, and called the office. For his money, Scolari should get an answer. He did.

"Franklin Investigations."

"Evening, Del. What do we have on Derek Marshall?"

"Precious little, boss, that's what."

"Well, give it to me."

"Okay, I canvassed his neighborhood. He's the invisible man. Rented apartment. Manager says he's always on time with the rent. Nothing else. I missed the mailman, but I'll catch him tomorrow. See if he can tell me anything. Neighbors know him by sight. That's about it. No wild parties. Haven't seen him with lots of girls. One thought he was seeing this one particular woman but hasn't seen her around in quite a while."

"How long has he been in the apartment?"

"Three years."

"Manager let you look at the rent application?"

"Leo, you know that's confidential. I couldn't even ask for that information."

"We prosper on the carelessness of others, Del. Did you ask?"

"Yes, and he was offended and indignant."

"Tough shit."

"Monday morning we'll go through court records and permits and licenses for the last three years, see if anything shakes out."

"Neighbors tell you anything else?"

"No, like I said, they knew him by sight, period."

"You find his car?"

"Yeah. Now that was a gold mine. Thing had stickers all over it."

"Such as?"

"Bush-Quayle. We'll check him out with Young Republican organizations. Also, Georgetown Law School."

"You run him through our directories?"

"Yeah, nothing. He's either a drone or modest."

"Call Walter O'Neil, tonight. Give him the name, see if he can get a law firm for the guy, maybe even someone who'll talk about him."

"Okay. I'm also going over to the school tomorrow, use the library, look up yearbooks, et cetera. See if we can locate a classmate. Alumni affairs will have to wait until Monday."

"How about NCIC?"

"Clean. No warrants or arrests. He's good or he's tidy."

"Anything else on the car?"

"Yeah, a sticker for something called Ultimate Frisbee. Nobody here knows anything about it. We're trying to track down an association for it, find out where it's played, then we'll interview people."

"Okay. We've still got three, maybe four days. How's the office doing? Are the other cases being covered?"

"Yeah, we spread them around. Clancy hired a couple of freelancers to start next week. Right now, me, Clancy, and Larry are pulling double shifts on this. Monday when the offices are open and the databases are up, we'll probably put the two new guys on it."

"Good. Any word from the St. Mary's registrar's office?"

"No. Same problem there. Closed for the weekend. Won't know anything until Monday."

"All right. Good work, Del." I gave him my number. "Call here day or night with anything. If you can't get me directly, have me paged. I'll be out tomorrow morning on a field trip with Marshall and Gina, but I should be around the rest of the day."

"All right. Talk to you tomorrow."

I slipped the phone under the netting. Plumped the pillows and opened my book. Living alone had made me a voracious reader, as if all my other appetites had mutated into a hunger for the words that would make me someone else, put me somewhere else, or at least help me to sleep. The more I read, the harder it was to keep my interest. Boredom crept over me like the slow death it was. I was an old jaded john needing ever kinkier tricks just to get it up, or over with. Pretty soon nothing would move me at all. Until then, I was grateful for Michael Malone and the jolts and length of *Time's Witness*.

I woke up to the telephone's insistent ring, crawled out of bed, and thanked the front desk for the call. A chameleon darted out from under the bed and headed out the door. "Nice seeing you," I called out, and hoped he'd had a bountiful evening keeping my room an insect-free zone. I dressed and hurried down to breakfast.

After a glass of soursop, I ordered salt fish and onions with bakes and lots of coffee. Derek and Gina were not in the dining room. Maybe they'd ordered room service, maybe they were sleeping in and wouldn't make it. I ate quickly and kept checking my watch while I had my second cup of coffee. Our driver had arrived and was looking at the activities board. Another couple came up to him and introduced themselves. I wiped my mouth and left to join the group. Derek and Gina came down the hill as I checked in.

Our driver told us that his name was Wellington Bramble and that he was also a registered tour guide with the Department of the Interior. The other couple climbed into the back of the van, then Derek and Gina in the middle row. I hopped in up front, next to Wellington, turned, and introduced myself.

"Hi, my name is Leo Haggerty."

"Hello, I'm Derek Marshall and this is my fiancée, Gina Dalesandro."

"Pleasure to meet you."

Derek and Gina turned and we were all introduced to Tom and Dorothy Needham of Chicago, Illinois.

Wellington stuck his head out the window and spoke to one of the maids. They spoke rapidly in the local patois until the woman slapped him across the forearm and waved a scolding finger at him.

He engaged the gears, pulled away from the reception area, and told us that we would be visiting the tropical rain forests that surround the island's active volcano. All this in perfect English, the language of strangers and for strangers.

Dorothy Needham asked the question on all of our minds. "How long will we be on this road to the volcano?"

Wellington laughed. "Twenty minutes, ma'am, then we go inland to the volcano."

We left the coast road and passed through a gate marked St. Mary's Island Conservancy—Devil's Cauldron Volcano and Tropical Rain Forest. I was first out and helped the women step down into the muddy path. Wellington lined us up and began to lead us through the jungle, calling out the names of plants and flowers and answering questions.

There were soursop trees, lime trees, nutmeg, guava, bananas, coconuts, cocoa trees, ginger lilies, lobster-claw plants, flamboyant and hibiscus, impression fern, and chenille red-hot cattails. We stopped on the path at a large fern. Wellington turned and pointed to it.

"Here, you touch the plant, right here," he said, pointing at Derek, who eyed him suspiciously. "It won't hurt you."

Derek reached out a finger and touched the fern. Instantly the leaves retracted and curled in on themselves.

"That's Mary, Mary, Shut the Door. As you can see, a delicate and shy plant indeed."

He waved us on and we followed. Gina slipped an arm through Derek's and put her head on his shoulder. She squeezed him once.

"Derek, you know I used to be like that plant. Before you came along. All closed up and frightened if anybody got too close. But not anymore. I am so happy," she said, and squeezed him again.

Other than a mild self-loathing, I was having a good time, too. We came out of the forest and were on the volcano. Wellington turned to face us.

"Ladies and gentlemen, please listen very carefully. We are on top of an active volcano. There is no danger of an eruption, because there is no crust, so there is no pressure buildup. The last eruption was over two hundred years ago.

That does not mean that there is no danger here. You must stay on the marked path at all times and be very careful on the sections that have no guardrail. The water in the volcano is well over three hundred degrees Fahrenheit; should you stumble and fall in, you would be burned alive. I do not wish to alarm you unreasonably, but a couple of years ago we did lose a visitor, so please be very careful. Now follow me."

We moved along, single file and well spaced through a setting unlike any other I'd ever encountered. The circular top of the volcano looked like a wound on the earth. The ground steamed and smoked and nothing grew anywhere. Here and there black water leaked out of crusty patches like blood seeping from under a scab. The smell of sulfur was everywhere.

I followed Derek and Gina and watched him stop a couple of times and test the railings before he let her proceed. Caution, Derek? Or a trial run?

We circled the volcano and retraced our path back to the van. As promised, we were back at the hotel twenty minutes later. Gina was flushed with excitement and asked Derek if they could go back again. He thought that was possible, but there weren't any other guided tours this week, so they'd have to rent a car and go themselves. I closed my eyes and imagined her by the side of the road, taking a picture perhaps, and him ushering her through the foliage and on her way to eternity.

We all went in for lunch and ate separately. I followed them back to their room and then down to the beach. They moved to the far end of the beach and sat facing away from everyone else. I went into the bar and worked my way through a pair of long necks.

A couple in the dining room was having a spat, or maybe it was a tiff. Whatever, she called him a *schwein* and really tagged him with an open forehand to the chops. His face lit up redder than a baboon's ass.

She pushed back her chair, swung her long blonde hair in an about-face, and stormed off. I watched her go, taking each step like she was grinding out a cigarette under her foot. Made her hips and butt do terrible things.

I pulled my eyes away when I realized I had company. He was leering at me enthusiastically.

I swung around slowly. "Yes?"

It was one of the local hustlers who patrolled the beach, as ubiquitous and resourceful as the coconuts that littered the sand.

"I seen you around, man. Y'all alone. That's not a good thin', man. I was thinkin' maybe you could use some company. Someone to share paradise wit'. Watcha say, man?"

I shook my head. "I don't think so."

He frowned. "I know you ain't that way, man. I seen you watch that blonde with the big ones. What'sa matter? What you afraid of?" He stopped and tried to answer that one for me. "She be clean, man. No problem."

When I didn't say anything, he got pissed. "What is it then? You don't fuck strange, man?"

"Watch my lips, bucko. I'm not interested. Don't make more of it than there is."

He sized me up and decided I wasn't worth the aggravation. Spinning off his stool, he called me something in patois. I was sure it wasn't "sir."

I found a free lounge under a bohio and kept an eye on Derek and Gina. No sooner had I settled in than Gina got up and headed across the cocoa-colored volcanic sands to the beach bar. She was a little pink around the edges. Probably wouldn't be out too long today. Derek had his back to me, so

I swiveled my head to keep her in sight. She sat down and one of the female staff came over and began to run a comb through her hair. Cornrowing. She'd be there for at least an hour. I ordered a drink from a wandering waiter, closed my eyes, and relaxed.

Gina strolled back, her hair in tight little braids, each one tipped with a series of colored beads. She was smiling and kicking up little sprays of water. I watched her take Derek by the hands and pull him up out of his chair. She twirled around and shook her head back and forth, just to watch the braids fly by.

They picked up their snorkels and fins and headed for the water. I watched to see which way they'd go. The left side of the bay had numerous warning signs about the strong current including one on the point that said Turn Back—Next Stop Panama.

They went right and so did I. Maybe it was a little fear, maybe it was love, but she held on to his hand while they hovered over the reef. I went farther out and then turned back so I could keep them in sight. The reef was one of the richest I'd ever been on and worthy of its reputation as one of the best in the Caribbean.

I kept my position near the couple, moving when they did, just like the school of squid I was above. They were in formation, tentacles tucked in, holding their position by undulating the fins on each lateral axis. When the school moved, they all went at once and kept the same distance from each other. I drifted off the coral to a bed of sea grass. Two creatures were walking through the grass. Gray-green, with knobs and lumps everywhere, they had legs and wings! They weren't toxic-waste mutants, just the flying gurnards. I dived down on them and they spread their violet wings and took off.

When I surfaced, Derek and Gina were heading in. I swam

downstream from them and came ashore as they did. Gina was holding her side and peeking behind her palm. Derek steadied her and helped get her flippers off.

"I don't know what it was, Derek. It just brushed me and then it felt like a bee sting. It really burns," Gina said.

I wandered by and said, "Looks like a jellyfish sting. When did it happen?"

"Just a second ago." They answered in unison.

"Best thing for that is papaya skins. Has an enzyme that neutralizes the toxin. The beach restaurant has plenty of them. They keep it just for things like this. You better get right over, though. It only works if you apply it right away."

"Thanks. Thanks a lot," Derek said, then turned to help Gina down the beach.

"Yes, thank you," she said over his shoulder.

"You're welcome," I said to myself, and went to dry off.

I sat at the bar, waiting for dinner and playing back-gammon with myself. Derek and Gina came in and went to the bar to order. Her dress was a swirl of purple, black, and white and matched the color of the beads in her hair. Derek wore lime green shorts and a white short-sleeved shirt. Drinks in hand, they walked over to me. I stood up, shook hands, and invited them to join me.

"That tip of yours was a lifesaver. We went over to the bar and got some papaya on it right away. I think the pain was gone in maybe five minutes. How did you know about it?" Gina asked.

"I've been stung myself before. Somebody told me about it. Now I tell you. Word of mouth."

"Well, we're very grateful. We're getting married here on the island and I didn't want anything to mess this time up for us," Derek said.

I raised my glass in a toast. "Congratulations to you. This is a lovely place to get married. When is the ceremony?" I asked, sipping my drink.

"Tomorrow," Gina said, running her arm through Derek's. "I'm so excited."

I nearly drowned her in rerouted rum punch but managed to turn away and choke myself instead. I pounded my chest and waved off any assistance.

"Are you okay?" Derek asked.

"Yes, yes, I'm fine," I said as I got myself under control. Tomorrow? How the hell could it be tomorrow? "Sorry. I was trying to talk when I was drinking. Just doesn't work that way."

Derek asked if he could buy me another drink and I let him take my glass to the bar.

"I read the tourist brochure about getting married on the island. How long does it take for them to approve an application? They only said that you have to be on the island for two days before you can submit an application."

Gina leaned forward and touched my knee. "It usually takes two or three days, but Derek found a way to hurry things up. He sent the papers down early to the manager here and he agreed to file them for us as if we were on the island. It'll be ready tomorrow morning and we'll get married right after noon."

"That's wonderful. Where will the ceremony be?" My head was spinning.

"Here at the hotel. Down on the beach. They provide a cake, champagne, photographs, flowers. Would you join us afterward to celebrate?"

"Thank you, that's very kind. I'm not sure that I'll still be here, though. My plane leaves in the afternoon, and you know with that ride back to the airport, I might be gone. If

I'm still here, I'd be delighted."

Derek returned with drinks and sat close to Gina and looped an arm around her.

"Honey, I hope you don't mind, but I invited Mr. Haggerty to join us after the ceremony." She smiled anxiously.

"No, that sounds great, love to have you. By the way, it sounded like you've been to the islands before. This is our first time. Have you ever gone scuba diving?" Derek was all graciousness.

"Yeah, are you thinking of trying it?"

"Maybe, they have a course for beginners tomorrow. We were talking about taking the course and seeing if we liked it," he said.

"I'm a little scared. Is it really dangerous?" Gina asked.

Absolutely lethal. Russian roulette with one empty chamber. Don't do it. Wouldn't recommend it to my worst enemy.

"No, not really. There are dangers if you're careless, and they're pretty serious ones. The sea is not very forgiving of our mistakes. But if you're well trained and maintain some respect for what you're doing, it's not all that dangerous."

"I don't know. Maybe I'll just watch you do it, Derek."

"Come on, honey. You really liked snorkeling. Can you imagine how much fun it would be if you didn't have to worry about coming up for air all the time?" Derek gave Gina a squeeze. "And besides, I love the way you look in that new suit."

I saw others heading to the dining room and began to clean up the tiles from the board.

"Mr. Haggerty, would you—" Gina began.

"I'm sure we'll see Mr. Haggerty again, Gina. Thanks for your help this afternoon," Derek said, and led her to the dining room.

I finished my drink and took myself to dinner. After that, I sat and watched them dance to the *shak-shak* band. She put her head on his shoulder and molded her body to his. They swayed together in the perfect harmony only lovers and mothers and babies have.

They left that way, her head on his shoulder, a peaceful smile on her lips. I could not drink enough to cut the ache I felt and went to bed when I gave up trying.

Del was in when I called and gave me the brief bad news.

"The mailman was a dead end. I went over to the school library and talked to teachers and students. So far, nobody's had anything useful to tell us. I've got a class list and we're working our way through it. Walt did get a lead on him, though. He's a junior partner in a small law firm, a 'boutique' he called it."

"What kind of law?" Come on, say tax and estate.

"Immigration and naturalization."

"Shit. Anything else?"

"Yeah, he's new there. Still don't know where he came from. We'll try to get some information from the partners first thing in the morning."

"It better be first thing. Our timetable just went out the window. They're getting married tomorrow at noon."

"Jesus Christ, that puts the screws to us. We'll only have a couple of hours to work with."

"Don't remind me. Is that it?"

"For right now. Clancy is hitting bars looking for people that play this 'Ultimate Frisbee' thing. He's got a sketch with him. Hasn't called in yet."

"Well, if he finds anything, call me no matter what time it is. I'll be around all morning tomorrow. If you don't get me direct, have me paged, as an emergency. Right now we don't have shit."

"Hey, boss, we just ran out of time. I'm sure in a couple of days we'd have turned something up."

"Maybe so, Del, but tomorrow around noon somebody's gonna look out over their heads and ask if anybody has anything to say or forever hold your peace. I don't see myself raising my hand and asking for a couple of more days, 'cause we're bound to turn something up."

"We did our best. We just weren't holding very good cards is all."

"Del, we were holding shit." I should have folded when Scolari dealt them.

I hung up and readied my bedroom to repel all boarders. Under the netting, I sat and mulled over my options. I had no reason to stick my nose into Gina's life. No reason at all to think that Derek was anything but the man she'd waited her whole life for. Her happiness was real, though. She was blossoming under his touch. I had seen it. And happiness is a fragile thing. Who was I to cast a shadow on hers? And without any reason. Tomorrow was a special day for her. How would she remember it? How would I?

I woke early from a restless night and called the office. Nothing new. I tried Scolari's number and spoke briefly to him. I told him we were out of time and had nothing of substance. I asked him a couple of questions and he gave me some good news and some bad. There was nothing else to do, so I went down to see the betrothed.

They were in the dining room holding hands and finishing their coffee. I approached and asked if I could join them.

"Good morning, Mr. Haggerty. Lovely day, isn't it?" Gina said, her face aglow.

I settled into the chair and decided to smack them in the face with it. "Before you proceed with your wedding, I have some news for you."

They sat upright and took their hands, still joined, off the table.

"Gina's uncle, Enzo Scolari, wishes me to inform you that he has had his attorneys activate the trustee's discretionary powers over Miss Dalesandro's portion of the estate so that she cannot take possession of the money or use it in any fashion without his consent. He regrets having to take this action, but your insistence on this marriage leaves him no choice."

"You son of a bitch. You've been spying on us for that bastard," Derek shouted, and threw his glass of water at me. I sat there dripping while I counted to ten. Gina had gone pale and was on the verge of tears. Marshall stood up. "Come on, Gina, let's go. I don't want this man anywhere near me." He leaned forward and stabbed a finger at me. "I intend to call your employer, Mr. Scolari, and let him know what a despicable piece of shit I think he is, and that goes double for you." He turned away. "Gina, are you coming?"

"Just a second, honey," she whispered. "I'll be along in just a second." Marshall crashed out of the room, assaulting chairs and tables that got in his way.

"Why did you do this to me? I've waited my whole life for this day. To find someone who loves me and wants to live with me and to celebrate that. We came here to get away from my uncle and his obsessions. You know what hurts the most? You reminded me that my uncle doesn't believe that anyone could love me for myself. It has to be my money. What's so wrong with *me?* Can you tell me that?" She was starting to cry and wiped at her tears with her palms. "Hell of a question to be asking on your wedding day, huh? You do good work, Mr. Haggerty. I hope you're proud of yourself."

I'd rather Marshall had thrown acid in my face than the words she hurled at me. "Think about one thing, Miss

Dalesandro. This way you can't lose. If he doesn't marry you now, you've avoided a lot of heartache and maybe worse. If he does, knowing this, then you can relax knowing it's you and not your money. The way I see it, either way you can't lose. But I'm sorry. If there had been any other way, I'd have done it."

"Yes, well, I have to go, Mr. Haggerty." She rose, dropped her napkin on the table, and walked slowly through the room, using every bit of dignity she could muster.

I spent the rest of the morning in the bar waiting for the last act to unfold.

At noon, Gina appeared in a long white dress. She had a bouquet of flowers in her hands and was trying hard to smile. I sipped some anesthetic and looked away. No need to make it any harder now. I wasn't sure whether I wanted Marshall to show up or not.

Derek appeared at her side in khaki slacks and an embroidered white shirt. What will be, will be. They moved slowly down the stairs. I went to my room, packed, and checked out. By three o'clock I was off the island and on my way home.

It was almost a year later when Kelly buzzed me on the intercom to say that a Mr. Derek Marshall was here to see me.

"Show him in."

He hadn't changed a bit. Neither one of us moved to shake hands. When I didn't invite him to sit down, he did anyway.

"What do you want, Marshall?"

"You know, I'll never forget that moment when you told me that Scolari had altered the trust. Right there in public. I was so angry that you'd try to make me look bad like that in front of Gina and everyone else. It really has stayed with me. And here I am, leaving the area. I thought I'd come by and return the favor before I left."

"How's Gina?" I asked with a veneer of nonchalance over trepidation.

"Funny you should ask. I'm a widower, you know. She had a terrible accident about six months ago. We were scuba diving. It was her first time. I'd already had some courses. I guess she misunderstood what I'd told her and she held her breath coming up. Ruptured a lung. She was dead before I could get her to shore."

I almost bit through my pipe stem. "You're a real piece of work, aren't you? Pretty slick, death by misinformation. Got away with it, didn't you?"

"The official verdict was accidental death. Scolari was beside himself, as you can imagine. There I was, sole inheritor of Gina's estate, and according to the terms of the trust her half of the grandfather's money was mine. It was all in Scolari stock, so I made a deal with the old man. He got rid of me and I got paid fifty percent more than the shares were worth."

"You should be careful, Derek, that old man hasn't got long to live. He might decide to take you with him."

"That thought has crossed my mind. So I'm going to take my money and put some space between him and me."

Marshall stood up to leave. "By the way, your bluff wasn't half-bad. It actually threw me there for a second. That's why I tossed the water on you. I had to get away and do some thinking, make sure I hadn't overlooked anything. But I hadn't."

"How did you know it was a bluff?" You cocky little shit.

Marshall pondered that a moment. "It doesn't matter. You'll never be able to prove this. It's not on paper anywhere. While I was in law school I worked one year as an unpaid intern at the law firm handling the estate of old man Scolari, the grandfather. This was when Gina's mother died. I did a turn in lots of different departments. I read the documents when I was Xeroxing them. That's how I knew the setup. Her mother's share went to Gina. Anything happens to her and the estate is transferred according to the terms of Gina's will. An orphan, with no siblings. That made me sole inheritor, even if she died intestate. Scolari couldn't change the trust or its terms. Your little stunt actually convinced Gina of my sincerity. I wasn't in any hurry to get her to write a will and she absolutely refused to do it when Scolari pushed her on it.

"Like I said, for a bluff it wasn't half-bad. Gina believed you, but I think she was the only one who didn't know anything about her money. Well, I've got to be going, got a plane to catch." He smiled at me like he was a dog and I was his favorite tree.

It was hard to resist the impulse to threaten him, but a threat is also a warning and I had no intention of playing fair. I consoled myself with the fact that last time I only had two days to work with. Now I had a lifetime. When I heard the outer door close, I buzzed Kelly on the intercom.

"Yes, Mr. Haggerty?"

"Reopen the file on Derek Marshall."

ACKNOWLEDGEMENTS: I'd like to thank the following people for their contributions to this story: Joyce Huxley of Scuba St. Lucia for her information on hyperbaric accidents; Michael and Alison Weber of Charlottesville for the title and good company; and John Cort and Rebecca Barbetti for including us in their wedding celebration and tales of "the spork" among other things.

Lost and Found

"So, how would you like another shot at Derek Marshall?"

Inside, you learned to speak once and listen twice. I listened.

"Not interested?"

"Not saying. What does a 'second shot' mean?"

"He's come out of hiding. He left San Francisco, drove to San Diego and jumped on a cruise ship to Mexico. He has a woman with him."

"You think he plans to kill her?"

"I don't know. That's one of the things I want you to find out."

I looked at the old man. I hadn't seen Enzo Scolari in six, maybe seven years. Time had leached a lot of life out of him. He was frail and bony. Waiting for my reply, he massaged the swollen arthritic knuckles of his hands. His wispy, white eyebrows were now as unruly as smoke.

Six years ago he had hired me to prevent his niece's marriage to Derek Marshall. I wasn't able to do that. She married Marshall and in short order he murdered her and became a millionaire. For two years after that I kept tabs on him, hoping that he'd step wrong and I'd be there to drop a net over him. It didn't happen.

"Why me?"

"I can't think of anyone better qualified, Mr. Haggerty. You know Marshall. You know how he works. You have a personal stake in this, or at least you did. And you're available. You can follow him wherever he goes."

"Marshall knows me, too. I can't get near him. He'll make me and that's the end of that."

"I don't think so, Mr. Haggerty. I knew you then and I would never recognize you now. You've changed quite a bit. How much weight have you put on?"

I shrugged. "Thirty six pounds."

"It looks good on you. All muscle. How did you do that? I hear the food is not fit for animals."

"I lifted weights four hours a day, seven days a week. That and good genes. I can turn shit into muscle."

"That seems to be the case. With your shaved head and goatee, sunglasses and a hat, he'll never recognize you."

I let it pass. "I lost my license. I can't carry a gun. I have no contacts anymore. I don't know how I could be of any use to you."

Scolari waved my words away with a swat of his bony hand. "You didn't get stupid, did you? You were a bright man. I'm betting you still are. You don't need a license or a gun, just your wits. As for contacts, I know all you'll ever need about Derek Marshall. I maintained my own surveillance on Mr. Marshall after he left Virginia."

Scolari touched the switch on his wheelchair, spun towards the desk and poured himself a glass of water. His hand shook so badly that he had to stop two inches from his mouth and let his head close the distance. He drained the glass and put it on the desk.

Scolari turned back to me.

"What was prison like, Mr. Haggerty?"

"Just like any gated community, Mr. Scolari. Too many rules."

"How does it feel to be back in the world?"

"I wouldn't know. I'm just out. I'm not back."

"Yes, well let me tell you about Derek Marshall. After he settled in San Francisco, I had our local office keep track of all the women he dated. After the first date we sent them a press kit, so to speak. All the clippings about Gina's death, the inquest, the unanswered questions. Most of them never went out with him again. There were a few that we could not dissuade. However, Derek Marshall spent many, many nights alone. I also tried to recover the money he got when Gina died. I was not quite as successful there. I have many business contacts all over the country. Those that I could influence in San Francisco made it hard for him to get loans or closed mutual funds to him. I ruined a couple of his investments; cost him and some other people quite a bit of money. All of this forced Mr. Marshall into a very low profile life style. He wasn't enjoying the spoils of his crime.

"I'm worried about this trip to Mexico. It's his first attempt to shake my surveillance. I want to know what he's up to. Is he planning to disappear? Who is the woman with him? Is she an accomplice to his plans? Is she in danger from him? That's where you come in, Mr. Haggerty. As I said, you know Derek, how he thinks. You have no ties to this area anymore, am I correct?"

I just listened.

"I kept track of you, too. You have no license, no job, and no career. No family. Your friends in the police department can't help you because you're a felon. Same with your friends at other agencies. No one can use you. You have no home, no money. Your lawyer got all that.

"I however, have a plane ticket for you, a car waiting at the airport in Tucson, and a cabin on the ship where he's staying. Right now they are wet-docked at Puerto Penasco for repairs. They'll be there for three days. I also have a company credit card for you. While you're on the job all your living expenses will be covered."

"What do you want from me?"

"Find out what he's up to. I don't want to lose him. That's

the first thing. Find out who the girl is. If she's in danger, warn her off. I don't want anyone else to go through what I've gone through."

"That's it?"

"That's it. Report to me as soon as you find out anything. I don't care what time it is. I sleep badly when I sleep at all. That's your 'second shot.' Are you interested?"

Scolari's offer beat everything else I had going. I was too old to be starting over from scratch.

"When's the next plane out?"

In the air over Tucson, I thought about my talk with old man Scolari. He was awfully eager to get me out here with Marshall. Why? Maybe he blamed me for Gina's death. Maybe he'd decided to have us both killed? No. I went to prison two years after Derek left. He never tried it then and he had plenty of time. Maybe he wants to set me up for Derek's death, do it that way? Why now? He can maneuver me into position a lot easier than before. Five years ago a lot more people would have cared about what happened to me, not now. Maybe he was tired of waiting and decided to make something happen? How sick was he?

Maybe what I should do is milk this for all it's worth. File dummy reports, stay away from Marshall in case it's a frame and see how long I can ride this until he catches on. They say living well is the best revenge. Besides, what's the worst that he could do, fire me? Why am I not scared?

We began to descend over Tucson. I looked out the window at the ground rushing up at us. Most crashes occur on takeoffs and landings. I watched all the way down. We bounced once on the runway, then settled down and began to slow.

Scolari had asked me how it felt to be back. I really didn't know. I remember thinking about Humpty Dumpty when I was sentenced. How some men shattered when they hit bottom, while others armored themselves all the way down and they didn't feel a thing. Not then, not ever.

My rental car was in a lot across the street from the airport. I threw my bag in the passenger seat, got in, and turned on the air conditioner. The airport information board said it was 110 degrees today. The rental agent had given me a courtesy map of the area. I unfolded it and decided on a route. I pulled out of the lot and entered the freeway traffic that ran by the airport.

I drove south out of America into Mexico. My last case had started in Mexico. It ended in the Maryland State Penitentiary Maximum Security Facility at Jessup. There was only one thing I knew for certain. I was not going into a Mexican prison.

I crossed the border at Nogales and headed towards Hermosillo. Halfway there I turned west towards Mexicali, then south again to the Gulf of California.

God must have had only a few crayons left in his box when he got to the desert. Everything was one shade of brown or another. Scraggly plants sprouted up on the hills that flanked the road. Each group of plants had its own shepherd; a tall cactus watching over it. Some were as straight and narrow as Giacometti's men. Others had arms: some up; some down; some both; signaling each other like giant green semaphores.

An hour or so later I saw the sign for the docks, pulled off the road and stopped at the guard's station. Razor wire ringed the area.

"Name sir?"

"Haggerty, Leo Haggerty."

"Yes sir. You are registered on the Calypso Moonbeam.

Drive straight ahead to the parking lot. Check in with security at the gangway."

I surrendered my passport, got my security pass, room key, and directions to my cabin. It was clean. It was bigger than I was used to, it was all mine, and I had the key to the door.

I dropped my bag on the floor and lay down on the bed. I took off my sunglasses and stared at the ceiling fan. Its blades seemed to move as slowly as the hands of a prison clock. It wasn't long before I was asleep.

I awoke lying on my back and looked at my watch. It was after four o'clock. I checked the map I had been given and found the lounge. I left the room and went there.

I sat in a soft chair and ordered a gin and tonic from the waitress. My seat allowed me to watch the entrance to the bar and the dining room. At the very least, I ought to see what Derek looked like these days. No use letting him surprise me. I sipped my drink and watched the people come and go. It was almost eight when Marshall showed up. The last seven years had not hurt him any. He'd put on a few pounds and erased his jaw line along the way. His hair was still fine and brown, but he parted it on the left now. The glasses were gone, so I guessed he wore contacts.

He had his arm around the waist of a tall blonde, whose pale blue eyes and bright smile stood out against her tan face like turquoise and ivory in the sandy desert. Derek laughed at something the maitre d' said, squeezed his friend to him and kissed her ear. I took a long slow pull on my drink and thought of Gina Dalesandro. I could still see her wiping tears off her cheek on her wedding day and asking me, "What's so wrong with me? Can you tell me that?"

I whispered what I hadn't said then. "Nothing Gina, not one single thing. I'm sorry I've darkened your day. I'm sorry I didn't do better." I hadn't been able to save her back then and I'd tried my best. This grinning bastard had murdered her and gotten rich doing it. I raised that drink to Gina's memory and asked her to "wish me better luck this time." I raised the rest to forget.

I nursed a port until Marshall and the girl were done eating and then followed them out of the dining room. They walked back to the cabins and entered room 116, a deck below me.

Still haunted by Gina Dalesandro, I went back to my room and called Scolari. It was 1:30 a.m. back east, and, good as his word he picked up on the second ring.

"Yes."

"Mr. Scolari, this is Leo Haggerty. I've located Derek Marshall. I saw him at dinner this evening. He has a woman with him. A blonde, tall and very tanned. Do you know anything about her?"

"No, we're still working on it. What else have you found out?"

"Not much. I'll follow him tomorrow, see if I can get a line on what he's doing here. If I have to I'll try to get closer to the woman, see if she's in any danger and warn her off."

"Careful, Mr. Haggerty. I don't want Marshall spooked. He hasn't made you, I presume?"

"No."

"We'll try to find out who she is and if she's in any danger."

"Call me here at anytime with any information you get. Especially on the girl."

"Of course, Mr. Haggarty. You'll be the first to know. Goodnight."

I hadn't lifted or run today, so I did seven hundred sit-ups as penance, showered and lay naked on the cool, clean sheets of the bed. I listened hard into the darkness. No one was crying, or cursing. No one was praying or screaming. No one was begging for the mercy that never came. In the middle of the night, I got up and left my room, just because I could.

I awoke around seven, slipped into a T-shirt, shorts and running shoes and trotted down the gangway. I showed the security guy my pass and headed for the guard's station. I passed him and turned right down the road and ran off into the desert. I came back an hour later.

I trudged back up the gangway. At the top, a woman was putting up a notice on the bulletin board. I stopped to read it.

She looked at me. "How far did you go?"

I shrugged. "Six miles."

"You take any water with you?"

"Nah, it's wasn't that far."

"Provided you don't turn an ankle, step on a rattler, and you stay on the road. But if things go wrong, you'll need that water because you're sweating quite a bit. Heatstroke and dehydration can drop anyone. You ever been out in the desert before?"

"No, I haven't. Maybe my ignorance has led to disrespect."

"Why don't you come on my hike this morning." She tapped the notice. "You'll learn more about the desert than you ever wanted to know."

Her chestnut hair was pulled back under a beige baseball cap and flowed out the back, thick and smooth as a thoroughbred's well-curried tail. Silvered sunglasses shielded her eyes like a beetle's shiny shell. I found that strangely reassuring.

"When is it?"

"Nine."

"Okay," I said, and walked away. I went into my room, stripped down and took a shower, ending it with the icy needle spray I knew so well was only one mistake away.

I had a light breakfast, then went outside to find my guide. She was standing out by the notice board alternately staring at her clipboard and looking all around to see who was missing. I'd once heard a camp counselor call it "urchin searchin'."

I pulled up in front of her.

"Looks like you're it."

"Hike still on?"

"Sure. Here, take this." She gave me a water bottle on a belt. I saw she had one on her hip, so I strapped mine on.

"We may as well start with the rules of the desert. They're real simple. This is God's country not man's. We're not welcome here. It's not user friendly. If you don't respect that, it will kill you. There are three absolutes: Never travel without water; never go out in the desert alone; always tell someone where you are going. Got that?"

"Got it."

"You ought to wear a hat. That shiny scalp of yours is a solar collector."

"I'll get one after the hike."

"Here put this on your head, like a do-rag." She handed me a bandana from her back pocket. "You look like you're in pretty good shape. Why don't we go out to those mountains over there." She pointed into the distance. "It's probably a couple of hours out. We can see a number of things on the way."

"Sounds good."

She held out her hand. "My name's Kiki. Kiki Davenport."

"Leo Haggerty." I shook it, and then tied the bandana around my head.

"Where are you from?" she asked and turned to lead the way. She had on a small fanny pack.

"Back east."

143

We left the road and walked out into the desert. After about twenty minutes she stopped by a twisted tree decorated with a fuzzy necklace.

"This is a chain fruit cholla. It's a kind of cactus. I like to start with them to show people the enormous variety of the cactus family."

"The big ones with the arms. They look like they're guarding the others. What are they?"

"Those are Saguaro. The largest of all the cacti. It's funny you should describe them like that. Saguaro means *sentinel* in Spanish.

"I find cacti fascinating. This is a very harsh environment. Great heat and light, very little water. The parameters for survival are very narrow. Not only do they survive, they thrive. And they do so in many, many ways. They remind me of how creative the will to live can be."

She looked out across the desert. "Here, let's look at this one." She walked off the path into the bush. I followed.

She looked like the land itself. All variations of brown, from her beige hiking boots, white socks and tanned skin, to her khaki shorts and cream shirt. She'd be hard to see at a distance. I made a note.

"This is a jumping cholla. Very, very nasty."

The cactus was covered with very fine spines so thick that they looked like a soft yellow fur. "Why?"

"This plant reproduces asexually. These last segments of the stalks get carried off by animals that brush up against them. The spines are hooked and so fine that they're almost impossible to get out. When the animal finally gets it off them it falls to the ground, roots and starts to grow."

"Why jumping cholla?"

"When it breaks off, it looks like it jumped onto you. The slightest contact leaves you covered in these spines. Bend down and take a closer look."

She squatted down and I got down next to her and looked at the tiny barbs on the spines. Six inches away, they were invisible.

I avoided looking at her but I could smell her; sweet and clean, flowers and spice.

"You go out into the desert, you should always carry a comb. That way you can get the cholla off if you have to. You slide the teeth down into the spines and flip it off. You can't use your other hand. They'll both wind up full of spines."

"I'll bet falling into one of these is a real mess."

"Oh yeah," she said, nodding in sincere agreement.

"Let's head for those rocks over there. It's a mile or so. We'll climb them, check out the valley beyond, and then head back." I followed her extended arm. She wore a large ring on her right hand, an oval, rose-colored stone in a heavy silver and gold setting.

I followed her back to the path and we set off in silence. For twenty minutes I walked in her footsteps up a gradual incline on a narrow, winding path. Eyes down, I watched her legs move, each step a precise placement on a flat rock surface. The steeper the incline, the closer the attention I paid. We stopped on a plateau.

"Look there," she said. I saw a paddle shaped cactus with several of its paddles half chewed off.

"Javelinas."

"What's that?"

"Javelinas, peccaries, wild pigs. They eat prickly pears— spines and all. They travel in packs. Nasty customers if you're hunting them."

"Are they interested in hunting us?" I asked.

"No. I suppose if you got between a mother and her young they'd charge and drive you off.

"They've got very sharp tusks, and they'd give you a bad bite. I had an old boyfriend who used to hunt them with a bow and arrow. When they were cornered, they'd charge. Then they were real dangerous. They were really fast and they'd be on you before you could get a shot off."

"You go hunting with him?"

"Yeah."

"Ever get one?"

"No. Too fast. One of them opened my leg up, though."

She pointed down to her thigh. I saw a long white scar on the inside. "Up near the artery. I left the javelinas alone after that. You ever hunt?"

I waited too long to answer. It was a simple question. "No."

"Funny, I'd have thought you did. You have that look."

"And what look is that?"

"Patient, watchful. A stalker. You don't say much. Most people talk my ear off on these hikes. They tell me all about themselves, ask me all about myself. You take information in but you don't offer any. That's hunter behavior. Plus, you don't look like a businessman."

"Really? Now why is that?"

"Your muscles. Getting those is a full time job. You wouldn't have time for an office."

"Maybe muscles are my business, like Arnold Schwarzenegger."

"Sorry. I've never seen you in any muscle magazines."

"You read that many of them?

She shook her head. "For years. The boyfriend with the bow and arrows. He was a body builder. Mister Southwest 1990."

"I like the way your mind works but I'm not a hunter. I'm just out here to relax and enjoy the scenery. So tell me, are there any animals to be worried about out here?"

She smiled, chuckled softly and shook her head. "Okay. Let's see. Everyone will tell you about the rattlesnakes, the Gila Monsters, the scorpions, and the tarantulas. They're all here, they're all dangerous, but you need to be stupid and unlucky to get bit. Simple rules for the biters: Look where you put your hands and feet; shake out your shoes before you put them on; don't reach into dark places, and watch where you step. That's about it, for them.

"Then there's cougars and bears. Bears aren't a big problem in the desert. Much more so up in the mountains. We do get cougars down here. They like javelina. They're pretty shy of humans and attacks are rare but not unheard of. If you meet one, stop, then back away slowly. Don't turn your back to them. Don't run. If they attack, protect your neck. Cats kill by asphyxiation. They'll try to bite your throat and cut off your air. Keep your hands up, protect your eyes and throat, and try to stay on your feet. If you can find something to hit them with, a thick stick or a heavy rock, so much the better. Keep backing away. We're not on their regular diet, so unless they're starving to death or protecting their young they're not likely to keep up the attack in the face of resistance."

She turned and headed up the path. As the grade steepened, we slowed as the footing got worse. I gave her more of a lead. No reason if she fell to take us both down the hill. We went into a cave made of fallen boulders and climbed up through an opening between the stones to the top of a giant boulder. Two rocks were on top of it in the center like the crown of a hat.

She walked over near the edge, squatted down and took the water bottle off her belt and squeezed out a long drink. I walked over next to her and did the same.

"Beautiful out here," I said.

"Sure is. I just love it. I don't ever want to leave."

"What brought you out here?"

She turned and looked at me. I saw my sunglasses in hers.

"An '85 Chevy with a black interior, a busted tape player and no A/C."

I laughed. She smiled. She sipped her water, then leaned back onto her butt, and crossed her legs Indian style. I stayed squatting. One time the warden wanted to talk to me about an accident in the laundry. He wanted to talk to me so badly that I was listed as escaped for two days. Turned out to be a mistake of course. I had fallen into a box in the power plant. It was only 30 inches deep but I couldn't get out. Not until the warden and I had that talk. Every day after that I practiced being folded up like a shirt in case I ever escaped again. I can squat a good long while.

"What do you like about it?" I said.

"It's empty out here. I like empty. You don't have to work to keep your distance. It's big and it's old out here. Not human time or human efforts. It helps me keep a good perspective on things, not take them too seriously. How about you? Do you like it out here?"

"Yeah, I like it out here. Like you said, it's empty. Empty is good. I don't ever want to be crowded again."

I looked around. You could see for miles in any direction. Dark clouds were forming to the south and the wind said they were headed this way.

I closed my eyes and tilted my face against the breeze.

"There's a storm coming. Summer storms are filled with lightning. We don't want to be up on the heights. Let's start down."

"I think I'll tempt fate a little longer. I haven't felt rain in a long time."

148

"Not smart. The storm isn't that far away. You'll get all the rain you want if we don't start back now. Monsoons can fill up these arroyos in a minute."

When I didn't move right away, she stood up and headed back down.

I sat on the hill and waited for the rain to come. The breeze picked up and caressed my face. A bolt of lightning flashed a jagged path to the ground. A thunderclap boomed almost immediately afterward. Time to go.

I caught up with her at the base of the rocks. "Uh, Mr. Southwest 1990 . . . you still with him?"

She shook her head. "No, he left me for Mister Southwest 1993."

I hadn't said this much to a woman in years. I decided to press my luck. Prison, like the desert, helps you with perspective. "Could I buy you dinner tonight?"

She thought about that for a minute. "Okay."

"What time should I come by?"

"Oh." She tilted her head. "You wanted to eat it with me, too."

I must have made a face.

"I'm kidding. I'm kidding," she said.

"Staff isn't supposed to fraternize with the guests. Why don't we meet off the ship? There's a little place in town called the Aztec Café. How about I meet you there, say eight o'clock?"

"Great."

She checked the sky. The clouds were rolling on while we stood still. "We really ought to head back."

"Sure." I followed her back into the desert. All the way back I wondered what color her eyes were.

At the ship's store I purchased a water bottle, some sunscreen and a soft, wide brimmed hat.

I found Derek by the pool, reading a book about moneyless investing.

He had a drink on the table next to him. His soft white body was starting to get a little pink: medium-rare. His legs were crossed at the ankles, and the upper foot tapped the lower one incessantly.

I walked around the pool and into the spa area. The weight room was beyond a pair of doors in the far wall. The blonde stood in line behind an enormously fat man. I brought up the rear.

The whale wanted a massage. He looked like he'd have to be stirred. I checked the blonde out head to toe, looking for any distinguishing marks. She had on a pair of clogs. They looked like hooves back in the 70's and they still did today. She adjusted her cover-up, and I saw a nice bruise on her right thigh. I glanced down into her bag, but it was fastened. She had a tennis bracelet on. It could have been diamonds, could have been rock candy for all I knew. No rings, but long, hot pink nails.

"The couples massage, how long does that last?"

"It's about an hour," the attendant said.

"Okay. We'd like to schedule one this afternoon. Cabin 116. How late do you do them?"

"We schedule the last ones of the day at five p.m."

"Okay, let's do it then. We'd also like room service at seven thirty."

"Do you want to order now?"

"No. We'll call it in later."

"Very good. Your masseurs will be Carl and Rita."

"Where is the Jacuzzi?"

"Through the doors into the ladies' locker room."

She picked up a towel from a woven basket next to the counter and glided off towards the locker room.

I took a quick glance at the schedule book to see what was entered. Just cabin numbers, no names. That made sense. Everything was automatically billed to the cabin to be settled up at departure.

"May I help you, sir?" asked a stocky girl with short dark hair wearing a green and beige uniform that made her look like a park ranger.

"Weights?"

"Through those doors."

"Anybody inside to spot?"

"No sir, we don't have free weights, just machines."

I nodded. I picked up a towel and walked into the weight room. It was empty and silent. I walked around the circuit of machines, looking at their maximum settings. No work here. I sat on a bench, pulled out my gloves and belt and tossed my bag into the corner.

I saw Marshall through the glass. He was having a nice vacation. I was having a nice vacation. He didn't have the jumpy, worried look of a man on the run. No furtive glances of the frightened schemer trying to lose a shadow. Maybe he's up here having a nice time with some bimbo. They go back to San Francisco, I go to San Francisco. This is a good gig. I'm paid to live the good life watching someone else live the good life. Don't fuck this up, Derek, I thought to myself. I could get used to this. A life sentence of pointless luxury. Guilty, your honor. Show me no mercy.

I did the circuit slowly, drawing out the negatives on each rep, squeezing the most work out of the machines. The weights slid smoothly, silently, up and down their spines like a steel bellows I inflated with each effort.

In the yard, you set your load by hand, hoisting each plate onto the bar, slamming it against the others, metal on metal, clanging like a cell door. When I finished my workout, I rubbed my face and scalp with my towel and draped it around my neck.

I looked around the empty room. Here the weight meant nothing. There you were watched by everyone. Sheer physical strength was important.

Early on I met all the animals. The spiders who run the joint; the great apes who did their bidding; the zombies; and the bunk bunnies. The great apes don't do the same time as everyone else. So I became a great ape. Things got better.

The fact that I was in for killing a cop didn't hurt my status any. I didn't correct anyone who thought it was murder, but I also didn't claim it. Inside you don't say anything you can't back up.

One thousand eight hundred and twenty-five days later, they opened a door and returned me to the world. Bigger. Stronger. Harder.

You go to the property room before you leave in your shiny black state suit. They hand you a bus ticket and then give your belongings in a brown manila envelope. They open it up and dump it out; your wallet, watch, some coins, a ring, keys, and a pen. They slide a form over for you to sign. I remember reading: "CHECK YOUR BELONGINGS. YOUR SIGNATURE CONFIRMS THAT EVERYTHING TAKEN FROM YOU HAS BEEN RETURNED IN ITS ORIGINAL CONDITION."

I looked into the bag. I turned it over and shook it. I tapped it with my hand. The guard asked me what I was looking for.

"Somehow, I don't think this is quite everything you took when I came in here."

"We didn't take anything you didn't deserve to lose," was his reply.

I stopped in front of the mirror and looked at myself. A

bullet head, a mask for a face, empty eyes and a miser's mouth. My shirt was soaked in sweat and hugged my wedge shaped torso, armor plated in muscle. Kiki was right. Everything that survives adapts to its environment. Well, I've changed environments again. Can I change myself again?

The blonde must have come out of the sauna by another door because I never saw her pass me but there she was sitting next to Derek. Derek's hand stroked lazy figure eights on her thigh with the tip of his index finger like a tiny figure skater.

I went back to my room, showered and lay down for a nap. At six I got up and dressed for dinner. I knew where Derek and his friend would be for the evening.

I sat by the pool and ordered a Salty Dog. I sat sipping it in the fading daylight and stared at the jagged peaks of the distant mountains. It looked like someone had torn off the edge of the sky.

I finished my drink and waved the waitress over for a second. She was dark skinned with thick black hair, held in place by a bright-multicolored ribbon. Her hair was stiff and wiry like a cord of very fine kindling. Her eyes were as dark as her hair without discernible pupils. I imagined her hair ablaze with gold and crimson flames.

"Another one, please."

She nodded, took the glass and left.

I drank steadily until the sun flattened itself on the horizon like the yolk of a dropped egg. My day now had a wavy, shimmery edge to it, like the air on a hot, still day.

I got directions to the cafe from the excursion desk and arrived a little before eight.

Inside, the big room was divided into three separate areas. To the left was a small dance floor. Something Spanish with pedal steel was playing on the sound system—Country-Mexican, I guess. A long bar ran across the back wall of the middle area. A couple of the men at the bar spotted me in the mirror and watched me walk across the room. I stared into their broad, flat Indian faces. They didn't like what they saw and returned to their conversation. A waitress in a white shirt with a string tie showed me to one of the tables in the dining section and handed me a menu. I glanced at it. Mostly Mexican, with some steaks, chili, and barbeque.

Kiki showed up a little after eight. She wore tooled mid-calf boots—the leather a brown and white patchwork—and a short, clingy white dress, sleeveless, cut low in the back. Her white Stetson had a turquoise ornament on the crown.

I stood up and pulled out a chair for her. She scooped her dress underneath herself and sat down.

"May I get you something to drink?" the waitress asked.

"I'm fine," I said. "I got an early start."

"Iced tea will be fine," she said.

"You look great." I nodded in agreement with myself.

Easy boy, you're just passing through. What would a good-looking young woman want with a beat-up old man like you? Nothing. Don't go thinking about it or wishing for it. Just do what you said you would. Enjoy some pleasant company, for a change. If you wanted to get laid, you should have lined up a pro.

"Thank you," she said and smiled. Her eyes were green.

"So what's good here?" I asked.

"Everything. I usually get the Carne Asada."

I sipped my water and just looked at her. Her face was a narrow oval with a thin straight nose and mouth. With her thick red hair, I thought of a fox. I could do this for hours, I thought. Not say a word. Just look. Prisons are the tower of Babel. Everyone scrambling over each other to be heard, to make their point, to tell it like it ain't. Silence reminds you what a sloth time is.

"Did you hear what I said?"

"I'm sorry. I wasn't paying attention."

"I could tell."

"I was, but not to what you were saying, just how you look."

"There was a time that would have pleased me, but I know I'm not that good looking. You looked at me like you'd never seen a woman before."

She drank her iced tea. "Let's see. How bad is this? You haven't felt rain in years, you hardly say a word about yourself, and you look at me like I'm a Martian." She paused then clapped her hands. "Hospital. You've been in a hospital. In a coma and now you have amnesia."

She shook her head. "No, not a coma. Where'd you get the muscles? I've got it. A monastery. Lots of time on your hands. You pump iron for Jesus. You're some kind of ninja monk."

"Why is this so important to you? I don't like to talk about myself. That's all. You're like a starfish on a clam. The harder you pull, the harder I'm gonna pull."

"No. You aren't a monk. Not now, not ever. I got it wrong again. When will I learn?" She took another drink, picked up her purse and pulled out her wallet. "I'll pay for the tea, thank you very much, don't bother to get up."

"What are you doing?"

"I'm leaving is what I'm doing."

"Why? What did I do?"

She put her elbows on the table and leaned forward to speak. "Just do me this, answer one question, okay?"

She didn't say tell the truth. "Okay, what is it?"

"You're a con, aren't you? You're just out of prison. That would explain things. Am I right?"

I weighed the effort in constructing and carrying off a

good lie against her green eyes, the wisp of hair that had eluded her French braid, and her fragrance riding across the table at me.

"That's it I'm outta here." She started up.

I reached out and grabbed her wrist. She stared down at my hand. She was shackled to me, unable to move.

"Don't go," I said, and released her. "Please. I'm sorry I touched you, that was wrong. Yes, I'm an ex-con, and yes, I'm just out of prison."

She sat down, rubbing her wrist.

"Did I hurt you?"

"No. You just scared me."

I shook my head, amazed at my stupidity. Maybe I did want to go back inside. "I'll pay for the tea. I'm sorry I scared you. You're the first woman I've spent any time with in five years. Just looking at you is enough for me. I can imagine that's not as much fun for you."

She stared at me, considering what I had just said. "What did you do?"

"Does it matter?"

"Yes. It does."

"What makes you think I'd tell you the truth?"

"I think you will. Let's leave it at that."

I exhaled long and slow, and closed my eyes to gather my thoughts.

"I was charged with felony murder of a police officer, a capital offense. I was found guilty of involuntary man-slaughter, and sentenced to and served the maximum, five years. Any questions?"

"Did you do it?"

I nodded yes. "Sure did. He was trying to kill me and a wit-ness I was protecting. There was a gunfight in the street. I was chasing him. He got hit by a car."

"You say you were protecting a witness. Were you a police officer?"

"No. I was a private investigator. She was a witness who could expose the involvement of the police and the district attorney in a pornography ring. He was sent out to kill her. He bought it instead."

"If that's true, why were you found guilty?"

"I couldn't prove the conspiracy part. By the time it went to trial, all the other witnesses had had fatal accidents. All that was left to see was that he was a police officer pursuing a legitimate warrant on a fugitive. I was assisting her in escaping. That's a felony. Chanda—that's my lawyer—she did a good job in getting it knocked down from murder to man two. For felony murder I'd have gotten the chair. Considering what could have happened, five years was a bargain. But then again, I don't often look at it that way."

She sat staring at me, her mouth pursed in thought.

"So," I said. "It's been nice having this talk. I'm glad we got that all cleared up. I won't try to stop you if you want to leave." I hoisted up a dead smile.

"I'll stay," she said.

"I'm glad. Why don't we order something?"

She ordered the Carne Asada and I followed her lead.

"You said you got it wrong again? What did you mean?"

"I can't say 'nothing' can I?"

"Not a chance."

"Thought so. My track record with guys isn't so great. There's a line out there between exciting and dangerous that always confuses me. My compass goes haywire and I always wind up on the wrong side of that line. That's what I meant. That's why I was being such a pain. I had all these questions about you. I figured let's just go straight to the bottom, avoid the whole disappointment part. That's really gotten old."

"If you had all those questions, why did you say 'yes' to dinner?"

"How else was I going to get them answered? Besides, you look like no two days with you would be the same. That's exciting."

Her food arrived, and she ordered a beer to go with it. I stayed with water.

"You know an awful lot about cactus. Are you a botanist?"

"No. I mean, I read a lot about them, but I don't have a degree or anything."

"You could have fooled me."

"Good. You see, I invented my job. So if I sound like I know what I'm talking about they won't replace me with a trained botanist."

"What do you mean invented it?"

"Well, I was living up in the desert with Ricky, Ricky Mendoza—Mr. Switch-hitter 1990. We both worked in gyms in Tucson. Anyway, after we split I didn't want to be part of that crowd anymore so I got a job as a trainer for the cruises. It was okay but I hated being indoors all the time and around all those pampered bitches, waiting on them hand and foot. I started going for hikes on my own whenever we put into port. People started going with me and they liked them. It got back to the cruise director. I made a pitch to make it my full-time job. And now it is. I'm always afraid I'll screw up and they'll replace me. So I read all the time: botany, zoology, geology.

"What about you? What are you really doing out here?" she asked.

"I'm working, following a guy who's on board. He murdered his first wife and got away with it. He even inherited her estate. I'm here to see that he doesn't do it again."

"What do you feel when you see a guy like that. Someone who got away with murder?"

"What do I feel? I feel like picking up a steak knife and burying it up to the hilt in his chest and then breaking off the blade. That's what I feel. Then I try not to feel anything. That's the way back inside. I don't want to go back inside."

"Are you working as a private investigator?"

"No. I can't do that anymore. I can't ever do that again. This is just something I'm doing until I can find a permanent job."

"Do you have any offers?"

"Oh yeah, I've got a permanent job waiting for me in Fresno."

"That's good."

"No, it's not. How shall I put this? Chief of Security for a west coast pharmaceutical distributor. How's that? The head of a biker gang liked my work in prison so much that they want me to handle security for all of their west coast runs. In return, I get the pick of the litter for my woman, a company chopper, and all the product my body can process. What's not to like?"

"You aren't going to do that, are you?"

"I don't know. Most of the time I think 'no'. Then there are some days I get up and think 'why not?' I was one of the good guys once. What did it get me? Maybe it's my way of getting to the bottom in a hurry, avoid all that pointless wishing and hoping that things will be different.

"The only thing I know for sure is that I'm not the man I once was. The man I am now is not an improvement. I'd like to get back the good things I lost, but it hasn't happened yet."

We finished eating and lingered over our coffee. I paid the check and escorted Kiki out of the café.

"How'd you get here?"

159

"Over there," she pointed to a white jeep in a corner of the lot.

"I'll walk you over."

"That's okay. I had a nice time. I hope you find those pieces that you're looking for."

"Thanks. Maybe your compass is starting to work a little better. You're still on the right side of things."

"Maybe," she said, smiling.

"Goodnight." I turned and walked away. Three steps later, I felt a hand on my arm. I turned. She was already backing away.

"Don't go to Fresno, Leo. That's not you. Keep looking. You'll find something better."

I started to speak, but she was already too far away, so I told myself, "I'll try. I really will."

The next day I saw Kiki after my run. She was taking two couples horseback riding. We exchanged smiles but nothing else. I was following Derek and his lady on a guided tour to some local ruins.

Throughout the tour, I kept my distance. I asked no questions and did nothing to draw attention to myself.

After lunch we went back to the ship. I was able to eavesdrop on Derek's plans to go soaring in the afternoon and got my own directions to the airfield. I spent the afternoon in the weight room and then just sitting in the lounge.

At four, I got into my car and headed for the airfield. Five miles from the dock and there were no signs of human life, except the dirt road running towards the distant mountains. Up ahead, I saw the dust of Derek's cab and kept my distance. I knew where he was going. And a car in the desert gives itself away.

I turned into the lot off the road and parked on the far side of the office, away from their car. A bi-plane idled on the runway by the office. A white plane was gliding in out of the still, blue sky. It bounced twice on its tiny wheels and then rolled to a halt when one wing tilted over to touch the ground. A young man, tanned and muscular with silvered sunglasses jumped out of the cockpit and began to talk excitedly with an older couple sitting on a bench under some trees. He shook the pilots' hand, walked over to the couple, and all three went to their car.

I watched Derek and the woman talk to the glider pilot and then to the pilot in the tow plane. The blonde shook her head 'no', and Derek pointed to the bench under the trees. He helped the pilot roll the glider over to the cable and attach it to the tow plane. Derek and the pilot got inside, and the blonde helped keep the wing level until the tow plane began to taxi down the runway. Then she walked over to the bench.

How long would Derek be up, I wondered? How far could one of these gliders go? They couldn't go too far. Not with Blondie on the ground. She wouldn't want to spend her afternoon sitting out here in the middle of nowhere. But suppose Derek wasn't coming back? No way to follow him. Can't ride with him. There's only one tow plane. By the time he gets back he could be anywhere. I began to manufacture possibilities in my mind. You take a parachute with you. You don't need a big landing strip. You can bail out in the desert. With a four-wheel drive vehicle you don't need to be near a road. These planes don't file flight plans. Nobody would know where you were going until you're up in the air.

I got out of the car and walked over to the office. The man behind the counter squinted up at me.

"Can I help you?"

"Yes. These flights—how long do they last?"

"Thirty minutes to an hour, depending on whether you want to do any fancy maneuvers."

161

"Is that the maximum?"

"Oh, hell no. Depends on how high up you want to go. I've ridden the thermals here for almost four hours."

"How far would a trip like that take you?"

"Two hundred, two hundred and fifty miles. Why? Would you like a trip like that?"

"I don't know. How much is it?"

"A hundred dollars an hour."

"You got any scheduled like that now? Before I put out that kind of money, I think I'd like to talk to someone who's done it, see how they liked it."

"Nah. Nothing on the books right now."

"Okay, thanks."

I turned to walk away but saw the blonde at the other end of the porch at the soda machine. She bent over to pick up her drink, looked at me for an instant without recognition, and walked back to her seat.

I got into my car, left the parking lot and drove back toward the ship. A half-mile away I found a flat, open space, turned off and drove into the desert. I turned around so that I could see the road and waited for a dust plume leaving the airfield. A half-hour later one appeared. I pulled back onto the road, followed it to the paved road and then back to the ship.

I sat in the bar and watched for them in its mirror. A half-hour later they walked in. I watched the woman pull him close to herself and whisper in his ear. I bowed my head and reached for some nuts. They walked past me towards the pool. Time to go before my cover gets blown. Once is nothing; twice a coincidence; three times is a pattern. I'd give them a day or so without me in their space. I waved to the bartender for the check.

"You've been following me all day. What is this? I told

162

them I'd make . . ." Derek, in full umbrage, had pulled up next to me.

I watched him in the mirror and spoke to his image, giving him only my profile to stare at.

"I have no idea what you're talking about." I picked up my drink and hid my face behind it.

He stared at the mirror. "No . . . Wait a minute. It's you. You can't fool me. Haggerty, Leo Haggerty. You son of a bitch. Old man Scolari sent you out after me." He pointed a finger at me.

I looked past him to see if heads were turning. They were. The blonde was standing at the far wall near the door. Her arms across her chest, she was worrying a nail.

"I won't be hounded like this. You have no right to harass me. This is stalking."

I focused on his soft, pale face, the color of outrage in his cheeks, his quivering lips, and his thin brown hair.

"I'm not stalking you, Derek. I'm not doing anything to you. I'm just out here on vacation, relaxing. It's nice to see a familiar face in a strange place." I smiled at him and began to raise my voice. "Old man Scolari didn't send me, Derek, Gina did. She can't rest, Derek. She wants to know why you killed her? Was it the money?" He stumbled, backing away from me, as my voice grew louder.

"What am I supposed to tell her? She loved you. Why did you kill her?" I smiled at everyone in the lounge.

Marshall disappeared into the hall. I returned to my drink. No sense in going anywhere. They'd just come to my cabin. I gobbled a few more nuts and held up my drink for a refill. No need to be parched when they arrived.

Ten minutes later, a gentleman in a suit came up next to me. I turned towards him and made my face a wall. I kept my hands in plain sight.

"My name is Munson. I'm chief of security here. We have a little problem. I'd like you to follow me to the captain's office."

"And if I don't?"

Munson stepped back so he'd have room to swing or draw. He had a high, square forehead and a flat nose dividing his broad, flat face. He looked like a mallet to me. A mallet that needed swinging, that cried out for John Henry to slam it against a steel spike. I grimaced as I suppressed that impulse.

"Then I'd have to call for backup and have you thrown into the brig."

"Really? You think so?" I started rocking, then stopped. "Let's do it the easy way," I said and followed Munson to the captain's office.

He opened the door and motioned me inside. I sat in the chair facing the desk. The captain, a Nils Lennartson, had a phone to his ear nodding at what he heard. He put the phone down and spoke to Munson.

"No need for you to be here, Tom. I can handle this."

Lennartson's hair was cut short and waxed stiff like a blonde bristle brush. Ruddy-cheeked and fair, he had the penetrating gaze of a man who had no doubts.

"Mr. Marshall says you are here to harass him. That you are an agent for his ex-wife's family and that there's a long history of that sort of thing."

I laughed. "*Ex*-wife? Oh she's *ex* all right; she's ex as in dead. Derek Marshall murdered her. I know because he confessed to me." I held up my hands. "Don't ask why he's not in jail. He was very clever. He killed her in a way that left no evidence. I'm out here at the insistence of his 'ex'-wife's guardian. Whenever Mr. Marshall shows an interest in a young woman, Mr. Scolari gets very concerned. He doesn't want another family to know the misery he's gone through."

Lennartson put his elbows on the desk and leaned forward.

"Let me make myself perfectly clear, Mr. Haggerty. I have no idea what went on before. Frankly, I don't care. There's nothing I can do about that. What I do care about is the ship's reputation and the comfort of its guests. I've informed Mr. Marshall that you are forbidden from coming within one hundred yards of him. If you disobey me, Mr. Haggerty, I'll either clap you in irons or turn you over to the local authorities. Gringos fare very poorly in Mexican jails. As for your concern for the young lady who is with him, I think your tantrum created so much attention that she's probably the safest person here. I know security will keep an eye on her from now on. You should be able to go about the rest of your stay without that on your mind. So there's no reason for you to be near Derek Marshall. Are we clear?"

"Yes sir, warden, we are clear." I stood up and left.

I went back to my room, showered, ordered room service, and put in a call to Enzo Scolari. It was after eight when he returned my call.

"Mr. Haggerty?"

"Mr. Scolari. We've got some problems here."

"Oh?"

"Marshall made me this afternoon, and now the captain has made it clear I'm not to be anywhere near Marshall or he'll arrest me. I can't even be an open shadow. I also think you're right about why he came up here. He's found a beautiful way to lose a tail. Soaring. You go up alone, and aren't subject to the same rules as engined aircraft, so you can't be followed. You parachute out in the middle of the desert to a waiting car, and you've got at least a half-day lead on anyone following you."

"Mr. Haggerty, it seems your usefulness has ended.

You're to leave the ship tomorrow morning and return the car to the airport. If you don't want to return to this area, feel free to convert your ticket to any other destination you'd like."

"Are you going to be able to get someone else out here that soon?"

"Don't worry, Mr. Haggerty, that's all been taken care of."

"Okay, when are they going to get here? I'll brief them on everything I've learned."

"That won't be necessary, Mr. Haggerty."

"What about the girl? Have you found out anything about her? What is she? Accomplice? Victim?"

"Mr. Haggerty, that is no longer your business."

"Wait a minute, that is my business. You don't want me out here because my cover's been blown, fine. You don't care if Derek Marshall disappears, lives the good life without ever paying for what he did, fine. I thought that was why you sent me out here, but I must have been mistaken. But don't tell me it's none of my business that *that* woman could still be a target. That's why I came out here."

"You're right, Mr. Haggerty, I'm sorry. You can rest assured that we've determined she's in no danger."

"That's nice, Mr. Scolari. Tell you what, though; I'm not convinced. How about a name and address? How is it she's here with Marshall? Give me that and then I'll rest assured."

"Mr. Haggerty, I don't have those details here with me. I'm at home. I'll call you with them tomorrow morning. How is that? Then you can leave without any concerns?"

"Fine. I'll be waiting."

I hung up the phone, sat there and stared at it. Fuck him. Fuck Derek Marshall. Why was I getting all churned up? Because my easy ride was over? Sure. This was sweet. All expenses paid. Did I really think this would last forever? If old man Scolari didn't care what happened to Derek Marshall, why should I? It wasn't my niece he murdered. I wasn't the law. He'd gotten away with that one. Once upon a time I'd hoped to catch him at something, anything, and to help put him away, for him to pay even a little bit for what he'd done, but I'd lost my chance at that when I went to prison. Just an empty threat I made a long time ago in another life. Who cares? Not me.

I took a long look around the cabin. So long good life. So long warm showers. So long heated towels, so long maid service, clean sheets every day. I pulled down my suitcase, threw it on the bed, opened the dresser and tossed everything inside. Zipping up that side, I flipped the bag over, went into the bathroom and scooped up my toilet articles and dumped them into the bag and closed it up. Packed. I had the impulse to just walk out, get in the car and leave, let Scolari clean up after me. But another night on clean sheets and a hot breakfast wouldn't hurt any. I opened up my plane ticket and fished out a piece of paper. Sitting up on the bed, I dialed a long-distance number.

"Yeah," was followed by a belch.

"Is 'The Kurgen' there?"

"Who wants to know?"

"Tell him it's Leo Haggerty, Slag told me to call." Slag was at the top of the prison food chain. He had no natural predators but time.

"Hold on."

I heard feet shuffle in the background, then someone picked up the phone.

"Yo, so you're out. Where are you?"

"Mexico."

"That's too bad. You coming up this way?"

"Looks like it. That job still open?"

"Yeah. There's a couple guys out here think it should be theirs, but if you're everything Slag says you are, you'll have no trouble convincing them otherwise."

"I got some business to clean up here first. You should see me in a couple of days."

"Alright. We'll party first, then we'll talk."

"Sounds good."

I went to the minibar, poured myself a gin and tonic, and turned on the TV. I muted the sound and just stared at the screen. I stared and I sipped, then I closed my eyes and got very still. Five years ago I could play a spider's web like a harp, play without anybody knowing I was there. At least I thought that, right up to "we the jury."

I was on another web now and I could feel it vibrate under my feet. Somebody was moving out there and it wasn't me. I played back everything that had happened since Scolari first called me, rethinking every slip, every stumble as a feint.

I went back to the bedroom and dialed the switchboard.

"I'd like the phone number for Kiki Davenport."

"I'm sorry we can't give out crew member's numbers."

"Can I leave a message?"

"I'll connect you with her voice mail."

"Hi, this is Kiki. I'm not available to take your call. At the tone, please leave your name and number and a brief message. I'll get back to you."

"Kiki, this is Leo Haggerty. I need your help. It's kind of an emergency. Call when you get in no matter what the time."

I hung up and waited.

Around 1:30, I put my drink down and then my head. At 8:30 I heard a pounding on the door.

"Leo, are you okay?"

I stumbled across the room and opened the door. She

didn't come in. "I didn't check my messages until this morning. Are you okay?"

"Yeah, yeah. I'm okay. Come on in. I need to talk to you."
She slipped inside.

"Does this have anything to do with Derek Marshall?"

"Yeah. How'd you know?"

"Everybody got briefed on it by Tom Munson. If you're anywhere near Marshall he's to be called."

"That's why I need your help because I can't go near him. I think he's being set up for a hit."

"If what you said is true, why do you care?"

"I'm not sure I do. What I do care about is being hustled out of the way so somebody can get a clean shot at him. I wanted him to pay for Gina Dalesandro. I don't think this has anything to do with her. I don't like the idea that somebody thinks I'll just bow out so murder can be done or that I'm too stupid to know what's going on. Besides, I'm still not convinced that the woman that's with him isn't in danger, also."

"Why don't you tell the captain? Let him take care of it?"

"Because I have nothing but hunches, and my hunches have nothing but questions dangling from them."

Kiki sat down on the sofa. "What do you want me to do?"

"Hear me out. I used to be pretty smart. These days I don't trust myself. But if this sounds plausible to you there may be something to it.

"When Derek Marshall blew my cover, he didn't recognize me at first. He said, 'I told them I'd make the . . .' He didn't finish his sentence. Then he recognized me. He was surprised that someone was there. He thought some 'they' had sent me and it was because he hadn't *made* something for them. Made what? Made it good? Made payments?

"He was reading some book on moneyless investing. Scolari said he'd ruined some of his investments, cost him and some other people a lot of money. Maybe more than he told me.

"If Marshall needs money, she could be a potential victim. If Marshall's a target, they may not care who goes with him. Especially if Scolari's not behind this."

"Why do you think Scolari is not behind this?"

"Let's look at what Scolari did. He hears I'm blown so he fires me. Okay so far. He shows no interest in how Marshall might disappear. *That's* why I'm supposed to be out here, so he can't escape Scolari's scrutiny. I tell him I'll brief my replacement; he says don't bother. He shows no concern for this girl until I raise it. Why? Because the 'them' Marshall thought sent me out here are going to whack him. So Scolari doesn't have to worry about him getting away or the girl being harmed by him. He just pulls me out of here so there's nobody watching, nobody in the way. That gives them the go ahead. Hell, I have no idea if Marshall's even in the wrong with these people."

"That's it?"

"Yeah."

"I can see why you didn't go to the captain. I can think of half a dozen other explanations that this guy Scolari didn't want to share with you."

"So can I, but this is the one that worries me."

"Okay, what do you want me to do?"

"Find out what you can about the girl. If you can get into the cabin while they're out, look in her purse, get a name, address, whatever. I need to know where she fits in. The other thing is to try to get to Marshall. See if he'll agree to meet me somewhere public. Away from the ship. I ought to warn him that he's a target and it isn't me who's after him. After that, he's on his own."

"All right. I'll go over to his cabin and try to talk to him or the girl, whoever's there. Where will you be?"

"I've got to check out. I'll go down the road towards town, sit in the first gas station I come to and wait for him there. If he comes. If he doesn't, I'll take the car back to Tucson. Then I've got a plane ticket to wherever."

"You going to Fresno?"

"I don't know. The job's still there."

"You called?"

"Yeah."

Kiki shook her head.

"When should I tell him to meet you?"

"I have to be off the ship by eleven. Say ten after."

"I'll call you here as soon as I get in touch with him."

"Okay."

She got up off the sofa and walked to the door. I went to open it for her. She turned in the space between me and the door, reached up to pat my chest, straighten out my collar. I looked down into her green eyes, at the little tug at the corner of her mouth where a smile was struggling to be and felt an enormous ache in my chest as a huge bubble of longing moved in my blood like a case of the bends.

Kiki kissed my cheek, spun under my arm and out the door. At nine thirty she called back. "I talked to the woman. Marshall was in the spa getting a fitness evaluation from Joey. He's the personal trainer. She said she'd give him the message. I also got a quick peek into her purse. She was putting on her makeup when I got there. Her name is Leslie Bowen. She lives at 931 Euclid Avenue in San Francisco."

"Great. Thanks."

At ten my phone rang again. It was Scolari.

"Mr. Haggerty. I've got that information you wanted. The woman with him is named Leila Kurland, she's from San Diego. Two priors for prostitution. Not a likely target for a man like him, wouldn't you say?"

"No, not the Derek Marshall we all know and love. I feel a lot better knowing she's okay. I'll be checking out at eleven, then I'll take the car back to Tucson. I have to stop and gas it up before I turn it in."

"Then what?"

"I don't know. See how far this ticket will take me I guess."

"Well, good luck Mr. Haggerty."

"Yeah, thanks."

I grabbed my bag, checked out, went to the car, threw it in the back seat and drove out of the lot. A couple of hundred yards up the road was a driveway that meandered up into the hills to a house that sat up above the Saguaro. I pulled into it and waited.

At 10:45 a white Camry nosed out of the dock's entrance. Leslie/Leila was behind the wheel. A moment of truth. The car turned east towards the mountains and flashed past me. I sat and watched it pull away.

She told Kiki she'd give Marshall the message. She's driving the other way. She didn't give him the message. She's in it with them. Or she did give him the message and he blew her off. Fuck them. It's their problem, not mine. They've been warned.

I pulled out and headed north towards America. I'd be in Fresno tonight. I turned on the radio, looking for something fast, loud and stupid. Look out bottom, here I come. You never bounce back as far as you fall. That's a law of nature. Doesn't matter if it's a basketball, a rock or a man. So why bother?

That worked for about five miles, but a cowlick of doubt kept popping up no matter how hard I tried to slick it down with bitterness or cynicism or self-pity. It just wouldn't go away. Once it came up with Kiki's face. That was easy to dismiss. No future there. Do it for yourself. Then it came back with a question. What would you have done five years ago? Would you drive away and let murder be done? What's different now?

"I am," I said to no one.

"Only if you let yourself be," was the reply.

If you never bounce back as far as you fall, then maybe you shouldn't fall any farther than you have to.

All important journeys begin with a U-turn, so I made one. I pushed the needle past ninety and held it there until I caught sight of Derek's car. I confirmed the tag number and then fell behind.

She was doing a steady seventy, going rapidly into the desert, but not so fast that anyone would notice. I looked ahead at oncoming traffic for an opportunity to pull alongside and force them over. Dust devils swirled off to either side of the road.

Almost immediately she turned south at an unmarked crossroads. I followed. We were still on paved road, but now there was no traffic at all. Then we had company. I kept flicking my eyes from the road to the mirror. The Camry hadn't changed speed, but the Jeep kept expanding in my mirror. I saw its turn signal flash as it moved to pass me. Smoked glass hid the occupants. I looked for the tag number. There was none. I went to slam on the brakes and let them shoot past me when the jeep hit me broadside and I flew off the road. The car slammed up and down as it bounced across the desert like a Brahma bull. I gritted my teeth and strangled the wheel trying to keep control. A giant saguaro stood in front of me, his lone arm up and extended towards me like a traffic cop. I threw myself sideways on the seat as I slammed into it. The giant green cop came slamming down on the roof, and everything went black.

I came to with a throbbing headache. The rest of me checked in as a battered presence. I was on my back and immediately tried to move my toes and hands. That was good. I flexed my limbs and felt their entirety. I opened my eyes and saw that the roof was gone. A bright light made me squint.

"Where am I?" I asked.

Surprisingly, a deep voice said, "You're in the hospital, Mr. Haggerty."

I turned towards the voice. I saw a badge on his chest, and the word *policia,* the black string tie, and the long black hair swept back over his ears, like a cutaway jacket behind a holster. His mouth was hidden behind a cookie duster.

"You're a lucky man. That Saguaro you hit must have weighed five tons. Crushed your car flat. You're damn lucky we found you. We weren't even looking for you."

I swallowed. My throat felt creased and raw.

"Water."

He handed me a glass with a straw. I sucked long and hard.

"Thanks. Who were you looking for?"

"Guy named Derek Marshall, a guest on the ship. He missed the boat when it departed. Captain called me because of some trouble with you. We got a call about a vulture dance in the desert, so I figured we ought to go check it out. Might be a cow, might be Marshall. We found you on the way there. Which brings me to my next question. What were you doing out there?"

You never tell the law the truth. Because there is no truth. Only your lies and somebody else's.

"I got lost. I wanted to go out into the desert, see it up close for myself, so I left the main road, do a little exploring."

"And what happened?"

"Some kind of pig ran across the road. I swerved to avoid

hitting it. Next thing I know, I'm aimed at the Saguaro."

I asked for more water. "You find Marshall?"

"Yeah, we found him, or what was left of him. Between the sun and the vultures he looked like a half-eaten piece of beef jerky when we got to him."

"How'd he die?"

"Stupidity, I'd say. We have no idea what he was doing out there. He was alone. No one knew where he'd gone. He had no water with him, although he did have a bottle of wine. We found that on the way to his body. Alcohol's the worst thing to drink in the desert. It just accelerates the dehydration. His car was just stopped. It had run out of gas. We guess he thought he could walk out, got disoriented, wandered deeper into the desert, got thirsty, drank the wine he had with him, got dehydrated, then sunstroke. Somewhere along the way he fell into a jumping cholla. His face and hands were covered in spines. Eventually he sat down and died. That's how we found him. Sitting up against a rock with his hands in his lap. They were covered in spines. He had spines in his eyelids, his lips. He was a mess.

"You're lucky we found you. You'd never have gotten out of that car by yourself. We needed a winch to get the Saguaro off you, then we had to use metal cutters to pry you out. Another day and you'd have been as dead as Marshall."

The cop got up to leave, then he turned back towards me.

"You see, that's the only reason I'm not arresting you. You couldn't have killed Marshall, and you wouldn't have staged that as an accident because nobody called us about you. You'd have died for sure. So I'm ignoring all the captain's stuff about you harassing Marshall, or the amazing coincidence of two accidents on that road at the same time. No evidence of foul play, but lots of stupidity, so we're gonna close it up as death by misadventure, unless you've got something you want to tell me?"

"No, I know justice when I see it."

The cop nodded goodbye and left. The door was swinging closed when Kiki pushed through.

She sat down in the chair, threw one leg over the other and clasped her hands around her knees. Her sandaled foot tapped away to silent music. "How are you doing?"

"I guess I'm okay. I've got this drip in me, but nothing seems to be broken."

"That's what the doctor said. You were pinned but not crushed. He thinks you can leave tomorrow."

"That's good. I don't know how I'll pay this bill, so the sooner I get out of here the better."

Her sunglasses were pushed up into her hair and she nodded in agreement.

"Oh, I've got your suitcase and your plane ticket. They gave me your belongings when they cut your clothes off."

"Thanks."

"Yeah, they weren't going to at first, but I told them you had been staying with me. Otherwise they were going to hold onto everything, and I figured you wouldn't want a policeman holding your ticket out of here, so I told him that and they gave it to me. I hope that was okay."

Her brow wrinkled like a raised blind.

"Yeah, that was good thinking."

"Well I'll go get your stuff."

"Kiki, thanks for coming. How will you get back to the ship?"

"I've got the company's jeep. I told the cruise director we were old friends, so he let me stay behind to make sure you were okay. I promised him I'd catch up at the next port of call."

"Where is that?"

"We're headed around Baja back to Ensenada. I'll probably get there before the ship does."

"So you wouldn't have to leave right away?"

"No, I wouldn't have to."

"You know if you were here tomorrow, you could have company for that trip back."

"Really? What would I want with company?"

"I don't know. I hear your compass doesn't work so well. A girl could get lost like that."

"Oh? And you don't get lost?"

"Oh, I get lost too. That's why you should have me along. That's how I learned what it takes to get found."

ACKNOWLEDGEMENTS: I'd like to thank the following people for the gracious donation of their expertise. Any errors are entirely my responsibility. Chanda Kinsey, defense attorney; Johnny Ringo of Carefree Jeep Tours; Paula Edgin, JoAnne Reiss and Arllys Filmer-Ennett, concierges at The Boulders; Sherry Mehalic of Travel Partners; and Rhoda K. Schutz.

The Black Eyed Blonde

I woke up with my nose in the newsprint and a telephone inside my head. I shook my head and the phone fell out onto my desk. My hand spider walked over to it, grabbed it around the throat, and silenced it.

"Hello," she said. Her voice fluttered all through both of those syllables.

When I didn't answer, she tried again. "Hello, Mr. Barlow, are you there?"

I checked the inside of my jacket to be sure and said, "Yes, this is Max Barlow."

"Oh, thank goodness, Mr. Barlow. My name is Angela DiLivio. My husband is Bruno DiLivio. Do you know him?"

I knew Bruno DiLivio. He was a gambler out of Vegas. He'd taken over Benny Voltaire's place. I wasn't sure how much more I wanted to know.

"Yes, I know him."

"I'd like you to follow him, Mr. Barlow. I think he's seeing another woman. If he is, I want you to get pictures."

"I'm sorry, Mrs. DiLivio, but I don't do divorce work."

"But Mr. Thornton said you were the best. You were the man I should talk to."

Good old Ray Thornton, throwing some work my way. Ever since he'd hooked up with Adrian Jones, he'd become Santa Claus to the rest of us working stiffs. And here it wasn't even November.

"I'm sorry, Mrs. DiLivio. Ray has me mixed up with another Max Barlow. Like I said, I don't do divorce work."

"Well, do you know where this other Max Barlow is?"

"No, Mrs. DiLivio, I haven't a clue."

"Well, I'm sorry to have wasted your time, Mr. Barlow, if that's even your name." She replaced the receiver indelicately.

"No problem at all," I said to myself.

I rubbed my eyes and stared at the top of my desk. So this was as far as I'd gotten. I was just going to stop by and type up my notes before I went home. Guess I didn't make it. I reached into my pocket and pulled out my notebook and the novel I had been reading. *Fast One*, by a guy named Paul Cain. Rumor had it that Cain was a screenwriter in town whose real name was Ruric. Rumor had it that even Ruric wasn't his real name. Maybe it was Barlow.

I flipped open my notebook. I'd spent all night watching a cop as a favor for a friend of mine from the D.A.'s office. Seems that the D.A. wasn't happy with the police investigation of a recent murder. They'd asked me to shadow the cop because he wouldn't know my face. He'd spent a long time over dinner with the decidedly ungrieving widow at Musso and Frank's before dropping her off at her house. I spent the next two hours following him as he drove aimlessly through our host, the City of Angels.

I went over to the sink in the corner, ran some water, and splashed it on my face. Toweling dry, I looked at the face in the mirror. We looked like the same guy, but we weren't. I did know where that other Max Barlow had gone. He'd disappeared soon after that visit from Delano Stiles.

I went back to my desk, spun the chair around so it faced east, and looked out over Cahuenga Boulevard. I closed my eyes and it was spring again. The late afternoon sunlight was streaming in so heavily it looked pooled, like butter, on the floor. And Delano Stiles was telling me about his wife.

He'd marched right into my office, sat down, leaned forward, and told me, "I need you to find my wife, Mr. Barlow."

I looked up from a chess diagram I had been studying and asked, "And why is that?"

"Because she's gone. She's run away, Mr. Barlow, and she's taken my son with her."

I took a moment to see what she was running away from. He was tall, slim, and well dressed in a pin-striped suit. His black hair was swept back and had a touch of gray at the temples. His strong, even features were marred by the presence of a ridiculous, pencil-thin moustache.

"Let's back up a step," I said. "What's your name, your wife's, and your son's?"

"I'm Delano Stiles." He stopped to take a deep breath. He sounded like he'd run up all six flights of stairs to my office. "My wife is Monica and our son's name is Brandon. He's five years old."

"How long has your wife been missing, Mr. Stiles?"

"A couple of hours, maybe. I got a call from a car dealer over on Wilcox. He said that she had come in and tried to sell her car. When he found out that the car was in my name he told her she couldn't sell it. He was calling me when she grabbed some suitcases out of the car and ran out of the showroom, dragging Brandon with her. As soon as I got the message, I drove right over and questioned the man. Then I went looking for them myself. But frankly, Mr. Barlow, I'm not the kind of man who can make people answer my questions. So I looked up detectives in the phone book, saw that your office was nearby, and came right over to see if I could retain your services."

"I'm sorry, Mr. Stiles, but I haven't any experience in divorce work. My background has been in insurance and criminal investigations."

"This isn't really a divorce case, Mr. Barlow. It's Brandon I want back, not my wife. He's only five, Mr. Barlow, just a little boy. It must be terrifying for him to be dragged all over strange parts of this city by a woman who's no longer thinking clearly."

"Why do you say that?"

"Because there's no reason for her to do something like this."

"Has she ever taken it on the lam before?"

"No. She's never done anything like this before. It's so . . . so impulsive."

Nothing Stiles had said so far had overcome my aversion to divorce work. Besides that, I still had seven bucks in the bank.

"I don't know, Mr. Stiles. Domestic stuff really isn't my line."

That's because it always seemed like legitimized blackmail. Two people trying to dig up as much dirt as possible so they could hold each other's noses in it until one of them cried, "Enough!" I was not about to be anyone's spade. But then again, maybe this one was different. I waited to find out.

"Are you married, Mr. Barlow?"

"No."

"Any children?"

"No."

"Then you can't know what it's like to lose one, can you? I love my son, Mr. Barlow. I need him with me. I don't want Monica back. I'll offer her a fair settlement. You won't have to be peeping at keyholes, I assure you."

I thought it over. He just wanted his kid found. I wasn't being asked to prove that the mother wasn't fit to walk among decent, god-fearing people, let alone marry or raise one.

"All right, Mr. Stiles, I'll take the case. If she's trying to skip town, she'll need money. Did she tap the bank accounts?"

"No, I called the bank before I came over here. The accounts are all in my name anyway."

"Does she have any money of her own?"

"You mean family money? No, her people are farmers, I believe. They're not even from around here. They're in Arkansas, Little Rock, I think."

"How did you meet her? It doesn't sound like you two traveled in the same circles."

"That's true. But out here in Hollywood all the circles seem to overlap, don't you think? Anyway it seems that way to me. Monica was a showgirl at Voltaire's. That's where I met her. She wanted to be an actress. I admit I was quite taken with her, Mr. Barlow. She's a stunning girl. These days I think she was more taken with my connections than with me."

As Hollywood marriages went this was no worse than most. It would last as long as her looks and his money made each other feel good. When that didn't work anymore they'd finally realize that they were strangers, get divorced, and go do the same damn thing again.

"Has she appeared in any movies? That might make it easier to track her down. People in this town are crazy about identifying actors and actresses. It brightens their days just being in the same city with them."

"No, she hasn't been in any pictures. Monica's dreams exceed her talents. Even my intercessions on her behalf can't change that. She seems to blame me for her failure. I tried to provide for her every need and want, and this is how she repays me."

Stiles was wandering off into his own melancholy reverie. I retrieved him with a question. "Does your wife have any friends she might turn to at a time like this?"

"No. Monica was, as they say, 'right off the bus,' when I

met her at Voltaire's. We married shortly thereafter. She never made any effort to get along with my friends. She just stayed at home and doted on Brandon."

I pulled out my notebook, flipped it open, and prepared to write. "What things did she take with her?"

"I asked the maid to check the house when I got the call about the car. She said that Monica took two suitcases filled with clothes for her and Brandon, some makeup, her jewelry, Brandon's teddy bear, and his favorite blanket."

"What were she and Brandon wearing?"

"Roxana, that's our maid, says she was wearing a teal blue skirt and a cream-colored silk blouse. Brandon had on white knee-high socks, khaki shorts, and a green and white striped shirt."

"Good. Do you have a picture of either of them?"

"Yes, I do." He pulled out his wallet, slid the photo out, and handed it to me.

Monica Stiles was sitting in a chair with her arms around her son. He was leaning back against her so that their cheeks touched. Brandon was a little towhead with deep dimples and the assured smile of a well-loved child.

A billowing tangle of blonde hair framed his mother's face. I studied that face. A broad, high forehead tapered past prominent cheekbones to a small square chin. Her full upper lip was wide and downswept. She would smile and pout magnificently. Her eyes were hidden behind large sunglasses.

"What color are your wife's eyes?"

"Black."

I looked at him.

"Yes, black. Monica's coloring is very unusual. She's a natural blonde, too."

"I'll need to take this with me," I said, tapping the picture.

"If you must. Please don't lose it, Mr. Barlow."

"I'll be very careful with it. Now what was the name of the car dealer who called you?"

"The man's name was Artie Schumacher. He's the general manager at Peabody Motors. They're on Wilcox, between Sunset and Hollywood."

"Okay. Where can I reach you today if I find your wife and son?"

"I'll be at my office the rest of the day. It's on Rossmore just opposite Paramount Studios." He gave me the direct line into his office.

"My fee is twenty dollars a day and expenses. If I don't find her today, I'd suggest you call Pinkerton's in Little Rock to catch her at the other end."

Stiles opened his wallet and began laying crisp twenties on my desk. "Here's twenty for your time today and forty against expenses. Please find her for me, Mr. Barlow."

"That's what I'm about to do, Mr. Stiles."

He rose and turned to leave. I had one question left to ask but I wasn't sure I needed to know the answer. With his hand on the doorknob, I decided to ask it anyway.

"Mr. Stiles, why is your wife in such a hurry to leave town?"

He turned slowly, and looking down at me, he said, "Mr. Barlow, I assure you that it's a personal and private matter between my wife and me. I'm sure you can respect that."

"Of course," I said.

I watched Stiles pull the office door closed behind him and stared at the bills on my desk. Los Angeles was the wrong town to be poor in. When the hoboes tried to enter, city hall made a fence out of the boys in blue and dared them to climb over it. With things as tough as they were, why would Monica Stiles put herself on the wrong side of money? When I found her, I just might ask her that.

I stood up, unclipped my holster, and locked my gun in my desk. I wasn't going to be shooting anybody today. With the money in my wallet, I locked up the office and went to work.

Peabody Motors was one block west and one south. Schumacher was bald and fat, and judging from the way he rocked on his feet, his shoes hurt, too. He confirmed everything that Stiles had told me.

I thanked him for his help and walked out of the showroom. On the sidewalk I tried to imagine myself trying to get out of town and standing there with two suitcases and a kid and no money in my pocket. She was a long way from Union Station or the airport. The bus station was only two blocks away, on Vine. Buses were cheaper and left more frequently. If Monica Stiles was still in town at all, she was nearby. That much I was sure of.

I drifted down Wilcox and crossed Sunset, looking for the places where she might have gotten money. On Santa Monica, I saw a pawnbroker's gold trident and went inside.

The man behind the counter had a loupe in his eye and a bauble in his hand.

"Excuse me," I said.

He put the stone down onto a velvet pillow and looked at me. "Yeah?"

I took out the picture of Monica and Brandon Stiles. "Has this woman been in this afternoon?"

He took the picture and studied it. "Not while I've been here, and I'd remember. She's a looker, that one is."

"Okay, thanks. Any other pawnshops in this area?"

"No. We're the only one up this way. Most of the others are over in Smoketown. What's the skirt trying to move, anyway?"

"Jewelry."

"Good stuff?" he asked hopefully.

"Yeah, real good." I opened my wallet and put a fin on the velvet pillow. I put my card on the bill. "If she comes in, you call me. It'll be worth your while."

He slipped the bill into his shirt pocket and glanced at the card. "Sure thing, Mr. Barlow."

"If I'm not there I'll be at Burt Levin's Tavern. You know it?"

"Yeah, the one on Vine, next to the bus station."

"That's right."

I left the shop and headed east on Santa Monica to Vine. As far as I could tell, Monica Stiles still had no money. Wearing a silk blouse and stockings she wasn't going to get much of a response if she tried to panhandle. I didn't feature her doing a smash-and-grab routine either, not with little Brandon in tow.

I wandered into the bus station and checked the schedule. The next bus east left at 7:30, two hours from now. I did a slow circuit through the terminal, but they weren't there. I thought about sitting still for the two hours and letting her come to me, but I still had a couple of moves left to make and the silly idea that I should earn my fee.

Burt Levin's Tavern was just up the block. I walked in, ambled around the bar, and nodded to Burt. He grunted around the cigar stuffed into his cheek and continued washing dishes. I fed the phone a nickel and called a house dick I knew. The shops were going to close pretty soon, and since Mrs. Stiles wasn't in the bus station the only places left for her to lie low in were the apartment hotels north of Hollywood Boulevard.

"Gramercy Place Apartments," a voice said.

"Is Costacurta there?"

"Hold a moment." I held.

"Costacurta," he rasped.

"Stan, it's Max Barlow."

"Yeah, Barlow, long time."

"I need a favor."

"What is it?"

"I'm looking for a woman. She's dragging a couple of suit-cases and a kid. Teal skirt, cream blouse. A good-looking blonde. You want to keep your eyes open and call some of your buddies in the other buildings. If you turn her up, call me at Burt Levin's, okay?"

"Sure thing, Barlow."

"Thanks."

I swiveled around on the stool and stared into Burt Levin's face. Burt had a bulbous drinker's nose that got so bright when he was angry it looked like a tomato wedge between his eyes.

"What'll it be, Barlow?" he growled. A shiv in the throat had left him with a one-tone voicebox.

"Whiskey."

Burt poured with a friend's heavy hand, and I sipped a bit before I took it back to the far corner booth and waited for the phone to ring.

I sipped and waited for almost an hour. When the call came in, it was Costacurta.

"Your girl's been made, Barlow."

"Where?"

"Over on Kenmore, near Hollywood."

"The kid with her?"

"No. Just the doll. She was walking toward the Morewood Arms Hotel."

"Thanks, Stan."

"Nothing to it."

I finished off my drink and went back into the rapidly spreading dusk. The Morewood was two blocks away and on the far side of Kenmore. I took up a position opposite the entrance of the hotel but didn't see Monica Stiles there.

She was walking up the sidewalk arm in arm with an older man who looked and dressed like her husband. Maybe she was learning to make friends. She was dressed as the maid had described, but she was wearing the sunglasses I had seen in the picture.

As they approached the front door, she turned her head toward me and ran her hand through her fine blonde hair. I saw a diamond on her left hand, gold buttons in her ears, a gold necklace that encircled her long, delicious throat and a large red pin to keep her blouse closed. I shook my head. She was wearing Little Rock and back for her, the kid, and the teddy bear, and she was doing the horizontal bop anyway. But that was Stiles's problem, not mine.

When they went through the Morewood's revolving front door, I walked across the street and used the lobby phone to call my client. I told him that I had located his wife and that his son was probably close by. He thanked me and said that he'd be there right away. I told him not to hurry and hung up. I wasn't here to take pictures or set them up for anyone else.

Back at my roost, I lit a cigarette and waited for her to come back out. About twenty minutes later she came flying out of the hotel, clattering down the steps on her high heels. Her arms were out for balance as if the stone was bunching and flexing itself under her feet.

I tossed the butt away and fell in behind her. She had a raging case of foot fever and I was afraid she'd spot me if I tried to close on her. So I slowed down and settled for just keeping her in sight.

She turned right on Franklin and ducked into a doorway. It was the side entrance to the Golden West Apartments. My place, the Hobart Arms, was only a block away.

Just as I got to the entrance and reached for the knob, the door retreated and I came face to face with Monica Stiles. She had a large suitcase in her left hand and a smaller one under her arm. In her other hand were her son's small fingers. He looked up at me, but he wasn't wearing that assured smile. He had that wide-eyed stare you get when your world is collapsing around you and you wonder if you'll ever be able to see over the rubble. He clutched his teddy bear to his chest.

"Excuse me," she said, "I've got to get somewhere."

I reached out and gripped her elbow. "I'm sorry, Mrs. Stiles. I can't let you leave."

Her head snapped towards me. "Let me go. You have no right to stop me like this."

"It's not you, Mrs. Stiles. It's the boy. His father doesn't want him to leave town."

"No," she shouted. "He can't have him. No. No. No." She swung her right hand at my face. I dodged the blow. She dropped the suitcases on my foot and pummeled me with both hands. I reached out and snatched her wrists and shook her hard. She whipped her head back and forth and tried to bite me. Her sunglasses flew off and I pulled her close.

Stiles had told the truth. She was a blonde all the way down and her eyes were black. But there was also purple and yellow and red there too.

"Rough trade at the Morewood?" I asked.

"No, you bastard. These came today with breakfast. Courtesy of your boss." The discoloration of her face was about right for a punch-out over bacon and eggs.

"Why'd he hit you?"

"How should I know? Maybe the sun came up too early. I gave up asking that question a while ago. I don't care what the answer is. I just want out. I can't take it anymore."

The boy, who had stepped into the darkness when his

mother swung at me, came forward and wrapped his arms around her and lay his head on her hip.

She stroked his head and murmured, "It's okay, Brandon. Mommy's okay." Her stare dared me to make a liar out of her. I passed on it.

"Where were you going?"

"To the bus station. Catch the seven-thirty back east. My people are in Arkansas. I have no one out here. Delano kept me a prisoner in the house. He wouldn't let me out for anything. He was so jealous of anyone who paid attention to me."

"Why didn't you hock the jewelry? You'd have been out of here hours ago."

"That's a laugh, mister. Don't you think I tried? They're paste. I couldn't get to Pomona on these. Delano never trusted me. He never let me have any money. I didn't realize that everything he's given me was a fake. The only thing I have that's real is Brandon."

"How did you know that the Morewood was a hot-sheet joint? You're supposed to be right off the bus."

"When I found out that the jewelry was paste, I was frantic. I had nothing else to sell. The pawnbroker saw how desperate I was. He told me about the Morewood."

"And what was his cut for doing you this kindness?"

"He said he'd get a piece from the front desk for each guy I came in with."

When this was over I was going to have a talk with the pawnbroker. Probably a short, painful talk.

"How much money do you have?"

"Just enough to get me and Brandon out of the state. It was easy enough to pick up the guys, but I couldn't do the rest. I only got into the room with the last one. I made him get undressed first. Then I took his wallet and ran out."

I thought about everything I'd been told today and was

ready to dismiss it all as self-serving half-truths. All except her black eye. That I believed in. I didn't care how she might have failed Stiles as a wife, there was no excuse for that. So I reached into my wallet and slipped out sixty dollars.

"Here, take this. It'll get you home and you can eat, too."

She reached out slowly and took the bills from my hand.

"Thank you. I don't know how I can repay you, Mister . . ."

"Barlow, Max Barlow. And you don't have to. The money isn't mine. I never earned it. I never found you."

I reached down for one of the bags, and when I turned I saw Delano Stiles striding across the street toward us. He had two Hard Harrys flanking him.

I pulled my car keys out of my pocket, turned, and pressed them into her palm.

"Go. It's the convertible on the corner. You can still catch the bus. Don't go to Little Rock. He'll be waiting for you there. Get lost."

She reached for the suitcase and I said, "Leave them or you'll never make it."

She tore a slit in her skirt, kicked off her heels, picked Brandon up and ran for her life.

I watched Brandon's face over her shoulder as she fled up the street and wondered why he didn't cry out for his dad.

Stiles pointed up the street and one of his goons sheared off in pursuit. I dashed out into the street and tackled him knee-high. He toppled over and slammed his head on the road. He was stunned for a second. I grabbed his collar, set him up, and closed his shop.

I heard footsteps behind me and rolled away. Stiles kicked at my head, but I grabbed his ankle, twisted it hard, and he fell over. I scrambled to my feet and saw the second guy standing in the intersection. My car was pulling away from the curb. He reached into his jacket and pulled out a pistol. He moved casually into his shooter's crouch and sighted down his rigid arm.

I ran up the street yelling, "No!" But I was too late and his aim too true. I saw my car close on him. He fired once, twice, and then slid sideways like a toreador as the car careened past him on its three good tires, veered sharply to the right, jumped the curb, and slammed into Monroe's Pharmacy.

The shooter holstered up and sauntered over to the wreck. I caught up to him, spun him around, and broke my hand breaking his jaw. Stiles ran past me and flung open the car's passenger door. The whoop of police sirens grew in the distance.

Stiles groaned, "Oh my god," and sank to his knees. I looked in the driver's window. Monica Stiles was crouched over her son. She held his head in her hands and was kissing him everywhere. Over and over she murmured, "Baby, Baby." But he couldn't hear her. Children's bones are soft they say, but no neck turns that far.

I walked over to the bus stop bench, sat down, and lit a cigarette. I took it out of my mouth, stared at its glowing red tip and wanted to put it out in my heart. Instead I waited for the sirens to drown out two sets of sobs.

They never did though, and these days I'm not the same man I was that day. The name's the same, and that confuses some people. That's why I have to remind them that I don't do divorce work.

FORENSIC
PSYCHOLOGISTS

RANSOM TRIPLETT

MATTHIAS WALDMAN

Not Enough Monkeys

"Dr. Triplett, Dr. Ransom Triplett?"

I looked up from my exam-covered desk. A young woman hugging a fat file stood in the doorway. I guess just looking up was enough for her, because she entered arm outstretched, hand aimed at the middle of my chest, and said, "I'm Monica Chao, I have a project I'd like to interest you in."

I rose from my chair, intercepted her hand mid-desk, and nodded to the empty chair on her right.

"I've just come from the state penitentiary. I've been talking with some of the staff there and we believe that a terrible miscarriage of justice is going to happen." She hoisted the file onto the desk, where it landed with a thud and lay still as a corpse.

"Actually, the miscarriage is ongoing. Dr. Triplett, they have an innocent man on death row there. He is going to be executed the first of next month."

"And?" I asked.

"And I want you, no, I hope you'll be willing to help me prove this. They're going to execute an innocent man."

"Excuse me, Miss Chao, how old are you?"

"I beg your pardon." She stiffened in her seat.

"What are you, twenty-four, twenty-five—twenty-six at the most? Am I correct?"

"I fail to see the relevance of my age."

"Humor me. Am I correct?"

She thought about it for a minute. "Close enough. Let's just leave it at that."

"First time to the penitentiary, yes?"

She nodded.

"And lo and behold, you found an innocent man there.

195

Ms. Chao, the prisons are full of innocent men; in fact, they are filled with nothing but innocent men. I have been practicing forensic psychology for almost twenty years; I have yet to meet a man in prison who did the crime. One million innocent men behind bars. Amazing. No wonder crime is on the rise. All the villains are still on the streets. Please, Ms. Chao, no innocent-men stories. I don't know what brought you to the prison, but the innocent-man story gets the inmate an hour, maybe two, alone with a lawyer. An attractive woman like yourself, they probably had a raffle to see who'd get to look up your skirt."

She slid one hand down from her lap to smooth her hem across her thigh. Satisfied that I was merely rude, she was about to fire a response.

I put up my hands in surrender. "Please, Ms. Chao. I get calls or visits like this all the time. If you want to interest me in a project, bring me something truly rare, a culpable convict, a man who says he did it, or better yet, the rarest of all—a remorseful man, a man tortured by guilt over the horrors he inflicted on other people. For that you have my undivided time and attention."

I looked down at the exam I had been grading. Her chair didn't move. "I don't know what else you have going on in your life, Dr. Triplett, that could be more important than saving an innocent man's life, but I'm not going to let you run me off with your cynicism." She pushed the file toward me. "Don't read it. It's on your head. If they execute an innocent man how will you explain that you didn't have time even to look at the file?" Her jaw was determined but her eyes glistened with oncoming defeat.

"I'm going to do everything I can for my client. He is not going to die because I didn't turn over every rock or look into every corner."

"And what rock am I under, Ms. Chao? Who sent you to me?"

"Mr. Talaverde did."

"Paul Talaverde? My old friend?" I smiled at the memory.

"Yes. I work in the pro bono section of the firm."

"What did he say?"

"I'd really rather Mr. Talaverde talk to you. It was his idea."

"No, no, no. You're going to do whatever it takes for your client, remember? This is what it takes; if you want me to read this file you tell me what Paul Talaverde said."

She smiled at me. "And if I do, you'll agree to read the file?"

I shook my head sadly. "No, you have no leverage here. I'm mildly curious, you're desperate." I pushed the file back at her.

"Okay, you asked for it. He said you used to be the best forensic psychologist around, but that you were burned out now. Actually, he said you pretended to be burned out, but that you could still be seduced if the case was interesting enough. He said that if that didn't work, I should try to shame you into it. You had always been vulnerable to that, and probably still were."

"Anything else?"

She looked away and pursed her mouth in distaste. "He said I should start with you because your contract at the university forbids you from doing private-practice work for a fee. So, if you took the case . . ."

"The price was right. Paul say anything else?"

"No, that was it."

"Then we're still friends. Tell him he was right on two counts. Now, I have a couple of questions for you, Ms. Chao."

She brushed an eave of lustrous black hair out of her face and clasped her hands around her knee, a perfect impression of the earnest student eager to please.

"Who did you talk to at the prison? You said 'we' believe there is a terrible miscarriage? Truth or seduction, Ms. Chao?"

"Truth, Dr. Triplett. Our firm got a call from Otis Weems, he was original counsel on this case, saying that one of the doctors at the prison had called him very concerned about Earl, that's Earl Munsey, the defendant." She pointed to the case file.

"Mr. Weems didn't want to get into it, you know the ineffective-counsel issues, so it was assigned to me. I went up to the prison to talk to the doctor. Then I talked to Earl Munsey. Obviously you think I'm a naive fool, but I'm convinced that Earl Munsey didn't do it and they are going to execute an innocent man."

"What did the doctor say?"

"He said Earl was deteriorating as the execution date approached."

"Deteriorating how?"

"You name it. He paced his cell at all hours. He wouldn't leave for exercise. He was convinced that they would move up the date and take him right off the yard. He stopped eating. Then last week he started crying all the time, calling for his mother. He started banging his head against the walls of his cell, he tore off his fingernails digging at the brick."

"You've never been on death row, have you?"

"No. Don't ever want to, either."

"It's ugly, very ugly. It's cases like this that make people question what we're doing. We destroy another human being's sense of dignity, reduce them to a gibbering gobbet of fear. Why? Then you remember what they did to some other human being and it gets real complicated. At least it does for me."

"Are you in favor of the death penalty?"

"I think in some cases it's just. There are some people who do things for which they should forfeit their lives. But then I don't believe in the sanctity of life. Suicide makes sense to me, so does abortion. What I think is neither here nor there. What you are describing happens all the time. The law prohibits the execution of a mentally ill person. But then, who wouldn't be mentally ill at the prospect of death by electrocution? The prison hospitals routinely medicate prisoners to near-comas as their dates approach so they won't act in such a way as to appear mentally ill and avoid execution. It's a hell of a choice for the doctors. Do nothing and watch your patients shit themselves like crazed rats and then get executed anyway, or trank them to the eyeballs so they're easier to kill. So far you haven't told me anything unusual to warrant looking into this case. It's interesting that the doctor called his attorney, most of the time they wouldn't bother. What's got you so convinced this guy is innocent, not just terrified?"

"When I got there to see him he was curled up on the floor, rocking back and forth, crying for his mother, saying, 'I didn't do it, I didn't do it,' over and over again. I just watched him through the window of his cell. When I went in he didn't even know I was in the room. Nothing changed. I told him who I was. Nothing. No new evidence, no claims that someone else did it or he was framed. He didn't ask me to represent him. Just rocking and crying."

"Did he know you were coming?"

"No. It was on the spur of the moment. The prison doctor had called his attorney, who called us. Mr. Talaverde asked me to go up right away. I didn't tell the doctor I was coming, neither did Mr. Talaverde. We didn't even agree to look into it, so his attorney couldn't have told him anything. I checked with the doctor. Weems hadn't gotten back to him."

"All right. Leave me the file. I'll read it tonight and call you tomorrow." She was right, I didn't have anything more important to do.

"Here's my home number," she said as she wrote on the back of a business card. "My son's been sick. I may not be in the office tomorrow." She slid the card over to me. I put it in the file.

I finished my workout, showered, changed, made a pitcher of gin and tonic, and set it on the patio table next to the file. I put a fresh, clean legal pad and pen on the other side. I poured a drink, sat down, and opened the Earl Munsey file.

Earl Munsey had been nineteen when he was arrested for the murders of Joleen Pennybacker, Martha Dombrowski, and Eleanor Gelman. Pennybacker was found in a model home by a real-estate agent, Dombrowski in an empty house by the residents when they returned from a trip, and Gelman in a rental condo, by the next occupants. At first the three women appeared to have been murdered where they were found, with the murder weapons at the scene: Pennybacker's skull crushed by a blood-covered wooden stick; Dombrowski shot in the head by the .32 caliber gun found next to her body; and Gelman bludgeoned by the fifteen-pound dumbbell near her.

Medical examination revealed that these were post-mortem wounds and that each woman had been strangled by a soft ligature, perhaps rubber tubing. They had all been sexually assaulted before death, with bruising of the genital area but no penetration. There were no hair samples or bodily fluids at the scene of the crime. In addition, each victim had been bled, probably by syringe, and splashes of their blood were found at the next crime scene. They had been murdered elsewhere and placed at the scenes.

I picked up the crime-scene psychological profile. The profiler had been Warren Schuster, trained at Quantico, now a consultant in private practice.

All three crime scenes had a number of similarities. The women were partially clothed and appeared to have been killed by surprise, in the middle of an activity: Pennybacker sitting in front of a makeup mirror; Dombrowski in the kitchen, in front of an open refrigerator; and Gelman in the foyer with money in her hand, perhaps making change for a delivery. The reality of the murders was quite the opposite. All three endured multiple, near-death strangulations along with repeated, unsuccessful attempts at penetration both anal and vaginal.

Schuster concluded that the crimes represented two levels of reality. One, the final scenes of partially clad women, surprised and quickly killed, was based on an actual event, probably from the killer's adolescence. The killer had been, perhaps, a peeping Tom who had been caught by a woman, maybe even reported to the police, hence the undress, the surprise, their being in the middle of ordinary activities. The postmortem wounds were the revenge of the discovered voyeur for her reporting him to the authorities, or laughing at him when she discovered him. The actual murders were the enactments of his fantasies. What he wanted to do to the women as he watched them. What he hadn't done the first time.

Schuster suggested they look for a white male, early twenties, with a history of sexual offenses such as obscene phone calls, exposing himself, peeping into houses. He would have an extensive collection of pornography, probably emphasizing sadomasochistic themes, and have at least one camera with telephoto lenses. I'd have said the same thing.

The police put that together with the commonalities of the locations and began to look at deliverymen, cable installers, cleaning services, utility repairmen, mailmen. They were linking the profile to those who had the opportunity to get into the locations with the bodies. They also videotaped the crowds that showed up at each crime scene.

There at the intersection of history, opportunity, and obsession stood Earl Munsey, a vocational-school work-study employee of Beauty Kleen Restorations, Inc., a cleaning service with contracts that included all three locations. At fifteen, Earl had been arrested on a charge that he had spied on a neighbor going from her bedroom to her shower. That charge brought forth three other complainants. He was convicted and given a suspended sentence and placed in a residential facility for a year. He continued with outpatient counseling and community-service hours cleaning the bathrooms at the city park. That led to his employment with Beauty Kleen. A search warrant of his parents' home turned up dozens of bondage magazines and videos, but no cameras. He also had a file about all the crimes sealed in a plastic bag and suspended from the floor vent in his bedroom into the ductwork. Earl had keys to all the locations, and although he was not assigned to the crews that were cleaning them, he could have easily gained access with the bodies. He was in the videotapes of the crowds at all three crime scenes. The neighbors all described Earl as a "strange duck," a "lurker," not a stalker, but always in the background, watching women, then scurrying off when their eyes met his.

I flipped over to the counseling notes from the residential facility. Psychological testing showed that Earl had an IQ of 82, was dyslexic, learning disabled by a sequential processing disorder, and attention deficit disordered. He had poor impulse controls, was often flooded by his feelings, used fantasy to excess to relieve chronic feelings of depression and emptiness. He was passive, easily suggestible, quite concrete in his thinking and rigid in his judgments. The therapist noted that Earl was unable to articulate why he had been watching the women and denied doing it even though there had been numerous witnesses. Therapy was eventually terminated as unproductive, and he was recommended for a job that was structured and did not involve contact with the public. That was the last anyone heard of Earl Munsey for three years.

The police had all they needed for an arrest. Earl was Mirandized and waived having an attorney present. Prosecutors would later argue that his psychological evaluation was not known to them at the time and that the standard error of the measure of an IQ of 82 could place it in the average range and his consent should have been considered competent. He was questioned by Detectives Ermentraut and Bigelow for almost forty-eight straight hours. At the end of which Earl Munsey signed a confession to the three murders.

I read the confession. There was no mention of how Earl Munsey lured the women into his van, which was presumed to be where the killings took place, or managed to keep from leaving a single piece of forensic evidence tying him to the crime. Earl claimed to have been in a fog and that it "wasn't him" who had picked up the women. The murders, however, were described in gruesome detail.

The prosecution charged Earl with capital murder while committing felony sexual assault, attempted rape and sodomy, and asked for the death penalty. Without too much protest from Otis Weems, they got it.

Clipped to the back of the file was a bag of photographs from the crime scenes. I looked at the backs and arranged them in order. There was no identification of who took the photos, Ermentraut or Bigelow.

First was Joleen Pennybacker on the floor in front of a makeup mirror. Perfumes and potpourri were spilled on the floor. She was nude except for a pair of fur wraps around her neck. Next to her was a bloody wooden stick matted with her hair and brains.

Martha Dombrowski lay on the kitchen floor clad only in a college T-shirt. Food from the open refrigerator lay around her, a can, ground meat, donuts, and a .32-caliber pistol that had left her with a small round hole in the middle of her forehead.

Eleanor Gelman was in the entrance foyer, also clad only in a college T-shirt. She had a twenty-dollar bill in her right hand, and there were some coins around her left hand. Next to her was a bloody, crusted dumbbell with five-pound plates.

I closed the file. Monica Chao had things to work with, especially the confession, but I didn't see how I could help her. The profile and crime-scene analysis made sense to me. I could see Earl Munsey doing this crime. Maybe the confession was coerced and there were gaps in it. Maybe they shouldn't have convicted him. Maybe she could parlay that into a new trial. That didn't mean he didn't do it. Not in the post-O.J. world.

I called Monica Chao and told her I had no ideas and that I would return the file to her. She asked if I could come by tonight. She had some more information that she had received by court order and she didn't want to waste time. I got directions to her place and drove over.

She opened the door and motioned me inside. Monica wore running shoes, jean skirt, and a cream-colored blouse knotted at the midriff. Her hair was pulled back into a glossy ponytail. A young boy, perhaps five, stood in the center of the living room.

"This is my son, Justin. Justin, say hello to Dr. Triplett." Justin approached with his hand out but a somber look on his face. We shook hands and he turned back to his game on the floor.

"Listen, I just wanted to drop this off. I'll let you get back to whatever . . ."

She ushered me into the kitchen. "Justin's upset right now. His father and I separated a couple of months ago. He keeps hoping we'll get back together again. Whenever somebody comes over, he's hoping it's his dad. When it's not, he's disappointed."

"Listen, I don't have anything to tell you. Not from a psychological point of view. You have the confession to work with . . ."

"No, I don't. Weems argued that on the first appeal. That and the consent. He lost. I don't have anything. Before you give up on this, look at what I got today at the office. It's the photos from Ermentraut and Bigelow. Along with their notes. The photos you saw were from the first officers on the scene, the patrolmen."

"Okay, I'll look at them," I said resentfully, ready to be out from under one of her rocks. "How late are you going to be up tonight? I'll drop them back when I'm done."

"You can do it here. I've got an office set up next to the living room. Justin and I were about to eat. Why don't you look at the stuff, stay for dinner, and tell me what you think. I'm making hot-and-sour soup and Dan Dan noodles, it's Justin's favorite."

"What's Dan Dan noodles?"

"It's a spicy chili peanut sauce over noodles. Very good."

"Okay. Where are the photos?" The sooner I started, the sooner I was done.

"In my office, on the desk. I'll let you know when we're

ready to eat." I walked out of the kitchen and across the living room. Justin was on his elbows and knees, staring down at a board on the floor before him. His chin rested in the cup of his palms.

I turned into the first door on the left, sat down at Monica's desk, and put the file next to her printer. I picked up the photographs. They were larger than the ones the patrolmen had taken. I propped them up side by side in front of the computer screen. I flipped up Ermentraut's notebook and read his notes.

Joleen Pennybacker: four bloodstains on floor; furs not part of house decor; potpourri?: lab says it's dried thyme leaves; perfumes: Escada and Opium, from the house; wooden stick: solid maple—look at local cabinetmakers, furniture repair shops.

I looked at Joleen Pennybacker: young, slim, ghostly pale in the harsh flashlight. The pool of blood under her head black, not red. Lying on her back, eyes wide, hands up, fingers spread as if startled by someone standing in front of her. Had she been sitting? Why no chair? The two furs draped over her shoulder and around her neck. Trying them on before she got dressed? A gift? The sensuous feel of fur on skin? The potpourri and perfume spilled on the floor. As if she'd pulled them over in a struggle or standing up to flee. Someone she'd seen in the mirror. The bloody stick that stopped her.

I picked up Martha Dombrowski's picture. I tilted it under the light then reached over and turned on Monica's desk lamp. In the corners, four dark stains. Just like the first scene. Repetition becomes ritual. Another indicator that these tableaux had symbolic meaning to the killer. He was putting order on his chaos. Shaping it to give him release from his hungers. For the moment.

Martha was older, softer. Again on her back. Nude except for the T-shirt. A college. I brought the photo closer: University of California. She, too, had her hands up as if startled and a pool of black blood under her head. There was food strewn around her and the refrigerator door was open. The dropped gun. She hears someone, has food in her hands, a midnight snack perhaps, turns, sees the killer. Only he is not a killer yet. She sees him watching her. She's going to report him, like the first one did. He can't let that happen. He shoots her. He drops the gun and runs. Ritual reenactments of his trauma, his shame, only he's rewritten the end. They don't tell, they die. He escapes to watch them again. Better yet, he does what he only dreamed of the first time. But he can't.

Even with them subdued, restrained, he can't get it up, can't put it in. A level of inhibition even this degree of control and power can't conquer. Twisted religious upbringing? What did Munsey's parents do to him?

Thank God they caught this guy. He'd have kept doing this until he was able to penetrate his victims. And then he'd have kept on anyway, just hyphenating his career: serial killer-rapist.

I looked at the notes. Food: can of baked beans, open with lid; package of ground meat; box of donuts. The food belonged to the owners of the house. T-shirt: University of California. Neither the victim nor the residents attended the school. Boyfriend? Killer? Blood not the victim's. Match for # 1. The gun was a .32-caliber H & R. No serial number. A later note said ballistics couldn't match it with any other killings and they hadn't been able to trace its owner.

The last picture was Eleanor Gelman. Again the four bloodstains. Again the body nude except for a college T-shirt. This time it's the University of Richmond. Was Munsey's first victim, the one who reported him, a college student?

She's on her back in the foyer. This time her hands have money in them. Coins all around the left one, dropped when she's startled, a twenty in her right. For whom? Where's her purse? I scanned the corners of the photo to see if it was on the floor or hanging from a doorknob. Why get it out to give to someone? She's only half dressed. So many questions but the answer is always the same—silence. Her head sits in a pool of blood. Satan's halo, viscous, sickly sweet, the light shining off bits of bone and brain. I looked at the dumbbell. There was a difference with this one. Her ankles were tied. With what?

I looked at Ermentraut's notes. Bloodstains not the victim's. Same as victim # 2. T-shirt—victim did not go to University of Richmond. Her son? Money: 7 cents—all pennies. Ankles: rubber tubing. Chemistry supplies? M.E. says consistent with ligatures on all three victims.

I stared at all three pictures. A triptych from Earl Munsey's unconscious. The same scene over and over again, unchanging forever. That's one definition of hell.

"Are you staying for dinner?"

I looked down. Justin stood there just as somber as before. Dark eyes peering up from under his bowl-cut black hair.

"I was going to. Your mom offered since I'm helping her with her work. Is that okay with you?"

Justin put his hand on my arm. "Do you know my dad?"

"No, I don't," I said gently.

"Oh." He turned away, then back. "Can you play with me? Just until Mom calls me to eat?"

I looked at the photos. Nothing there. I might as well play with the little guy. His dad would if he were here.

"Sure. Just until your mom calls."

I pushed away from the console and followed him into the living room. A sliding-glass door and surrounding windows let plenty of light into the room and it bounced off the dark parquet floor. A large-screen TV sat in the center of the far wall surrounded by a built-in bookcase. I scanned the books: cookbooks, exercise books, books on divorce and child-rearing, romances, mysteries, arts and crafts, everything but law books. A low, cream-colored leather sofa and chair set encircled a wood and glass coffee table. A free-form cypress base with bronze claws gripping a palette-shaped glass top.

Justin sat down in between the table and the sofa and picked up a plastic frame. I thought about squeezing in next to him but chose an adjoining side of the table. His mother poked her head around the corner.

"We'll eat in just a couple of minutes." Then she lifted her head up towards me.

"Anything?"

"Where do you stand on feeding the messenger?"

"We feed them in these parts. Good news or bad."

"I still don't see anything."

"Okay."

Justin scooted over towards me and handed me the frame. It was covered with numbered plastic shingles.

"How do you play, Justin?"

"It's a memory game. You have to remember where the matching pictures are. When they match you take them off the board."

"Show me. We'll do this one for practice. It won't count, okay?"

"Okay. See, here is a pony, and this one is a pony. So I take them off." He lifted two numbered shingles, revealing the ponies. Off they came, revealing another layer under-neath.

"What's this, Justin?" I asked, noticing that he was sitting right up next to my leg and starting to list to starboard. I hoped that he wouldn't climb into my lap, so I called out for help.

"How's dinner coming?"

"Couple more minutes, that's all." And so the *Titanic* was lost.

"This is the next part," he said, now looking up at me from the space between the board and my chest.

"Once you uncover the board, you have to guess the puzzle. That's hard. I have a good memory, but my mom gets the puzzles right. That's how she wins. She's really smart. She's a lawyer."

"I'm sure she is, Justin. Since this is just practice, I'm going to look at the puzzle. Maybe I can show you some tricks. Help you beat your mom."

"Cool," he said and clapped his hands.

I pulled the backing up and looked at it. "You know, Justin, if your memory is good, you might try to uncover the corners first. That puts a frame on the puzzle. It's a lot easier to figure out from the edges in instead of the middle out."

A chill went down my back and out my arms as the picture in my head disappeared and a great white shape rushed to breach into recognition on the vast empty sea of my mind.

I stood up, handed Justin the board, and hurried back to the office. Sliding into the chair, I pulled an empty legal pad in front of me and stared at the pictures.

"Aren't we going to play anymore?" Justin asked forlornly, from the doorway.

I looked over my shoulder. "I'm sorry, Justin. This is very important. I'll play with you when I'm done. I promise. Okay?"

"You promise?"

"Yes. I promise, Justin."

He stood there trying to decide the worth of my word,

weighing it against the collection of promises he already held. He turned and walked away. I heard the shingles spill onto the wooden floor.

His mother appeared in the doorway. "What happened? He just ran into his room. Dinner's on."

"I'm sorry. I was playing with him when I got this idea about Munsey and the murders. I bolted over here to try it out and I told him I couldn't play with him now. I'll just scoop this stuff up and take it back to my place. Let you and him get on with dinner."

She came towards me. "Do you have something?"

"No, no. I have an idea. I need to try it out. It's probably nothing. I really need to get on it while it's fresh, before I lose it." I started to take the pictures down.

"No, no," she said, palms up in retreat. "Stay here. I'll close the door. We'll be quiet. Do what you have to. We don't have any time to spare. If you've got an idea, run with it. Do you want any food?"

"No, thank you. How about a cup of coffee? You might want to put on a pot. This could take awhile."

"Sure. Coming right up." She shook her fists in excitement and disappeared.

I wondered if this scene had been played out before, with her husband. The disappointed child, the abandoned dinner, work demands taking priority. Eventually sliding from a separation that was impromptu and random to one that was formalized and permanent.

I didn't need food. I was burning up excitement as fuel, the same excitement I felt every time I had panned golden nuggets of meaning out of the onrushing blur of life. So far, that had turned out to be the one enduring passion of my life.

I drew diagrams and schematics, scribbled translations and made lists and erased them all. The hours wore on. The refills of coffee told me so. The trash can filled, then over-flowed. I kept drawing and writing. Eventually, the tide of erasures receded and I was left with a single page of work. The clock said two a.m. when Monica knocked on the doorframe.

"How's it going?"

"Gone as far as I can. I'm done."

"Want something to eat?"

"No, thanks. I'm caffeinated to the eyeballs. I can't eat when I'm wired like this."

She slid down along the wall until she sat cross-legged on the floor. She sipped from a steamy mug. "So?" she said, dipping her head in anticipation, her eyes as somber as her son's had been.

I took off my glasses, rubbed my eyes for a minute, put the glasses back on, and turned to the pictures.

"I was playing that game with Justin and telling him how frames help solve puzzles, when it occurred to me. There were frames on these murder scenes. See here." I pointed to the bloodstains around each body. "They aren't from the victims. Ermentraut's notes say that, or I think they do. They're unnecessary to the scene. There's plenty of blood all over the place from the head injuries. Why the frame? What does a frame do?"

Monica shrugged. "I don't know. I've never actually been at a crime scene."

"A frame tells you what the field of information is. What's inside is important, what's outside is not. Serial killers don't frame their work. They know what's important. They arrange it just so. They remove what's irrelevant. When it's just right, when it's satisfying, they stop. That's the 'art,' if you want, in the composition.

"If Schuster's right, then this is Earl Munsey's ritual

reenactment of his shame, changed to include his fantasized torture and rape and revenge. Very satisfying. This is a scene by Earl for Earl. There's no need for a frame. Suppose, just suppose, this isn't a construction for the killer's own use, own pleasure. Who is it for? It's a construction. There's no question about that. He brought the bodies, the weapons, the blood, the props. Who's going to see this? The police. It's a message to them. They need a frame. They have ignorant eyes. They don't know what to attend to, what to ignore. He's helping us poor dumb bastards along. He's jumping up and down, waving his arms, saying Here I am, here I am."

"Did you figure out the messages?" A tentative, hopeful smile emerged across her narrow oval face.

"I think so."

"What do they say?"

"Bear with me. I have to explain this step by step. The logic seemed inescapable to me when I was doing it. But delusions can be quite logical, too. You have to understand it and believe it. If I can't convince you, you can't convince anyone else.

"The typical way of interpreting a crime scene for clues to the killer's personality is actuarial and symbolic. What do most serial killers have in common? What are the significant correlates? What needs do certain acts satisfy? For example, why mutilate the face? Why take souvenirs? And so on. We're talking about translating their hidden, obscure inner language because they're talking to themselves, not us.

"Suppose this guy is talking to us. He speaks our language. How do we read? Left to right. Top to bottom. So I looked at what was inside the frames. Here is Joleen Pennybacker."

I picked up the photo and used my hands to frame her body. "Left to right: furs, body, potpourri. Top to bottom: perfume, bloody stick. Gibberish, right? That's what I've been doing all night. Trying every different category that might describe each element, trying to make sentences out of them."

"Have you?"

"Yes."

"What do they say?"

"First, there are rules to the messages. All languages have grammar and syntax. Ignore the bodies. They're irrelevant, zeros, place-holders. Without them there is no crime scene. No crime. He killed these women as bait. To draw us in as an audience. That's why there's no penetration. His driving need isn't sexual, it's narcissism. He demonstrates his power by leaving an abundance of clues that nobody gets. He's diddling us, not them. He's been laughing at us for two years now."

"Those poor women. You're saying he killed them just to show us how smart he is, that he could get away with it. This is incredible." She shuddered.

"Don't say that. It has to be credible. Otherwise Earl Munsey fries for this. His eyes explode, his blood boils, his hair bursts into flame. And this bastard laughs all the way to hell.

"This is Joleen Pennybacker. Furs; thyme, not potpourri. It was all dried thyme; scents, not perfumes. The murder weapon, a blood-covered stick, a red stick. Furs, thyme, scents, red stick. *First time since Red-stick.* He's announcing his appearance. He's telling us where he came from. I did this one and I said, Triplett, you're crazy. You've tortured the data beyond recognition. You're the infinite number of monkeys. *Voila!* Random hammering on the keys and we get *Hamlet.* Once, perhaps. What if they're all meaningful and related? God couldn't make enough monkeys to pull that off."

I picked up the next picture. "This is Martha

Dombrowski. Remember, ignore her body. Left to right: can, not food, not beans; look at the T-shirt: University of California, U C is visible, the rest needs a magnifying glass; and meat. Then: a donut and a gun. Can UC meat. Donut a gun. *Can you see me? Done it again.* Again. Number two. It only makes sense as the second of a series. They either both make sense or neither of them does."

I exchanged photos. "Here's Eleanor Gelman. These coins, I counted them. All pennies. Copper. Coppers. The shirt: University of Richmond, same maker. UR, then a dumbbell. The twenty, that stumped me. Money, greenbacks, dollars, currency, a bill, Bill, his name? It's Jackson's face on the bill. See how her thumb is pressed over it. Then her ankles. Tied? Knot? Tube? Hose? Bound." I stopped to see if she was convinced. She looked like she was trying to suppress a grimace. Her plum-colored lips darkened.

"*Cops, you are dumbbells, Jackson bound.* He's going to Jackson. That's where his next victims will be found. Some town named Jackson."

I leaned back. Monica looked into her cup. No help there.

"I know: A tale told by an idiot, full of sound and fury, signifying nothing. Perhaps, but I know one thing for certain. A demonstrable scientific fact."

"What's that?"

"If I'm right, Earl Munsey couldn't have killed those women."

"Why?"

"He's dyslexic, and he has a sequencing disorder. He reverses letters and words. He couldn't put a rebus together."

"A rebus?"

"That's what I think they are. It's a kind of puzzle where images stand for the syllables of words.

"We're halfway home. If I'm right, then Earl Munsey is

indeed innocent. Now we have to prove that I'm right. But that's for tomorrow," I looked at the clock, "or later, whichever comes first."

"You can crash here if you want. I made up the bed in the guest room."

"No, I don't think so. Besides, wouldn't that get you in hot water with your ex? Most custody orders forbid overnight guests of the opposite sex."

"Yeah, well, John isn't in any position to dictate terms to me. Not with him out every night being true to his new gay identity. I may have been just a treatment plan for John when we were married, but I'm a whole lot more trouble now." She nodded, agreeing with herself.

I remembered why I quit doing custody work and switched to criminal. Too much violence in the custody work.

"I just think it'd be confusing for Justin to find me here when he wakes up. Tell him I haven't forgotten my promise. I'll play with him next time I'm over." I wondered if she'd remember to do that. If not, I'd call him myself. If you couldn't keep your word to a child your priorities were in serious disarray.

I put my work in the file, took my mug to the kitchen pass-through, and wished Monica good night.

"Thank you for everything. Even if you can't prove your theory, I appreciate how hard you've worked, and I'll tell Earl you did all you could. But I have faith in you. If it's there, you'll find it, that's what Paul Talaverde said about you."

"Yeah, well, even a stopped clock is right twice a day. I'll call you when I know something." I waved and turned down the steps.

"Good night, Dr. Triplett. And good luck."

She was still outlined in the doorway, her head resting

against the frame, when I drove away.

The first thing I did the next day was call Ermentraut. He was in court, so I left a message. Then I tried Bigelow.

"Homicide, Detective Bigelow."

"Detective, this is Dr. Ransom Triplett. I wonder if I could have a couple of minutes of your time."

"Couple of minutes, sure. What about?"

"Earl Munsey."

"Oh Christ. Are you one of those bleeding hearts that thinks we shouldn't execute this bastard? Let me tell you something. I was there. At the scene. At the morgue. I saw what he did. I'll sleep like a baby the day they serve him up the juice of justice. Goodbye . . ."

"Whoa, whoa, just a second, please. This is not about whether he should be executed. I've been going over the file as a consultant to his attorney. Personally, I think you guys have the right man."

"Damn straight we do. And another thing, that confession was pristine. Clean all through. We never touched him. We read him his rights. What were we supposed to do? Talk him out of it? Oh no, Mr. Munsey, that would be unwise, here, let us call a lawyer for you. Why don't we just stop trying to catch anybody? He freaking confessed. What do these people want?"

"Well, detective, I just want to ask you a couple of small questions, so I can explain them to his attorney. It just might put this whole thing to rest."

"Okay, what is it?"

'The things that were around the body. That Munsey planted at the scene . . ."

"You mean like the gun, the tubing, that stuff?"

"Yeah. Did any of that lead anywhere?"

"No. The stuff at the first scene came from the model home. Except the herbs that he spilled. We took his picture to local groceries. Nothing. The food was from the owners. The gun was a Saturday-night special, cold, no serial numbers. We hit all the gun shops, the known dealers. No one could ID Munsey. Same thing for the tubing, the dumbbell. He could have gotten them anywhere. Yard sales—hell, he could have stolen them out of a garage. None of that stuff went anywhere."

"Last question. The blood spatters on the floor. Detective Ermentraut's notes aren't clear. The blood spatters at the scenes aren't the victims'. Whose were they?"

"Uh, let me remember. I think it was victim number one's blood at the second scene and number two's at the next one. Yeah, that's right."

"Could you tell me the victims' blood types?"

"Yeah, hold on. We pulled that jacket on account of people like you. This one is not gonna get away."

I doodled on my pad. Zeros, large ones, small ones. Then I linked them. All the little naughts going nowhere. Earl Munsey was moving slowly, inexorably towards eternity.

"Okay. Here's the lab report. You want the DNA markers and everything, or just the type?"

"Blood type is fine."

"Girl number one was O positive. Girl number two was AB. Girl number three was B positive. No, that's the stains. The girls were AB, B positive, and A."

"You ever find the third girl's blood?"

"No. He must have stashed it somewhere. We figure he'd have used it at the next scene. But then there wasn't a next scene."

"Thanks, detective."

"No problem. Six days and it won't matter anymore."

"Yeah," I said and hung up. Unless you're wrong. Then six days from now it'll matter forever.

I spent the next two days pursuing my theory without any success, although my geographical knowledge was enormously enriched. I learned that there were eighteen Jacksons in the United States, strung from California to New Jersey and from Minnesota to Louisiana. Almost all were small towns with few homicides and not one that looked at all like my rebus killer.

Then I tried Red Stick. Make no mistake about it. There is not one Redstick, U.S.A. There are six Red Oaks and five Redwoods and I called them all. No murders at all like mine.

I sat on the porch, watching one of Earl Munsey's last four sunsets. A gin and tonic slowly diluted on the table next to me. I had nothing. A theory that tortured me with its plausibility, that I refused to accept as a statistical chimera, a product of just enough monkeys scribbling associations to three pictures. Maybe it was data rape, me forcing myself all over the pictures. They yielded up a facsimile of meaning, enough to get me to roll off, grunting in satisfaction, while they lay there, mute in the darkness, their secrets still unknown.

Well, it hadn't been good for me, either. We were running out of time and I had no ideas, bright or otherwise. The phone rang.

"Dr. Triplett. This is Monica Chao. I was wondering how you were doing. We're running out of time."

"I know. How am I doing? Not well at all. I've called every Jackson, every Redwood, every Red Oak in the country. Nothing. I don't know what else to do. Maybe it's all a mirage, an illusion. They aren't rebuses at all. The fact that I've created these sentences is a monument to human inventiveness in the face of complexity and ambiguity. Or I'm right. They are rebuses and I'm just not good enough to translate them correctly. Maybe we need more monkeys. I don't know. Whoever the killer is, he and I don't seem to speak the same language."

I forgot all about Monica. I felt an avalanche slowing, turning on itself, turning into a kaleidoscope, slowing further, settling, stopping, halted. The pattern blazed through my mind. I began to laugh, a cleansing cackle of satisfaction. Had I seen the truth or only applied even finer filigree to my delusion? One call would tell all. I heard someone calling my name in the distance.

"Monica, I have to go. I'll call you right back. I think I've solved it. I hope I have."

I dialed the operator, got the area code I wanted, and then dialed information for the police department's central phone number. I was shuttled through departments toward Homicide.

A voice answered, "Thibault."

"Baton Rouge Homicide?" I said, savoring each syllable.

"Yeah. Who is this?"

I gave my name. "Detective Thibault, I'm working on a case here in Virginia. A man's going to be executed in four days for a series of murders up here. Some last-minute evidence has emerged that may link him to murders elsewhere. Baton Rouge in particular. If so, they would have been at least three years ago. Were you in Homicide then?"

"Doctor, I investigated Cain. I've been twenty-seven years in Homicide in this city. There ain't hardly a murder here I don't know something about, but they're also startin' to run together. I'm due to retire end of the year. I hope this one had a flourish, or four days won't do it."

"Our killer," I said, glad to relinquish ownership, "had an unusual MO. He only killed women and then he placed the bodies in conspicuous locations, where they were sure to be found."

"Got to do better than that, Doc. That's half of our murders. How'd he do 'em?"

"He strangled them after an attempted sexual assault. But at the crime scenes there were weapons found, or rather planted, so that it looked like the victims had been killed where they were found. Clubs, guns, that sort of thing."

"That doesn't ring any bells. Anything else?"

"He took some blood from each victim and he'd spatter it around the next crime scene."

Thibault was silent for a minute. When he spoke his voice was strangely hoarse. "Your boy's gonna go when, four days, you said?"

"Yeah, why?"

"Let me ask you a question. Your first victim, what kind of blood type?"

"AB, but—"

We finished the sentence in harmony. "The bloodstains were O positive."

"Yes," I said, flooded with elation. "When did these killings occur?"

"They started five years ago. There were four of them over the course of a year. Then they stopped."

"That's great. Do you have the lab work on these stains?"

"Yeah. They're in the file. I'd have to go dig it out, but I could fax it to you. Take an hour or so."

"If the blood's a match, our guy couldn't have done it. He was in a residential facility that whole year. This is great. Listen, I don't want to be rude, but I've got to call the lawyer with this news."

Thibault's voice was thick and weary when he spoke.

"As soon as you know, Doc, call me right back. You see, if

your boy didn't do it, and that's our blood at the scene, then I've got a call to make. 'Cause our guy didn't do it, either. And his next of kin aren't going to like that one little bit."

ACKNOWLEDGEMENTS: I would like to thank the following people for their help with this story: noted defense attorney Peter Greenspun; Dr. Jane Greenstein; Constance Knott; Officer Adam K. Schutz; Dr. Mark E. Schutz; and my son, Jakob Lindenberger-Schutz, who solved it in a flash.

Expert Opinion

It was winter when the first call came in. That brief lull in domestic warfare that comes right before Christmas. No one wants to be in court that time of year. Not the lawyers, not the families. It has to be a life or death emergency to get on the docket. No judge wants to be playing Solomon in the manger.

I looked out my office window. The sky was gray and cloudy. The air was cold and dry without a hint of snow. Walking to my office, the day had the look and feel of marble.

The phone rang twice before I picked it up.

"Dr. Triplett, this is Larry Fortunato. I'm an attorney in Lawrence, New Jersey. I'd like to use you in a case."

"I'm sorry, Mr. Fortunato, but I'm buried in work right now. I'm not taking on any new cases."

"How long until you can?"

"I won't be starting any new cases for another six weeks, maybe two months. Can I refer you to anyone?"

"Not really, Doctor. You're the one we want."

"Is one of the parents down here?" I asked, wondering why a New Jersey lawyer was so keen to use me here in Virginia.

"No, the parents both live up here. I did some research. Your name kept coming up as the best, so I figured we'd go with the best."

"That's very flattering. What kind of case is it?" May as well find out what I was best at. I wasn't going to take the case regardless of the answer.

"It's a sexual abuse case. Mother claims the father abuses the little boy."

"There are some very good people up your way. There's—"

"I know doctor, but believe me we called all of them. I asked them the same question. If it was your kid, who would you want to do the evaluation? You ought to feel pretty good about this. Your name is always the answer. Well, not always. Some shrink across the state isn't too crazy about you, but I heard you blew him away in court a couple of times."

"That is nice to hear. This is a hard area to keep a decent reputation in. People don't really want evaluations done. They want verification of what they already know is true. A lot of messengers get killed in this line of work."

"No problem of that here, Doctor. Neither of the parties would be retaining you. It's the little boy's—"

"Don't tell me. I don't want to know. Even if I took the case, I wouldn't want to hear anything without all the attorneys on the phone. These cases are like tar pits. You make one false move and you can't undo it. These cases are littered with the bones of evaluators who screwed up."

"Okay. I respect that. Let me ask you one question. Hypothetically, if you were to take the case, how much would it cost?"

"My hourly rate is two hundred dollars. Not knowing anything about this case, I'd tell you the range is eight to twelve thousand dollars. These cases are very, very draining. I can only do two or three at a time. They take at least two months to complete. If I was taking any more of these that is."

"Of course. Sounds like you need a little R and R."

"Yeah." I needed more than that. I needed a new how and why, but that was none of his business.

"Well, thank you for your time, Dr. Triplett. Take care of yourself."

I cradled the phone and surveyed the cases on my desk. First up Tiffany Pearlman. A child so damaged that she could scarcely go a day without harming herself. Overdoses, auto wrecks, pregnancies, poetry in her own blood. A walking death notice lacking only a date. The county had no money to underwrite treatment. The parents were bankrupt from trying to pin the blame on each other. She was a slow motion suicide heading downhill. If I was lucky, I'd get her committed the first week of January and buy her a little time. She, of course, thought that she was fine and it was the rest of us who were crazy.

The rest of the pile was more of the same. Their trials were strung out over the next month. After that I was going to take some time off. See if I could reinvent myself.

The envelope was on my secretary's desk a week later. She wasn't in on Wednesdays so no one saw who delivered it. A large manila envelope with my name typed across the front. I got these packages all the time. First thing a divorce lawyer tells their client: keep a journal. Each parent documenting the outrages perpetrated by the other. Each hurt brooded over lovingly. No slight too small to remember or small enough to forgive. However long they spent preparing their case, it took at least twice as long to recover any sense of proportion. If they ever did.

I took the envelope into my office. I peeled it open and dumped out the contents.

The money was old and in wads held together by rubber bands. One fell on the floor. I picked it up and looked at the door. It was open. I felt naked and closed the door.

There was no letter in the envelope. Nothing. This was definitely not Publisher's Clearinghouse. I picked up a brick. All hundreds. Did banks ever give people hundreds? I thought they were for interbank transactions. I did a quick total. Six thousand. Twelve bricks. Seventy-two grand.

The phone rang. I picked it up and said nothing. "Dr.

Triplett. You received a package today." The voice was smooth and even and unknown.

"Who is this?"

"That package contained an amount of money twice what you would earn from your caseload for the next two months, am I correct?"

"Who is this? I'm not going to answer any questions until I know who this is?"

"This is your new client, Dr. Triplett."

"Oh, no, you're not. I don't work like this. You tell me who you are and where to send this money. I don't want it."

"You can't return it, Dr. Triplett. No one will accept it."

"Then I'll give it away. I don't want it."

"If you give it away, it will be considered spent. Lie back and enjoy it, Doc. You've been bought and paid for." After a moment of silence the voice returned, softer. "Take a deep breath, Doctor. Count it again. That's a lot of R and R, Doctor. We'll be in touch."

I hung up the phone. My heart and mind were racing. I felt like I was swimming through Jell-O with my mouth open.

This was not happening to me. I looked at the money. Oh, yes, it was. I'm a psychologist. I don't even do criminal work. I obey the law. I don't even get traffic tickets. This is insane. There has to be something I can do.

I looked at the bricks of money again. Seventy-two thousand dollars worth of serious intent. Maybe I should call the cops. And tell them what? I was being forced at twice my hourly rate to perform unknown services, for an unknown person. I'm sure there is a crime in there somewhere. Any ideas, Officer? Sure. If they want you to do something illegal, or they threaten you with bodily harm, you call us. Gross overpayment won't do? No.

I had to talk to this guy the next time that he called. That's what I do best—talk to desperate people. People backed into corners, people who felt they had nothing to lose or everything to lose and no way to win. People who could not compromise or negotiate or yield. That's what I did every day. End conflicts, build bridges, put doors into corners. That's what put this guy onto me now. This time I was one of those people. I'd use my skills to get myself out of his life and him out of mine. I felt better already. I had a plan. I knew what I was going to do. I was good at this. The best, he'd said.

I looked at the money. First things first. This had to be put into the bank. I had to be able to return it and that meant guaranteeing its safety. My office safebox wouldn't do, neither would the one I had at home.

I scooped the money into the bag, put on my jacket, turned off the lights and locked the office door. Outside, I fiddled with my key ring, looking for the front door key. I found it and locked the dead bolt. As I withdrew the key from the sticky lock, I heard a voice.

"Dr. Triplett?"

I turned toward the voice. There were two of them. Left wore a butterscotch leather jacket over a chocolate turtleneck. His face was deeply pitted. Could have been acne, could have been shrapnel for all I knew. His hands were at his side. Right was the talker. His head cocked slightly to one side, a smile on his face. "Dr. Triplett, would you step this way please?" He turned sideways and pointed to a black limousine with tinted windows.

I looked from Left to Right. "And if I say no?"

Left reached up and pulled away his jacket to show me that the question had been rhetorical.

"Right here on the street. You'd shoot me?" I asked Right.

"In a fucking heartbeat, Doc. You have no idea how angry

Mr. G is with you. Getting shot is the least of your worries. Step this way, please."

He stepped off the curb and opened the door. All I could see was a pair of legs in the middle of the rear seat and an empty bench facing backwards toward the legs. I stepped between Left and Right, holding my bag like it was my lunch. Right's cologne was cloyingly sweet. I ducked my head and slipped onto the bench with my bag of money in my lap. Right slid in next to me and pulled the door closed. Left came around the car, opened the other door and sat down next to me. I was pressed between them, feeling the pressure of their arms and legs against me from my shoulders to my shoes. I couldn't move.

My host stroked his beard slowly, rhythmically, like he was petting himself. He lifted his chin, pursed his lips in thought and then backhanded me across the face.

My eyes watered and my muscles tensed. The pressure on me from both sides increased. I relaxed.

"Who the fuck do you think you are? Huh?" he asked. He was short and stocky, with black hair that swept straight back from a widow's peak. With his sharp, curved nose, thick neck and bulging eyes, he looked like a great horned owl. I felt like a field mouse. His hands were pale and square with short, thick fingers.

"I asked you a question. Who the fuck do you think you are?"

"I think I'm terrified, that's who."

"That's good. You should be. You should be wondering if you're ever gonna get out of this car."

He leaned back against the seat. "I called you and told you I had a problem. A serious fucking problem, and you were too fucking busy to help me. What do you think? You're too good for me?"

The pale hand flew and my head snapped back. I closed my eyes to stop the spinning.

"I came to you with respect," he said pointing a single finger at me. "We did our homework. You're the best. You gave us a price and we doubled it. In cash. Up front. But you're still too busy for me, for my problem. How'd you get so special, Mr. Terrified? You feeling special right now?"

"No," I whispered.

"So tell me, what is it? I ain't good enough for you? My money ain't good enough for you?"

I took a deep breath. Telling him that his attorney had never gotten around to giving me his name was not going to derail this tirade. "It had nothing to do with you or your money. I'm full. There's only so many of these that I can do at one time. I'm in the middle of three cases. I have to finish them. They've got court dates."

"So? You think we couldn't fix that? You don't think we could arrange a continuance or two? Talk to the lawyers, the docket clerks if that's what you needed? Did you come back and say that was the problem, could we work with you on that? No. Nothing. No interest. Just blew me off. Too busy. You busy right now, Mr. Terrified? I'll bet you are. Busy holding your water, is what."

My companions snickered.

"Since you're not too busy all of a sudden, let me tell you about my problem."

I smiled weakly. "Sure."

"When I was younger, I met this girl. You don't need to know her name. A stripper. Whew, God was she hot. Anyway, that's another story. She got knocked up. Said the kid was mine. Now I'm married. I got two kids of my own. Coulda been mine, I'm not saying that. But I tell her you push this and he's an orphan. Let it be and I'll keep an eye on him. I'll look out for him. She's a smart girl. I don't hear from her again. Until a few weeks ago. She calls me up outta the blue. Says my son's in trouble. I gotta help him out like I said. So I say okay, what's the problem. She says he's getting divorced. I start laughing. That's the fucking problem? No, she says the wife claims he's diddling the kid. Won't let him have no visitation. It's killing him. He grew up without a father, now he'll grow old without a son. Help him. Help him. You said you would. He's your own flesh and blood. Look at him, just see him once and then deny him. Look me in the eye and deny him. Fuck." He shrugged and rolled his eyes. "She gave me the address. I went by. Stopped me cold. I seen him walking down the street. It's like I'm watching myself. Little things. The way he walks. The way he laughs. He looks just like me at his age. Okay, he's my son. So I introduce myself to him. I tell him I'm a friend of his mother's, that's all. We sit down and talk. He tells me his wife, she's getting boned by her boss and she wants out. She says she's gonna take the kid. He pulls out his wallet, shows me a picture. What do I know? Kids, they all look alike. He tells me his name. The kid's got my first name. It was his mother's idea. Now so far neither of my other two kids are married. This is my only grandchild, a grandson. With my name. I say how's she gonna do that? She's sucking some other guy's dick and she's a fit mother, c'mon, am I right?"

I nodded in the understanding that passeth all reason.

"He says she's saying the boy don't want to go with him on visits. That when he comes back, he's got nightmares. He wants to sleep with her. That his daddy's mean to him. That he touched him where nobody should touch him. That his butthole's red and sore when he comes back. My son, he gets down on his knees. We're in a restaurant. He gets down on his knees and he swears on his mother's life that he never touched the kid. That it's a fucking lie. I tell him to get up, he's drawing eyes. I tell him I'll talk to her. Hear what she's gotta say. I'll get to the bottom of this."

He leaned back. "You got any questions. Anything else you want to know?"

"No. Not now. If I do, I'll ask, if that's okay, of course."

He smiled broadly. "Of course it's okay. That's why we're here isn't it? I tell you my problem and you listen and ask questions, right? I mean, I'm not paying 400 dollars an hour to a deaf mute, am I?" The smile spread. I was invited to reply and managed a wince of relief.

"Okay. So I go meet the wife. Jesus, what a bitch. I tell her how I'm Vito's uncle and I hear that they're having some problems, maybe I can help. Well, she unloads on him. He's never been a provider to her. He's always losing jobs. She's worked two jobs to make ends meet. She also says he's never been a real man in the sack. She thinks he's maybe a little light in the loafers." He wagged his left hand and pursed his mouth in distaste. "She liked the way he was at first—real gentle and all. But then she realized he was a mama's boy. His mother, she never let him out of her sight. She was always afraid he wouldn't come back, like the father. She was always running his life, calling him at all hours and him always going over there. She got tired of playing second fiddle to the mother. On top of that he was never interested in her as a woman. She had to get him drunk to do it and even then he wasn't flying at full mast. So I ask her about her boss. She says he's just a friend, that Vito's paranoid that she's sleeping around 'cause he wouldn't give her what she needed. She says they just talk. I ask her about the kid. She tells me the same story as Vito. I ask if there's anybody else has seen this stuff. She says no. She took him to the doctor's to check out his butt. She said they couldn't see nothing wrong. They stuck some camera up his butt, a colosto—something. I don't know."

"A colposcope. It's called a colposcope." My voice sounded like it was being piped into the car.

"That's right." My host smiled.

"That's good. It's a specialist's instrument. Somebody with some training took a look at him."

"Maybe, that's good. I don't know. All I know is my grandson has some camera shoved up his ass. He's three years old for Christ's sake. What the fuck is this?"

When I didn't answer, he went on. "She says she ain't gonna let Vito see the boy without a supervisor. A fucking supervisor. And not his mother. She doesn't trust his mother on account of their relationship. He's gotta go down to welfare and get a fucking social worker and pay to see his own kid. If he doesn't agree she's gonna call child protective services and have him charged with child molesting.

"Child molesting. My son molesting my grandson. Can you believe this shit? I asked if I can see the little boy. She asks why. I say I want to talk to him a second, that's all. She says she wants to be there. Okay, fine. She brings the little boy in. He's cute. He's got these big, dark eyes, in this little face. He looks like a little bird, you know what I mean? Very serious face. He's watching me. He's sitting on his mother's lap, holding on to her with both hands. I try to catch his eye, get him to come over, sit in my lap, talk. He keeps turning his face away. She says he's shy. I think fuck, she's gonna make him a freaking mama's boy just like she complains about Vito. So I take out a silver dollar I got in my pocket, that and a couple pieces of candy I brought just in case I want to talk to this kid. He looks at the mother and she says, go, it's okay. So he comes over and sits on my lap. I give him the dollar, tell him if he's a good boy he can keep it. I ask the mother to step outside, give me a little privacy with the boy. She don't like that, so I tell her to go to the front window, tell me what she sees. She goes over to the window, comes back, pats the boy on the head and leaves. Smart woman."

Left and Right chuckle with amusement at the memory.

"So I ask the kid some questions. His daddy, he ever stick anything in his butt? He ever touch his pee-pee? Why don't he like to go over his dad's house? Don't he know that if he's lying his old man could go to jail? Why would he want to do that?

"The kid just looks at me with those big eyes. He don't say nothing. I give him a piece of candy. He takes it and puts it in his mouth but he still don't say nothing. Now all this time, I'm very calm. He starts to cry. He wants his mommy. I tell him we ain't done yet. He can't see his mommy until we're done. He's gotta answer my questions first. The fucking kid starts to lose it. He gets down and goes to run to the door. I gotta grab him by the shirt. He's crying, I pick him up in the air and I shake him until he shuts up. I tell him I'm his grandfather and when your grandfather asks you a question you answer him. He just started screaming for his mother and he wouldn't shut up. The mother started screaming for the kid. This wasn't getting anywhere. I wanted to smack them both. I gave the kid back to his mother and told her not to talk to anyone about this, that I'd fix the problem.

"The bitch, she overheard me tell the kid I'm his grandfather. She calls Vito and tells him, 'You know that old man came by, your uncle, he's your fucking father.' Vito, he calls me, he says stay outta my life. You think you can just snap your fingers and make it all good. No thank you. I don't need your fucking help. You didn't have time for me, well now I ain't got time for you." He shook his head in disbelief. "So here we are."

Here we are indeed. Just click my ruby slippers three times and I'm gone. "What do you want from me?"

He looked at me incredulously, as if I had just barked or honked like a goose. "Ain't you been listening? I want to know what's happening here. There is no way anybody is gonna molest my grandson, no way. But if Vito ain't doin' it then there's no way he's gonna have a fuckin' social worker with him, watching him like he's some kind of pervert.

"This is my family. My son wants to be with his son, he's gonna be with his son. I gotta know the truth. What's happening. Then I know what I gotta do. I gotta know now. If my son didn't do it then he should be out in the park with his son right now, this minute, throwing him a ball, whatever they want to do. If he did do it, then it isn't gonna happen again, ever. That's what I want. I ain't waitin' two months for you to get around to me. I want the truth, and I want it now."

"What if you can't have that?" I asked, aware of a faint stirring of pleasure at his impotence.

"What do you mean?"

"I mean, what if the truth can't be known. Can't be proven. What if there's doubt about if anything really happened?"

"No." He shook his head rejecting that possibility. "It either did or it didn't happen. That's all you gotta tell me. I gotta know for sure. I can't be worrying the rest of my life, I made a mistake; that's he's sticking his fuckin' cock up my grandson's ass—you hear me? That ain't gonna happen." He got right in my face and jabbed home each word with the end of a finger, typing out his frustration on the keyboard of my chest.

I reached out and grabbed his wrist. "I get the point. Now you're paying me a lot of money to help you with this problem. Do you want my expert opinion or do you just want to break my ribs?"

Our eyes met like two dogs over one bone. Neither of us looked away. I let go of his wrist and he sat back. "Okay, what's your opinion?"

"When I asked you what you wanted, you said you wanted the truth. Suppose that isn't possible? Suppose you will never know without a doubt what happened? Can you accept that? Can you live with being wrong, with not protecting your grandson or with ending your son's relationship with his child for no good reason?"

"No, that's not acceptable. Those prices are too high. I want the truth. If I know the truth, I know what to do and what I do will be right."

"Then I can't help you."

"What do you mean you can't help me? You're supposed to be the best, you wrote the book, you know all there is about this shit. You're a fucking doctor, for Christ's sake."

"But I'm not God. Maybe I do know all there is, but that's a lot less than what we need to know. Even if I had an opinion about what happened, even if that was a result of all the research I know and all the skill I have, that would just be the best we can do right now, I could still be wrong. I can't guarantee you the truth, nobody can. If you can't accept that then I can't help you."

He shook his head like a buffalo beset by flies. "I don't get it. Why is this so hard? Okay, I don't know how to talk to little kids, but you do. That's your job."

I had to stifle the impulse to talk down to him, to rub his nose in his need, to hit him with fists of sarcasm, and remember that somewhere inside there was a confused parent trying to do the right thing for his kid, doing his best no matter how far it fell from being good enough.

It was also my best chance of seeing the outside of this car.

"This is why it's so hard. First, you have no witness. What-ever is or isn't happening, the only ones there are the boy and his father. He isn't going to confess. He hasn't. He denies it. Maybe it's the truth, maybe it isn't. What are you going to do? Torture it out of him? Even if he says he did it, you'll never know if that was just to end the pain. You can torture people into saying what you want to hear but not into telling you the truth. Pain trumps truth, unless you're a saint. There's no physical evidence. They checked out his butt and didn't find any fissures. But that doesn't prove anything. There's all kinds of abuse that doesn't leave physical evidence. He could be masturbating the boy or fellating him, or having the child do him. The nightmares, the fears, wanting to sleep with his mother, not wanting to go with his father, that means nothing. You see that very often with kids of his age when parents separate, especially if there's a lot of conflict. They don't want to leave the mother if she's been the primary care-taker, but after the transfer they have a good time with the dad. They return and they want to reestablish that closeness with the mother, they regress, they want to sleep with her. You don't have to have sexual abuse to explain all of that. That's one of the biggest problems. There's no set of symp-toms that separates sexual abuse from other phenomena *and* that *always* shows up with sexual abuse. Sexual abuse is a complex thing. Is the violent rape of a ten-year-old girl by a stranger the same as a father masturbating in front of his sleeping six-year-old son? No, but sexual abuse covers both things. Some kids are abused, there's no physical evidence, they make no disclosures and no one notices anything wrong from the outside. That's why this is so hard. Not only that—"

"What about him telling his mother that his daddy touches him?"

"So far, all we have is her word that he said that. Suppose I interview him and he says nothing. Does that mean she's lying, or it didn't happen, or just that I couldn't get the information from him? Suppose he recants. He catches on that everybody's upset, that he might never see his dad again, that he loves his dad, that he wants his dad so badly he'll put up with that other stuff, that it isn't so bad after all. It takes a lot for a kid to give up on a parent, usually it's the other way around. Does that mean it didn't happen? No. I've had cases where the victim was in one room recanting to me, while next door the parent was confessing to the police.

"Suppose the kid does make a disclosure to me. I do a clean interview, no suggestions, no leading questions, I get a disclosure but not a lot of details, it's a little inconsistent, the effect's unremarkable. Not a great disclosure. Does that mean nothing happened? No. Kids are abused and may never give a 'great' account of what happened to them. You get the picture? This is a high wire act on a razor blade over a minefield. Very hard to keep your balance and anywhere you come down could blow up in your face."

My host sat silent and slack, pummeled by something he couldn't bully into submission.

"I'm not done yet. Let me throw a wrinkle into all this. Suppose I make a mistake, then what?"

"What do you mean?"

"You know what I mean. Suppose I tell you your son didn't do anything. That's my expert opinion. You tell the wife that he can have visits with his son. A year later they rush the boy to the hospital with a torn anus. What are you going to do?"

A smile appeared and disappeared, as enigmatic and unmistakable as the Mona Lisa's. "I'd kill you, you fucked up like that."

"Right. So the smart play for me is to tell you that your son did molest the boy. If I'm right, he doesn't get a chance to do it again. If I'm wrong, how will you ever know? The boy is being protected from something that never happened. And it keeps on not happening. I don't even need to do an evaluation. I just have to look out for myself and cover my tracks. You said it yourself. I'm the best there is at what I do. Who's gonna catch me? I go through the motions. I build a case. The evidence could go either way. I say your son did it. Now you have to worry about whether that's what I truly believe or what I want you to believe because it's best for me. You can't have certainty, it's not there. Not for you, not for me, not for anyone.

"This is not me being too good for you. This is not about me or you. This is about the truth. The truth is the same for all of us, you, me, everybody. Nobody can get a leg up on this one. What you want, I can't deliver. No one can."

"So, what should I do, Doctor? What's your expert opinion?"

"I think you have to accept that you may never know for sure what happened. That you can live with the possibility of being wrong. If you can, then an evaluation can be a useful thing to do."

"And if I can't?"

"Then raise him yourself. That's the only way to be certain." Like an open parachute on the ground, I quickly packed up my frustration before it blew me away.

"Or maybe you decide it isn't your problem. You don't have to fix this. Just because someone presents it to you doesn't mean you have to accept it. It's not your problem until you accept it as one. You said your son didn't want your help anyway."

He looked at me like I was a talking ferret.

238

"My son is accused of diddling my grandson and I'm supposed to nod my head and say my, my isn't that something. You all get back to me when you sort that out. It isn't my problem. You're in my prayers. That's what's wrong with you people. I hear this, it is my problem. I'm not gonna walk away from it. I'm gonna fix it. That's what I do best, Doctor. I fix problems. That's why people come to me. You think I'd be where I am today if I said well, that's tough, wish I could help you with that. Come back next time with an easy one. Sorry doesn't feed the bulldog, Doctor. Problems need fixin'. Tears and sympathy, that's for women."

He leaned back and reached into his pockets. "So, what do I do with you? You think you earned that seventy-two grand?"

I pushed the envelope toward him. "Absolutely not. Here, keep it. I don't want any of it."

"Really? You sell yourself short, Doc. Maybe you didn't solve my problem, but you cleared up my thinking. That's worth something. How long we been talking, Tommy?"

Left checked his watch. "About an hour Mr. G."

"Okay, that's what, four hundred? Yeah. Tommy get that out of the bag."

Tommy reached in and counted off four one hundred dollar bills and handed them to me.

"That was for services rendered, Doctor. That means that all of this is privileged and confidential, am I right?"

The question itself was a pardon and a release. "Absolutely. Not a word of this to anyone."

"Now, get out."

No one moved, so I leaned over Tommy, grabbed the door handle, unlocked it and stumbled out into the afternoon's fading light. I turned around and tempted fate. "Just for curiosity's sake, what did you get out of all this?"

"Watching you twist and turn on my hook reminded me that when you bring a problem to me, you make a problem for me. And there's a price for that, too."

I closed the door and the limousine pulled away. Low and sleek, it turned the corner and disappeared.

I had my life back, just as I left it. Or so I thought.

A week later, I was sitting on my patio, drinking a cup of coffee and eating a bagel. The sun was bright overhead, the air crisp and cool. Winter and spring had a truce. I was skimming the newspaper. There it was, midway down page A8:

> Vito and Carla Battista were found shot to death in a parking lot outside Ms. Battista's lawyer's office, where the estranged couple had just left a meeting. Police believe the murders were a botched carjacking. The couple's only child, Salvatore, age 3, is in the care of his grandfather, reputed mob boss, Salvatore Giannini.

The State versus Adam Shelley

FORENSIC EVALUATION

This is the report of the evaluation conducted by the forensic team of the behavioral sciences division at Goldstadt Medical Center on Adam Shelley (DOB 10/31/92).

Social History

Adam's mother was Mary W. Shelley, age 19 and a college freshman. She sought genetic screening of a possible pregnancy and was informed that unusual chromosomal defects were identified. She then filed for an abortion under the rape exemption. Her request was denied because the rape was not reported within the 7-day state guidelines for the exemption to be valid. An assault report had been filed with local police but there was no mention of a rape. Subsequent to the rejection of her request she apparently sought out an illegal abortionist in the city of Charlotte. She was arrested for fetal endangerment as part of the "sting" operation of the Department of Health and Welfare, which had established "apparently" illegal abortion shops across the state. A Sanctity Of Life motion was filed by the Fetal Defense League and Miss Shelley was committed to the Jesse Helms Memorial Reproduction Center for the duration of her pregnancy.

While in the center Miss Shelley suffered serious head trauma from either a fall or a possible suicide attempt. She was placed under the care of Dr. Henry Frankenstein of the neonatal intensive care unit. Although she was brain-dead, Dr. Frankenstein was able to sustain Miss Shelley as a viable carrier for the fetus. In fact it was during this case that Dr. Frankenstein developed many of the techniques now used in the induced coma treatment for chronic miscarriage, prematurely, and pre-partum agitation in committed patients.

Subsequent to the birth of her child, Miss Shelley was maintained on life support systems and then transferred to the Raleigh-Durham Neurovegetative Center where she is still a resident. No father was ever named.

The child was named Adam Shelley by his legal guardians, the State Department of Social Services Child Protection Unit. He was raised in the pediatrics unit of the Helms Center until the age of seven. This was occasioned by the severity of his medical needs. (See findings under Physical/ Medical Information.)

At age seven he was placed in long-term foster care with the DeLacey family in Winston-Salem. This was felt to be an appropriate placement, as the father was blind and the family already had a disabled daughter, Agatha, in addition to a son, Felix. The placement seemed to go well and there was discussion of legal adoption by the DeLacey family. Unfortunately an incident occurred with a young friend of Agatha's. The child, Marian Ludwigsdottir, was two years younger than Adam. One afternoon she came to visit the children, who were under the care of Mrs. DeLacey. She called them all in for a snack and, when Marian did not come in, she went out and found her dead in the family's above-ground swimming pool. The death was formally ruled accidental and no evidence linked Adam with the death, but the DeLaceys asked that he be returned to the care of the State.

At age nine, Adam was placed outside the Helms Center for a second time. This placement was with the Sweet Love of Jesus Youth Home run by the television ministry of Billy Ray

Washburn. Adam was there for almost two years. During that time he made several suicide attempts, including one near-fatal laceration through the large vein in his eyestalk. There was some consideration that this was an expression of guilt over the death of the Ludwigsdottir girl; however, Adam never expressed any knowledge of her death.

Unfortunately this home was raided by the police in the summer of 2005 when it was discovered that certain of the children were being selected out by the staff and housed in a separate building for use as sex partners by Reverend Washburn and members of his ministry board of directors. There was no evidence uncovered that Adam Shelley was abused in this fashion. However, there were unconfirmed reports from other children that Adam was physically abused by a staff member named Fritz Harmann, and that videotapes of his abuse were shown to stimulate some of the men before they molested other children. No copies of the videotapes were ever found. What cannot be disputed is that at the time of the raid by the State Police the body of Fritz Harmann was found hanging in his room, dead of a broken neck. It is also a fact that Adam Shelley was a resident of this special ward.

Brief attempts were made to place Adam in residential schools where he could receive multi-modal therapy for his disabilities. Because of his history, age and appearance it was determined that family placement was entirely out of the question. No matter where he was placed Adam was not welcome. He was tormented by other students, no matter what their disabilities. Ultimately he was returned to the Helms Center's Adolescent and Youth Services.

While a resident there he became aware of the connection between his birth and Dr. Frankenstein. Another resident showed him the *People* Magazine article about Dr. Frankenstein's work that made reference to his early discoveries, and his original ground-breaking work on Mary Shelley and the birth of her son, Adam.

Adam showed little overt interest in Dr. Frankenstein or his birth. Pediatric records show that he entered puberty rather late, around thirteen. Shortly thereafter, violent outbursts against staff and other residents increased. Adam was placed in solitary confinement, and was so secluded when he made his escape from the Helms Center and went on his rampage.

Physical/Medical Examination

Adam Shelley is a well-nourished fourteen-year-old white male. He stands 6'7" and weighs 274 pounds. Whether his unusual size is part of his condition or a separate distinguishing feature is impossible to say.

Adam presents a mixed picture of various congenital Dysostoses, including Cleidocranial, Craniofacial (Crouzon's Disease) and Mandibulofacial (Treacher-Collins Disease or Franchescetti's Syndrome). Such a combination raises the possibility of exposure by the mother to mutagenic agents such as toxic waste or radiation. Mother's medical record, however, does not show similar symptoms.

EEG and CAT-scan were conducted while sedated, so the results are not definitive. Adam refused to cooperate with the medical examination and so had to be tranquilized by use of a dart gun and then placed in restraints. No idiopathic or otherwise unusual brain activity was noted, nor were there lesions or tumors. The history for epileptiform seizures is negative.

Visually Adam presents with acrocephaly or tower skull, enlarged parietal and frontal areas of the skull and extremely exophthalmic eyes, actually sitting on soft stalk-like protrusions. Stereoscopic vision is very poor and may well contribute to his general clumsiness and problems with gross motor articulation.

External ears are malformed; the growth of and enfolding of extraneous tissue interferes with proper reception of sound. The tissue should be considered tumor-like and surgical procedures are tantamount to pruning with rapid reappearance of the tissues.

Nostrils and sinus cavities are incomplete and not fully separated. Sense of smell is rudimentary. Highly arched cleft palate and defective dentition makes articulation extremely poor.

Early medical records show 27 separate surgeries to repair defects or halt worsening conditions. Present appearance represents maximal improvement. Rapid growth as an adolescent threatens to create further difficulties. In light of the current situation, it should be pointed out that it is unusual for such an individual to live to his current age, and maximum expected lifespan would surely not be past early twenties.

Although Adam's size is very unusual, he does not seem to suffer from Giantism. Testosterone levels are normal and genital size and structure are normal and proportionate. Neither is he abnormally hirsute. Endocrine explanations for his behavior do not seem warranted, nor would hormonal treatments, such as chemical castration, be effective.

Development, other than the massive, congenital and irreversible craniofacial deformities, seems within normal limits.

Psychological Functioning

Attempts at formal psychological testing with Adam were unsuccessful. He was presented with the Wechsler Intelligence Scale for Children—Revised (WISC-R), the Rorschach using the Exner Method and the Millon Adolescent

Personality Inventory (MAPI), and destroyed the materials. Menacing gestures towards the staff psychologist led to a termination of the testing.

Structured interviews were attempted with Adam on one side of a shatterproof plexiglass barrier. Due to the constant mucosal drip from the incomplete sinuses into the throat and other dental and palate deformities, articulation of words is extremely poor and verbal communication quite limited. A review of early school records showed at least average academic performance. In fact an early administration of the WISC-R, adapted for written responses, at age 7, just prior to the placement with the DeLacey family showed a verbal IQ of 107, Performance IQ 111, Full Scale 109, well within normal limits. There is no evidence available to us that Adam did not possess the requisite cognitive abilities to understand the consequences of his actions.

Adam was monitored by video cameras during his entire stay at Goldstadt Medical Center. Detailed analysis of vocalizations and movements showed no pattern of responses to internally generated stimuli, either as visual hallucinations or auditory command hallucinations. Instead he roamed his cell in repetitive movements much like any other higher-order zoological specimen is apt to do. Attempts to dislodge window bars or to bend the bars of his door have been unsuccessful and have decreased during his incarceration. Most of the time he sits on the floor in the far distant corner of his cell. He either cries or raps his head against the wall. Recently he has begun to pluck obsessively at his garments. No suicidal behavior has been noted but because of his early history it cannot be discounted. Constant video surveillance and the spartan nature of his quarters mean that a successful attempt is highly unlikely.

There has never been any observed history of the use of

drugs or alcohol. Blood work taken when he was apprehended showed not even trace elements of any psychoactive drugs either prescribed or illegal. A claim of diminished capacity is not supported by any evidence.

We are not privy to much of Adam Shelley's psychological make-up. This has always been the case and it is even more so now that he actively refuses to cooperate with our evaluation. No content analysis of his fantasies is possible.

His appearance has set him apart from others since birth. The lack of a stable, consistent and nurturing maternal relationship has probably impaired his capacity for all subsequent object relations. His history shows greater and greater isolation, dating from the failure of the DeLacey placement. His possible involvement in the death of the neighbor girl raises the question of early impulsivity and poor self-control even within a familial setting. That loss may have been the cause of the suicide attempts he later made. This would point to the inner experience of guilt, loss, depression and some rudimentary capacity to empathize and identify with other people. He has seriously limited ability and almost no experience in developing required social skills.

He probably experienced some degree of object hunger and experienced the end of those relationships as a loss and some depression and guilt as an expression of personal responsibility. Unfortunately his behavior since then does not point to the continued existence of such internal structures or capacities. The death of Fritz Harmann may be explained as retribution for the abuse he inflicted; however, the records at The Helms Center show no remorse, guilt or affect of any kind at the event. Indeed Adam has steadfastly refused to ever discuss anything about his stay at the Sweet Love of Jesus Youth Home.

I think it would be appropriate to consider Adam as at least an antisocial personality disorder (DSM III-R 301.70) with very limited capacity to connect or empathize with others. Previous therapy attempts with Adam have been uniformly unsuccessful. Initial attempts foundered on his sensitivity to the reactions of the therapist to his appearance. He would test these therapists by getting very close to them, opening his mouth, and exposing his rhinolaryngeal cavity to them. Eventually, he gave up on therapy and refused to participate. His condition at this time should be considered permanent and not subject to remediation. The prognosis of coerced psychotherapy is notoriously poor.

Violence Assessment

This assessment will utilize a combined clinical and actuarial prediction model. Current data sources cannot be used, as Adam Shelley has refused to co-operate with the evaluation. We must rely upon interpretation of the evidence compiled by the police during their investigation.

Actuarial Variables

Age: Currently Adam is fourteen. While at one time this would have been considered early onset of a history of violence, this is no longer the case. What is of more importance is whether to date the first violent episode to the death of Marian Ludwigsdottir at age 7 or the death of Fritz Harmann at age 12. The evidence in these matters is highly equivocal. A cautious interpretation, attempting to minimize the probability of a false negative, would use the age of onset as 7. This is still statistically rare and an ominous prognostic sign.

Sex: Male. Unremarkable. The finding that at least 90% of all violent episodes are male activities has been a durable one.

Race: Caucasian. This factor weighs against a prediction of risk. Statistically, in the United States, more violence is committed by minority group members. What is consistent with previous race studies is that both offender and victim(s) were of the same racial group.

Socio-economic Status: As an adolescent it is premature to definitely assign Adam Shelley to a particular social class. However, based on other highly correlated factors, a reasonable prediction can be made. 1. Family of Origin—Adam has been raised, with brief interludes, as a ward of the state and in institutional settings. Ultimate social class attainment for adults with this background correlates very highly with the distribution for children of single-parent unskilled labor families. 2. Educational/Occupational Level—Adam has never attended public schools. He has been educated as part of his treatment in residential hospital settings. Converting his current education achievements to public school equivalents, we believe him to be at least two years behind, possibly four. Likely occupational status is low. His lack of schooling, poor socialization and appearance would make it hard for him to work even on an assembly line. Due to his size and prodigious strength a case might be made for a higher standard of living in an isolated high-risk job such as a Game Warden in a sector with a high incidence of poaching and food hoarding.

Clinical Variables

History of Violence: Our approach relies upon a modified Kleinholz-Wessel Model. Case assumptions are that probability increases with each event, becoming a certainty at N5, and that the most important features of the pattern of events are: 1. Recency, 2. Severity, 3. Frequency, and an escalation in those features.

Most Recent Episode: The roots of the most recent episode of violence lay in a series of letters written by Adam Shelley to Dr. Henry Frankenstein. These letters were in the possession of Henry Clerval, Dr. Frankenstein's personal attorney. He informed the police that it was his advice to Dr. Frankenstein that he not reply to the letters because he felt that they were a precursor to a malpractice suit.

The essence of the letters (there were three) was Adam's belief that Dr. Frankenstein had an obligation to him to "locate and provide others of my kind" to ease the loneliness he felt due to repeated rejections by other people. The second letter contained vague threats against people in general but without any named victims. The last letter concluded with a vow to "ruin your life as you have ruined mine."

It was only three weeks after sending that letter that Adam Shelley escaped from the Helms Center. Dr. Frankenstein's home address was in the telephone book. It must be concluded that Adam made his way there on foot that evening. There were no reports of anyone sighting him en route.

Dr. Frankenstein had just recently been married, for the first time, to Elizabeth Lavenza. His wife had been an intensive-care nurse at the hospital where Dr. Frankenstein was Chief of Neonatology.

In the home that evening were Dr. Frankenstein's younger brother, William, a close personal friend, Victor Moritz, who had been best man at the wedding, and his father, Alphonse Frankenstein.

What follows is the official recreation of the crime scene by the police forensics experts. It is believed that Adam Shelley hid by the large bushes alongside the garage. When Victor Moritz opened the garage door to park the car he had borrowed, Adam Shelley slipped into the garage and hid in the shadows. Victor Moritz left the car and went into the house through the inside door. It was at that time that Adam Shelley gripped Victor Moritz from behind and strangled him with his bare hands.

Entering the house, it appears that Adam Shelley was seen by William Frankenstein, who screamed and attempted to flee the house. He was caught by Adam Shelley, who seized him by the neck with such force that while shaking him the spinal cord was severed and the spine itself broken at the topmost cervix. The boy's body was flung into the fireplace.

William's father, Alphonse, apparently awakened by the sounds of the struggle, came upon the scene of his son being murdered and suffered a sudden, massive and fatal heart attack.

Dr. Frankenstein and his wife were last seen leaving a party at 10:30 p.m. They probably arrived home around 10:50 p.m. Adam Shelley made no effort to hide the bodies and apparently waited for them in the darkened living room.

When Dr. Frankenstein entered the house, he was struck a blow on the side of the head and knocked unconscious. What follows is from the final statements by Dr. Frankenstein before his death en route to the hospital.

Dr. Frankenstein and his wife, who had passed out, were carried upstairs to their bedroom. Mrs. Frankenstein was placed on the bed and the Doctor bound to his desk chair with his neckties.

When he came to, he found Adam Shelley stroking the breast of his still unconscious wife. He demanded that he stop, and the boy laughed at him. He reminded the Doctor of his request that he provide him with others like himself and that he hadn't even bothered to respond. He said that he had originally planned to come to the house and kill Dr. Frankenstein for "forcing life upon me, a life beyond the reach of love," but now he had fashioned a more fitting revenge. He would let Dr. Frankenstein live but would take his wife and make her his own. He intended to make her pregnant and thereby create a family for himself in his own image, children to love and be loved by in return. Obviously Adam's plan was doomed. He had no appreciation of how hard it would be to create another like him even if he were the father.

Adam Shelley then proceeded to rape Elizabeth Lavenza Frankenstein in front of her husband. While this was going on Dr. Frankenstein managed to work free from his bonds and threw himself at Adam Shelley. They struggled and Adam hoisted the Doctor overhead and threw him down the flight of stairs, where he suffered major cranial trauma.

Elizabeth Frankenstein attempted to flee out an upstairs window, but was caught by Adam Shelley. Leaving the house, with Mrs. Frankenstein over his shoulder, he stopped and dipped his fingers in Henry Frankenstein's blood and left a message on the mirror by the front door: "If not love, then fear me."

He then fled into the rapidly falling December snow. Henry Frankenstein managed to drag himself out of the front door of the house, where he was seen by a neighbor across the street who called the police.

Adam Shelley became the immediate object of an intensive statewide manhunt. The next day he was cornered in a nearby barn and captured. Before he surrendered, he held the body of Elizabeth Frankenstein overhead and broke her neck.

Prediction of Future Violence

Drawing on the psychological and medical findings, the social history and the recreation of the most recent violent episode, we offer the following predictions.

Violence exists as a potential within us all. There is a constant dynamic flux between those forces that inhibit its expression and those motives that it expresses. Violence occurs when a particular external situation or set of relationships destabilizes the balance of forces within an individual. A prediction of future violence must attempt to describe those forces, the stability of their balance, and what the likelihood is of a provocative situation occurring.

Adam Shelley is a permanently disfigured young man who interprets the reactions of others to his appearance as rejection. Although at one point in time that rejection may have resulted in hurt and sadness, it now sparks anger and rage. Adam's appearance is not alterable. Frankly, it is unlikely that the response to him by others can be altered either. Therefore social interactions pose a constant risk of provocation. Therapy to alter his responses to others is unlikely to be successful.

None of the emotions of "conscience" seem to operate within Adam Shelley at this time. He has shown no remorse or guilt over any of his actions. Whatever rudimentary capacity for empathy he may have had now seems gone. He views himself as something other than a human being, reducing his capacity to identify with them. Fear of retribution does not seem to motivate him. Indeed, it may be argued that he would seek out and welcome retaliation as an indirect form of suicide.

Adam's history of violence shows an increase in recency, severity and frequency. One may characterize the early episodes as accidental or retributive, but the deaths of William Frankenstein and Victor Moritz were merely expedient as means to his end, and that of Elizabeth Lavenza Frankenstein lapsed into the sadistic.

Conclusions

In sum, Adam Shelley seems a boy lacking in internalized inhibitors to violence, likely to run into many provocative situations, and now with a history that makes it almost certain that he will resort to violence again. Technically, the crimes that Adam Shelley is charged with constitute a mass murder, although his transportation of Elizabeth Lavenza Frankenstein argues for a classification as a spree killer. It is the opinion of this team that if allowed to return to society Adam Shelley would pose a constant high risk to kill again.

A number of mitigating conditions were explored in regards to criminal intent. No unusual brain pathology was noted, nor any neuro-hormonal disorders. Diminished capacity due to substance abuse, intentional or otherwise, was ruled out. Intelligence was deemed adequate to distinguish right from wrong. There was no evidence of psychotic process or command hallucinations. The crimes in question cannot be deemed to have arisen from an irresistible impulse. The original threat occurred in a letter mailed three weeks prior to the attack. There is clear evidence of planning and intentionality. During the crime, Adam Shelley reiterated his motive when he wrote in Henry Frankenstein's blood, "If not love, then fear me."

Recommendations

Reviewing the evidence accumulated by this team we must conclude that Adam Shelley was criminally responsible for the deaths of William, Alphonse, Elizabeth and Henry Frankenstein and Victor Moritz. We also conclude that he poses a constant high risk to kill again if released into society.

Despite his age, we cannot find any reason to reduce his sentence or grant a stay of execution.

M. Waldman, M.D., Ph.D.
Chief, Forensic Services
Behavioral Sciences Division
Goldstadt Medical Center

THE POLICE

AVERY BITTERMAN

MAX KINCAID

Christmas in Dodge City

Sharnella Watkins had never walked into a police station in her life. She'd been tossed in delirious or drunk, carried in kicking and screaming, and marched in on a manacled chorus line. But walk in on her own, never. That would have been like sex. Another thing that if it was up to her, she'd never do.

She checked both ways before she crossed the street, searching for witnesses, not traffic, and clattered over on her nosebleed heels.

She knocked on the bulletproof plastic at the information center.

The desk sergeant looked up from his racing form. "Help you, ma'am?"

"I'd like to talk to that detective, the big one. He's bald and he gots a beard down in front, ah, you know, ah Van Dyke they calls it, oh yeah, he wears glasses, too."

"That's detective Bitterman, ma'am, and why would you like to talk to him?"

"It's personal."

"Well, he's working now. Why don't you come back when his shift ends?"

"When's that?"

"Six o'clock."

"I can't wait that long. Can you give me his phone number? I'll call him."

"Sorry, ma'am, I can't do that. Unless you're family. You aren't family, are you?" The desk man sniggered. Big Bad Bitterman and this itty-bitty black junkie whore.

"No, I guess you're not. Sorry 'bout that." The desk man

looked down, trying to root out a winner in all those optimistic names.

Sharnella knew the truth would be pointless, but along with a nonexistent gag reflex, the other gift that had kept her alive on the streets all these years was the unerring ability to pick the right lie when she had to.

She leaned forward so that her bright red lips were only inches from the divider and sneered. Then, shaking her head, she said, "You think you're so smart. Well, lets me tell you something. It ain't me what needs him. He's been looking for me. He wants to talk to me. And now, I'm telling you both, to go fuck yo'selves. I ain't coming back, and I ain't gonna talk to him and . . ." She got close enough for the desk man to count her missing molars: "I'm gonna tell him it was your sorry bullshit what pissed me off and he should see you 'bout why he can't solve no cases no more."

The desk man had been following her little breadcrumbs of innuendo and found himself ending up face to face with Mount Bitterman. The explosion wouldn't be that bad. Bitterman had made enough enemies that if he declared you one, you'd as likely be toasted as shunned. Bitterman never forgot and never forgave.

The desk man had endured too much inexplicable disappointment and loss to risk an angry Bitterman.

As Sharnella turned to walk away, the desk man said: "Hold your horses, bitch. This is his number at headquarters." He wouldn't write it down for her, hoping her memory would fail. She'd be fucked and Bitterman would have no cause. As she backed away, mouthing the numbers to fix them in her disloyal mind, the desk man said, "You know Bitterman only listens to the dead. I hope you find him soon."

Across town, Detective Avery Bitterman reached down and pulled on his dick. One of the advantages of a closed front desk. He'd notice himself doing this more since his divorce. A dispassionate review told him that it wasn't for pleasure but rather to reassure himself that he was still all there, a feeling he had less and less often these days.

The receptionist at headquarters told him that he had a call from a Sharnella Watkins and that she said it was an emergency. "Put it through," he said.

"Is this Detective Bitterman?"

"Yes, it is. How may I help you?"

"You probably don't remember me, but I remembers you. You arrested my boy Rondell. You was the only one who didn't beat up on him. You wouldn't let nobody hurt him."

Bitterman shook his head, remembering. That's right, ma'am. I wouldn't let them lynch him. I thought it would be more fitting if your son got sent to Lorton, where he could meet the two sons of the woman he raped, sodomized, and tortured to death. Those mother's sons and some friends tied him down, inserted a hedge shears up Rondell's ass, opened him up and strung his intestines around him like he was a Christmas tree. When, to their delight, this didn't kill him, they poured gasoline over him like he was a sundae and set him on fire.

"No, I do remember you, Sharmella."

"SharNella." She knew she was right to call this man. He remembered her. He would help her.

"It's my baby, Dantreya. He's gone, Mr. Bitterman. I know he's in some kind of trouble . . ."

What a fuckin' surprise. "Ma'am, I'm a homicide detective. You want to go to your local district house and file a missing persons report. I can't help you with this."

"Please, Mr. Bitterman. They won't do anything. They'll just say, 'That's what kids do,' and with me as a mother why not stay out all night. But he's not like that. He's different than my others. He's a good boy. He goes to school. He's fifteen and he never been in no trouble. Never, not even little things. He likes to draw. He wants to be an artist. You should come and see what he draws. Please, Mr. Bitterman, he's all I got left. It's Christmas tomorrow. I just want my baby home." Wails gave way to staccato sobbing.

Sharnella's tears annoyed Bitterman. I'm a homicide detective, that's what I do, he said to no one. I can't deal with this shit. It ain't my job. Come back when he's dead. Then I'll listen.

"Ma'am, I'm sorry. I understand how you feel. But the beat cops can keep an eye out for him. You tell them where he's likely to go. That's your best bet, not me. I'm sorry. I gotta go now."

Bitterman hung up over her wailing "No's." Where was he going to go? He was head of the cold case squad. These days, everything was a cold case. Arrest and conviction rates were lower for homicide than for jaywalking. The killers were younger, bolder and completely without restraint. The law of the jungle, "an eye for an eye," would have been a welcome relief. The law of the streets was "an eye for a hangnail." Everything was a killing offense. Motive was nothing, opportunity and means were ubiquitous. Children packed lunchbox, thermos, and sidearm in their knapsacks for school. The police were the biggest provider of handguns. Three thousand had disappeared from the city's property rooms to create more dead bodies that the medical examiner's office couldn't autopsy, release or bury. That for Bitterman was the guiding symbol of his work these days. Handguns on a conveyor belt back to the streets, and the frozen dead serving longer and longer sentences in eternity's drunk tank.

The phone jerked Bitterman back from his reverie.

"Mr. Bitterman, this is Sharnella Watkins. Don't hang up

on me. I can help you. My boy's gone, 'cause they want to kill him."

"Who's they, Sharnella?"

"The 6th and O Crew."

"Sharnella, you said your son had never been in trouble. The 6th and O Crew is nothing but. Why am I listening to this?"

"He didn't do nothing. He was coming home from school with a trophy he got at a art show, and Lufer tried to take it from him, but my baby wouldn't give it to him and when Lufer tried again he hit him with it and knocked him down and my baby ran off. He said Lufer went to get his gun and was yellin' that he'd kill him for sure. And he would, that boy's purely mean. He kill you for no reason."

"Sharnella, this still doesn't help me. Get to the help-me part or I'm hangin' up."

Sharnella had never given a policeman a straight answer in her life. But her baby was in danger. Sharnella never stopped to think why she felt so differently about this child, her fourth, than any of the others, only that she did and that his death, after all the others, would kill her too.

"This boy, Lufer Timmons. He's killed a bunch of people. That's what everybody says. Everybody afraid of him. They say he's the Crew's main shooter. But he does it when it ain't business, just 'cause he likes it. And he said he'll kill my boy. Doesn't that help you, Mr. Bitterman?"

The Crew favored death as a solution to all its problems. Giving the delivery man a name was a help. "Tell you what, Sharnella. You go over to the station house like I said and give 'em all the information about your son. Bring a picture, a list of all of his friends and where they live, and where he's been known to hang out. Tell them to fax me a copy of all that. I'll look into it."

261

Her story was probably 90 percent bullshit and 10 percent horseshit for flavor, but Bitterman knew he'd check it out. You turned over every rock and picked up every squiggling thing. That was his motto: No Corner Too Deep, No Corner Too Dark.

Bitterman tried to remember Sharnella from her second son's trial. She'd started dropping babies at fourteen and was done before twenty. That'd make her around thirty-five now. She looked fifty. Flatbacking and mainlining aged women with interest. Beginning as a second-generation whore, Sharnella's childhood had been null and void; her prime had passed unnoticed, one sweaty afternoon in a New York Avenue motel.

Bitterman was more aware of time than ever before. He'd lifted and run and dragged his ugly white man's game to basketball courts all over the city. Elbow and ass, he rebounded with the best even though he couldn't jump over a dime. No one ever forgot a pick he set or an outlet pass that went end to end, but he remembered not to shoot too often or try to dribble and run at the same time. His twenties and thirties didn't seem all that different, but now at forty-five he knew he wasn't the same man. Bald by choice, rather than balding. Thicker but not yet fat, slower both in reflexes and foot speed. Maybe mellowing was nothing more than realizing that he couldn't tear the doors off the world anymore. The long afternoon of invincibility had passed.

Sharnella's second son, Jabari, had killed a rival drug dealer in a rip-off attempt that also killed a nursing student driving by. Her only daughter, Female, with a short "a" and a long "e," so named by the hospital and then taken by Sharnella, who liked the sound of it, had died of an overdose of extremely good cocaine at the age of sixteen. Everything she delivered died or killed someone else.

Bitterman called down to Identification and Records.

"Get me the file on Lufer Timmons. If there's a picture make a copy for me and send it up with the file. And see if there's a file on Dantreya Watkins."

Bitterman sat at his desk awaiting the files, massaging his eyes.

Bitterman had tried to catch a case of racism for years, a really virulent one, but to no avail. He had mumps when he needed anthrax. It would have made his job so much easier. No sadness for the wasted lives, no respect for the courage of the many, no grief for the victims, no compassion for the survivors.

He'd been a homicide cop in a black city for almost his entire adult life. He'd seen every form of violence one person could do to another. He'd seen black women who'd drowned their own babies, and ones who'd ripped their own flesh at the chalk outlines of a fallen son. Men who'd shot and stabbed an entire family, then eaten the dinner off their plates and men who'd worked three jobs for a lifetime, so their children wouldn't have to. Bitterman just didn't get it, how anyone could conclude that they were all of a kind, that they were different and less. He wished he could, it saved on the wear and tear.

When he opened his eyes again, he saw the Lufer Timmons file on the desk and a note saying no file on that Watkins. Maybe he was his mother's pride and joy.

Lufer Timmons had been raised by strangers, starting with his parents and moving on to a series of foster homes, residential treatment centers, detention centers and jails. Now at seventeen, he was well on his way to evening the score with a number of crimes to his credit starting with the attempted rape of his therapist at the age of eleven.

Bitterman studied the picture of Timmons. Six one and a

hundred sixty-eight pounds. He had a long face with deep crevices in his cheeks, thin lips, a thin nose, prominent cheekbones, and bulging froggy eyes. Bitterman pocketed one photo, Xeroxed the page of known associates and family and put the file in his desk drawer. A call to operations yielded the very pleasant news that one of his known associates was currently in custody at the downtown detention center.

Bitterman drove slowly along "The Stroll" looking for Sunshine, as in "put a little Sunshine in your day," her marketing pitch to the curbside crawlers. Sunshine was a six-foot redhead, natural, with alabaster skin, emerald green eyes and surgically perfected tits. Bitterman had decided that Sunshine was going to be his Christmas present to himself. He wasn't even sure he wanted to have sex with her. He just wanted to look at her, all of her, without having to hurry, like when she was on display, so he could memorize her beauty. Lately he'd been thinking about what he had to show for forty-five years, and all the fucks of a lifetime hadn't stayed with him as sharply as his memory of her on a warm summer's eve, leaning against a lamppost, trying to stay one lick ahead of a fast-melting vanilla cone. Her tongue moving rapidly up the sides of the cone until anticipating defeat, she engulfed the whole mound and sucked it out of the cone. Beauty baffled Bitterman. It seemed fundamental and indivisible. He could not break down his response into pieces or explain it away by recourse to another force or power. Sunshine was perfect and her beauty touched him in a way he couldn't avoid. He hoped that she wouldn't be easy to find. He knew that she would turn out to have bad teeth and bray like a donkey.

Lafonzo Nellis was waiting for Bitterman in interrogation

room six. Bitterman sat down and the guard left.

"So, Lafonzo. Tell me about Lufer Timmons."

"Fuck you."

"Glad we got that cleared up. Let me give you some context, here, Lafonzo, before you get into more trouble than you can get out of. Because it's Christmas, God gave me three wishes. The first is a known acquaintance of Lufer Timmons in custody, that's you. The second is to have you locked up but not papered. The third is up to you. See, if you don't talk to me, that's okay. I hear that Lufer is a reasonable man, fair with his friends, not likely to do anything rash. I'm gonna leave here, head over to 6th and O and start asking about Lufer, and talking loud about how much help you were to me. The street bull who brought you in hasn't papered you yet. He can let you go and he doesn't have to explain a thing. You're just DWOP: Dropped Without Prosecution. Now, I hear that a lot of your buddies saw you get busted and righteously, too. How you gonna explain being out of here right after we talk? Huh?"

"You ain't got the juice to make that happen."

"Oh, yeah. You been around, Lafonzo. Let's get a reality check here. You know that a street bull's got two jobs. His shift and court time. Court time is time and a half. You sit on your butt, you drink coffee, you tell lies, you hit on the chippies, nobody's shooting at you, and it's time and a half. Now, I just promised that guy I'd list him as a witness on my next two homicide trials. They're usually three or four days each. Easy time, easy money. What do you got to offer him?"

Lafonzo had a friend who was a cop and he'd pocketed $100,000 in court time and he'd only made three arrests all year. Lafonzo had a vision of trying to 'splain everything to Lufer. Lafonzo made his mind up immediately and forever.

"Okay, okay. What do you want to know?"

"We'll start with the easy stuff. I got a picture of Lufer from his last arrest. Look at it, tell me if he's changed any."

He slid the picture across the table. Lafonzo didn't pick it up. "Yeah, that's him. He ain't changed none."

"Okay, so tell me about him. What's he like?"

"He's a crazy man. I mean, what you want to know? He's in the Crew, 6th and O. You know what that means. I don't got to tell you. Let's just leave it at this, if there's trouble, Lufer fixes it. Period. Understand?"

"We're getting there. If I was to go lookin' for him, where would I find him?"

"Dude moves around a lot. See, there's plenty of other people, like to find him, too, you see what I'm saying. If he has a pad, it's a secret to me."

"What kind of car does he drive?"

"A 'Vette, a black one."

"You know the year, the tags?"

"No, man. Why should I care?"

Bitterman knew he'd find no such car legally registered to Timmons.

"Okay, where does he hang out? I'm gonna put a man at 6th and O with his picture every day from now on. So where else will he show up?"

Lafonzo was running out of room for evasions; a full-blown lie was called for here. But present danger prevailed over the future.

"They's a few bars he fancies. Nairobi Jones, Langtry's, the Southeaster."

"What else can you tell me? Any trademarks, things that he favors?"

"I don't know. He always wears that long coat. You know, the ones that go down to your boots."

"A duster?" Bitterman was finally interested.

"Yeah."

"What color?"

"Dark. Dark red."

"Like burgundy?"

"Yeah."

"What's it made of?"

"Leather. Musta cost plenty."

"What about a bandanna?"

"Yeah, that too. He wears it around his neck, not on his head."

Glory to God. The red leather duster and the bandanna could make him "Johnny-Jump-Out," wanted in six daylight shootings. Bitterman put what he knew from the files together with Nellis's information and began to understand his quarry a little better.

"He fancies himself quite a shootist, doesn't he?" Bitterman began. "No back of the ear, hands tied, in a dark room for him. I admire that. Straight up in your face, shoot and shoot back. He must have quite a reputation in the 'hood. You don't fuck with Lufer Timmons, do you?"

"What do you need me for? You seem to know everything."

"That I do, Lafonzo. I know that Lufer steals a car when he's gonna whack someone. He's got a driver he trusts. He cruises the streets till he finds his target, then he jumps out, which is why we call him 'Johnny-Jump-Out.' No pussy bullshit drive-bys for our Johnny, no, he jumps out, calls the target by name, pulls his piece and does it right there, trading gunfire on the street, broad daylight, then back in the car and he's gone. Cool customer, our Lufer, drawing down on a man telling him you're gonna kill him and then doing it. Nice gun he uses, too, .44 Magnum. Holds on to it.

Does he wear a holster, Lafonzo?"

"Yeah."

"Tell me about it."

"What for?"

"Because I want to know, Lafonzo."

"It's on his left hip, facing the other way."

"A cross-draw, how elegant. And so cocky. Most guys just shoot and throw down. He doesn't think he's gonna get caught. I know he wears armor because one guy hit him right in the chest before Lufer put one between his eyes."

"So how come you know so much, you ain't got him yet?"

"All we had was an M.O. No pattern to his killings. Now, I know that there isn't one. Lufer gets hot, you get shot. Now I've got a name, a description, and some places to look for him. He got a name for himself? All the great ones had nick-names. What about Lufer?"

"Fuck, man, he don't need no nickname. You hear Lufer Timmons looking for you, that's like hearing the Terminator wants you."

Bitterman pocketed his photograph and smiled at Lafonzo. "I guess you'll be wanting to spend some time in-doors, right?"

Lafonzo sat up straight. "Don't you be putting me out there, now. That motherfucker'll kill me."

"Relax. I'm not gonna screw around with you. I'll make sure you're papered and held, maybe get you a nice high bond you can't post. How's that sound?"

"Great. Fuckin' great. Thanks."

No other city in the world had as much of its population behind bars. Even the bad guys prefer to be in jail rather than on the streets. Bitterman was optimistic about nailing Timmons. A guy so caught up in building a reputation wouldn't be able to wait for it to be bestowed upon him. He'd help it along with plenty of boasting. All they had to do was find the right pair of ears. Secondly, he liked his gun too much. Holding on to that was a mistake. If they found that, they'd match it to bullets in his six victims. Once he was off the streets, they'd go back and talk to the deaf, dumb, and blind who'd seen and heard everything and convince just one of them to talk. Once gone he would not be coming back.

Bitterman left the detention center to get an arrest warrant from a judge. If he got it soon, it'd make the 3 p.m. roll call for the next shift. By tomorrow morning, every active duty officer on the streets would be looking for Lufer Timmons. A Christmas present to the city.

Dantreya Watkins had been going about this all wrong. He'd approached the "gangstas" on the street looking for a piece and received the short course on urban economics: Desperation drives the price up, not down. Once his ignorance of makes and models was established, his "brothers" tried to sell him .25-caliber purse guns for four hundred bucks. Poverty only served to delay his fleecing. After three unsuccessful tries, he knew enough to ask for a .380 Walther. That seemed to be a respectable gun. He found a kindly gentleman who sold him such a gun and a full clip of ammo for three hundred bucks, which was all the money he could steal from his mother.

It wasn't until later, in an abandoned warehouse when Dantreya squeezed off a practice round and saw the cartridge roll out of the end of the barrel that he learned that the clip was full of .32 caliber ammo and completely useless. Dantreya was now armed with a three-hundred-dollar hammer.

Dantreya's descent into the all-too-real world, far from the comics he read, rewrote, and illustrated in his room was now complete. He was waiting nervously at the side of his friend TerrAnce's house for TerrAnce to get his father's gun for him. In exchange, Dantreya had offered TerrAnce his entire collection of *X-Men* comics, which they would go get as soon as TerrAnce lifted the gun from his father's holster in the closet.

TerrAnce pushed open the ripped screen door with his shoulder and, holding the gun carefully in both hands, took the steps, one at a time. He walked around the side of the house and approached Dantreya, both hands grasping the trigger and pointing the gun at him. Dantreya stepped aside as gracefully as any matador and took the gun out of his friend's hands.

"Thanks man," he said, as he spun the chambers of the revolver. The bullets looked like the right size. Now, all he had to do was find Lufer Timmons. His older friends could help with that.

TerrAnce looked at him expectantly. Dantreya slipped the gun into his jacket and shrugged, "Hey man, I gotta go. I'll get you your stuff and bring it right back."

That said, he took off across the street and ran up the alley away from his friend TerrAnce, now crying with all the disappointment an eight-year-old has.

Bitterman pulled up to the corner of 6th and O. He got out and put the cherry on the roof to simplify things for the locals. Up here, a white man with an attitude had to be crazy or a cop. Bitterman wanted to make sure they made the right choices.

Fats Taylor was poured over a folding chair.

"The fuck you doin' up here, Bitterman?" Fats asked, his chest heaved with the effort of speech.

"Just came up to hear myself talk, Fats. You bein' such a good listener and all."

"I hear everything, sees everything, and knows everything." Fats chuckled and smiled.

And eats everything, Bitterman thought.

"I'm looking for a faggoty little nigger, name of Lufer Timmons, you know him?"

Fats's face sealed over, as smooth and black as asphalt in August.

"Well, you listen, Fats, and I'll talk to myself. This little queer thinks he's a real pistolero, a gunslinger. Well, I think he's a coward. I know who he's shot, where, when, and why. Pretty tough with kids, and cripples, spaced-out druggies, welshing gamblers that don't carry. You tell him I'm looking for him, Fats. And you know who I've put in the ground."

Bitterman closed his show, went back to his car and drove away. Fats could be counted on to spread the word, emphasizing every insult. A punk like Timmons; to whom respect was fear and fear was all, wouldn't let this pass. Bitterman was already wearing armor and would until Lufer was taken in. Although facing a .44 Magnum he might just as well be wearing sun block.

Bitterman repeated his performance in Nairobi Jones and the Southeaster.

For fun, in Nairobi Jones, he told them he was Charlie Siringo, the Pinkerton who single-handedly tracked the Wild Bunch until they fled to South America. In the Southeaster he was Heck Thomas, one of the legendary "Oklahoma Guardsmen."

Bitterman wanted Lufer to stay put, and challenging him would do that. He wanted him angry and impulsive, so he insulted him. He wanted him confused, so he multiplied his pursuers.

Bitterman drove over to Langtry's via all the "cupcake corners" in the first district. His latest ex-partner had suggested that the politically correct term for these young ladies was "vertically challenged," and they should be so described in all police reports. Bitterman got himself a new partner. He'd seen only a few working girls out on the sidewalks. Cold weather and the new law that allowed the city to confiscate the cars of the johns caught soliciting had forced one more evolution in the pursuit of reckless abandon. Now the girls drove endlessly around the block until they pulled up alongside a likely customer. The negotiations had more feeling than the foreplay to follow. Then a quick sprint to lose a police pursuit and the happy couple was free to lay down together, take aim and miss each other at point-blank range.

Sunshine's Mercedes was off line. Bitterman figured she was probably curled up with some rich young defense attorney in one of the city's better hotels. Next to a Sugar Daddy John, a Galahad Defense Attorney was a girl's best chance to get off the streets and get some instant respectability. Just another reason to hate those scumbags. Bitterman gave up after talking to Betty Boop. She'd shown up around the same time as Sunshine, and Bitterman had fancied her, too. Now her looks had gone like last week's snow.

Bitterman pulled up across the street from Langtry's and started over when he saw Sunshine's Mercedes. He turned back and got into his car to consider his options. If she was in Langtry's alone, he'd pick her up and put her somewhere until he was done looking for Lufer and then celebrate Christmas Eve with her. If she was somewhere else nearby and he went in looking for Lufer, he'd miss her when she came out. He didn't like that plan much. Of course, she could be with someone else already. As long as it wasn't some fuckin' defense attorney he'd flash some badge, heft a little gun and requisition her on police business. Bitterman decided that this year the city could wait to get his gift.

He hadn't been this excited since he was four years old and came down in the middle of the night to see if Santa had brought the baseball glove that would make him Willie Mays. Just give me this one thing, Lord, just because it's something I can ask for. Everything else I lack is so huge, so vague, so damned close that I don't even know what I'm looking for.

Dantreya Watkins hurried halfway down the alley, then slowed and moved cautiously along the wall to the intersection with the street. He was trying to think of what his heroes would do. Batman would swoop from the dark and knock Lufer down, then disarm him, tie him up, and leave him for the police. The Punisher would kick down a door and come in guns blazing. Dantreya tried to conjure courage but all he got was a tremor in his legs and a wave of nausea. He turned back to the alley and threw up all over his shoes. Courage had not delivered him to this place. He had nowhere near enough money to pay for Lufer's death, and he could not imagine running away to live elsewhere. He could leave his world as a superhero, but not as himself. Like his mother, he had an allergy to the police and would not take a step toward one. He knew Lufer was a guarantee of death, only the date on the death certificate was missing. His fears and beliefs, what was impossible and what was certain, had brought him to this alley. His mind had painted him into a corner and it didn't bother with a small brush.

The tremor in his legs increased and Dantreya gripped the pistol in his pocket even tighter, hoping that would slow down the shaking that surged through him. He thanked God for the gun. Without it he knew he was a dead man looking to lie down.

Forty minutes later Lufer Timmons in his long red duster

273

pushed open the door to Langtry's and stepped out onto the sidewalk. Avery Bitterman sat up, cursing his luck that Timmons would be the one to show first. Timmons held the door and his companion stepped out into the night. She really was lovely, a thick mane of brick red hair, pale skin and deep dimples when she smiled. Sunshine, in her knee-high boots, towered over Lufer, who traveled up her length slowly, appreciating every inch of her. He was gonna love climbing up this one. Lufer wasn't particularly fond of white meat, but that crazy honky who'd been jivin' with him put him in the mood to fuck this bitch cross-eyed, then maybe mess her up some. Called him a faggot, a punk. He'd show him who the real man was. First he'd teach this white bitch about black lovin'. That'd ruin her for white dick. Then he'd go find that motherfucka, kneecap him, make him beg for the bullet, then shove his gun all the way up his ass before he did him. Lufer smiled, goddamn that felt good. Life was good to Lufer, offering him so many avenues to pleasure.

Sunshine slipped her arm through his and they walked down the street, Lufer showin' off his prize and she whispering in his ear about what she had in mind for him. Bitterman let them pass his car, then got out and walked up the opposite sidewalk. Oh my, he said to himself as he felt something leak out of him. Sunshine was still as beautiful as ever, but her smile as she lay her head on Lufer's shoulder was not one he wanted anymore. He couldn't kid himself about what they would mean to each other, not any longer anyway.

Lufer pushed open the door to a three-story walk-up between a Brazilian restaurant and an erotic lingerie store. Bitterman pulled out his radio, gave his location, who he was watching, and called for backup. If he'd been able to see down the alley across the way, he'd have seen a slim figure back away, turn and run to the fire escape and quickly begin to climb.

Bitterman crossed the street and stood by the door to Timmons's crib. He opened his jacket and thumbed back the strap on his holster. A level-three vest was supposed to be able to stop a .44 provided it wasn't too close, but they said the shock would flatten you and you got broken up inside even if there wasn't penetration. Where the hell was backup, Bitterman thought.

He scanned the street in both directions and saw nothing. Right now he was the thin blue line.

A shot rang out, then another, then a scream and a third one.

Bitterman yelled into his radio, "Shots fired, I'm going up." He pulled the door open and heard things falling, scuffling and screaming from above. Both hands on his pistol, he followed it up the stairs. He hit the second floor and pointed his gun at all the doors and then up the stairs.

The noise was coming from the door at the far end. Bitterman closed rapidly and pressed himself against the wall. He reached out with his right hand and touched the doorknob. It was unlocked.

"Wonderful, I get an open door but no backup," he said to himself.

Bitterman slowly turned the knob. The noises had stopped.

No banging, no screams. When it was fully turned, he flung it open and stepped through into what he hoped was not the line of fire.

Lufer was on the floor. His pants were down around his knees. Sunshine was under him, twitching. Lufer's cannon was in his hand and there was a bullet hole in the sofa. There was also one in his neck, and the blood was pooling under his chin.

Bitterman saw a young boy to his left, holding on to a snub-nosed .38. The gun was jumping around like it was electrified. His left leg tried to keep time but it couldn't. There was a large stain on the front of the boy's pants.

"Put down the gun," Bitterman barked, but the boy didn't respond.

Bitterman searched his face. His eyes were wide open and unfocused.

"Put down the gun," Bitterman asked, more gently but to no avail.

The boy was clearly freaked out by what he'd done. Maybe he could get close enough to disarm him.

"Son, please put down the gun. You're making me nervous the way it's shaking there. I don't know what happened here, but I know he's a bad man. Why don't you tell me what happened here."

Bitterman edged closer to the boy, who was facing away from him. Maybe he could get his hand on the gun, then hit him in the temple with his pistol. At this range he couldn't afford to let the boy turn. Even shooting to wound him wouldn't work. An accidental off-line discharge could be fatal this close. Should he tell him he was going to reach for his gun, or just do it? And where the fuck was backup anyway?

Bitterman moved slowly toward the boy until he was about two feet away. If he turned on him he'd have to shoot him. He had no choice. Why wouldn't he just put the gun down and make this easier on both of them?

Bitterman slowly reached out for the gun. The boy's eyes snapped into focus and he tried to pull away. Bitterman grabbed for the gun. It swung up towards his face, he pulled it down towards his chest and slammed the kid in the head with his pistol. The .38 went off and Bitterman fell back gasping. Dantreya Watkins hit the floor and lay still.

Bitterman, on his back, reached up and touched his chest. He could feel the .38 embedded in the Kevlar. God, did he hurt and was he glad he could say it.

He lay there on his back, like a Kevlar turtle, his hands clenching with the pain of each breath. He saw Sunshine push Lufer Timmons up off of her, until she was clear of his now and forever limp penis, roll out from under it, stand up and stagger to the door without a backward glance. Bitterman tried to call out to her for help but could only groan instead, as she banged her way down the stairs. The front door slammed and Bitterman lay there in the enveloping silence waiting for the sounds of backup: screeching tires, sirens, pounding footsteps. Above all else he wanted there to be someone in a hurry to find him. Bitterman closed his eyes and whispered, "Merry fucking Christmas."

Open and Shut

"Just how deep did they bury Kincaid?"

"Across the river. Permanent midnights. He's a clerk at the jail infirmary."

The chief shook his head. That was as far away from the action as you could get and still be a police officer. You sat alone at a desk with a silent phone waiting to push papers around three times a month. You slept in the day. That would have cut Kincaid off from contact with just about everyone in the department.

"How long has he been out there?"

"Two years, Chief." Assistant Chief Morlock was reading from Max Kincaid's personnel file.

"Did he ever apply for a transfer?"

"The first year. He was rejected. He didn't try again."

"Why didn't he resign?"

"Too close to retirement would be my guess. Besides, who else would take him after the stunts he pulled?"

"That's true. Well, wake him up and tell him to get down here. His exile is about to end."

In the dark, Max Kincaid felt for the phone as if it were a hooker with time left on her meter. "Yeah?"

"Sergeant Kincaid. This is Chief Stalling's office. The chief wants you in his office in an hour."

"You've got the wrong number." Kincaid unplugged his phone and went back to sleep.

Twenty minutes later, a battering ram was testing his front door. Kincaid rolled out of bed, walked across his efficiency apartment, and viewed the proceedings through his peephole. *My, my,* he thought. *They've got my old lieutenant down here.* Avery Bitterman was one of the few officers Kincaid would listen to, or at least he once was. Bitterman was leaning against the far wall, massaging his scalp. Two uniforms were banging on the front door in tandem. Kincaid thought about reporting a disorderly-in-public to the station house and giving everyone a shitload of paperwork to do but decided against it. The pleasure would be pale and brief, and Bitterman was one of his last friends.

"Good morning, Officers," he said, swinging the door wide open. "Anything I can do for you this fine summer day? Sorry if I was a little slow getting to the door. I've only been asleep for . . ." He checked his watch. "Fifty minutes."

"That's enough. I'll talk to Sergeant Kincaid." Bitterman pushed off from the wall. The two officers turned and walked down the hall. Bitterman moved past Kincaid, into the apartment. He sat at the card table next to the kitchenette. "Sit down, Max. You might be interested in what I have to say."

Kincaid pulled out a folding chair and stared at Bitterman. They had worked Homicide together for ten years, until everything came apart. He hadn't seen him in over a year, but Bitterman still looked the same.

"Been awhile, Avery. How've you been?"

"Don't ask. Chief Stalling asked me to come over and roust you as a personal favor. He's pissed about the phone call but he's willing to cut you a little slack. That's because he thinks he needs you. That's a real fragile thought, Max. Listen carefully. This is a one-time offer. You know there's been a directive to retrain and re-qualify all officers in firearm procedures. To do that, they either have to hire new instructors at the academy or reassign officers. Reassignment is cheaper. He wants you to be one of the instructors. That's the offer. Max, it's day work, you can use your skills, and it's a chance to practice what you preached."

Kincaid walked around the proposal, looking for its tripwire.

"Why me? I'm the last person on earth they'd want over there."

"I'll let the chief explain it to you, Max. Just get dressed, I'm supposed to deliver you personally."

Kincaid arrived at headquarters within the hour he'd been originally allotted. The chief's secretary announced his arrival as soon as he walked in.

Chief Stalling looked up briefly and said, "Take a seat, Sergeant." Kincaid did and stared at the top of the chief's head while he read the file on Max Kincaid. When he looked up, Kincaid marveled at how much he looked like a fruit bat. Jug ears, pug nose, all those uneven teeth in that brown face. Kincaid realized he hadn't been listening.

"Excuse me, Chief; could you repeat that?"

"Am I boring you, Kincaid?"

"No sir, it's just that I'm still a little fuzzy. I'd just come off duty when Lieutenant Bitterman showed up."

"What I asked you is whether you wanted a transfer to the academy. You'd be senior firearms examiner and sit on the weapons-use review team."

"Sir, why am I being offered this position? I can't imagine that you'd want me anywhere near the academy. You've got my file there, you know the history."

"That's exactly why I'm offering you the transfer. You made a lot of enemies when you were doing deadly-force investigations. Your memos pissed off a lot of people. Turns out you were right about a lot of things. You know the mayor has mandated complete retraining and re-qualification of all officers—I repeat, *all* officers—in proper firearm procedure. I read all your memos, Kincaid. I'd think that you'd jump at this opportunity. You'd be able to train officers so they wouldn't be a danger to themselves, their partners, or the citizens. It's what you said was needed."

"So I'm the poster boy for the department's new get-tough policy. If you read those memos, you know I was especially critical of management. You hired hundreds of officers without background checks just so the budget allocations wouldn't get lost. Many of them were never properly trained on firearms. Hell, the shooting range wasn't open for how long, a year? Most officers have never been re-qualified. You know that a number of women officers were qualifying on their backs. Yeah, we've got people out there with guns and the authority to use them but no skill or judgment, and I'm all for getting them off the streets, but I won't whitewash the department. They were sent out into a combat zone without the tools to do the job. That's management's fault. Was then, is now."

"Are you through? In case you hadn't noticed, I was not part of that 'you' you so eloquently denounced. I was brought in to change the way things are done. I'm asking you if you want to be part of that change. You take care of your end of this and I'll take care of mine. You look old enough to remember this line, Sergeant: 'If you aren't part of the solution, you're part of the problem.' So, what'll it be?"

Kincaid was silent for a while. "When do I start?" He'd been saying yes inside ever since Bitterman told him of the offer, but he didn't want anyone to know how hungry he was.

"Effective immediately. You have a weapons-use review scheduled for one o'clock. It's a homicide. You can move into your office as soon as you like. Cherise will handle the paperwork. The case file on the shooting is on her desk. Take it on your way out. Dismissed."

"Yes, sir." Kincaid stood up and left the office. He picked up the file and began to read it in the elevator. Out on the street, he blinked at the sunlight, at all the people on the streets. He'd slept through all of this for two years. The solitude, the darkness, hadn't been all bad.

He crossed the street, entered the support-services building, and took the elevator to the top floor. Weapons-Use Review was a secured section. He showed his badge, signed the book, and deposited his weapon in the safe. The receptionist told him that his office was 704 and the door buzzed open. He walked back, following the numbers on the doors. 704 had a window on the back wall that offered a view into another office across the alley. The furniture was strictly functional: gray steel desk, gray steel shelves, gray steel file, a chalkboard for crime-scene diagrams. There was a microphone sticking out of the desk, like an antenna on a bug's head. The tape recorder would be in the upper right drawer. He'd move it over as he was left-handed. One chair for the officer, one for counsel or union rep. He sat behind the desk, moved the phone to the left side, and checked the drawers. His predecessor had cleared out everything but the dust. Fortunately, Max asked little of his surroundings and put little into them. He'd be functional by one o'clock. He called the academy.

"Director Hansen, please. This is Sergeant Kincaid."

"Max. Bruce Hansen. I hear you're coming over here. Is that so?"

"God's truth, Bruce. I need to schedule a time on the range. Get myself re-qualified."

"What for? Christ, you've forgotten more about procedure than most officers ever learn."

"Maybe, but the word from on high is *everybody* retrains. I need to *show* that I'm qualified, not just say so. And I need to be more than qualified. I need to be better than anyone else. When I tell some A.C. that he's failed and he has to turn in his piece, I want to be able to show him there and then how you do it. I've been off the street for two years, Bruce. That's a lot of rust."

"Okay. How about four o'clock today? I'll have Hapgood be your examiner."

"Thanks, Bruce." Max figured he'd wait a week or so before he suggested to his new boss that all examiners should be on the course at least once a week to work on their own shortcomings.

The next phone call would be much harder. He punched in Vicki's number.

"Hello," he heard.

"Hi, Vicki. It's Dad. I'm glad I caught you. Are you in-between classes?"

"Yeah. Where are you calling from?" She hadn't recognized the number on her screen, which increased the likelihood that she'd answer the call.

"My new job. I'm at the academy. It's day work, like normal people. Monday through Friday. I wanted to let you know right away. Maybe we could do something this weekend. It's been quite awhile, you know."

"Yeah, it has, Dad. Quite awhile. Only thing is, I've got some plans for this weekend. I'm going to the beach with a bunch of friends. They're counting on me and I've already paid for the room, so I'd be out the money if I didn't go."

Kincaid picked up right on cue. He wouldn't want such a reasonable excuse to fall flat between them. "Of course, honey. I understand. It's late notice. I just wanted you to know what my schedule is. We could go out to dinner some night when you don't have a lot of homework, or a weekend—do something together. Are you still playing soccer?"

"Yes, Dad. I still play soccer. Every weekend. Have since I was nine years old."

"Well, I'd like to come see you play. When is your next game?"

"We've got a State Cup game next week. It's down in Roanoke. Why don't you wait until there's one nearby. I'll send you a schedule."

"Thanks. That's great. You have my address, don't you?"

"I have your address, Dad. Look, I've got to go. I'm going to be late for my next class."

"Sure, honey. Have fun at the beach." He almost said "I love you," but no one was listening.

Officer Delbert Tillis entered Kincaid's office at one o'clock. He was tall and thin, with a flattop and a pencil-thin moustache. His features were soft and blunt, and his ears flared out at the bottom like Michael Jordan's.

"Sit down, Officer Tillis. My name is Sergeant Max Kincaid. I'm interviewing you as part of the weapons-use review team. This team will collect evidence and make a finding as to whether the shooting was justified or not and whether you will be subject to any disciplinary action. Because a person died as the result of you discharging your weapon, Homicide is also investigating this and will present their evidence to a district attorney, who may indict you criminally. The information from our investigation may be turned over to the district attorney. You have the right to have an attorney present for this interview, or a member of the police officers' union. Do you waive that right?"

"Yeah. I've got nothing to hide." Tillis stared straight at Kincaid.

"For the record, state your name, badge number, and present assignment."

"Officer Delbert P. Tillis, Junior. Badge number four-one-oh-nine, assigned to the second district." Crisp, confident.

"This interview is being tape-recorded. You or your attorney is entitled to a copy of the transcript of this interview. Why don't you tell me everything that happened?"

"Where do you want me to start?"

"It's your story. Start at the start, go to the end. I'm not going to interrupt you or ask any questions." Too often, questioning improved the quality of the story. Kincaid wanted it to be all Tillis.

"Fine, whatever." Tillis looked annoyed.

Kincaid set a pad in front of himself and adjusted the volume on the recorder. His notes would mostly be diagrams, converting the officer's words to actions. He'd note inconsistencies between approved procedures and the report with brief questions. Later, he'd read the transcript and compare his thought processes as he moved through the story with what Tillis had to say, looking first for plausible differences and then for the lies.

"I saw the guy sitting in the car. He looked like he could have been sleeping, or hurt, or dead. I didn't know what. The place was deserted, man. I didn't have no backup. I didn't know what I was walking into, so I pulled out my piece and I came up alongside the car, and, you know, I tapped on the window with the barrel, just, like, to startle him, to see if he woke up, and, *bam,* the thing went off. You know how the piece is, man, it went off. I didn't even pull the trigger. Shit, man, you gotta believe me, I did not mean to kill that guy. It was an accident."

Tillis was leaning forward in his chair, palms open as a sign of his transparency. His eyes had been fixed on Kincaid's blank face the whole time he spoke.

"How long have you been on the force, Officer?"

"Four years."

"All in the second?"

"Yes."

"When was the last time you were qualified in weapons procedure?"

Tillis looked away. "I don't remember."

"Were you notified, were you scheduled?"

"Yes."

"Did you shoot?"

"Yes."

"How many times?"

"Two."

"Did you qualify?"

"No."

"Do you remember what the proper procedure is for the use of a firearm as a door knocker?"

"No."

"No? There is none. It's a gun. How many times have you done this, Officer? Knock, knock, open up—whoops, guess I shot you. Didn't mean to. Sorry."

"None. It's never happened before."

"Lucky you. Where's your piece, Officer?"

"Homicide took it at the scene."

"Let's go back to the start. I'm a little fuzzy there. You said the place was deserted. What were you doing there?"

"I saw this guy's car there, by itself; so I went down to check it out. You know, maybe it was kids doing the nasty. I'd roust 'em, move 'em out of there. It ain't a good neighborhood."

"Where was the car again?"

"Parked at the end of the road."

"Right. So you went down there." Kincaid looked at his notes. "From where?"

"From the street, man. I was driving by. I just picked up some food at Mickey D's."

"Were you on duty, Officer?"

"No."

"A little bit slower this time. You see the car from the street. Then what?"

"I pulled down the road till I got to the car."

"You see anything in the car?"

"No, it was dark. So I pulled up alongside. I got out and walked towards it. That's when I see the guy."

"And the gun goes off. Then what?"

"Then what? I freak out, man. I reach in the door, the window's all gone, open it up, and he falls out into my arms. I mean, he's dead. I know that right away. Half of his head is gone. I just lost it, man." Tillis looked down and shook his head.

"Lost it how?"

He shrugged. Kincaid leaned forward. "I need your words, Officer Tillis; you lost it how?"

Kincaid turned up the volume on the recorder to catch Tillis's whispered reply. "I just dropped him, right there in the dirt. I jumped back, my heart was pounding. His head had flopped over and all I saw was this big hole, and blood, and bones, and all this soft gooey shit, so I dropped him and he fell in the dirt. And I'm thinking, I shot this guy, I killed him, and I can't even pick him up out of the dirt. He shouldn't be lying there like that. It wasn't right, but I just couldn't pick him up. I couldn't. I just went around the car and got my radio and called it in."

"You ever shot anyone before, Officer Tillis?"

"No. I've never discharged my weapon in the line of duty."

"Has the department psychologist spoken to you yet?"

"No. I'm supposed to see him tomorrow."

"How do you feel about that?"

"I don't know. What good is talking about it? It's done. I did it. Nothing's gonna change that."

"You'd be surprised. Talking about things can make a big difference. Killing a man, that's a heavy load to carry alone. Especially an accident. I think that's even tougher than murder. Murder, you get what you want. An accident, jeez, what a waste. But, hey, I'm no psychologist."

Kincaid reviewed his notes and leaned back in his chair. "Listen, why don't we wrap it up right now. I'll get this typed up and the team will review it. If I have any more questions, you'll be at home, right?"

"Yeah."

"This is Sergeant Max Kincaid. Interview terminated at one fifty-one p.m."

Tillis pushed away from the desk. He stood up and shook his head with sadness as he said, "You gotta believe me. I'm telling the truth. I didn't mean to kill that guy."

Kincaid nodded. "I believe you, Officer Tillis."

Alone, he buzzed the front desk. "I have an interview tape that needs to be transcribed. How do I get that done?"

"That's part of my job, Sergeant. Is there anything else you need?"

"Yeah, get me Officer Tillis's personnel file—and who's handling this investigation out of Homicide?"

"Uh, that would be Detective Seymour."

"Seymour? Don't think I know him."

"Probably not, sir."

"When will the report be sent over?"

"Detective Seymour will be bringing it over this afternoon."

Kincaid left the building and walked around the corner to

a sandwich shop and ate a "U-Boat" for lunch: bratwurst, sauerkraut, and mustard on a roll; side of German potato salad. Tillis's file was on his desk when he returned. Pulling the window shade up, he rested his heels on the window ledge while he read. A knock on his door turned him around and upright.

"Come in."

A tall, broad-shouldered woman with short, spiky blond hair opened the door. She wore a camel pantsuit over a black turtleneck. Her eyes were a pale blue-gray. Like ice water.

"Sergeant Kincaid? I'm Detective Seymour. Angela Seymour."

They shook hands and Seymour slipped into a chair.

"How much of your investigation have you completed?" Kincaid asked.

"Crime scene and forensics. We're doing a background on the victim and we took a statement from Tillis at the scene. How about you?"

"Formal statement. I've been reading his personnel file. How do you see it?"

"Forensics and crime scene match his story. There was residue on the window fragments. That's where the shot came from. The clerk at Mickey D's said he'd just picked up some food. His tire tracks and footprints match the story. He pulled up alongside the car, walked around, shot him, opened the door, the body fell out, he walked back and called it in, that sort of thing. The tape of the call seems consistent. You know, 'I shot him. I shot him. It was a mistake. I didn't mean it.' He was real shook up. The timing was right. The guy was still warm when we got there."

"How about the gun? Street-ready?"

"Yeah. The magazine was full, so there was one in the chamber."

"This guy is a field manual for screw-ups. You couldn't handle this situation in a more incompetent fashion. He sees this car at the end of the road. Off-duty, he goes down without calling anyone; parks alongside, not in the rear; doesn't ask the guy to step out of the vehicle; uses his gun as a door knocker. I've been looking at his record. No history of use-of-force complaints, no history of improper discharge, no distinctions of any kind. Officer Tillis is a very thin, very pale blue line. I'm going to check his record at the academy. See what kind of training they were doing when he went through. He's never re-qualified since he got out. I don't know if his negligence is more his fault or ours."

"He learned the right way. We were in the same class. But if they didn't require him to re-qualify, he wouldn't do it. Delbert did enough to get by, nothing more. On one hand this surprises me, and on the other it doesn't. I don't see Delbert letting his Big Mac get cold to check out a stack of corpses, much less a parked car. That reminds me, what did he say about seeing the car?"

Kincaid flipped back through his notes. "He saw the car from the street. He was driving by after he picked up the food."

"Never happened." Seymour grew animated. Kincaid knew that feeling when the first lie raised its head above the smooth surface of a case. Something to chase, to hunt back to its lair, see if it had family. Seymour began to talk with her hands, and Kincaid noted that she had rings on all of her fingers.

"I drove by the alley and missed it when we responded to the call. You can't see anything from the street."

"How very curious. Then what brought Officer Tillis to that dark and lonely place? What was the victim's name?"

"Ronnie Lewis."

"What do we know about him?"

"Nothing yet, but we're working on it."

Kincaid checked his watch. He had to be at the range by four. "Listen, I've got to go, uh, let me give you my card." He pulled out his wallet, took out a card, flipped it over, and wrote on the back. "This is my home number and my number here. Call me if you find out anything. I'll do the same." He handed her the card.

She reached into her jacket and pulled out a card case and gave him hers. As she was leaving, she turned back. "I've just got to ask. How did you ever manage to write that on the watch commander's forehead?" She was referring to the final incident that sent him across the river. He had written "750," the code for dereliction of duty, on the watch commander's forehead. Something he didn't notice until, perplexed by the stares and snickers from everyone he met at the station house, he went into the locker room and saw it in the mirror.

"I'll never tell. Who knows, I may be called on to do it again."

"Well, it was appreciated by some of us. The guy was a complete asshole. The rumors of how you did it got pretty extreme."

"Well, maybe you'll tell me about them someday."

"Only if you tell me the truth."

Kincaid drank two large cups of coffee before heading over to the range. He was crashing. One hour of sleep and his biological clock was busted. He hoped that the coffee would just keep him alert, not shaky, when he shot. The drive over reminded him of one benefit of midnights. Empty streets. At three a.m. you were fifteen minutes from anywhere. At three p.m. you were fifteen minutes from the next intersection. Rust and caffeine notwithstanding, Kincaid qualified easily.

At his best, he had shot a rapid-fire perfect with his weak hand and unmarked targets.

Kincaid made it back to his apartment by six, knocked down a couple of gin and tonics as sedatives, reheated a pizza, and wondered how long it would take to train his body to sleep at night. After dinner he took out his Ruger .44 Magnum and worked on one of his teaching exercises: fieldstripping and reassembling a sidearm with his eyes closed. He could do it with a dozen different weapons. He could do it with one model while lecturing about another. If he'd known his way around his wife's body like that, he might still be married. Or at least on speaking terms.

Morning came and Kincaid went to his office. He wasn't expected to start his examiner's duties until the following Monday. In the meantime, he wanted to get as far into this case as he could. Tillis's file revealed that he was a native son. This had been one of the biggest problems with the recruitment push of five years ago. Local roots and no background checks meant that a lot of thugs got guns and badges, and those thugs had long histories with many of the local drug crews. Far too often, it was those loyalties that ruled—not the oath, the paycheck, the brotherhood of blue. No officer had, as yet, murdered another to further a criminal enterprise, but police had served as security for drug couriers, killing rivals and warning of raids.

Kincaid read on. Tillis lived nowhere near the scene of the shooting, nor was it in his district. God knows there were other Mickey D's in this town. What brought him to that location? Kincaid knew that things would get much more interesting if Tillis and Lewis knew each other. From that fact you could breed a motive, and negligence would be murder.

At ten, his phone rang. It was Seymour.

"You wanted to know about Lewis. Three priors. Nothing heavy."

"Tillis arrest him?"

"No. I looked at Lewis's entire jacket. Tillis isn't mentioned anywhere. He wasn't second officer, or station clerk. He didn't handle crime scene, forensics, property, or records. Nothing."

"What are the dates on those arrests?"

"Ten February this year, six July ninety-six, and twenty-three October ninety-one."

"What were the home addresses for Lewis on those arrests?"

"Same as now: Sixty-one East Markham Terrace."

"Nowhere near where he was shot. Anything from the M.E.? Drugs in his system? Recent sexual activity?"

"Nothing. You think Tillis was cruising and Lewis threatened to out him? Or Lewis propositioned him and he panicked?"

"No idea. I'm just curious about what brought those two guys to that place at that time. I'll settle for God's will if I have to, but it's never my first choice."

"I'll keep looking into Lewis. Maybe Tillis gave him a ticket. We're pulling his driving record. What are you doing?"

"I'll check into Tillis's background a little more, see if I can put them together, even if it's a fifth-grade study hall. Listen, could you fax over a copy of Tillis's statement at the crime scene and his call in to dispatch."

"Sure. Let me know what you find out."

"Will do. Oh, by the way, he was strapped to a seat."

"Who was?"

"The watch commander."

"No." Seymour was both puzzled and impressed.

"Yes."

★ ★ ★ ★ ★

There was a knock at his door. Kincaid said, "Come in." The receptionist came in, a squat black woman with short, tightly curled hair, parted on one side.

"Here's that transcript you wanted, sir." She handed him a stack of papers and the tape.

Reaching out, he said, "Thank you. I should have introduced myself earlier. I'm Sergeant Kincaid, and you are . . . ?"

"Shondell Witherspoon." Deep dimples split her cheeks each time she spoke.

"Pleased to meet you, Ms. Witherspoon. When Detective Seymour's fax arrives, I want to see it right away, and I need the department psychologist's phone number."

"That would be Dr. Rice. He's at extension two-one-oh-one at headquarters."

"Thank you."

Kincaid dialed the number as Witherspoon pulled the door closed.

"Support Services."

"Dr. Rice, please."

"Dr. Rice is on vacation. Can anyone else help you?"

"This is Sergeant Kincaid at Weapons-Use Review. Who's handling post-incident debriefings while Rice is away?"

"No one, Sergeant. The other staff positions haven't been filled. Dr. Rice will be back next week. Is there anyone in particular you're interested in?"

"Officer Tillis. When is he scheduled to be seen?"

"I don't know. He hasn't called this office and didn't respond to my calls. I was just typing up an A71 notice for him to appear. He has ten days, then he's put on leave."

"Ask Dr. Rice to call me when he's returned."

"Will do."

Kincaid opened Tillis's personnel folder and looked at his assignments over the last four years—especially the dates of Lewis's arrests in '96 and '01. He called Tillis's station house. While he was waiting to get through, he opened the desk drawers to see if he had a lockbox for his interview tapes.

"This is Sergeant Kincaid. Get me the duty clerk, please."

"This is Binyon, what can I do for you?"

"I'm checking assignments. How far back do your records go?"

"Not very far, Sergeant. We used to keep them here before the computer center opened downtown. They were kept up in the attic, but we had the pipes burst last fall, you know, that record cold spell back in October. Anyway, everything got soaked and it all kind of turned into big bricks of paper mâché. All the pages got glued together so we sent them to the incinerator."

"Thanks." Kincaid was switched over to procurement. Tillis had never requested money for a confidential informant, so he hadn't been using Lewis that way.

There were no paper records connecting them or ruling out a connection. Kincaid was still wondering where he was going to store his tapes when he saw a possible solution to his problem.

It took Kincaid the rest of the afternoon to put Lewis and Tillis together, and it was late in the day when he returned to the office to get Detective Seymour's fax. Kincaid read Tillis's statement and the transcript of his radio call. They were a match with what he'd said in the interview. Kincaid was glad he hadn't relied on Seymour's memory. Two lies and a damaging truth. A motive was gestating. Buoyed by that thought, he called the morgue.

"Medical Examiner's office."

"This is Sergeant Kincaid. You've got a body there,

Ronnie Lewis, shot by an officer. Anyone come by to look at his belongings?"

"No. Homicide's in no hurry. They know who did this one."

"I'm coming by to check them out now."

"Whatever."

Kincaid was now unquestionably poaching on Seymour's turf. His job was procedures and personnel—Tillis. She could also investigate Tillis for criminal purposes, but Lewis, the victim, was exclusively hers.

The morgue was down by the river, cut into the slopes so that much of the building was underground. This reduced the energy required to keep the building and its occupants cool. Hot, muggy summer days would send half a dozen citizens over with lead passports and no luggage.

Outside, Kincaid slipped on his new pair of sunglasses. He'd had to buy sunblock also as he adjusted to being out during the day. Thirty cursing minutes later, he walked into the cool, dark entrance hall to the morgue. The visitors' entrance was a ramp with railings. There were benches at both ends. Too many grief-stricken family members had fallen on the stairs at the old morgue. He pushed through the double doors and was refreshed by the chill air. Property was at the end of the hall. He signed in and had the clerk get Ronnie Lewis's belongings. Kincaid felt the clothing to see if anything was sewn into a seam or pocket. Nothing. He felt the length of the belt for bulges, pried off the heel of a shoe. More nothing. All the victim had had in his pockets was fifty-three cents in coins, a wallet, and a ring of keys: one to a Ford; one, probably, to his house; the third to a deadbolt, perhaps, or a storage unit or any of a dozen other possibilities. Kincaid opened the wallet. It contained thirty-six dollars in cash, a driver's license, a social security card, a receipt for a money order, and a picture of a young woman with verandah-sized breasts and an inviting smile. He turned it over. There was no name or phone number. A subway pass. A video-store card, an ATM card, and some business cards stuck behind the cash. Kincaid wrote down the names and numbers, returned the cards to their place, and left.

Back at the office, he called the impound lot to see what was in Lewis's car. Nothing of any use—an ice scraper, a couple of flares, jumper cables, tire-pressure gauge, some change in the ashtray, the owner's manual and some local maps in the glove compartment. Kincaid asked if the maps had any locations circled or routes highlighted. The clerk said yes but none of them were to the crime scene or Tillis's residence and he'd already told that to Detective Seymour, don't you people ever talk to each other?

Kincaid dialed the numbers on each of the cards he'd taken from Lewis's wallet. The first was to an out-call exotic dancer agency. They weren't sending anybody to visit Mr. Lewis until he paid up for the last visit. Kincaid told them to close the account and kiss the hundred bucks goodbye. They had no account for Officer Tillis. The second card was for a bail bondsman who hadn't heard from Lewis since his last arrest. That bond had been paid for by his mother, who'd invoked her own three-strikes-you're-out rule and told Ronnie he was on his own.

Next up was a disconnected line for Novelties Unlimited. The last card was for a lawyer, Malcolm Prevost. Kincaid asked the secretary to get Mr. Prevost and tell him it was a police matter.

"This is Malcom Prevost, what can I do for you?"

"It's about Ronnie Lewis. Is he a client of yours?"

"I doubt it. I don't do criminal defense work. I'm a personal-injury lawyer and the name doesn't ring a bell."

"Could you check, please? We found your card in his wallet."

"Hold on a second."

Prevost returned and said, "He called this office last week, Friday. I was in court—it's motions day. Anyway, my secretary set up an appointment for him for this Thursday."

"Did he say what he wanted?"

"I'm sorry. That's confidential, Sergeant."

"Let me help you with that. Ronnie Lewis won't be able to complain. Other than meeting his maker, he's not available for anything. We're investigating a conspiracy here. Right now I like you for co-conspirator, or accessory before the fact, at the least. Tell me why he called and I'll downgrade you to helpful citizen."

"Fine, fine. All he said was that he wanted me to represent him. He said that he'd been shot by a police officer."

"Did he say anything else?"

"No, that's all."

"Well, here's a hot tip, Counselor. Don't take any calls from his next-of-kin."

Kincaid was walking past the receptionist's desk when her phone rang. He thought about letting it ring but decided that if it was Seymour he'd just as soon get it over with.

"What the hell were you doing over at the M.E.'s office?"

"Stepping on your toes, Detective." Mea culpa as judo, an old bad habit.

"You don't think I can do my job?"

"Not at all. Homicide's a busy unit these days. I've got time to make this case a priority, so I pushed on it."

"Thanks for nothing, Kincaid. I'm Homicide, you aren't, and this shit won't help you get back here. This is why no one missed you when you got sent across the river."

"I'd say I'm sorry but it wouldn't be true. I can't remember if I'm impulsive or compulsive. Either way, I'd rather piss you off than stop myself. It's nothing personal, ask my wife." Change was a hard turn of the wheel on a lifetime of momentum, his therapist had said. He'd blown straight through another intersection again.

"Maybe not to you, but it is to me. I've shared my last piece of information with you, Kincaid, and it is personal."

"Let me make it up to you. I'm going to interview Tillis again tomorrow. He knew Lewis and I can prove it. Why don't you watch it behind the glass? Run with whatever I get."

"Oh, I will. After I nail your feet to the floor. What time?"

"Nine o'clock."

Seymour hung up and Kincaid called Tillis and set up the appointment. He went to the range and shot five hundred rounds' worth of tranquilizers and then went home. At home, he watched a first-round game of the women's World Cup. It used to be that the women's play was mercifully free of the ludicrous dives, cynical fouls, and feigned injuries of the men. When a woman went down, she was fouled. If she stayed down she was hurt, period. But big money had changed all that. Maybe Vicki'd like to watch a game with him, was the thought he drifted off to sleep on.

Tillis sat down in the interview room. Kincaid was not obliged to tell him that he was being observed but he had to tell him that the session was being taped. Angela Seymour pulled her chair closer to the glass, turned the volume up slightly, and flipped open her notebook. If she got anything out of this interview she wouldn't have to wait for a transcript.

"Officer Tillis, who was the man you shot?"

"Don't know. His ID said he was Ronnie Lewis."

"You ever met him before?"

"No. He was a stranger to me."

"That so? This interview is conducted just like any internal-affairs investigation. If you lie to me, you can be dismissed. Did you ever meet Ronnie Lewis before?"

"No. I never met the guy, that's the truth." Delbert's voice rose with righteous conviction.

"No, Delbert. That's not the truth. Let me tell you what the truth is. You knew Ronnie Lewis. You met him at least twice. You were on transport the last two times he was arrested. Transporters don't have to sign anything as long as there's no injury to the prisoner. Reasonable that you'd think there was no way to connect you two, but I matched up the arrest times on the paperwork with the dispatch calls on the runs. They keep the tapes of those calls for three years, Delbert. I heard your voice on them. You knew Ronnie Lewis. You knew Ronnie Lewis was down at the end of the road when you went there."

"I did not." Tillis's voice quivered as the impossible became the inevitable.

"Delbert, you couldn't see the car from the road. You had no reason to go down there unless you knew someone was there." Kincaid stopped. "This is important, Del. This is premeditation. This isn't positive policing, this isn't street initiative. You went down there to meet a man you already knew. We're waving goodbye to negligence, hello murder two."

"Murder two? Are you nuts, man? I told you I shot the guy. It was an accident. I didn't mean it."

"That's the beauty of it, Delbert. I believe you, I really do. Have from the beginning. It was an accident, *and* it was murder."

"You're crazy, man. I don't have to listen to this bullshit. I want my union rep here. If you're so damn certain of all this, why hasn't Homicide picked me up? That dyke bitch would love nothing better than to bust my ass. I was with her at the academy. She was a ball-cutter then, she's a ball-cutter now."

"That was the hard part, Delbert: motive. Motive and intent, that's what I needed. You can stop the interview now if you want. We can wait for your union rep to get here. I don't care if you don't say another word. You might want to hear what I have to tell you alone, though—without him here. See, I don't think they're going to be too eager to rush to your defense. Are they?"

Tillis stared back, impassive, defiant, but wondering if Kincaid could back up his words.

"I wanted you to be a simple schmuck, Delbert. A poorly trained, unqualified guy who had no business being a cop, sent to do an impossible job without the tools. I could have pounded on your failures like a drum while I preached my personal brand of truth. You were almost as big a victim as Lewis. That's what I wanted to see, but you wouldn't let me. No, you're anything but simple, Delbert. You've failed to qualify twice. Once more and you're out of a job. I'll bet you're not independently wealthy. Your friend Ronnie Lewis is not a captain of industry either. How do a small-time hood and a marginal cop turn that around? Work with what you've got. Here's the best part, Delbert. I'll even spot you being careful about your plans, but you should have used a better quality target than Ronnie. He called an attorney to represent him in a shooting. Last week. So Ronnie's either clairvoyant or incredibly stupid. I'll go for number two." Kincaid watched Tillis try to stifle his disbelief at Lewis's stupidity and greed.

"You like that, huh? What a fool. Couldn't wait to get shot first, then line up the lawyer. Who knows, maybe all the good ones would be taken. Here's where your accident becomes murder. I see an insurance fraud here. You shoot Lewis. He sues the city for what? A million dollars? Isn't that typical these days? You two split the proceeds. Your ineptitude and lack of training provides the necessary element of negligence. Hell, my report would have been your best piece of evidence. This shooting was definitely unjustified. In fact, let me tweak this one a little bit. You get a lawyer and sue the department for negligence in your training—you shouldn't have been allowed out on the streets with a weapon. Hell, I'll stipulate to that. You double-dip your ineptitude and walk away a millionaire. Now that's a golden parachute. Every other cop on the force pays your severance pay. I don't think so."

"You haven't said a word about murder, Sergeant. It's what it always was—an accident." Tillis even smiled a bit, confident that Kincaid was blowing smoke and couldn't prove the points he was making.

"Murder it is. A person killed in the commission of a felony is murder two. Fraud's a felony. You knew him; you went to a secluded place to meet; your partner had lined up an attorney to represent him in a gunshot case. That's a conspiracy. You were to provide the bullet. And you did. That makes it murder. And an accident. You meant to shoot him, not kill him. I said I believed you."

The door to the interview room opened and Detective Seymour walked in. She had her right hand extended toward Tillis. She moved her index and forefinger together like scissors and went, "Snip, snip.

"Delbert Tillis. You have the right to remain silent, anything you say can and will be used against you in a court of law . . ." The Miranda warning went on as Tillis shook his head.

"What tipped you off? Why even bother to look into this? I mean, what could have been more open and shut?"

Kincaid knew that all violent deaths were best approached as open and shut: with an open mind and a shut mouth. "It was something you said, Delbert. From the very first, you said it was a mistake. You didn't mean to kill him. That's right. It was a mistake. You didn't mean to kill him. But you never said you didn't mean to shoot him. That's what bothered me."

This one is for Adam, who when he saw the light, his spirits rose and he was young again.

SERIAL KILLERS

VERN BIGELOW AND GARNET SIMMS

Meeting of the Minds

Vernon Bigelow came over the rise and could not believe his good luck. It was on him like one of his spells, and he had to double clutch and downshift or he'd have blown right on past.

He pulled his rig off the road and came up behind the metal-flake blue Firebird. A white rag was tied to the antenna. He sat in the cab and looked for the driver. Not in the car, not up ahead. He glanced in his rearview mirrors. Nothing behind him. He turned off the engine, reached down and grabbed a short iron bar from next to his seat, and unlocked the door. You can't be too careful, he reminded himself. Being a Good Samaritan got a lot of people killed, and he wasn't going to be one of them. He jumped down from the cab and walked around its big red hood, patting it like it was the nose of his number one dog. He put almost a hundred thousand miles a year on this rig and it had brought him some mighty profitable loads, mighty profitable indeed.

Vernon walked alongside the Firebird. Low and wide, its body gleamed and sparkled like a giant beetle. Nobody in the backseat sleeping, no "Call the Police" card in the rear window.

Just a pair of big old custom speakers in each rear corner.

He felt the hood. Cool. It had been here awhile.

Vernon looked up and down the road and saw no one. The sun was in retreat and would vanish in thirty minutes. Orange and purple pastels smeared the bellies of the clouds above.

There wasn't much traffic on this road at high noon, he mused; after dark there wouldn't be any at all. Thirty miles in either direction to the nearest towns. Nothing but woods and fields on either side. A farmhouse now and then back off the road. Tobacco and corn hadn't been taken in yet, but the cotton was all gone. Fluffs of white all over the ground, debris after the pickers had been through.

Vern pulled the driver's handle. The door was unlocked. He opened it and looked inside. No car phone, no CB. Behind the front seat were an old rag and an empty plastic grocery bag. Vern took one last look around, put the bar in his pocket, and ducked his head inside. He popped open the compartment between the bucket seats. A couple of maps, some napkins, a pencil, a petrified mint, and the car's papers. The shifter curved up from the floor like a giant metal talon with an eightball impaled on the end of it.

Vern opened the pouch of papers. All the warranties were on one side. The other had the safety inspections, the emissions inspections, the insurance ID card, and the registration. He started to pull that out.

"God, am I glad to see you."

Spooked, Vern jerked himself upright and reached for the iron bar in his pocket.

"Jesus Christ, you scared the shit out of me," he yelled back at the woman standing in the field facing him.

"Sorry 'bout that," she yelled back.

"Where the hell were you?" he asked.

"In the woods. I couldn't wait any longer. Must be my lucky day. I was sure I'd leave and somebody'd come by and just keep on goin'. I've been standing out there with my thumb out for forty-five minutes."

She high-stepped it across the soft ground, gingerly crossed the ditch by the side of the road, and then stood on the other side of the car.

Vern wished he'd seen her by the side of the road, thumb out. He'd a pulled over, unlocked the door, and helped her into the cab. She'd get in, flash him a smile, thank him for being so kind. He'd tell her this was no place for a girl to be all alone. What with it getting dark and all. He wished he'd seen her like that, but this was all right too. She had on a pair of bluejean shorts, tight, with the bottoms rolled up, and a white blouse pulled up under her breasts and tied in a knot, so her stomach showed. She could have been tighter, but she was okay. Her breasts looked like they were okay, too. Soft, but not too droopy, big but not too big. Hell, what was he thinking, he couldn't remember a breast that wasn't okay.

Vern reminded himself not to stare, it put people off, and asked, "What's wrong with your car?"

"I don't know. It ain't my car."

"Well, let's open her up and see what's wrong."

Vern reached under the dashboard and released the hood.

He walked around the car to the front, pulled up the hood until the hydraulic support rod caught. He wiped his hands on his jeans and stuck one out.

"My name's Vern, Vern Bigelow. What's yours?"

The woman didn't take his hand. She took a step back and Vern noticed her right hand was in her purse.

"Okay." He flashed a big grin. "That's cool. You should be cautious, out here all alone, broken down, me a stranger, things bein' the way they are these days." He held up his hands. "Why don't you go on over there a ways, keep on going until you feel safe, and I'll look under the hood here. Okay?"

She took a couple of steps back, so that she could easily keep the car between them.

Vern scanned the car's engine for anything obvious. "Can't see anything wrong. Why don't you get inside and turn it on?" He'd been watching her out of the corner of his eye the whole time. What was in her purse? he wondered.

She came around the far side of the car, then in two long

strides slid into the front seat and locked the door.

Vern came around the hood. "Turn the engine on. If you don't do that I can't tell what's wrong."

She just sat there staring at him, doing nothing.

"Lady, if you don't turn the car on, I can't help you."

Still nothing.

Vern looked around. It was dark now. He couldn't even see a house light in any direction. He walked up to the front window and leaned over.

"Tell you what. You just sit in there with your hand in your purse. What are you gonna do, spray perfume in my face? I'm gonna go back to my truck and leave you here. While I'm driving down the road, I'm gonna be thinking about how scared you must be and it'd be pretty mean to leave you out here all alone. That might lead me to stop in town and call the police and have them come out and pick you up. Then again, I might start thinking about how you wouldn't even do me the courtesy of starting your car when you were all locked up safe inside, and all I was trying to do was help you. I spend too much time thinking like that and I know I won't stop anywhere and call anyone."

Vernon stood up and turned to walk away.

He spun back, pulled the iron rod from his pocket, and swung it ferociously at the glass. Inside, the woman threw her hands up in front of her face and screamed.

Vern tapped the glass lightly. "One last thought. This glass won't protect you. When they say shatterproof, it just means the glass won't explode in on you and cut you or blind you when someone hits it, like with an iron rod, or a baseball bat, or a hammer, or a rifle butt, and then pushes the glass out of the way to reach in and pull you out through the window."

Vern smiled, pleased with himself. "Just thought you'd want to know that before I leave."

He walked back to his truck, unlocked the door, took a step up, and swung himself into his chair like he was mounting a horse.

He put the rod back in its place and turned on his lights. Dumb broad, serve her sorry ass right if something happened to her, he thought. Something real bad. She didn't know common decency when it fell out of the sky on her. Decent people knew decency when they saw it, 'cause they practiced it. You couldn't appreciate what you didn't practice. Vern Bigelow knew that to be the truth.

Vern turned his engine on, checked his rearview mirror, and prepared to follow his headlights, his own personal moons, into the darkness. There was a pounding on his other door. Vern leaned over and looked down. It was her. He opened the door.

She brushed a wayward swatch of dark red hair out of her face and then raked it back with inch-long crimson nails. It hung down her back in a long braid, like a bell pull.

"First, you gotta . . ."

"Garnet Simms, but everyone calls me Red," she said, taking his hand and climbing in beside him. No smile. No thank you, Vern noted.

"That's pretty fortunate, you turning out to have red hair and all."

"Not really. All the kids in my family got red hair. My mother was running out of names—Scarlett, Ruby, Rusty, Rose—by the time I came along. That's enough about me. What's your name again?"

"Vern, Vern Bigelow."

"How'd you happen to be coming up this godforsaken road, Vern? I'd just about lost hope of ever being picked up. You ain't haulin'."

"No. I just dropped a load in Weldon. Going to pick up a

311

sealed one down at Morehead City, at the port there. Figured I'd take the scenic route. I spend most of my time on the interstates. You from around here?"

"Why do you ask?" she said, turning to face him.

"No reason. But like you said, this ain't a main road or nothing. I don't ever see much traffic here, except other rigs that are overweight and late, bypassing the stations, and locals. Locals, it's just out one driveway, up the road a couple of miles to another driveway."

"No. I ain't from around here."

Vern finished looking Garnet over. She was wearing clunky platform shoes. He hated them when they first came around, and he still hated them. Damned ugly things to find at the end of a woman's legs. She had no rings on her fingers. Funny, what with her spending so much time on those nails. That bag of hers was a regular satchel.

Garnet let him check her out, and when he got to her face she gave him one of her starter smiles. One without any teeth or dimple to it.

She hadn't checked herself out in a mirror, except in the Firebird, since early in the afternoon. Her hair needed to be brushed back and refastened. She hated it when it got in her face. If it was up to her, she'd have chopped it all off. But then things weren't always up to her, were they?

Garnet knew she wasn't pretty. She was attractive. That was a bit more than plain, which beat ugly by a long shot, but still short of pretty. With pretty you didn't have to work so hard, you could coast along behind pretty. She knew plenty of girls who did that. Beautiful? Beautiful killed her. It was a crime, being beautiful. Like stealing. She'd thought about plastic surgery for a while. If God shafted you, you could always do it yourself. But surgery was expensive. She knew. She'd looked into it and Garnet was no closer to having that kind of money than the day she'd left home.

No, attractive was just a slight pull, like two real tiny magnets. You had to boost that signal. Fortunately there were lots of boosters around. Clothes, your walk, bad habits, smiles, touching their hands for no reason, letting them help you with everything, makeup, giggles, certain ways of looking at them, listening to their every stupid word. Enough of that and they didn't see the crooked teeth, the acne that ruined your junior year, the overbite, the nose that was too something, every damn thing that didn't add up to pretty.

Vern smiled back. That was better, he thought. A thank you would have been in order, but he'd let that pass.

"Your car all locked up?"

"Yeah, but I told you it wasn't my car."

"Okay, your boyfriend's then."

"It ain't my boyfriend's neither. I didn't turn it over 'cause I didn't have the keys!"

"Then what were you doin' out here?"

"I told you. I was hitchhiking. I hadn't got a ride in almost an hour. I've been walking up the road, thumb out. I had to go so I hiked back into the woods. That Firebird was here when I got here. You saw that rag on the antenna. Something broke down, the guy probably got a ride to town to get it towed and ain't come back yet. That's all. I figured I'd hang around awhile, try to cop a ride when he got back. Then you showed up, and got all pissy."

"I'm sorry. I thought you were a bitch and here I was, just trying to be helpful. You could have said all that."

"Yeah, well, you were right about me being out here by myself. I was scared. So I just locked myself in. Your little trick with the pipe didn't help none neither."

"Yeah, well, sometimes I just go off, I guess. I didn't hurt you though. I just wanted to make a point. Let you know you weren't being so smart, you know."

Garnet smiled. "Let's just let bygones be bygones, Vern. What do you say? Start over?" She held out her hand.

Vern smiled back. This was gonna turn out okay. "Sure. Let's start over. My name's Vern, can I give you a lift somewhere, little lady?" He shook her hand and felt the edge of her nails as they slid across his palm.

"Thank you, Vern, my name's Garnet, and I sure would appreciate a ride."

Vern put the Kenworth in gear, pulled around the Firebird, and headed towards Scotland Neck. Behind them the crows and starlings were settling silently into the trees.

Vern got comfortable, put both hands on the wheel, and drove smoothly down highway 301. Garnet scanned the cab, careful not to let her eyes light on him. She thought he'd be real sensitive about that. The cab was clean and bare, not like most she'd been in. No candy wrappers, beer cans, ripped maps, magazines, or crap on the floor. No pictures taped to the visors. Some smiling cow hefting her breasts like the catch of the day to look at when the sun was too much to face.

Vern was trying to ignore her, she concluded. Most guys started asking stupid questions right after she got in. Couldn't just let her ride, had to know all about her. Sometimes she rolled the window down and leaned her head out. Her hair streamed away, like it did with drowned bodies. She felt the tug and tingle along her scalp, behind her ears.

Vern was different. Silent, contained, not eager to know her, probe her with questions. Just let her be. She took the time to map him with her eyes. He had funny hands, pink, clean, and hairless, like he washed them a lot. Most men went to her straight from the toilet or from under the hood, like her skin was no different than porcelain or cast iron.

Hard to read his face with that beard. A regular wolfman. Not a speck of skin showing from his throat to his nostrils.

"You want any music?" Vern asked.

"Uh, that's okay . . ." she stammered.

Vern turned the radio on. They were between signals. He hit the Seek button. Tony Bennett crooned into the cab. Vern grimaced and hit the button again. Rap bounced off the windows. "God, I hate that stuff," Garnet said and shuddered. Vern agreed and sought another channel. "Police report a . . ." Garnet reached to change the channel but Vern beat her to it.

"I hate the news. News sucks. Nothing but bad news on it. Who wants to listen to that anyway? Long as it ain't happenin' to me, I don't need to know. You know what I mean?" Vern stared straight through Garnet, looking for an answer she didn't have.

"Yeah. I guess so. I don't know. Sometimes it's interesting, what's going on out there. You know, you hear about things, maybe makes you a little more cautious. Maybe you can avoid something bad."

"Trust me. Bad news doesn't work that way. If it's out there, it's got your name on it and it's gonna find you no matter what. Shit happens and there is no explaining it. End of story."

Garnet looked out the window. She knew he was right. She knew it with a certitude that grew each and every day.

Scotland Neck came and went in less than a minute. A downshift series, a right, then a left, and it was all behind them.

"Hamilton's next, then Williamston. Where are you going to?" Vern asked.

"Morehead sounds good. I'd like to see the ocean."

"Well la-de-da. Aren't we something? Ain't you got somewhere to be?"

"No. I go where I want to, when I want to. Like my mother said, I'm free, white, and twenty-one. Nobody can tell me what to do."

"Free, white, and twenty-one. Don't you got life by the tail?"

"I ain't saying that, it's just I ain't got anywhere I got to be. You said you were heading to Morehead and I thought I'd like to see the ocean."

"Don't you have a job?"

"No. I got fired. That's why I was hitching. I was gonna go back home. But, the more I thought about it, that wasn't such a good idea. I'd just have to listen to my folks go off on me about what a loser I am. But you came along, and now I can go sit on the beach and listen to the ocean. I'd rather do that. I can always get another job."

"What were you doing?"

"I was waitressing. Slavery for white folks. My boss thought I should be nice to him for four twenty-five an hour. I thought he should try living with nine fingers. Like you said, end of story."

Hamilton at night was invisible. Vern blew past the Reduce Speed sign, caught a green on the only light in town, and was gone. Twenty miles later they snaked through Williamston, past the peanut farms, the homes with the wrap-around porches, the Piggly Wiggly store, down to the inter-section with the coast highway.

Garnet leaned her head against the window and began to drift off. She'd been on the road since early that morning.

"You getting tired?" Vern asked hopefully.

"I guess. It's been a long day."

Vern pointed back over his shoulder. "Got a bed in the back. You could take a nap. I'll wake you when we get to Morehead."

316

Garnet mulled that over. "No, that's okay. We can't be that far from Morehead. What is it, an hour and a half?"

"About that. You sure? It's a comfortable bed. Nice and soft."

"No thanks. But I appreciate the offer. You use it often?"

Vern shrugged. "Now and then. It's nice to have right there if you need it. Just pull over to the side of the road. Climb in, lock everything up, and it's your own private hideaway. You can do what you want. I don't do a lot of interstate hauling, but I'll pull a double, back to back, Asheville to New Bern, and spend an overnight at a truck stop. If I'm on my way home after a run like that, I'll just pull over to the side of the road and check out for a while."

Garnet slipped a long crimson nail inside her lips and ran it over the edge of her canine tooth. "You married?"

Vern shook his head.

"You must get lonely out here, driving all the time by yourself, place to place, nobody to go home to."

"I didn't say that," Vern snapped.

"I'm sorry. I guess I just figured . . ."

"Well, you figured wrong. You asked if I was married. I ain't. That don't mean I'm by myself."

"Sure. You're right. I got that wrong." Garnet put her palms up in surrender.

They drove on in silence towards the town of Washington. The moon shone down on the cotton that littered the fields like ripped Kleenex. Vern wished he was back in the mountains. The snow-covered mountains that rose like the spine of a great beast whose white skin showed through its thick black fur.

A police car passed them going the other way in Washington. It had so many antennas it looked like a fishing boat. Vern and Garnet eyed it as it approached and then each followed it in a side-view mirror. Vern caught Garnet checking him out. He smiled the way his mother taught him to. The one he used when he'd done something wrong and his father's rage was en route, being delivered long distance by his good right arm.

"Sorry I snapped at you like that, you weren't wrong. I just don't want to talk about it."

"That's okay. I was just making conversation." Garnet grinned. She hoped it disarmed him.

Vanceboro passed, then New Bern. They crossed the Neuse River, passed the signs for Tyron Palace, and took Carolina 70 towards Morehead City and the ocean. As the outskirts of New Bern receded, they entered the Croatan Forest. Twenty-one years ago a man came into this forest and buried his family there. Dogs dug them up a couple of days later, as it was a shallow grave. He was in quite a hurry, people said. They never found him though. Croatan was an awfully big forest, Vern remembered.

On the edge of the forest a neon yellow arrow pointed into the trees. Garnet followed the arrow to a trailer in a clearing. A single bulb dangled from a branch over the corrugated siding. Its cone revealed the word "Girls" in plump, hot-pink letters on the trailer door. Rule number one, she thought, in heaven there will be no double-wides.

Havelock began with a long, half-empty strip shopping center, then some fast-food places, an enormous pawnshop, and culminated with the entrance to the air base.

"We're almost there," Vern said. "Twenty minutes maybe."

"Great. Drop me off at a motel. Someplace cheap, okay?"

"Hell, you don't need to do that. You can use the cab."

"Uh, no thanks," she said. The courtesy spread thin over a cringe.

"Hey, I'm just trying to be nice. I'm pretty wired. My pickup isn't until two tomorrow. I'm gonna get something to eat, chew the fat with the guys, probably go to a bar, play some pool, maybe cards. I don't usually crash until six. Catch some z's until noon. Load up and hit the road. You'd have the cab to yourself. Lock yourself in." Vern shook his head. "Christ, you sure got a suspicious mind. I mean, if I'd wanted to hurt you, I had plenty of chances to do it by now, right? I mean, look at you. You're half my size."

Garnet burned at that indignity. She was a giant, a huge storm of a woman, trapped in this tiny body. It was somebody else's body, not hers. She could escape it, but not for long. It always found her in the end. Someday she would lose this body for good. She would be big. Very big.

"And don't flatter yourself, anyway," he sneered.

"Screw you too, Vern. I was going to apologize and just say I needed a shower, I feel pretty crummy, and I'm not a good sleeper. I toss and turn a lot. Your cab is just too small and I wouldn't want to inconvenience you. But now I'm not going to say that at all. I'm tired of your being nice and having to get a pat on the back for it all the time, like you're always doing everybody such a big favor. I mean, picking up a hitch-hiker, one-half your size if I remember correctly, isn't like finding a cure for cancer, you know. So thank you very much and let me out here."

Vern pressed his foot down on the accelerator as he ground his teeth together. Harder, faster, harder, faster.

"Fine. You win. Don't let me out here. Kill us both instead. That's pretty bright."

Vern froze his rage. Huge molten flares of lava, trapped inside him. Brittle, hard, with nowhere to go. Brighter than you think, bitch. Run your goddamn mouth. Get all them smart words out, now. That ain't what's gonna be coming out

319

soon. Everybody thinks they're so damn smart and Vern
Bigelow's so damned dumb. God, I love being underesti-
mated, he thought. Please, go on there, all smug and self-
righteous. You got all the answers, huh? Oh, wait till you hear
my questions.

Vern relaxed and the truck slowed down. "No, I'm not
going to just let you out here. I said I'd give you a ride to
Morehead City and that's exactly what I'm going to do.
There's going to be no doubt that I'm a man of my word," he
said without looking at Garnet.

Ten minutes later, Garnet murmured, "Thank you," to
the windshield.

Morehead City began to coalesce along the roadside, first
with small businesses, then large warehouses taking advantage of low rents. Discount furniture, self-storage places, flea
markets. The motels came with gas stations and fast food at-
tached.

"Here, this is fine, right here," Garnet said, pointing to a
one-story concrete L. Doors and windows alternated as drea-
rily as days and nights would inside them. Skinny metal poles
supported an overhang that had peeling shingles sitting up
like a bad toupee in the wind. The office was at the far end of
the lot.

Vern turned in and stopped his rig. "Listen, you and I
haven't hit it off real good, and every time I say something
you turn it upside down and look for something else in it. But
I'm gonna do it one more time 'cause I'm just like that. Why
don't you let me go down and register in the office? Just for
myself. That way he won't know there's a woman down here
all by herself. You're awfully skittish about things and I'm
just thinking this way you're a lot less likely to get hassled by
any of his friends, have something bad happen to you." Vern
stared straight ahead in mock deference, mock formality.

"That's a very good idea, Vern. I appreciate that. Thank you."

"Okay, why don't you just scrunch down here so he can't see you and wait until I come back."

Garnet crouched below the window level as Vern rolled the rig slowly toward the office. He parked under a burned-out light and stepped down from the cab.

Five minutes later, he climbed back in, backed out, and drove around the corner. He parked in the last spot, in front of door number one. He asked for the room farthest from the road because he was such a poor sleeper. The manager nodded, knowing what that was like.

"Okay, wait until I open the door. I'll come back to get my bags out of the cab. You slide out and go in with me. In this darkness, nobody'll see you."

Garnet whispered, "Thanks."

Vern left the cab door open, opened the room up, and pushed the door wide. The blinds were drawn across the small front window. He'd put on the light when they were both inside. He walked back to the cab. "Okay, c'mon out," he whispered and reached up to grab Garnet's waist to help her down. She pushed across the seats, legs first, and felt him reach for her and hold her in his strong arms. Her legs slid down towards the ground. She was glad she wore shorts and not a skirt. Skirts betrayed you. They wouldn't keep still. As soon as her feet hit the ground she moved past Vern, free of his grip but still in his shadow. Up close, he was bigger than she'd thought.

Vern closed the door and they lockstepped across the sidewalk into the room.

Vern closed the door behind them. Garnet's shape emerged from the darkness. Thin strips of light were lashed across her from her waist to her scalp. She was bound by the thinnest of cords, Vern thought.

"Please turn on the light," she whispered, ruining the moment.

Vern flicked on the lights. Garnet released the grip on her bag and it slid around on her hips. She looked the room over. The walls were an avocado green. The carpet was a brown that could go six months without being vacuumed and nobody'd notice.

It was reassuring. She'd spent many a night in motels like this. Even worked a few days in them as a housekeeper. Little chain dangling from the doorframe, copy of the innkeepers' law posted on the door. Who writes that shit? she wondered. Probably the same guy who wrote the mattress tag.

"Seems nice enough," Vern said and walked over to the bathroom. He flicked on the light. "You got the basics," he said over his shoulder.

"Oh joy. Has the toilet been sanitized?" she asked.

Vern lifted the seat. "Your seal of protection is intact."

They both laughed. Vern looked back at Garnet, her eyes narrowed, her mouth open. Her head lifted back, the cords of her neck stood out. He liked watching women's faces. They were so expressive. Not like men's. Theirs were masks: flat, cold, closed. He'd seen so many expressions on so many faces. Laughter was nice, but it was not his favorite.

"How much do I owe you?" she asked.

"Hey, don't worry about it. Why don't we go out, get a bottle, come back, kick back and relax."

"No thanks, really. How much do I owe you for the room?"

Vern flicked his eyes around. Could she get to the door before he did? Was there anything she could throw at him?

No, not even an ashtray. How about the Bible? He looked down and pulled open the nightstand drawer. There it was.

Must be an army of them Gideons running around. How come he never met any of them?

Vern slid forward between the bed and the dresser. Closer, closer. His eyes on hers. This was one of the best parts. Snake and mouse time. Every bad dream comes true, every fear is realized. The pit opens right up under your feet, the ground melts away. That sweet moment of realization of just how wrong your life has gone. Not so smart now, are you?

Garnet moved toward him. She arched her back a little, just enough to move her breasts a little, get him to notice them.

Vern stopped and looked at her. She was close enough to touch. He watched her breast rise and fall with her breath, the swell of her hips in her shorts. He was breathing through his mouth and stopped to swallow.

"Maybe that isn't such a bad idea after all. We'll get something to drink, come back here, and figure out what I owe you. I'm sure we'll figure something out, right, Vern?"

Garnet leaned forward and put her hand on Vern's collar, patting it and then his chest. Vern reached for her and his face bore down on hers. She gritted her teeth and turned away. The smell. It was always there. They couldn't wash it off. She couldn't wash it off. She was going to vomit.

"Um, look, Vern, why don't you get comfortable on the bed here, put on some TV. Let me go freshen up a minute. It's been a long day. I'm hot and sticky. I'll feel better. Just give me a minute, okay?"

"Okay. Sure, go on, freshen up. I'll wait here." He stepped aside and Garnet scooted past him into the bathroom and closed the door.

Vern sat on the edge of the bed, picked up the remote control, and switched on the television. Preoccupied, he began changing channels. He looked around the room. He never did it in rooms. Always his cab, his lair, his den. Alone, private, safe. Dark and Close. He did much of it by feel anyway. So, maybe this time he'd do the easy stuff here. She seemed willing enough. It had never happened that way. He wasn't sure he'd like it as much. Only one way to find out. He'd still finish her in the cab. Had to be that way. They'd seen him check in. But they hadn't seen her. He nodded and smiled at his own cleverness.

Garnet threw up in the toilet, then flushed it. She washed her face with water and looked into the mirror. *There's no way out of here. There's no other way.* She knew it. She'd looked into his eyes and seen it there. He was going to do it whether she wanted to or not. Just because he wanted to and he was bigger. He could make her do it. Just like they all could. Like they all had. It was now or never.

Vern stopped changing channels when he recognized the car. Metal-flake blue with a white rag on the antenna. The bathroom door slammed open and Garnet rushed at him. He turned and stood to meet her. She had something in her hand. A dumbbell. He raised his arm, but too late. She hit him with all her might and detonated a darkness all around him.

Vern came to. He was on the bed. God, did his head hurt. He moved it slowly from side to side. He was alone. She got away. Thank God he hadn't tried anything. Even if she went to the police, there was nothing they could do. He never touched her. He was innocent. This had happened before, missed attempts. None this close though. Usually something spooked them before he closed, and they ran. I wonder what time is it? He tried to read his watch but his arm wouldn't turn. Vern tried harder and realized he was cuffed to the bed. He tried the other arm. Trapped! He turned his head from side to side even though his head exploded each time.

Garnet came out of the bathroom. She sat on the bed and pulled her bag into her lap. The TV was still on. She took the remote control and searched for the late news.

"Police outside of Weldon found the body of local automobile racer George Reynolds in the woods near his car today. He is the latest victim of the serial killer working the North Carolina back roads."

Vern strained to turn his head toward the TV. "What are you gonna do? What are you gonna do?" His voice rose.

Garnet pinched his nostrils shut and then stuffed George Reynolds's underpants into his mouth.

"What am I going to do?" she said dreamily, and looked around for the little body she had once again managed to escape. "Let me show you." She opened her purse and spread out her answer on the nightstand.

About the Author

Benjamin M. Schutz is the author of the acclaimed psychological thriller, *The Mongol Reply*. Before that he wrote novels and short stories about private eye Leo Haggerty. These works have been honored with a Shamus award as best P.I. novel of the year for *A Tax in Blood*, and both a Shamus and Edgar Allan Poe award for the short story "Mary, Mary Shut the Door." Only one other short story has received both these awards. His non series short stories have appeared in such distinguished anthologies as *Crème de la Crime*, *A Century of Noir*, and *Mystery: The Best of 2001*. He is a forensic psychologist and lives in the Northern Virginia suburbs of Washington, D.C.